Dark Water

*Book 2 in the
Aztec Elements Series*

by

Philip Dickinson

**Grosvenor House
Publishing Limited**

This book is published by
Grosvenor House Publishing Ltd
28-30 High Street, Guildford, Surrey, GU1 3EL.
www.grosvenorhousepublishing.co.uk

A CIP record for this book
is available from the British Library

ISBN 978-1-78148-371-8

To my sister, for all her encouragement
and critique, harsh but fair.

And to my wife, for her love and all the
great years we've had together.

To Lucy,

Don't get any ideas !

Phil .

Acknowledgements

Once again, I owe thanks to many people who chivvied me along, provided moral support, feedback and gentle mocking in just the right measures. Once again my sister, Melanie, has provided the bulwark of belief balanced with proper heavyweight critique. Several other kind souls provided input after reading early drafts of *Dark Water*; they include Jean Norton, Laura Donkersley, Alexia van der Schans, Sandy P (A.K. A. Makeitsonbrone), Sarah Ghinn and Mark Crowther.

Owen Benwell has created a masterpiece again. The cover design for *Dark Water* is utterly magnificent and totally captures the mood of the novel. Not only that but it looks breathtaking alongside the reworked cover to *New Fire*, which now also shows itself to be one of the codices in the Aztec Elements series.

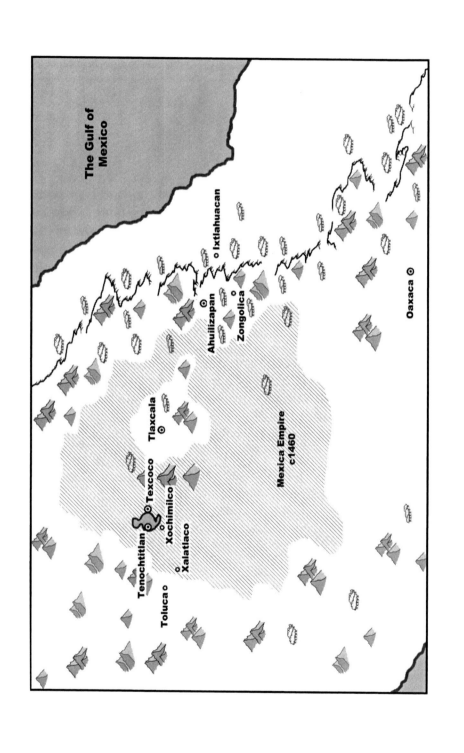

The Gulf of Mexico

Ixtlahuacan

Ahuilizapan

Zongolica

Oaxaca

Tlaxcala

Texcoco

Tenochtitlan

Xochimilco

Xalatlaco

Toluca

Mexica Empire c.1460

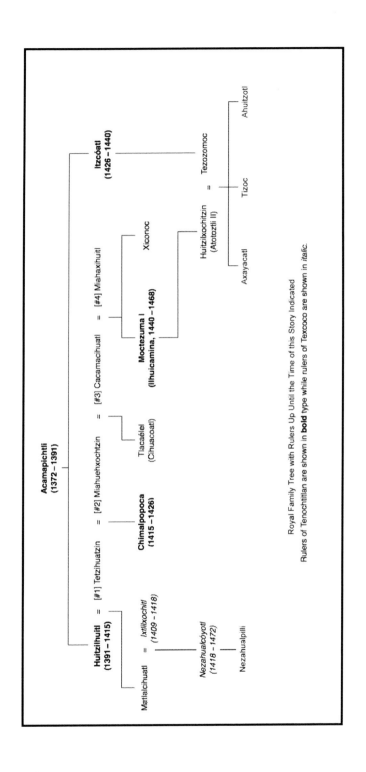

Royal Family Tree with Rulers Up Until the Time of this Story Indicated

Rulers of Tenochtitlan are shown in **bold** type while rulers of Texcoco are shown in *italic*.

Acamapichtli
(1372 – 1391)

Huitzilhuitl = [#1] Tetzihuatzin = [#2] Miahuehxochtzin = [#3] Cacamacihuatl = [#4] Miahaxihuitl
(1391 – 1415)

Mettalcihuatl = *Ixtlilxochitl*
(1409 – 1418)

Chimalpopoca
(1415 – 1426)

Tlacaélel
(Cihuacoatl)

Moctezuma I
(Ilhuicamina, 1440 – 1468)

Xiconoc

Nezahualcóyotl
(1418 – 1472)

Nezahualpilli

Axayacatl

Huitzilxochitzin
(Atotoztli II)

Tizoc

Tezozomoc

Ahuitzotl

Itzcóatl
(1426 – 1440)

=

Nahuatl Names

Heart of the Jaguar's name is Ocelotyolotl in Nahuatl.

The second part of Moctezuma Ilhuicamina's name translates as Archer of the Sky, but his people referred to their leader and other important rulers as 'tlatoani', He Who Speaks.

Tlacaelel was a gifted military leader who was promoted to first advisor to the tlatoani long before his half-brother Moctezuma took the throne. The holder of this post was also known by the title of Cihuacoatl, or Woman Snake.

The name Axayacatl translates as The Face of Water.

Iquehuacatzin's name is pronounced ee-kwe-wah-katsin. His brother's name, Mahchimaleh, is spoken the way it looks.

Huitzilopochtli, pronounced wee-tsil-au-potch-tli was the God of War and Sun God. His shrine held pride of place atop the Great Temple alongside only one other, that of Tlaloc, God of Rain.

Quetzalcoatl, the Feathered Serpent, was adopted by the Mexica from previous civilisations in the region, notably Teotihuacan. He was credited with creating the Fifth World, the time of people, and was the god of commerce.

Mictlantecuhtli was the Aztec god of the dead and guardian of the underworld, Mictlan.

Chapter 1 – Tenochtitlan

Bleak dreams of abandonment faded into muddled consciousness. Clawfoot rubbed his eyes. The indistinct image of the parents he'd never known faded, but the darkness refused to budge. It was still night time. He felt a hand on his shoulder shaking him.

'Wake up, Clawfoot. You're going to be late for the ceremony!' The urgent voice was like a slap in the face.

'The sacrifice!' Clawfoot leapt to his feet and nearly bowled the old man over. Eternal Flame, Clawfoot's mentor, had come to find him. His frail silhouette was dimly visible against the meagre starlight that bled into the room from a high window. 'Where in the name of Mictlan's testicles is Angry Lizard? He was supposed to wake me.'

'I don't know,' confessed Eternal Flame. 'The others are waiting for you at the shrine. I thought something like this might have happened, so I came to get you.'

'That eater of dogshit is trying to get me killed,' growled Clawfoot, feeling for the ceremonial robe that lay beside his palette. Angry Lizard was a warrior priest, the second son of the brother of Azcapotzalco's ruler and therefore a nobody, but he was a dangerous nobody because of the noble birthright he lost when his family had gifted him to the priesthood. There were five ranks between acolyte and the high priest of Huitzilopochtli and at the grand age of thirty-three summers, Angry Lizard had only reached the second level. Clawfoot had already reached the same level at the age of sixteen, a meteoric rise that had earned him more enemies than friends. He could not have cared less about their friendship, but their attempts to undermine his progress through the ranks were becoming more and more dangerous. It had been Angry Lizard's duty to wake Clawfoot because it was his turn on the morning vigil. The idiot would have had nothing to do from midnight to dawn but pray and watch the sky for messages from the gods, small streaks of light that sparked and raced across the heavens, so he would have no excuse.

'It could just be an accident. He's forgotten.'

Clawfoot shook his head. 'No. He knew how important this was to me.' The old man was unable to comprehend the level of mutual hatred that existed between Clawfoot and his fellow priests. He tugged the long robe over his shoulders.

'Come on! You're going to be late!' said Eternal Flame.

'You said that already,' complained Clawfoot as he followed the old man out of the door. He cursed when he saw the bright blue star of Tlahuiz, already high above Huexotzinco. He would be late.

'Soon, Clawfoot. Very soon!'

'After the sacrifice, I'm going to find that stinking piece of offal and feed him to the crows.'

'You will do no such thing!' squawked Eternal Flame as he hurried from the accommodation block. 'You have enough enemies already.'

'Maybe this time I'll make sure I have one fewer.' They were trotting now, the best pace that the ancient priest could manage.

Clawfoot heard the old man sigh.

'There is too much violence in you. Your mind needs to be focused on the ceremony. Where are the gifts?'

'I placed them in the shrine last night,' said Clawfoot.

'The rabbit?'

'Yes.'

'It's all prepared and waiting in the shrine?'

'Yes,' snapped Clawfoot. 'It's all exactly as you have made me practise so many times.'

'Not there now.' Eternal Flame's breathing rattled under the strain as he tried to keep up. Clawfoot stopped and the old man collided with him.

'What did you say?'

'If you prepared the shrine last night, someone has cleared it away.'

Unable to put his anger into words, Clawfoot left his mentor gasping for breath as he raced up the steps of the Great Temple. The blue gauze of dawn was a thin streak above the western horizon as Clawfoot reached the platform. Sunrise was no more than a few heartbeats away as he sprinted past the chacmool towards the shrine of Tlaloc, which the order of Huitzilopochtli was forced to share, while their own shrine, no more than twenty paces away, was entirely buried under the towering stonework that would support its replacement. Three warrior priests were escorting a fourth man, the Blessed One, towards the entrance, which meant that the sacrifice had not begun.

Clawfoot crossed the threshold where the gloom of the shrine was held at bay with four pitch-soaked brands that burned in sconces around the room. The stench of rancid blood assailed his nostrils. It was a disgusting smell, but today Clawfoot decided that it suited his rage. Everything had been set for this morning's dedication; everything had been planned with his usual attention to detail. Thanks to the futile vendetta of a second-rate priest, the whole thing would be ruined. There would be a reckoning.

Five disapproving stares met Clawfoot's entrance; the five experienced priests selected to hold the offering down once he was brought to the shrine, the same five men who would rule on Clawfoot's performance. Their robes were black and forbidding and all had their hair tied tightly back, which served to accentuate their severe expressions. He knew them all well enough to understand that none of them would grant him any favours, especially in light of his late arrival. Although the most senior clerics of the order were impressed with the speed of Clawfoot's learning, progression up the ranks was not easily won. Clawfoot avoided their opprobrium by checking for the minor gifts he had set out last night. There were a few wilting flowers trampled into the stone but nothing else. No salted meat of rabbit dressed in leaves of the Mesquite bush, no fruit and no pitcher of octli. At least the altar was still clean, a solid block of night-blue stone, waist high and half the length of a man, that Clawfoot had been up half the night polishing. It looked like a vast, glistening gemstone of the gods.

One of the officials approached. He was a broad-shouldered man with streaks of grey in his hair. Disappointment leaked from him like pus from the boil on his neck. This was Clawfoot's designated second, the priest who would have stood in for him if he had been delayed any more and the man who would report back to the high priest afterwards. The knot in Clawfoot's stomach tightened.

'Are you ready?' croaked the official.

'I am, Venerable Father.'

'There are no gifts. The ceremony is late.'

Ready with a bitter retort, Clawfoot opened his mouth, then thought the better of it. *Just get the offering underway*, he thought to himself. 'Fetch the Blessed One.'

The official nodded and signalled to the men outside. He and the other four priests gathered around the altar, while Clawfoot stood facing the entrance.

Moments later the Blessed One was brought before them. He stumbled and had to be caught. He was a paunchy man of late middle age, a captive warrior from the Tlaxcalan states. Firelight revealed the scrawny man's unfocused gaze and the thin stream of spittle that dangled from his lower lip. The man had been drugged too heavily. Clawfoot wondered if Angry Lizard or one of the others had a hand in this. It would have been easy enough for them to wreak this sabotage. He put his hands on the man's shoulders and looked into his eyes, liquid pools beneath drooping lids. Tracks of moisture streaked his face. He had been crying.

'I am your father,' Clawfoot spoke the opening line of the ceremony.

The man named as the Blessed One didn't react. His head rolled slightly, as though he was trying to locate the source of the voice. Clawfoot had dispatched three humans over the last year in training for this event. All had been plied with quantities of octli, the sacred drink made from fermented maguey pulp, that helped to make them more compliant, but none had been this far gone; this man could barely stand. This was Clawfoot's first true offering to the gods. He couldn't allow anything more to go wrong. His future depended on it. He had no parents, no family making generous contributions to the priesthood. There would be no cushy role for him if this didn't work out. Ever since he had been snared by a gang of Catchers, priests whose self-appointed job was to rid the streets of homeless orphans, Clawfoot had been convinced that he would be sold on as a slave or, worse still, offered up to the gods on one of the holy days. After a brief spell, incarcerated in the catacombs under the temple complex, hope dwindling with the passing of the summer, the high priest had unexpectedly paid a visit. Of all the caged wretches, it was Clawfoot who had caught his eye. The high priest must have seen something unusual in him because the next day, Clawfoot was offered the chance to escape slavery and sacrifice if he was willing to become a priest. He had accepted, believing his luck had turned, but life as an acolyte was tough, particularly in the Order of Huitzilopochtli. The God of War cared little for the weak as the elders were constantly reminding their charges. The onerous succession of prayers, devotions and sacrifices were set against a backdrop of horrors promised to those who repeatedly fell short. It was not uncommon for the priests to pick out one of the young men for 'special treatment'. There was no secret as to their fate. Excision of a man's heart in a ritual sacrifice was a tricky business and the initiates were always in need of practice.

Clawfoot was no stranger to terror. Years of sleeping rough with the relentless threat of starvation and disease had taught him resilience. What began as hard work conducted under duress had eventually become the gift of knowledge as he had begun to study alongside the real scholars. His eyes had been opened. He understood the origins of each of the Five Worlds and could recite the precedence of the pantheon of gods, from the Creator Pair to Mictlantecuhtli right through to the latecomer Quetzalcoatl. He could scribe all but the most esoteric texts. Clawfoot's teachers delighted in his thirst for knowledge, especially his mentor, Eternal Flame, so it wasn't long before he leapfrogged the indolent third or fourth sons of noblemen. They were no match for his zeal. He made them look stupid without even trying. The priesthood was a blessed relief from the squalor of life on the street. He had a safe place to sleep and as much food as he needed.

Clawfoot had found a way out of the gutter and nothing was going to stand in his way.

He slapped the Blessed One savagely across the face, earning shocked gasps from the older priests. The harsh treatment seemed to work because the man managed to focus on Clawfoot.

'I am your father,' repeated Clawfoot.

One of the priests poked the offering in the ribs.

'Honoured Father, I am your son.' The response was slurred, but at least the ceremony was underway.

'You are the Blessed One.'

'I am the Blessed One.'

He had been trained, but Clawfoot remembered the words of his mentor. 'Deep in their souls,' the old man had said, 'everyone knows the words. They are imprinted deep into our flesh.'

'I will show you the path,' continued Clawfoot.

There was another delay. The Blessed One wobbled slightly. 'I will follow it.'

'The light of the ancestors will guide you on your way.'

'I will follow the light.'

'You will carry a message to Huitzilopochtli, Light of the Sun and God of War.'

'I will carry a message,' the man drooled.

A sense of calm enfolded Clawfoot as he guided the Blessed One through the remainder of the dedication. In spite of the man's intoxication it was clear that the conditioning was working because he remembered all the lines. Even Clawfoot's anger with Angry Lizard dissipated. Some of the world's chaos would be stilled tonight through this sacrifice. The squalling mess of humanity would be cleaned, a little, as one life was returned to the gods; a gift to the givers.

When the dedication was done, the Blessed One was stretched reluctantly across the altar. His eyes had rolled up into his head and his lips moved constantly now, but no sound came forth. The man had some rudimentary understanding of what was going on. He kept trying to scratch the backs of his hands, but four of the priests had a hold of him now. On the very cusp of meeting the gods, how could one not be nervous? The official presented the ritual blade to Clawfoot. Each specific religious occasion had its own blade. This one was a heavy jade bludgeon. The handle carved into its body was sensuously smooth and cool to the touch. Beneath the handle, two cutting edges met in a vicious point; one of them long and smooth, for slicing open the belly, while the other was short and set with serrations that were designed to rasp into the victim's breastbone. Clawfoot didn't like it. Jade wasn't as hard as obsidian and didn't hold its edge well.

'Ready the Blessed One.'

The official moved to take hold of the Blessed One's head. He bent it back over the end of the altar, which caused the offering to arch his back towards the ceiling of the shrine.

Clawfoot located the sacrificial knife over the man's chest, raised it high and then brought it down in one smooth movement backed with as much power as he could muster. A grating thud was accompanied by a high-pitched whoop as the air was forced from the offering's lungs. Clawfoot twisted the blade and felt a satisfying crack. This was the 'release' that the elders spoke of when breastbone sheared in half. It was a strike of rare perfection. Quickly, Clawfoot pulled the blade free and used a slicing motion under the bottom ribs and turned the incision into a cross shape. Now blood pumped from the wound, spraying Clawfoot and the priest beside him. The offering shuddered, still too winded to draw breath and scream. The priests on either side reached into the man's chest and pulled. The ribs peeled back. Clawfoot reacted quickly, before the gouting blood obscured the prize. He thrust the blade up between the lungs, reached his left hand into the top of the mess and located the heart, warm and still beating. He hacked determinedly around the top of the heart and pulled it out, splashing blood everywhere. A gasping rattle escaped the dying man. He convulsed once and lay still. Eternal Flame released the man's head and calmly collected a bowl from an alcove set in the wall of the shrine. He held it out.

'This is the gift of life,' said Clawfoot. He had dropped the ceremonial blade and was holding the heart above his head in both hands. It had stopped beating, although blood still poured from the severed arteries, making rivulets down his arms.

'Oh Huitzilopochtli, sun-bearer and bringer of warmth. Hear our plea. We return this precious life back to you as a token of our devotion. Blood of the gods brought life to the world, so we make our payment.' He lowered the heart into the bowl. 'Nothing that we have is ours. Everything that we are is yours. Men are born into this world and quickly pass, while you continue your track across the heavens. Thus has it been since Quetzalcoatl shaped the Fifth World and thus we beseech you to keep it. Accept this gift, given willingly, as a symbol of our love for you.'

The other priests dipped their fingers into the bowl and smeared red stripes across their cheeks. Clawfoot spoke the rest of the dedication and then all the priests processed out to the chacmool that stood at the top of the temple steps. Eternal Flame was waiting there. He shot a questioning glance at Clawfoot who ignored him. The contents of the bowl were transferred carefully into the one held in the statue's hands. The rim of the sun had just cleared the horizon above Texcoco; its rays lit the Great Temple with an unearthly incandescence. The new stonework that soared above the priests on the old temple top glowed as though lit from within. The dedication to the gods was complete and the priests who had assisted Clawfoot went into a huddle to discuss the outcome. Clawfoot was beginning to relax when Eternal Flame tapped him on the shoulder.

'It went well?'

'The cut was well made and the offering was made before sunrise.'

'The poor presentation will count against you. Huitzilopochtli will not be pleased.'

'I set everything out, I told you. Someone stole it and if there's any justice in the world, Huitzilopochtli knows who and is making plans to punish him, even as we speak.'

Eternal Flame looked suspiciously at Clawfoot. He looked as though he was about to say something and then thought the better of it. The priest who had officiated came over. His face of disappointment was like a wet cloth that had been trampled into mud.

'To atone for being late, you will stay here and help the young ones clean up.'

'Wait—'

'Oh, and I've warned you about the proper address for your elders.' Here he gave Eternal Flame a flinty look. Clawfoot's mentor had long ago given up trying to get him to address him using the honorific. Eternal Flame didn't care, but Clawfoot was always being taken to task for his lack of formality with others.

'Yes, Venerable Father.'

'Better. So, for insubordination, you can also take the head for cleaning…before you take your morning meal.'

Clawfoot bowed, wondering whether there would be any food left by the time he was done. In the end, it wasn't so bad. Eternal Flame corralled the acolytes who arrived on the temple top and herded them towards the shrine. They were wary of Clawfoot because of his reputation for violence, but they were keen to impress the elders, so the altar was immaculate within a short space of time. They even mopped around Clawfoot as he removed the Blessed One's head. When everything looked under control, he picked up the head by its hair, wrapped it in a sack and left the young initiates to run rings around his old mentor. He wondered, not for the first time, at how astonishingly heavy a human head was. At the base of the temple steps he turned right and skirted around the skull rack that dominated the square. It had recently been enlarged to make more space for the skulls of sacrificial victims. Six men lying head to foot would barely have stretched its full length, while three would have just measured its width. Skulls were cemented onto the corner posts to give it the strength and between them rose a hundred or more wooden poles to which the cross-pieces were attached that held the skulls. This is where the head Clawfoot was carrying would end up once it had been picked clean.

Beyond the rack was the scholastic wing of the priests' accommodation and here, Clawfoot found the doorway that led to its basement. This was the domain of the Master Curator who, amongst other duties, was responsible for preparing victims' heads for the skull rack. The Master himself wasn't in, but one of his students took possession of the bundle that was dripping blood at a steady rate. He advised Clawfoot in dolorous tones that it wouldn't be stripped and mounted on the skull rack until the new moon. Apparently there was an unexpected shortage of maggots.

It was on the way out that Clawfoot had an idea. A section of the Master Curator's ill-lit corridor was devoted to human remains that resulted from his experiments. An entire skeleton, fascinating to Clawfoot, held pride of place; its skull had not been sent to be mounted on the rack. Next to it was the most perfect example of a human skin that he had ever seen, a leftover from one of Xipe Totec's grisly festivals. Opposite them were some dried organs, barely recognisable in their shrivelled state, but above them all, draped along the length of the corridor like a grotesque, desiccated snake carcass, was what Clawfoot knew to be human intestines. This was his inspiration. He hurried back to the Great Temple and found the acolytes who were gathered around the corpse they had dragged to the base of the steps. They were cheerfully drawing lots to decide who would convey it to the mud scrapers at Xaltocan. Clawfoot persuaded them to let him cut out a long length of intestine and they watched, horrified and fascinated in equal measure, while holding their noses at the smell of excrement. A short while later the whole slick and bloody mess of tubes was installed under the straw pallet that Angry Lizard used for a bed.

Petty revenge plus a plentiful supply of tamales and salted fish in the refectory improved Clawfoot's mood a little, but he wasn't able to completely shake the feeling of gloom that prevailed. He should have been celebrating his first official devotion to the gods with a human offering, but instead, his head was cluttered with half-remembered dreams of parents who had died or abandoned him when he was an infant, and his stomach was full of bile, caused once more by his contempt for his fellow priests. To make matters worse, Clawfoot was worried about the morning's events. The older priests were more guarded in their dislike for him than the middle ranks, but they certainly saw no reason to favour him over any other candidates. The morning's dedication had not been exemplary.

The sudden appearance of the high priest in the refectory brought a deathly silence to the usually noisy morning meal and filled Clawfoot with a horrible foreboding. Feathered Darkness was accompanied by four of the Silent Watch, his own hand-picked warrior priests, men sworn to a vow of silence and committed to protect the high priest of Huitzilopochtli with their own lives.

One hundred and twenty gnostics, warrior priests and acolytes paused to see which unfortunate victim would be summoned, perhaps never to be seen again. Many of them turned to stare at Clawfoot. Evidently, news of the morning's proceedings had spread. The God of War's first minister on earth, known to the common people as 'Heaven's Knife', swept the querulous ranks with a hawk-like gaze until he too lit on Clawfoot. One pale finger curled, beckoning. Clawfoot swivelled his head but discovered that everyone was carefully inspecting their bowls for scraps, all except Angry Lizard who smirked at him from across the room. He swallowed drily, got to his feet and followed as the high priest stalked from the room.

Chapter 2
The Jungles of Totonaca

The humid air pressed in on Shield of Gold and his skin was slick with sweat. The air reminded him of the steam baths in Tenochtitlan, except that there was no way to step outside of it here. This was his first sortie into the jungles of Totonaca as the army of Mexica pushed towards the coast. He was standing on one of the raised platforms ringing the temporary arena that had been erected on a patch of low-lying swamp. It was flanked by the town on one side and a dense, jungle-covered slope on the other.

'Twelve cacao beans,' said Two Sign suddenly. The big Eagle Knight had been silent for a while, watching the captive from Ahuilizapan who'd been brought out and led around the gladiatorial ring. He was a big man with a misshapen nose and his forehead wrinkled over bushy eyebrows, giving his long face a quizzical expression.

It was such an outrageous wager that his friends were lost for words. Last Medicine, the grizzled old warrior-turned-advisor, raised his eyebrows at Jaguar in disbelief and both of them took another look at the man who was about to die.

The prisoner's ankle had now been secured to a massive stone ring by a length of hemp that would allow him just enough room to fight and dodge his opponents' blows but no more. He was short and stout around the middle, like many of the jungle dwellers. His face had been daubed with white paint so that the only distinguishing features were his soot-blackened lips and the narrow slits of his eyes. He was dressed in a simple white loincloth and an insubstantial, ceremonial shoulder-guard made of cotton and blue feathers. His head was cleanly shaved up to a circle of his scalp at the back from which a long, warrior's queue

12

hung. As the men who had brought him in stepped back, a priest bowed briefly and handed him a wooden club that was also adorned with blue feathers. Shield of Gold thought that the prisoner looked surprisingly calm for someone who was expected to fight to the death with such an inadequate weapon.

This was the fifth and last gladiatorial bout of the day. As Shield of Gold was only fourteen, he'd never seen this form of trial by combat before, but the three older men had warned him that they only ever had one outcome. They had been proved right. The previous warriors of Ahuilizapan had fought bravely, but none of them for long, each succumbing to the first of the four Mexica knights who had been granted the honour of combat in 'The Marking with the Sword'. There was a subdued air among the local men. They stood in a ring, forming the edge of the arena with more behind them, standing on blocks of stone that had been moved into position to create a rough circle. It was obvious that the confidence in their own warriors had been undermined in the early rounds.

'You're betting that this one will beat two opponents?' Jaguar asked Two Sign.

'Reckon so.'

Last Medicine, the oldest of them, hawked and spat at his feet.' He doesn't look that special to me.' He scowled, causing a whitening of the cicatrice of scars that ran down from where his left ear used to be and across his neck. As usual, Shield of Gold struggled to tear his gaze away from the grisly war wound, simultaneously appalled and fascinated. Twenty years as a Jaguar Knight had taken its toll on Last Medicine. His skin was a dark mahogany from the years out on campaign, fighting on one border or another and his face was wracked with a myriad of wrinkles and deep lines. Although he still had a stocky, solid frame, he used a staff to hide a pronounced limp. Shield of Gold knew from the tales Jaguar told about the old man that there was hardly a place on him that hadn't suffered a wound at some point.

'What would you know?' rejoined Two Sign with a snort.' You can barely see past the end of your own nose anymore!'

'That may be true, but I've still taken a tlatoani's ransom of cacao beans from you so far today.'

The two middle fingers missing from Two Sign's right hand didn't diminish the rudeness of the gesture that he made.

'I'm out,' said Jaguar, shaking his head.' I've already lost more than I can afford.'

'What about Tlacaelel's newly appointed messenger?' asked Two Sign.

'No thanks,' Shield of Gold squeaked and then bit his tongue in anger. His voice was breaking, and it tended to waver if he was put under stress or had to shout. Somehow, he couldn't quite get used to being included in the group. From Heart of the Jaguar, who was twenty-three, through Two Sign, who had seen nearly forty summers, to Last Medicine, the old veteran of nearly fifty years, there was a span of three generations of warriors, all three of whom had already attained legendary status. All three shaved their heads in the traditional style of Mexica warriors, with a patch at the rear grown long into a queue that was neatly tied and folded at the back of their heads. Shield of Gold felt embarrassed to be standing alongside them. He had a thick mop of black hair and was wearing a tunic that barely reached his thighs. The others wore the longer style that was only permitted to those who had proven themselves in battle.

'Last Medicine?'

The old advisor began to reply, but his words were drowned out as thousands of spectators surged to their feet and roared in approval as the first Jaguar Knight swaggered into the ring. His costume was so pristine it could only have been specially made for the occasion. The sleek dappled gold pelt of a once beautiful animal gleamed, shining so radiantly it almost looked wet as it draped the warrior's head and shoulders. A soft leather loincloth was tied neatly around his waist and draped elegantly down to his knees. Greaves of thick leather, covered with more jaguar skin, protected his lower legs. He held his obsidian-bladed sword aloft and turned slowly on the spot, grinning from under the snarling, toothed cowl. The crowd cheered again at the magnificent sight. Leaping Fire was well known and was obviously determined to capitalise on the attention.

'Look at his costume,' breathed Shield of Gold in awe. 'Nothing is more fearsome than the jaguar.'

'Appearances can be deceptive, Shield of Gold. The jaguar may have sharp claws and teeth, but the tapir kills more people.'

'Is that true?'

Jaguar nodded.

'It makes you wonder,' drawled Last Medicine, 'why Tlacaelel has never set up the Knights of the Tapir.'

Two Sign snorted. 'Watch out! Here come the tapir warriors. Are those spears they carry? No, they come with their own spits.'

Shield of Gold joined the men in their laughter, but the distraction was short-lived.

Leaping Fire advanced on the Ahuilizapan warrior in what, even to Shield of Gold's untrained eye, looked like a dangerously casual manner. As this was the last gladiatorial bout of the day, this captive would be an experienced fighter, one of Ahuilizapan's finest, and likely to give a good account of himself. Leaping Fire danced around, jabbing his sword, but the local man refused to be goaded into action prematurely, another sign that he was a veteran. He never once tried to use one of the wooden balls he'd been given as missiles; the previous rounds had shown that they were worse than useless. Perhaps this was why Two Sign had raised the stakes so high. Few of the spectators appeared to have spotted this and they shouted at Leaping Fire, urging him to get stuck in. The Jaguar Knight gathered himself and struck. The warrior from Ahuilizapan parried the blow with his club and then lashed out, low, almost catching Leaping Fire on the knee.

The near miss didn't have any effect on the Mexica's attack. Confident in the longer reach and deadliness of his weapon, he remained on the attack and rained a succession of blows down on the Ahuilizapan. The local man blocked repeatedly with his feathered club but was driven back against the stone he was tethered to. Perhaps Two Sign had got it wrong after all. This man was already finished and the three other knights, waiting outside the arena, would not get a turn today.

The Ahuilizapan warrior fell clumsily across the granite block and Leaping Fire swept his sword up on high to finish him

15

off. The crowd leapt to their feet baying for blood, but at that moment, the prisoner kicked Leaping Fire in the stomach and doubled him up, then followed with a blow to the side of Leaping Fire's head. The Mexica lurched sideways and suddenly the spectators all jumped to their feet again with a collective gasp. The strike hadn't been very powerful, but Leaping Fire was clearly dazed and crucially, he was still in range of his opponent. The combatant from Ahuilizapan wasted no time. He rolled from the platform and swung his club backhanded, catching the Jaguar Knight full in the face. The crunching of bone was audible through the shrieking of the crowd.

Shield of Gold saw Two Sign twitch an eyebrow at Last Medicine. It was a look that said 'What did I tell you?'

The local man snatched up his opponent's sword and placed it on the stone behind him; then, reaching out to the extent that his tether allowed him, he grabbed the knight's leg and dragged him closer before he could crawl out of reach. All around Shield of Gold, the spectators were howling and stamping their feet. Their horror now turned to adulation for the underdog as they bayed for the blood of their own champion. Confused, Leaping Fire tried to rise, when the best option would have been to roll or scramble away. His face was a ruined, bloody mess. His nose had almost been ripped off and hung to one side by a flap of skin.

The man from Ahuilizapan recovered the sword and assumed the killing stance. Jaguar could see why this man had been chosen for the last combat of the day. He put his hand to his mouth and joined in the whooping.

'Dispatch him! Dispatch him!' called the excited crowd.

Shield of Gold glanced up to his left. There, in the small enclosure reserved for Ahuilizapan's ruling classes, stood Imixquitl. His long forehead and pinched face betrayed no emotion, but members of his family and the high-ranking officials beside him showed no such reserve. Although they were ringed in by a guard of the most intimidating Mexica knights available and bound by a humiliating oath, sworn upon their most sacred gods, to bow to their new ruler, Moctezuma, their hero's success in the arena had provoked them into such a frenzy that it looked as though they would hurt themselves. The common folk of Ahuilizapan were no less enthusiastic. Arms were raised all around the arena, imploring their combatant to make the killing blow.

The triumphant warrior swung his arms, simultaneously pulling back in one, expertly fluid motion. The razor-edged shards of obsidian severed Leaping Fire's head and half of his shoulder from his body. The noise in the small arena was deafening and predictably, several scuffles broke out, as the more optimistic gamblers tried to claim their winnings from disgruntled and disbelieving neighbours. The four friends sat down again.

'It looks like I'm in trouble,' said Last Medicine ruefully when the noise had settled down a bit.

'So much for your Jaguar Knight.' Two Sign grinned at Jaguar. 'I thought you trained them better than that.'

'Leaping Fire was arrogant and paid with his life.' Jaguar looked angry.' The next man will have seen this. He won't make the same mistake.'

'Who is next up anyway?' asked Shield of Gold.

'One of my men, Gilded Serpent,' said Two Sign, watching as the corpse of the Jaguar Knight was dragged away. One of the priests who was officiating offered another cup of fortifying octli to the man from Ahuilizapan. 'Let's see if the Eagle Knight does any better.'

'I don't recognise that name,' said Shield of Gold, his voice dropping unexpectedly low, mid-sentence.

'He's one of the rangers,' said Jaguar. 'They travel huge distances in small units. They don't spend much time back at home.'

'Ah...' said Shield of Gold.

'So what do you think, young man?' asked Last Medicine, favouring him with a smile. He was either ignorant of the enmity between his friends or had chosen to ignore it.

Shield of Gold swelled with pride. It was a huge compliment having the veteran ask him a question. Shield of Gold echoed Jaguar's view. 'He won't make it past the next one!'

Ever since Jaguar had rescued Shield of Gold from a disease-infested house five years ago, he had turned up every evening at Jaguar's home to politely ask whether Jaguar's family business had any work for him. Several moons waxed and waned and then finally, Jaguar agreed to take him in to the family business as an apprentice. Nearly a year later, it was clear to everyone, including Shield of Gold, that he hadn't the creative abilities of even a blind axolotl; Jaguar's wife had insisted that some other work be found for him where he wouldn't be able to damage the tools and waste the precious jade stone. Shield of Gold's depression at the outcome didn't last long. By then, Jaguar had been asked to join Tlacaelel's retinue as a bodyguard and it was then that he learned that the general was also in need of a runner, his current one being unfit for duty after breaking his ankle on the high road to Toluca. Shield of Gold had been overawed in the presence of the tlatoani's half-brother, but everyone had been pleased to see that he swiftly took to his new duties. Whilst in Tenochtitlan he had to spend the mornings at telpochcalli, but when he had done with the morning lessons at the military school, he went to Tlacaelel's rooms in an old section of the palace to report for duty. Finally, if there was time at the end of the day, Shield of Gold returned to Jaguar's family to see if there were any errands he could run for the workshop.

Jaguar smiled and patted him on the shoulder.

'What?'

'Nothing,' replied Jaguar.

The priests were leaving the arena, taking Leaping Fire's sword with them and leaving the original wooden club behind. Gilded Serpent waited at the entrance to the ring.

'It's settled then,' rumbled Last Medicine, as though the high priests themselves had consulted the celestial heavens and pro-nounced upon the matter.' You might as well hand over the money now, Two Sign. What I don't understand is why you would bet against your own man.'

Two Sign's mouth shaped an obscenity, by way of response, but it was lost in the uproar. Everyone watched, transfixed as the Eagle Knight walked into the arena.

Leaping Fire's replacement wore eagle plumage, his face staring out from the open beak, above which glared unblinking eyes and below which the feathered cowl descended to conceal the warrior's shoulders, adding to the image of a giant bird. The result was both alarming and mesmeric.

Gilded Serpent circled his opponent warily. The crowd had fallen silent again, waiting with bated breath to see if the man from Ahuilizapan could repeat his earlier success, but he looked less sure of himself this time. Several times, Gilded Serpent jabbed at his opponent to test his reactions, and then retreated to a safe distance, beyond the reach of the tethered warrior. Each time, the blunt end of his sword was batted away. Gilded Serpent kept this up for a while as the spectators began to get restless. Suddenly, the Eagle Knight switched his sword to his left hand and made a powerful swipe at chest height. Surprised by the change of direction, the man from Ahuilizapan could only counter with a weak block, the impact jarring him through his crude club. Gilded Serpent switched hands again and swept the glassy shards of his sword in a glittering, deadly arc at his opponent's thigh. The local man blocked the shot again, but the impetus of the heavier sword dashed the club from his grip. The heavy clattering of the impact reverberated around the ring.

Shield of Gold stared as if spellbound. The spectacle was both terrifying and thrilling. He tried to imagine himself taking on four of the most ferocious enemy warriors one after the other and managing to stay alive. *It must be possible*, he thought, focusing on the combatants as the warrior from Ahuilizapan lunged at Gilded Serpent. This was the fighting spirit that Two Sign had seen in the man and why his wager had been such a large sum. Most people, when put in a life-threatening situation displayed a will to live, but for some, it burned in their hearts like an unquenchable fire. Two Sign would have seen thousands of warriors come and go. He'd trained with the best and earned many scars. He'd lost the middle two fingers of his right hand and many friends besides. Shield of Gold knew that Two Sign and Last Medicine were survivors and understood that they recognised that spark in others.

The two gladiators grappled on the ground and for a moment, it looked as though the local man had the advantage; he had Gilded Serpent pinned down. They both had a grip on the sword and for a moment, it looked as though the Mexica warrior might go the same way as his predecessor. It was hard to see exactly what happened next because of the view from where Shield of Gold and the others were sitting, but it looked as though the man from Ahuilizapan had to change his grip fractionally. It wasn't much of an opening, but it was all Gilded Serpent needed. He arched his body and partially dislodged his opponent, then let go of the precious sword for just long enough to grab a handful of sand and cast it into the face above him.

There was a howl of agony as the local man involuntarily let go of the sword to paw at his eyes. Gilded Serpent threw him off, got to his feet and then moved out of range, taking his sword with him. He let his opponent stagger to his feet, eyes streaming with tears and filth. The crowd started stamping their feet again and calling for the man from Texcoco to put an end to it. He dutifully obliged. He feinted right. The local man could do nothing but put his hands up to protect himself. Half blind, he saw the change of direction too late and was unable to stop the vicious sword slicing into his other side where it bit into unprotected chest. A solid, meaty thwack was heard around the arena and the man on whom Two Sign had bet a small fortune fell on his side with a groan. Suddenly, everyone was on their feet again, waving their hands, gesticulating or patting each other on the back in acknowledgement of a bet well placed. Last Medicine collected his winnings from a disappointed-looking Two Sign.

'Enjoy that?' asked Jaguar.

Shield of Gold nodded his head tentatively. 'Will the priests flay him afterwards?'

'Of course. We are feasting Xipe Totec after all. They'll present the skin to his captor when they've cleaned it up.'

Shield of Gold shuddered. 'Have you ever worn the skin of one of your captives?'

'No. I've never had that honour. Tlacaelel does not permit me to take part in ritual combat.'

'I suppose Tlacaelel values you too much.'

'Hmm,' was all Jaguar said in response.

'Don't you miss it? The action. The thrill of battle.'

Jaguar looked Shield of Gold in the eye.' No.'

'Really?' Shield of Gold sounded incredulous. 'But you're a hero! People sing songs about you. Your men sing a song about you. They call you "The Falling Claw".'

Jaguar laughed and patted Shield of Gold on the shoulder.' My men exaggerate. I've told you before not to believe all the stories you hear. Besides,' he added, 'I have a family now.'

Shield of Gold nodded but kept his eyes fixed on the priests who had filed back into the ring.

Four warrior priests of Xipe Totec glided into the arena, unhurried. Each wore a human skin stretched tightly over their head and chest and tied at the back with strips, cunningly cut in zigzags from the donor's skin. It was just possible to see the eyes of the priests, glinting through the dark eye holes in the fleshy masks they wore. The short tunics they wore beneath the skins were scruffy and black with accumulated blood and filth. They could bear the cloud of flies that swarmed in attendance, trying to land on the rotting edges, and seemed to be able to ignore the skins and the fresh blood patches from the preceding offering.

Shield of Gold couldn't shake the image of himself in the ring, trying to stay alive, armed only with a feathered club.

'Jaguar.'

'Yes?'

'Would you survive all four?'

Jaguar gave it the briefest consideration. 'No, but Two Sign might. The stories you've heard about him *are* true.'

'And if one of the fighters defeats all four warriors, they send in a left-handed warrior?'

'Yes. It's very hard to defend against without a shield, especially if you're tired.'

'Hey, you two! Quit yakking!' growled Last Medicine, who was straining to hear the incantations of the priests. 'You're like a pair of old women.'

Jaguar winked at Shield of Gold conspiratorially. Down on the sandy floor of the arena, the priests had bundled the man from Ahuilizapan, groaning piteously, onto the stone to which he was still attached by one leg. With one man at each corner, they bent him back so that his chest was exposed, while the senior cleric produced a sacrificial knife: an ugly, bulbous thing more like an axe. He began to chant an incantation and offered the weapon up to the sky. His victim lay still, although whether this was because he was badly wounded, couldn't move for the men restraining him or had simply given up the fight, Shield of Gold couldn't tell.

'This is going to go badly,' whispered Jaguar.

'Why's that?' asked Shield of Gold, puzzled as to what badly could mean in this situation.

'Tlacaelel told me that this priest doesn't know what he's doing.' Jaguar pressed on, ignoring Last Medicine's scowl. 'The high priest won't risk sending his most experienced men here. He claims they are too busy with the main ceremonies in Tenochtitlan. This man' – Jaguar nodded in the direction of the impending sacrifice – 'doesn't know one end of a knife from the other.'

The priest's incantation floated over the heads of the spectators.
'You are the body,
We are the skin.
You are the flesh,
We are your kin.
We give you our blood,
You feed the corn,
You shape the mud
Our children are born.'

There was a loud crack as the priest brought his knife crashing down on the man from Ahuilizapan's chest. There was a brief pause and then a keening sound could be faintly heard coming from the victim. The priest raised his unusually shaped weapon again as the high-pitched whine rose to a shriek that shredded the air and raised goosebumps all over Shield of Gold. The knife-wielder struck again. This time, the noise ended abruptly with a grunt. Shield of Gold heard a third strike hit home. He couldn't see very much. His view was obstructed by the crowd and he had the impression that everyone was holding their breath.

Jaguar nudged Shield of Gold. 'Told you so!'

Shield of Gold felt an uncharacteristic flash of irritation. He was trying to get a look at the proceedings and didn't want to be distracted. There was a noise of murmured approval from spectators at the front. He briefly caught sight of a dark hand held up high, holding a dark oozing mess, then his view was entirely obscured as the spectators leapt to their feet. For the fourth time that afternoon, the crowd roared their approval so loudly that Shield of Gold felt sure the gods themselves were joining in.

Chapter 3 – Tenochtitlan

Outside the accommodation block, two warrior priests of the Silent Watch intercepted Clawfoot and escorted him along behind the rapidly disappearing high priest and his own two armed men. Clawfoot had only spoken to Feathered Darkness three times before and he was vaguely worried that, unlike on those occasions, this time there were no other senior priests or tutors present. They left the towering pyramid of the Great Temple behind them and caught up with the lead group as they cleared the north gate in the Serpent Wall, but the high priest pressed on. He led them down to Fragrant Water – a badly misnamed canal – where a long canoe was tied up. While two of the warrior priests prepared to cast off, Feathered Darkness at last turned his attention to Clawfoot.

'How old are you?'

'Sixteen, Venerable Father.' Clawfoot's usual contempt for polite address was held carefully in check.

The high priest was looking at the construction site where the Great Temple was being enlarged. He had a long mane of black hair that softened the cruel, angular lines of his face. They were roughly the same height and Clawfoot judged him to be about thirty years old, although the streaks of grey in his hair made him look older. It was young for a high priest, but there was no doubting the man's authority. After Moctezuma, tlatoani and ruler of all the Mexica people, Feathered Darkness was the most powerful man alive. Still with his eyes fixed on the temple, he spoke again.

'You were nothing more than a street rat when I took you in.'

'Yes, Venerable Father.' Clawfoot recalled his capture as though it were only yesterday.

'Would you like to go back to that life?'

'No,' said Clawfoot, clenching his fists. This was it. Feathered Darkness had abducted him from the streets all those years ago, so some kind of universal balance would be maintained if he was the one to eject Clawfoot, although an escort from the city in a canoe seemed odd.

'The Order of Huitzilopochtli is your home.'

It could have been a statement or a question. Clawfoot thought about Little Maize and found he wasn't sure of his feelings for her anymore. Perhaps the embers they had nursed, leftover from their shared poverty, were gone, snuffed out in the cold, hard reality of life. There were three routes to a good life: nobility, which neither of them possessed, prowess in warfare, which they were not trained in, or a place in the priesthood. Fate had favoured Clawfoot; he felt sorry for her, but there was no room in his life for emotional attachments. He realised that whatever he had felt for her back in the days they had been in the gang he had carefully and deliberately extinguished. He knew he would have to tell her soon, but the simple words he had rehearsed would be much harder to say face-to-face. Feathered Darkness was right. His place was in the priesthood.

Before Clawfoot had time to answer, Feathered Darkness indicated that they should board the canoe. Two of the warrior priests had taken up poles and stood at the ends of the slender craft; the other two remained on the dock. Clawfoot sat on a narrow bench facing the high priest. He knew better than to ask where he was being taken. He didn't think it likely he was about to be sacrificed, but if he was, knowing it in advance wouldn't help. He closed his eyes and breathed deeply, trying to slow his heart. He listened to the plop and gurgle of the poles dipping into the water and contemplated the contrast between the late morning sun that was warming his back and the puddle of bilge water cooling his bare feet. As the canoe left the city behind and slid out into the chinampa, soft, earthy smells told their own story of the frantic preparations underway for the growing season. Farmers and their indentured labourers could be heard singing or cursing as they worked the raised fields that were criss-crossed by the network of canals surrounding Tenochtitlan.

'Eternal Flame tells me that this morning's dedication to our Lord Huitzilopochtli was a disaster,' said Feathered Darkness.

Clawfoot bristled at the negative portrayal of events, but an argument with the high priest was out of the question. 'It was very nearly late, Venerable Father.'

Feathered Darkness stared hard at Clawfoot for a while and then turned to look at the fields. He was clearly disappointed. 'You remind me of myself when I was young,' he said after a while. 'All that suppressed rage.'

Clawfoot realised that he had been grinding his teeth.

'You're always picking fights and you are disrespectful to your fellow priests. These are not good traits if you wish to rise further through the ranks.'

It was a reprimand. He had not passed the test.

'I advise you to take control of your demons if you have any desire to succeed. Don't get me wrong, I'm not suggesting that you can change your nature, but you must master your emotions. For now though, you may need some of your aptitude for violence for the task I'm giving to you.'

'You have a job for me, Venerable Father?'

'Yes,' replied the high priest. 'Look on it as a way of redeeming yourself.'

Clawfoot's heart soared with renewed hope. 'I'm honoured, Venerable Father, but surely you have older, more experienced people.'

'Of course.' Feathered Darkness waved a hand dismissively. 'But this will be a delicate mission. I need someone new, someone less recognisable and frankly... more disposable. Does that trouble you?'

'You mean that it's dangerous, Venerable Father.'

There was a pause and the high priest eventually blinked. 'Just so,' he replied.

'Then I'll have to make sure I do not fail,' said Clawfoot, injecting a confidence into the words that he did not feel. He wondered what the task would be, certainly nothing like the simple errands he had done before. That in itself was something to be thankful for, he decided.

'If you succeed, this morning's...problem will be overlooked and your passage to the next level will be complete.'

Relief flooded Clawfoot. 'Thank you, Gracious Father. I will do my best.' Reaching the third rank at the age of sixteen would be an extraordinary achievement. Only one rank would separate him from the most senior priests.

'I've heard reports of your work, not just from Eternal Flame, coordinating events for the recent feast day in honour of Xipe Totec, and the high priest of Tlaloc has nothing but praise for you, helping him with his preparations for the Feast of Hueytozotli.'

'Thank you, Venerable Father.'

Feathered Darkness scowled. 'For all your talents you seem intent on self-destruction. You're always getting into fights, you arrive late at the most important test of your skills to date and you fail to prepare the shrine properly, although I am willing to consider Eternal Flame's suggestion that someone wanted you to fail.'

Clawfoot nodded gratefully.

'This task I need you to do is too important. You must not fail. Do you understand?'

'I understand, Venerable Father.'

Feathered Darkness blinked once, then faced the front of the canoe again. 'We're going to meet Lord Xiconoc. Do you know who he is?'

Clawfoot nodded. A detailed knowledge of the Colhua history and family tree was compulsory learning in the priesthood. 'He's Moctezuma's brother.'

'And he's the most successful merchant alive today,' added Feathered Darkness, staring at Clawfoot as though watching for the information sink in. 'He earned a name for himself as a warrior fifteen years ago and was anointed as one of the Lord Protectors by the great Itzcoatl himself,' continued the high priest. 'Since then, he's used his status as an ambassador to build a commercial enterprise that stretches from the east coast to the west. Even now, his merchant convoys go out way beyond the boundaries of the empire that Tlacaelel is so busily extending. His pochteca, aided in part by our priests, barter and haggle with the Oaxacan's in the south, negotiate with the people of Tuxpan far to the north and even treat with Mayans in the distant reaches of the Yucatan. It is said that half the gold in the city has been brought here by Xiconoc's caravans in the last ten years; much of that goes directly to his brother's coffers in the form of taxes.'

'A powerful man,' reflected Clawfoot. 'Why does he want to speak to us?'

'He wants help getting hold of the one thing he doesn't yet have… his brother's throne.'

Clawfoot frowned. 'He wants to be the tlatoani? Excuse my ignorance, Venerable Father, but is this something the Order of Huitzilopochtli should be involved in?'

'Hmm… a sensible question but one that serves to illustrate how much you still have to learn. Remember that when Eternal Flame next accuses you of being arrogant.'

'Yes, Venerable Father.'

'There are many reasons why we should discuss such matters with him or any other member of the leading families. Firstly, we depend to a large extent on the patronage of the nobility. Some we could safely discard, while the loss of wealthier ones like Xiconoc would create difficulties for us. Secondly, today's would-be usurper could be tomorrow's tlatoani. It's advisable to remain friends with such people. Thirdly, information is power, although it must be carefully managed.'

'Is he dangerous to us?'

Feathered Darkness spat over the side of the canoe. 'Yes, but fortunately he has secrets.'

'Secrets that you know and can use as protection?'

'Good,' said Feathered Darkness. 'It seems my trust in you is well placed. Yes, Xiconoc has a voracious appetite for women. I have numerous reports of his bizarre games that even extend as far as Tezozomoc's wife.'

'Atotoztli?' said Clawfoot, genuinely shocked. 'But she's his niece?'

'Yes. And behaving in a most un-sisterly manner,' said the high priest. 'I have a man in Xiconoc's household who witnessed the two together on several occasions. You may be young, but I expect you've seen more than most boys your age, living on the street as you did.'

Clawfoot nodded, unsure of where this was going.

'My source told me that in one game, they muzzled and tormented a young anaconda. Then Xiconoc wrapped it around Atotoztli's neck. The snake was so angry that it began to throttle her and then Xiconoc mounted her. At the last moment, as the woman began to turn blue, he pulled a pre-positioned wire through the snake's body…sliced it in half and covered the pair of them with blood. My informant swore an oath to me that he'd never heard a woman moan so loudly.'

Clawfoot was trying to absorb all this when a shout rang out across the water. Crew members of a barge were gesticulating wildly as they bore down on the priests' canoe. The heavier craft was laden down with fresh manure and did not look very manoeuvrable. A staccato exchange of words ended as the crew in the barge realised with horror that they were about to sink an important priest and so began to take evasive action. Feathered Darkness looked unconcerned as the boatman in the prow of the advancing vessel rammed his pole deep into the mud and leaned his weight onto it, straining to turn the front of the vessel away from the impending collision. For a moment, nothing happened, and then the barge began to respond, yawing sideways and losing its momentum until it ploughed gently into the steep bank of the canal and came to rest.

Clawfoot stared at his mentor. The high priest hadn't moved so much as a muscle during the near disaster. The threat of collision and a dip in the canal hadn't been enough to worry him. That calm demeanour was what Clawfoot needed in the face of this task, whatever it was.

Apologies from the men on the barge faded behind them and before long, the journey was over. The warrior priests who were poling the canoe steered it towards a wooden jetty newly built out from a well-groomed plot of land. The two men kept the craft steady against the simple wooden pontoon with their poles, while a third man secured it to a post. Four dilapidated canoes wallowed alongside a grand, multi-hued affair that was decorated along its length with leering monkeys.

'Wait by the boat,' Feathered Darkness directed the warrior priests. 'We're in no danger here. Come,' he added to Clawfoot.

They climbed the half-dozen steps up from the jetty to the top of the field where they found a nobleman speaking to a man who Clawfoot reckoned must be a gardener. They made an incongruous pair. The nobleman was dressed in finery that would have been more appropriate for Moctezuma's court. He was middle-aged and his expanding midriff and thighs told a story of excess. His face was just beginning to catch up with the excesses of the rest of his body, as though it had only recently learned of its privileged lifestyle. Jowls had begun to appear and his eyes had taken refuge behind a fleshy nose. His hair was tidily swept back into an ornate clip with small but expensive feathers of ochre and russet. His long, yellow cloak draped to his knees was pinned at the breast with an extravagant gold brooch in the likeness of Quetzalcoatl, the feathered serpent god. By contrast, the gardener was a rangy man of advancing years, stooped under a mop of matted hair, caked with the earthen detritus of his toil. He was plagued by a nervous twitch on the right side of his face that triggered every couple of sentences and made his mouth twist as though he was eating sour fruit.

'I thought maize was supposed to come *from* the fields instead of the reverse!' fumed the nobleman. 'How many more sack-loads must I pay before this place starts to yield something?'

'There was a lot of work to do here, My Lord,' the gardener pleaded nervously. He had noticed Feathered Darkness and Clawfoot, but his employer had not. 'You know that most of the payments have been used to buy supplies and the paid workers have all been let go. All the men here are mayeques who live on your land. As to the work, we have hammered three thousand new posts in all around this plot. The edges of the chinampa had decayed, as you know. We have hauled nearly one thousand canoe loads of silt from the lake and mixed it with another six hundred canoe loads of the finest excrement from the sewers before grading it with the old soil that had become infertile. We've planted over seven hundred new willow saplings to stabilise the banks…' The gardener's voice tailed off.

The nobleman must have noticed the man staring beyond his shoulder because he turned and caught sight of Feathered Darkness. He dismissed the gardener with a wave of one arm that was thick with gold bangles and then walked over to clasp Feathered Darkness' hand.

'So good of you to come, Venerable Father.'

'Lord Xiconoc.' Feathered Darkness inclined his head fractionally.

Clawfoot was not introduced, so he stood a respectful couple of paces back.

'My sister advised me to cultivate a garden.' Xiconoc gestured around him at the reclaimed plot. 'She told me it would bring me peace, but she lied. It has brought me nothing but trouble.' He tried a wan smile, as if he had just shared a joke.

Clawfoot surveyed the rebuilt chinampa. For all his recent studies with the priests, learning history, geography, mathematics and astronomy, he knew nothing of farming or of raising crops. In spite of that, it was obvious that a lot of work had been carried out.

'Quite a project you've undertaken here,' observed Feathered Darkness.

'There was no choice,' replied Xiconoc sadly. 'My application for a piece of land nearer the city was turned down and this, which was the only other one large enough for what I have in mind, was in a shocking state.'

'I thought commerce was your thing, not farming,' said the high priest.

Xiconoc laughed briefly. 'You're right. I should have stuck with merchandise and numbers. However, it's not food I'm trying to grow here but a garden with flowers and trees collected from across the land.'

'An excellent idea,' exclaimed Feathered Darkness.

A ridiculous idea, thought Clawfoot, unconvinced by his master's apparent enthusiasm. Moctezuma already had a spectacular garden with all manner of plantings and an aviary with a dazzling variety of brightly coloured birds. It was a popular attraction with a constant stream of visitors from far and wide. Clawfoot couldn't imagine people flocking out to this island, so distant from the city centre.

'Are the omens good, Venerable Father?'

'With your leave, Xiconoc, I shall have my learned associate respond. Clawfoot here is a gifted pupil. The telling of someone's horoscope is a delicate business that takes our priests about ten years to learn. Brother Clawfoot mastered it in three. He shows such extraordinary promise that I may have to have him murdered to prevent him from becoming a threat to me.'

The nobleman stared for a moment and then guffawed with laughter. Clawfoot looked his master in the eye, but the older man's expression was as bland as if he'd been commenting on the weather. It sent a chill deep into Clawfoot's bones.

'Well then, young man... er, Venerable Father,' Xiconoc prompted.

Clawfoot inspected the surroundings briefly before turning in on himself. He closed his eyes and allowed the deep undercurrents of life to send images to him as he had been taught. The trick was to allow his mind to be guided by the multifarious nuances of the horoscope produced by the conjunction of the seasonal calendar with the religious one. Once the framework was in place, additional details could be layered in, specific to the subject to whom the horoscope was being pitched.

'My Lord, your endeavour is poised between the darkness of Tepeyollotl and the playfulness of the Old Coyote,' said Clawfoot. 'Today is ruled by the jaguar and the deer, which requires me to warn you of capricious danger... a day for caution. Happily though, the next trecena belongs to Xōchitl, the holy flower. That will be a good time for creativity, a good time to make things and in view of the flower motif, a most auspicious time to be constructing a garden.' Clawfoot bowed, wondering whether he'd done enough. The priests who taught him would have been satisfied, but Feathered Darkness was bound to be more critical.

Xiconoc's eyes narrowed. 'A day for caution!' He glanced between Clawfoot and Feathered Darkness as though suspicious of a threat. His frown held for a few heartbeats and then he smiled broadly. 'Of course. What day doesn't require caution?' He bent at the waist as much as his corpulent frame would allow and bowed to Clawfoot, thanking him for the advice.

Clawfoot looked to Feathered Darkness for approval, but the high priest was watching Xiconoc.

'This is a pleasing location,' he said to Xiconoc after a while. 'It's a shame I'm not able to visit these parts of the city more often. Sadly my duties permit little time for such indulgences.'

'Of course,' replied Xiconoc. 'The office of Lord High Priest of the Sun and the God of War must be a terrible burden.'

'We are both busy, Lord Xiconoc,' said Feathered Darkness. 'Shall we get down to business? I hope you haven't come to ask me for a blessing on your endeavour. If you want a good yield, you should have asked for the priest of Xilonen, the goddess of young maize and seedlings, or perhaps the high priest of Tlaloc, to send rain.'

Xiconoc scowled.' No, no, it's nothing like that. Besides, it's too early. The planting has only just begun. This whole project has taken far longer than I was led to believe. Come. Let's walk a little.' He indicated a path across the tilled earth towards the far side of the plot. 'Does he have to come with us?' The nobleman tilted his head back at Clawfoot.

'I have an idea that he will be useful to us both. You can rest assured,' added the high priest. 'Anything you can say to me may be heard by Clawfoot.'

'I see. Well, I'm sorry to drag you out all this way, but it was the safest place I could think to talk without being overheard.' Xiconoc saw that Feathered Darkness had nothing to add, so he continued. 'I thought well of your predecessor, you know. He would have been impressed with what you've done.'

The man was being cautious, watching the high priest for a reaction. Feathered Darkness merely nodded, which Xiconoc took as a good sign because he picked up where he had left off. 'You had a lot of work to do after his death, repairing the relationship between the sect of Huitzilopochtli and the tlatoani. It's obvious that you've worked hard to win back Moctezuma's trust after

Cloud Face's…unfortunate fall from grace. I've heard it said that you shared many of Cloud Face's beliefs.'

The low grumble Feathered Darkness emitted made it clear that Xiconoc had strayed into dangerous territory.

'Of course,' Xiconoc explained, 'some of his ideas were a little extreme, but he did love our city and our people!'

'Where is this going, My Lord?' Feathered Darkness asked, his voice an icy blast in the gathering warmth of the day. 'We've already established that we both have heavy workloads.' He cast a meaningful glance across the garden project. 'Let's get to the heart of the matter.'

'Yes, of course. My apologies, Venerable Father.' Xiconoc led them through a meadow and joined a path that followed the water's edge. 'I have heard reports of dissatisfaction in the tlatoani. I need to know what you have heard.'

'Dissatisfaction?' said Feathered Darkness. 'From what quarters?'

Xiconoc stopped abruptly. 'Don't toy with me, priest! This is too important. I know that you inherited your predecessor's network of informants and you've been busy expanding it too. I have spoken to you once before about this, so it can hardly come as a surprise. My brother's reign is not universally popular.'

'You're concerned for him?' asked the high priest.

Xiconoc resumed the stroll along the water's edge. 'Of course.' He waved an arm across the expanse of the city. 'Like every loyal Mexica citizen, I love our tlatoani. He's my brother after all. I wish him a long and happy reign, may Tezcatlipoca protect him.'

'What is it you propose? Should we be providing him with extra protection or is it a succession plan that you have in mind?'

'My brother has a great many people to protect him,' said Xiconoc softly. 'The Grey Privy Knights and the loyal ranks of Eagle and Jaguar Knights. No, joining ranks with them would be the wrong thing to do. For now, I'd like to know your thoughts on what we'd do if something *were* to happen to him. How do we ensure that whoever sits on the throne is the right choice?'

'And who would the "right choice"be, My Lord?'

Xiconoc laughed, trying to make it sound casual. Clawfoot found it the easiest thing in the world to despise the man.

'Your tone suggests that I favour my own appointment, so I won't lie; it has occurred to me, although there are one or two other possibilities.'

'Several,' said Feathered Darkness severely. 'Tlacaelel, for example, or perhaps the princes, Iquehuacatzin and Mahchimaleh, eh? They have both been schooled in the ways of kingship for just such an eventuality.'

'Yes. Yes, that's true,' conceded Xiconoc, 'but Tlacaelel would not represent change. He and Moctezuma think as one and as for the princes, don't make me laugh! Iquehuacatzin spends most of his time in the steam baths with boys half his age. I don't see the Calpullicalli warming much to him. The clan elders are somewhat... traditional in their views. As for Mahchimaleh, he may have a reputation on the battlefield, but all the brains went to his brother!'

'What about Axayacatl?'

'Tezozomoc's son?' scoffed Xiconoc. 'Ridiculous! That would be tantamount to putting his mother in charge. Don't get me wrong, I love my niece dearly...'

Clawfoot caught a meaningful glance from Feathered Darkness. Xiconoc didn't notice and carried on.

'...but I don't think she or her son are the right people to rule the Mexica, the greatest people in the world.'

Feathered Darkness clasped his hands behind his back. 'And the replacement is needed now?'

Xiconoc bristled. 'I never said that, but there is discontent.'

'People always complain.'

'This is different,' insisted Xiconoc. 'A lot of people are calling for change.'

'Well, they may have to wait a while,' observed the high priest.' Your brother appears to be in excellent health.'

Clawfoot followed the two older men as the path rose on a shallow incline. Willow saplings had been planted at regular intervals to keep the bank from slipping into the canal. He tried to stay close enough so that he could hear what they were saying whilst keeping a respectful distance. Feathered Darkness would undoubtedly question him later, expecting total recall of the conversation.

'I've heard that he is planning a trip to Ahuilizapan to see our army.' Xiconoc sounded thoughtful. 'That's a dangerous journey, passing by the rebel states of Tlaxcala and going into enemy-held lowlands. They'll be travelling through the jungle too,' the merchant added. 'I've been there. My trading convoys have travelled those lands; I know what they're like.'

Feathered Darkness stopped and Clawfoot nearly collided with him.

'I can see why you wanted to come out here to discuss this. You want my help to make sure the tlatoani doesn't return from Ahuilizapan.' He gazed out across the chinampa as though on the lookout for eavesdroppers. 'Have you mentioned this to anyone else?'

'Of course not,' Xiconoc shot back. 'I have many friends, but we both know that my cause will be stronger if I have your blessing first.'

Feathered Darkness nodded. 'And what if you have misjudged me? Greater men than you have paid with their lives for treachery of this kind. It would be a simple matter for me to report this conversation to Tlacaelel or directly to your brother.'

'You think that would buy you back into his inner circle?' Xiconoc gave the high priest a pitying look. 'I think you underestimate the damage your predecessor did. It will be a long time before the traitor Cloud Face's legacy is forgotten.'

Clawfoot knew the story of the previous high priest's treachery had led to a military disaster in which the might of the Mexica Empire had nearly been defeated. Although it was a taboo subject within the Order of Huitzilopochtli, he had also received schooling from priests of Tlaloc and Xipe Totec and they were a good deal less shy about the facts.

'The tlatoani knows the value of our work and he respects me.'

'He tolerates you, priest.' Xiconoc jabbed a finger at Feathered Darkness. 'You serve a purpose and no more.'

Clawfoot was amazed to hear the nobleman's tone of voice. Such a degree of disrespect anywhere within the Serpent Wall, the boundary between the holy centre of Tenochtitlan and its surroundings, would mean certain death. Even the high priests of the other orders wouldn't dare speak to Feathered Darkness like this. It was unsettling, yet at the same time it made him seem more human.

The two men stared at each other for a long time. Clawfoot pretended not to notice.

Eventually, Feathered Darkness offered a thin smile.' Let's agree that we both have only the best intentions for our people, our city and the Triple Alliance, yes?'

'I don't know why we treat Texcoco and its puffed-up poet-ruler as equals, but otherwise, yes, I agree.'

'Excellent!Let's also agree that if either of us felt that our people were being held back in any way, we'd be eager to find a way to fix the problem, whatever that might be.' Xiconoc nodded, so Feathered Darkness continued. They had started walking again and were following a raised path that ran between the freshly turned plots. 'Tell me what changes you would make if you were tlatoani.'

All it had taken were a few words and the tension that had been building eased.

'The first thing I would tackle is the Tlaxcala states,' began Xiconoc. 'I have no problem with the push for the coast, but our armies are leaving a dangerous enemy at their backs. The tribes of Tlaxcala are merely encircled, not subjugated. We should crush them before moving on. I know what they're like. I know what they're capable of. Every few days one of my trade convoys is ambushed by these bandits. If Tlacaelel is so clever, why can't he see this? It's like kicking an ants' nest. You kill a few, but the ones left behind become all the more determined to bite you.'

'You've raised this before in the Great Council, My Lord. Tlacaelel argued that the people of Tlaxcala have been contained and that there are greater rewards to be had by subjugating the great lands along the coast. Furthermore, their proximity means we always have a ready supply of sacrificial tribute.'

'Not all the clan heads are behind this plan,' insisted Xiconoc. 'As to the captives, think of the mighty haul we'd take if we crushed the Tlaxcala! If I had my way you'd have thousands of them to offer up to the gods. How would you like that? Our Lord Huitzilopochtli's birthday celebration this year could be the greatest tribute we have ever paid!'

For all his lessons with the priests, Clawfoot knew very little about Tlaxcala, but the prospect of defeating them within a year seemed unlikely. They had been a thorn in the Mexica side for a long time.

'A pleasing idea, Lord Xiconoc,' replied Feathered Darkness. 'Do you think that sacrificial tribute from the frontier could make up for the loss of the local supply?'

'Of course it could,' scoffed Xiconoc. 'That's just it. Everyone has become used to the old way of doing things. No one wants to try anything different.'

'Perhaps you're right. Perhaps we all need a bit of a shake up.'

Xiconoc was obviously encouraged and was becoming more animated. 'My brother's the worst of the lot. He's a lazy piece of shit! He slouches about in his palace summoning an army of slaves to do his bidding and arranging parties. Tlacaelel disappears off into the distant jungles and meanwhile, halfway between the two of them, they create a sanctuary for our enemies! This obsession with conquest on our furthest borders makes trouble for us closer to home. Our city is filthy and full of foreign traders who gain admittance because of the bad deals we've struck with their rulers. Our merchants are squeezed out of their own marketplace by outsiders.'

Clawfoot could see that the merchant was warming to the topic. Maybe others had heard this speech.

'Worst of all,' continued Xiconoc, 'we share the spoils of war with Texcoco! We should be rid of Nezahualcoyotl and his courtiers and administer the east bank of the lake ourselves. That way, we would get to keep all of the tribute.'

'Not quite all. You're forgetting Tlacopan's share,' the high priest pointed out. 'Anyway, a large part of any Texcoco tribute would go towards the cost of running the place.'

'True, true. So the overall benefit would be reduced a little.'

'In short, you propose to supplant your brother and sort these problems out yourself.'

'It's just an idea, you understand,' said Xiconoc. 'Nothing more than an idea.'

'I see,' rejoined Feathered Darkness after a lengthy pause.

They had reached the far corner of the field where two canals crossed. Clawfoot saw Xiconoc gazing at the field that lay across the narrow stretch of water and noted his envious expression. That plot had been planted early and had somehow avoided the frosts. The plant life over there looked vibrant.

Feathered Darkness noticed too. 'Come, you mustn't despair, Lord Xiconoc. Yours will look like that next year,' he encouraged. 'Now, let us suppose for a while that I was to support your plans, whatever they are... what would I stand to gain from this alliance?'

'A good question. It's my impression that the spiritual destiny of our people should be guided by one person and the political and commercial aims led by another. Wouldn't you agree?'

'That makes perfect sense.'

'This way,' said Xiconoc. He turned right and headed east, in the direction of the city. 'At present, the leadership in both these areas is confused. Tlacaelel leads the armies, yet he must undo all his plans if the tlatoani does not approve. You are the high priest of the Order of Huitzilopochtli and yet my brother claims to be appointed by the gods to rule over the earth.'

The high priest nodded.

'I would simplify things. You would occupy one role and I would occupy the other.'

'But—'

'No,' Xiconoc interrupted. 'My brother may claim some divine provenance, but I can assure you that I make no such assertion. I am of flesh and bone, raised by mortals. I utterly lack the power to communicate with the gods, so I shall leave that to you and concentrate instead on the business of state: negotiations, brokering deals, overseeing the laws of our people and managing our armies.'

'A return to the old ways?' said Feathered Darkness, clearly surprised.

'Just so. Would you accept that burden?'

Feathered Darkness bowed. 'That would be an honour, Xiconoc, not a burden.'

Xiconoc smiled, gaining in confidence. 'We will forge a new leadership, small but strong. No clans, no committees, no fuss.'

'Brother Clawfoot!' said Feathered Darkness suddenly.

Clawfoot was taken by surprise. He had been trying to picture the portly merchant sitting on the throne and passing judgement on miscreants and criminals. The picture hadn't been a good one.

'Lord Xiconoc would have an alliance, Brother Clawfoot. What do the auguries hold for alliances?'

It was another test. Clawfoot wondered what the high priest wanted him to say. He hoped that he had not missed any hints. 'It is a propitious time to look to the ways of other people and a bad time to remain stuck in one's own routine. Although the calendar makes no reference to alliances at present, the night sky provides some guidance. I'm sure you're aware that the Scorpion represents strength and independence and, since it is at its lowest in the sky at present, you may conclude that this is a good time to develop partnerships and build new alliances.'

'He's pompous for one so young, isn't he?' observed Xiconoc.

Feathered Darkness ignored the comment. 'The Heavens support your plans, therefore so do I.' Apparently Clawfoot's pronouncement was acceptable. 'So tell me, is the tlatoani really risking his life with a trip to Totonaca? He is always well guarded. The Grey Privy Knights are always at his side.'

Xiconoc's sandals slapped as he followed the line of the canal. Clawfoot and Feathered Darkness made no noise in their bare feet.

'Things are not as orderly in the outlands as they are here in Tenochtitlan,' the nobleman replied after a while. 'Even short journeys through the jungle can be treacherous and when it rains, sometimes it's impossible to see the man two steps ahead of you. There are frequent mudslides and sinkholes, a thousand times more snakes than we have here in the valley and hostile villages on every bend of the river. Expeditions frequently get lost and separated.'

'Yes, I know. I've only strayed outside the valley once. I did not enjoy it,' added the high priest with a sour expression. 'Nevertheless, if you leave everything to chance, the tlatoani may still come through unscathed. Bold plans require bold actions and yet, here you are, nearly two hundred miles from where the action needs to take place.'

'You know me better than that.' Xiconoc wagged a finger at him. 'Neither of us operates like that. We both have capable people working for us. I have a man in Ahuilizapan, well placed and eager to do some dirty work, and more on their way.'

'Who would that be?'

'Never you mind,' said Xiconoc sharply. 'When you need to know, I will share that information with you. For now, just believe me when I tell you that I have chosen capable people with access to the tlatoani.'

'I hope you have. This sounds like a job for a small army.'

'Very astute,' said the merchant, 'and that's where you come in.'

'Ah.'

'Yes. You stand to gain from this as much as I do. It's only reasonable that you lend a hand. As you said, we need to field enough people to secure the outcome we need...'

'But not so many that our involvement cannot be kept secret!'

'Indeed,' replied Xiconoc. 'War makes the situation in Ahuilizapan unpredictable. My people will benefit from some support from the priesthood.'

The two men made an unlikely partnership, so it made sense to Clawfoot that only something as significant as the overthrow of the old order would bring them together.

'I can spare three men. I will send young Clawfoot with two of my warrior priests. Will that suffice?'

'I had hoped you would commit more of your men, Venerable Father,' said Xiconoc. 'But perhaps that will do, as long as I can count on your support in another matter.'

'And what would that be?'

41

'Ah.' Xiconoc made a sad face. 'Things closer to home are trickier. Politics are harder to manipulate. There are certain council members who would not look favourably on my accession.'

The shocked look on Feathered Darkness' face didn't convince Clawfoot.

'Yes, yes, it's true. Some will be persuaded with a little money; others may need more primitive forms of coercion.' Xiconoc smiled and the sunlight glinted from a gold canine. 'I'm sure your spies have already plenty of grubby secrets we can use.'

Perhaps more than you would like, thought Clawfoot.

They stopped at the next corner of Xiconoc's plot. The canal they had been following crossed a wider channel. Light danced across the ripples as numerous craft plied up and down it and on the far shore, nets spanned a regiment of poles standing neatly along the shallows. Although they would have been cleared early that morning, several ducks and what looked like a heron had already become ensnared.

'May I make an observation?'

'Of course!' replied Xiconoc, cheerfully. 'That's exactly what I need you for: advice.'

'I may be able to bring pressure to bear on one or two individuals,' said Feathered Darkness smoothly, 'but this is not a game where the movement of one or two pieces on a board will tip the balance. This is nothing less than a battle for the hearts and minds of the people.'

A disturbance over by the nets distracted them. Clawfoot saw that one of the ducks had managed to untangle itself and dropped into the water. It bobbed about for a while, shrugging and quacking crossly before stretching its wings and flying straight at them.

'Eh? What's that then?' called Xiconoc, stooping beneath the whirring wings.

'The Mexica need a father figure at the head of the family,' replied Feathered Darkness after the noise of the bird had receded. 'If you want the people to see you as their father, you would do well to have a woman at your side.'

'Pah! I have four concubines,' spat Xiconoc. 'What need have I of a wife?!'

One of Feathered Darkness' eyebrows rose reproachfully.' My...sources suggest you regularly have need of *someone's* wife.'

Xiconoc's jaw gaped and then his temper suddenly flared and he raised his voice, shouting for the first time.' How dare you! You keep your spies away from me and don't ever talk to me like that in front of others!'

Clawfoot inspected his nails very closely. He remembered the story of the snake, sliced in two as it strangled Tezozomoc's wife, and decided he couldn't trust the expression on his own face. He didn't really care what Xiconoc thought of his involvement in the conversation, but there was no point in antagonising him needlessly.

'Please!' said Feathered Darkness, raising his hands in a placatory gesture. 'This young man grew up in the gutter,' he added, pointing at Clawfoot. 'Nothing shocks him.'

Clawfoot acknowledged the comment with the slightest of bows. He hadn't seen much fornication and sexual abandonment while he'd been a street urchin, but there was no sense in disagreeing with his mentor at a time like this. Clawfoot understood that Xiconoc's forbidden relationship was useful leverage, but the notion of copulation filled him with disgust. It was haphazard, too complicated, too emotional for his liking and included a range of unpleasant bodily fluids. No. He'd done the right thing detaching himself from Little Maize. He would leave the business of creating life to others and stick to the purer purpose of dispatching those so created to the afterlife.

'I meant—' the nobleman began, bellowing.

'I know what you meant!' interrupted the high priest. 'Do you think I care that you're fucking Tezozomoc's wife?' he added. 'You can rut with his daughters and his sons too as far as I'm concerned, as long as you don't let anyone else find out. Your public appearance will just be that much more endearing if you had a queen. You know that the clan heads will look more favourably on a family man for the highest post.'

Xiconoc sighed and looked out over the chinampa with a thoughtful expression.

There was a good view of the Great Temple from this stretch of the canals. It rose majestically from the low sprawl of

43

Tenochtitlan with a plume of dust rising above it that served as a reminder of the ongoing construction work. Clawfoot was suddenly overwhelmed with the memory of the morning's events. His first ceremony on the top of the magnificent building had been a success, no matter what Eternal Flame had wanted him to believe. Clawfoot had taken the beating heart from a man and returned it to the gods. It gave him a tight, tingling sensation in his loins, a physical arousal that felt good. Eternal Flame and other experienced priests had tried to describe the feeling of power; a visceral kind of joy that welled in Clawfoot's core seemed too animal, too base to be a thing of divine benefaction.

'Trust me.' Feathered Darkness was still trying to persuade Xiconoc. He pointed along the edge of the canal, indicating that they should resume their stroll. 'If you seriously want the throne, you must be a man of the people here in Tenochtitlan. You need a wedding ceremony and a wife that the common people will look upon adoringly—'

'Where should I get this wife?' interjected Xiconoc. He seemed to have conceded the argument.' None of my concubines are suitable. The matchmakers have tried many times to no avail and then there's the small matter of cost. These marriage ceremonies are ruinously expensive, especially when one has such illustrious family members as I have to impress.'

'I have a suggestion, My Lord, and I think it will help you in that respect too,' said Feathered Darkness. 'Choose a commoner, a girl from one of the orphanages. She won't have any family to worry about.'

'What?!' Xiconoc spat in disgust. 'You would have me marry a mayeque?'

'Think about it,' exclaimed Feathered Darkness.' It's been done before by the high-born and well-to-do merchants wishing to display their humility. It always goes down very well with the people. Some of these arrangements even lead to lasting love. Remember Itzcoatl's brother-in-law? When his second wife died, he chose Heavenly Amaranth from the House of Ordered Progression – sadly closed down in recent times – and they were happily married for twenty-three years!'

Xiconoc fell silent and stared out across the chinampa. Clawfoot could see that he was giving the idea serious consideration: a beautiful, innocent young girl, an adoring crowd applauding the generous nobleman with a humble heart. The girl would doubtless look up to the older man adoringly and dote on him, that is, thought Clawfoot, until she discovered his bizarre sexual proclivities. An orphan would have no troublesome brothers-in-law to invite into the business and the marriage would be a cut-price affair, free from parasitic family members... on her side anyway. Xiconoc's broad smile suggested that he had just arrived at the same conclusion.

'What are these girls like?'

'I have heard that there are many fine *young* ladies at the Sisters of Penitence.' Feathered Darkness was careful with his use of emphasis. 'I know the woman who runs the Sisters of Penitence. I'll put in a good word for you, eh? Then in a few days' time, you can arrange a visit and see for yourself.'

Chapter 4 – Tenochtitlan

Little Maize tried to contain her anger. She took a deep breath and looked around at the dismal outhouse that served as a kitchen. One small window under the eaves, surrounded by cracked limestone plaster, let in the pale early dawn light. Earthenware bowls and cooking instruments lay scattered everywhere. The fire in the hearth had been allowed to go out, an upturned pot had disgorged its salt across the floor in one corner, while in the centre of the room a puddle of lime water was soaking into the floor, a disaster left over from the night before. Little Maize knew who was responsible. Her life felt like one long battle to contain the damage that White Moon was trying to wreak in it. Perhaps, thought Little Maize, this was White Moon's attempt to prevent her from getting to the assembly this morning. She looked at the other two girls who were on the early shift.

'You two get on with grinding the corn,' she snapped. 'I'll fetch some others to clear up this mess.'

'What shall we use?' whined the younger of the two girls she'd brought with her. 'Everything's filthy!'

The thirteen year old was already hurrying out of the open door and into the courtyard beyond with a bucket to fetch water, but the eleven-year-old girl was just standing there in her threadbare, pale-blue dress with a dejected look on her face. The fine fuzz of hair on her head marked her out as new to the Sisters of Penitence. Mother insisted that all the girls were stripped naked and shorn on admittance so as to create the effect of a symbolic rebirth, but everyone knew that it was to get rid of lice. This girl was an orphan, like the others, but she was lazy and Little Maize, who had been worked hard in her time at the refuge, could not abide indolence. She took pride in her work. After five years, Mother had entrusted her with the position of Second Maiden with eight younger girls in her care. Their house was entitled 'Maidens of the Lake'. The other five houses were named after mountain, river, sky and stars, and each was run by one of the older girls who, like Little Maize, had been a resident for several years. Little Maize's job was to wake the girls in her care and set them to their chores as the sun rose.

Little Maize gritted her teeth and leaned into the strike. The cane caught the girl squarely across her back. She whimpered and leapt away in search of implements to grind the corn with. The older girl returned with water and set about clearing an area on the cluttered floor where they could work.

'That's right, get on with it! I'll be back soon with others to deal with this.' She gestured at the stacks of dirty crockery. At least there wasn't much food waste to dispose of. Mother was far too mean and the girls too hungry to leave anything edible behind. 'If this pile isn't gone by the time we sit down to eat,' she said, meaning the stack of fifty cobs, 'you two will go hungry again.'

Little Maize made her way back to the sleeping quarters and woke three more of the young ones for the task of cleaning up the kitchen. All the older girls were gone, already headed for the main hall, one of only two large rooms in the bizarre collection of buildings that was the refuge. The Sisters of Penitence had been a small affair at its founding by the great Itzcoatl, but as the city had sprawled, so the refuge had grown in a haphazard way, all paid for now by its principal benefactor, Lord Moctezuma. Little Maize twitched her cane at the bare legs in front of her and urged the girl to a run. She prayed that she would not be the last one to arrive at the assembly. Last night, Mother had sent round an instruction for the older girls to gather before the morning meal on the following day. No explanation had been given. It was not the only unexpected development though. There was more exciting news that Little Maize wanted to concentrate on. After almost a year without contact, Clawfoot had suddenly got word to her that they should meet. Since their capture by priests, they had been able to speak no more than a handful of times. Clawfoot's routine as an acolyte was as gruelling as hers, but at least he was free to come and go. Little Maize was a prisoner, in everything but name. Even now that she'd risen to the post of one of Mother's Seconds, she wasn't allowed to visit the market without a chaperone, a duty sternly undertaken by the three older women who ran the refuge for Mother. It was just luck that one of Huitzilopochtli's priests was a teacher at the refuge and came every tenth day with his litany of madness. Yesterday, he'd had a friendly smile and a message for Little Maize that her Clawfoot would come to see her on the following day.

Little Maize barked a series of orders at the flustered girls, leaving them in no doubt that her vengeance would be terrifying if the kitchen wasn't spotless on her return, and then sped off back down the corridor again until she reached the entrance to the hall. She dashed inside, ignoring the glares of the two dozen people already gathered there and made her way to a familiar patch of the worn, mud-brick floor. It looked as though she was last after all.

On a chair, made from tightly woven reeds with an ornamental back-piece that sported a few tatty brown feathers, sat Mother.

'We're being honoured with a guest,' said Mother, a humourless smile cracking her leathery features and exposing the stumps of her few remaining teeth. Spidery fingers tugged ineffectually at her shawl. She glanced down at her dress with a critical eye and, seeing nothing there pertinent to the situation, turned her flinty eyes on the assembled girls.

'My good friend Feathered Darkness visited me yesterday...'

Little Maize wanted to snort in contempt. *I'll join the cult of filth eaters if the old woman has any friends at all*, she thought. She couldn't imagine two less likely bed-fellows. None of the girls reacted to the news and that seemed to anger the old woman. Her voice took on a shrill note.

'What? Have you forgotten who the high priest of Huitzilopochtli is?'

Some of the girls gasped in shock when they finally understood who the visitor would be and Mother looked more satisfied.

'Yes, that's right.' Her voice was like a rattlesnake moving over dried leaves. 'You may also know him as Heaven's Knife.'

Little Maize knew the name from long ago. She would never forget his cruel, sharp face, the dark eyes and the unkempt, sinister black hair. Feathered Darkness was the one who had captured her brother Indigo who had never been seen again. He was also responsible for the Catchers who had trapped her and her beloved Clawfoot and had them dispatched to their separate prisons. She couldn't recall if he had been the high priest at the time, she had been very young, but everyone knew Heaven's Knife now. She saw two of the younger girls reel in terror. A visit from a high priest could only mean one thing. Some of them would be chosen for sacrifice to the gods.

Mother did smile then. Her dark eyes twinkled, deep in their sockets and her lower lip folded over her toothless mouth until it almost touched her nose. She cast her eyes around the room, looking for signs of weakness, making a mental note of which girls needed toughening up. Little Maize prayed that her fear was well concealed, but doubted it all the while.

White Moon, First Maiden and Mother's favourite, spoke up, as if to demonstrate her bravery.

'The Feast of Huitzilopochtli is many trecena away, blessed Mother. What ceremony does this concern?'

'No ceremony this time, child,' the old woman croaked. 'I'm sure you have all heard of Xiconoc, Huitzilihuitl's eighth child and Lord Protector of the Realm, one of our tlatoani's brothers and one of the richest men in Tenochtitlan?'

Mother had phrased it as a question, but all the girls knew of Xiconoc. Royal lineage was one of the things the Sisters of Penitence had to learn by heart. Little Maize hated those lessons. Pointless facts about people she would never meet and who their myriad, over-stuffed relatives were. Mother reminded them all who Xiconoc was anyway and then proceeded to explain that he was due to visit in five days' time.

'He's coming to choose a bride!' she cackled.

Little Maize was genuinely surprised. In the five years since her capture and incarceration, twenty-five girls had been married off, but only three of them to living men. The remainder had been betrothed to one god or another, none of them living more than a full cycle of the moon.

'Yes, that's right,' said Mother, seeing the astonishment on the faces all around. 'The great warrior and merchant, rich beyond any of your wildest imaginings, has decided to show his humility and deep attachment to us ordinary people. He will come here and choose his wife from amongst you.' The old woman sat back against her rough-hewn wooden throne and allowed her words to sink in.

It meant nothing to Little Maize. She would not be chosen and was grateful for that. Her dreams of escaping the torment of this cursed place revolved around Clawfoot. Somehow he would find a way to free her. Just then, Little Maize caught White Moon smirking at her from alongside Mother's chair, as if reading her thoughts. It was as though the older girl wanted to remind her of her place. They didn't live in the same house anymore and for that, Little Maize was grateful beyond words, but White Moon's place as First Maiden meant that she still had occasion to abuse her. Nowadays she had other, more pliable, young flesh to press herself upon and most of the trouble she gave Little Maize resulted from her position as Mother's favourite. Occasionally though, White Moon would happen across her, almost by accident, and Little Maize was forced to succumb to the older girl's predatory advances. The thought made her burn with shame. She had tried to fight back, but she wasn't strong. The years on the street had taken their toll on her frame and the meagre diet in the refuge wasn't going to set that right. At seventeen, White Moon was two years older and had a weight advantage that she used to good effect. Little Maize could not understand how there could be so much malice in such a beautiful girl. She tried to quell the bile gathering in her stomach and focused on Mother's words.

'I want this place cleaned as never before,' the old woman said, using her fiercest look. 'For the next five days, you will do double duties. I want every room, corridor and hall scrubbed clean from top to bottom. Every basket and every chest must be emptied out, the contents cleaned and put back neatly.'

Mother's list of instructions continued and Little Maize's attention began to wander.

'I can't imagine he'll find anyone worthy here,' clucked the old woman. 'I swear to the Earth Mother herself that I have done my best with you lot, but I've never been cursed with such a bunch of ugly ingrates!' She cracked her gap-toothed smile at White Moon then, as if excluding her from the list of the accused.

Little Maize fervently prayed that Xiconoc would take White Moon for his bride. To her, it seemed like the least upsetting outcome of them all. She certainly didn't want to be betrothed to a man she'd never met, even if it got her out of the Sisters of Penitence. How would she ever be able to be with Clawfoot? Little Maize pictured a fat, slovenly nobleman with nothing but rhetoric and gilded plumage to his name. Then she thought of Clawfoot and how they had been when they had lived together on the street with her brother, Indigo, and the young boy Shield of Gold. Back then it had seemed so hard, but with hindsight, she realised that it had been a blessed time. They had answered to no one and had never had to clean anything. True, they had nearly starved to death several times, but they had had the run of the city.

Mother was still ranting. 'I want to be sure you understand how great an honour it would be to be chosen. I rescued each and every one of you from the gutter! If it wasn't for me and the generosity of our Lord Moctezuma who funds this humble establishment, you would all be dead, or worse, slaves in Heuxotzingo.' She pointed a bony finger at Light of the Just, one of her Seconds who stood at the front. 'Imagine! The lucky girl will be mixing with the cream of Mexica society in a few weeks' time with dozens of slaves at her beck and call. Make sure you remember your home, your origins here at the Sisters of Penitence. When you have a chance, make sure your lord and master sees fit to grant us the means to continue our good work here at the refuge!

'I will see to it that you all have clean dresses to wear and I will send White Moon out to gather flowers to weave into your hair. You see how well I look after you, eh?'

Little Maize couldn't believe her ears. Mother never spent money on the girls. She only had two grey, rough-spun maguey fibre dresses, both of them third- or fourth-hand, obtained nearly two years ago when one of the girls had been picked as Tlaloc's bride.

All the girls began chattering excitedly as soon as they were sent from the hall. Even Little Maize felt some of the relief that whomever was picked was not to be led to the Great Temple.

She had no illusions about her beauty. When she was in her second year at the refuge, Little Maize had come across a battered copper mirror in the central courtyard. Convinced that it was one of Mother's trinkets, Little Maize had hidden it in the rafters of a storage shed, hoping to gain some credit by handing it in when it was reported lost. That day never came and so, when rare opportunities arose, she would take it out and polish it until she could see her reflection in it. She hadn't much liked what she had seen. She had an elegant face, longer than the traditional rounder shape of the Mexica people. Her nose was too big though and the flecks of green in her brown eyes gave her the look of a witch, at least that's what some of the other girls had said to her when she first arrived. Clawfoot had never said anything unkind. Little Maize felt sure that he found her attractive. When they had been together on the streets, she'd caught him looking at her that way he had: a strange, intense look and a slightly furrowed brow. Whenever it had happened, he'd always turned away immediately, as though embarrassed.

Little Maize was so preoccupied with her thoughts that she didn't see White Moon until it was too late and bumped into her.

'Don't go getting any ideas,' hissed White Moon.

'What?' Little Maize was shocked. She wondered how her tormentor could have known about her meeting with Clawfoot.

'You're never going to get out of this place,' said White Moon. She reached up and caught hold of Little Maize's hair, twisting her head to one side. The passageway was deserted. Little Maize turned her body sideways, desperate to avoid the older girl's questing hand.

'I—'

'You're not even from round here. He'll never pick you,' added White Moon cruelly.

Little Maize was staring in horrified fascination at White Moon's face. How could such evil reside in such perfect features? Her lustrous lashes were compressed to menacing narrow slits over her dark brown eyes and her small nose and perfectly formed lips were puckered into a contemptuous sneer. Suddenly, Little Maize realised what White Moon had said.

'I didn't think he would.'

'Good, because Mother hasn't given me quite enough cacao beans to get new dresses for all of us.' White Moon bared her perfect teeth in a radiant smile. 'You'll have to do without, but it would be wasted on you anyway. Xiconoc will be looking for a princess. He won't want a filthy slave girl like you!'

She pushed Little Maize away roughly, as though she had suddenly grown bored. She turned on her heel and stalked off a couple of paces before looking over her shoulder.

'Oh, how is the kitchen work coming along today?' she asked, one eyebrow cocked slightly. 'Do make sure it's spotless by nightfall. I'd hate for you to have to do it all again tomorrow, but you know the rule... if the task isn't done, your house keeps it another day.'

Little Maize's girls had to work harder than ever to complete their chores, but just before the sun dipped below the chain of mountains in the west, the kitchen was spotless, ensuring that tomorrow's tasks would not be hindered by today's unfinished business. Little Maize shooed her charges to their meagre evening meal and made it to the lakeside entrance to the walled compound that was their home.

'Where have you been?' said Clawfoot. 'I haven't got long.'

'I'm so sorry,' said Little Maize, trying to keep the desperation out of her voice. What she needed was a good long talk with Clawfoot, not a hurried exchange through a broken gate. Her gaze devoured him. He had changed so much. He was a head taller than she was now and he stared down at her over his angular jaw line. His nose, broken during their capture by the priests, had healed with a slight kink to it. She was a little shocked at the ragged look his ears had developed due to the repeated blood offerings that were required of initiates to the priesthood, but his mane of black hair gave him a rugged look that Little Maize decided she liked. He needed a wash, but she didn't say so for risk of souring the mood.

'White Moon is still making trouble for me. She made a mess of the kitchen, or had someone else do it. I had to make sure it was cleaned up.' It sounded boring as she said it and it made her cringe inside.

'Oh.'

Clawfoot looked so serious. Little Maize smiled shyly, hoping to provoke that wide grin she used to love so much when they had lived rough, scavenged for food and made their own rules up. Of course he wouldn't understand the extent of the torment that she faced. She was too ashamed to tell the whole truth about White Moon's unwelcome advances.

'You look good,' she ventured.

'Uh, so do you.'

Little Maize noticed his eyes straying to the front of her shift. Her breasts were fuller since his last visit. She felt her cheeks burn. 'You seem a bit distant. Is there something you want to tell me?' She hated herself for hurrying Clawfoot, but she had no idea how long they would be able to speak. Someone was sure to happen along at any moment.

'Yeah, well... I'm sorry I haven't come to see you recently. I thought I'd better, you know, come...'

There was something else. 'Is there something the matter?'

'No... no, nothing like that,' said Clawfoot. 'It's just that the priests have entrusted me with a mission.'

'That's great news, isn't it?' Little Maize was delighted for him. Clawfoot had been given a hard time when he'd been captured by the priests. He had hinted at beatings and lonely night-time vigils on freezing temple tops and Little Maize felt sure that, like her, Clawfoot hadn't told of the worst of it. Now it seemed that he'd finally earned their trust; not that she trusted any of the priests of course.

'Yes, but I have to go away, perhaps for many moons. Please,' he added, looking furtively over Little Maize's shoulder at the gathering shadows, 'you cannot speak of this to anyone.'

'I'll take your secrets to Mictlan's shades,' whispered Little Maize, reaching through the gate to touch Clawfoot's arm. She was elated that he was confiding in her.

'The tlatoani, Lord Moctezuma, is going to inspect the armies of the Triple Alliance in the jungles of Totonaca. A trade convoy is accompanying the royal caravan and I've been asked to join one of the older priests to provide spiritual guidance.'

Little Maize giggled, amused at the image of her best friend Clawfoot playing along with the holy men. Clawfoot frowned at her and she suddenly realised he was taking it seriously.

'Will you really be gone for many moons?'

'Yes. Possibly.'

Clawfoot didn't seem upset at the prospect and Little Maize grew concerned that she might be losing him. She wanted to give him hope. She wanted to remind him that they'd lived together and roamed the streets as one. Little Maize wanted to tell him that they would be together again, but she didn't trust her voice. She didn't think she would ever escape from the Sisters of Penitence, except as an offering to the gods. As the thought occurred to her, a terrifying image sprang to mind of Clawfoot officiating on the top of the Great Temple, wielding a cruel blade as the other priests bent her back over the altar. She gasped and put a hand to her mouth.

'Are you alright?' asked Clawfoot.

'Yes. Yes, I'm fine,' replied Little Maize and started babbling about the only thing she could think of to change the subject. 'There's a nobleman coming to choose a bride.'

'Err...yes, I know.'

'What? How can you?'

'I was with the high priest two days ago when he suggested it to Xiconoc.'

It was the only interesting news that Little Maize had to tell him, so the fact that he already knew about it made her feel depressed. She told herself that was absurd and that it didn't matter and tried to cheer herself up by imagining the consequence for one of the girls.

'At least someone will escape from here,' she said, as brightly as she could manage.

'Perhaps it will be you, Little Maize.'

'I don't want him to pick me!' Little Maize held Clawfoot's arm tightly. 'Clawfoot! Let's run away together.' Suddenly, her facade crumbled. Years of self-sufficiency fell away and her raw, painful need came to the surface. She looked into Clawfoot's earnest face. 'This gate isn't locked and I don't own anything.

We can go…now. We can find a place somewhere in the mountains where no one ever goes and build a house. We can grow maize and squashes and trade with nearby villages. It won't be much, but we'll be free again.' Little Maize could hear the desperation in her own voice and it nearly broke her. This was the dream that she had nurtured all these years and in the dead of night after White Moon had had her way. She had to make him see.

'Little Maize…' said Clawfoot with an apologetic face. He stopped and tried again. 'I want to go to Totonaca. I want to do this mission for the priests,' he added softly. He reached back through the bars of the wooden gate and held her arm, squeezing it gently.

'Well go then.' Little Maize fought the tremor in her voice. 'And when you get back, then we can go. I'll wait for you. I don't care how long it takes.'

'We're not allowed to have women.'

'What are you saying?' cried Little Maize fiercely. 'You're not one of them! You told me that yourself the last time you visited. You're not a priest.'

Clawfoot hung his head sadly. 'I… I have to go, Little Maize. I'll come and visit you again… I promise.'

A dark vortex opened up in Little Maize's soul and devoured her from the inside. Clawfoot was lying; she could sense it. She managed a strangled response of some kind, but it didn't sound like words, not even to her. Her vision clouded over and she clutched at the rotting gatepost as Clawfoot turned and trudged off into the gloom.

Chapter 5
The Jungles of Totonaca

It was pouring again. Every day, huge clouds boiled up, high above the emerald jungle, then coalesced to drench the waiting landscape. Raindrops lashed the long grass as though Tlaloc's lifeblood was falling in torrents from the murky sky. Jaguar could even hear the distant clatter as the onslaught raked the treetops at the jungle's edge. He picked his way carefully towards Tlacaelel's tent from the crudely built barracks that housed his company of men. Snakes often fled to higher ground in such weather. Jaguar didn't like snakes. Totonaca was teeming with the things and there were far too many places for them to hide. Back in the valley that surrounded Lake Texcoco there was less greenery and there were a great many more people. The snakes that lived there had the decency to hide at the sound of approaching footfall. Since the army had set out from Tenochtitlan two moons ago, ten men had died from snake bites.

Tlacaelel's tent was staked out in a clearing and stood on a platform made of cut logs. The unhappy men standing watch recognised Jaguar and nodded deferentially before moving aside. He pushed through the flap. Inside it was humid but mercifully free from rain. Jaguar squeezed what water he could from the end of his queue near the doorway to avoid dripping all over the reed mats that carpeted the room. Oil lamps helped to augment the dim light that penetrated the tent fabric.

Last Medicine and Two Sign were already there along with the other captains. Jaguar noted that the older men had adopted long tunics impregnated with beeswax to keep the rain off. No one looked comfortable. One was either damp with sweat from the cloying heat or soaked by the frequent rain in this cursed part of the world. Jaguar wore only his loincloth with a belt and dagger at his waist and the spotted skin headdress that marked him as the commander of the Jaguar Knights. The less clothing one wore, the less there was to dry out.

Xipil, one of Two Sign's trusted captains, a distinguished veteran with a stout chest and a damaged eye, was midway through a report about his reconnaissance trip to the east where the mountains ended in a broad plain that stretched as far as the eye could see. Beyond that far horizon was said to be the sea that only a handful of adventurous merchants had seen. Tlacaelel was listening intently, stopping the man every so often to ask a question. Like the men he commanded, the general's head was shaved, except for the back of his scalp where the hair was tied in a queue, doubled over to halve its length and keep it neat. Jaguar decided there was definitely more grey in that hair than when they had set out sixty days ago. All of the warriors treated him with respect verging on reverence whenever he spoke. The younger warriors kept their eyes to the floor.

'Ixtlahuacan lies another day's march from the foot of the mountains,' said Xipil. 'It is not a city like Tenochtitlan, not even as large as Ahuilizapan, but it is a wealthy town. We saw traders bringing many birds and animals to sell in the marketplace. Many people come from the coast with shells and strange fish and we even spoke to one man who said that the Tlaxcala used to visit often to buy gold and precious stones.'

'Any villages along the way?'

'Three, My Lord,' replied Xipil. 'Three villages between the pass just north of here and where the river kinks to the east.'

Tlacaelel nodded. 'The smaller villages on the river do not matter. Once we take their capital, they will soon dance to the same drumbeat. How many fighting men do you think they can muster?'

'Eight hundred people, but perhaps no more than two or three hundred capable warriors.' The scout knew what information Tlacaelel was after. 'Our local man went into all three villages pretending to be searching for his wife and daughters. He claimed that his family had run away from his own village when they heard about the advancing Mexica.'

'Did they suspect anything?'

The scout grinned. 'They let him leave, so I don't think they did.'

'Good. We may have need of him again.' Tlacaelel turned his attention to Jaguar. 'What have you to report?'

'Lord Tlacaelel, I travelled south along the Broken Ridge towards Zongolica. There were twelve of us and two local men. The town was exactly as described to us. It occupies the valley floor between steep ridges. The hills are thick with fruit trees. All of the flat land between the ridges has been cleared and turned over to farming, so a surprise attack may not be possible.'

'Did you send in one of the local men?'

'Lord Tlacaelel, I am sorry but our guides tried to escape so we were forced to kill them.'

Tlacaelel looked annoyed. 'Couldn't you have recaptured them?'

'No, My Lord, we were too close to the town. We couldn't risk them hearing the noise and raising the alarm. I gave the command for my men to take them down with arrows.'

'So we have no information from Zongolica. That is not good.'

Jaguar held a hand up to placate the general. 'We still managed to get the information we needed.'

'How so, without local people to infiltrate the town?'

'I did it, Lord Tlacaelel,' said Jaguar. 'I went into the town myself.'

'Didn't the townspeople recognise you as an outsider?'

'No, My Lord. I have no lip plugs or ornaments that mark me out as Mexica. Also, my skin is lighter than many of our people—'

'Aye, too much of your youth spent in a dingy workshop,' interrupted Two Sign with a sneer.

Jaguar ignored his friend. The Eagle Knight had been in a bad mood since the games when he'd lost his bet with Last Medicine. '...so I'm more like these folk who live beneath the trees and these cursed clouds,' he added. 'I waited until the evening rains began and, leaving my sword and shield with my men, I walked along the main street into town.'

'Didn't they challenge you?' asked Two Sign.

'They did.'

'What did you tell them?' Tlacaelel shot back. 'We have all learned some of the local dialect, but surely even your Totonacan is not good enough to pass as one of the natives.'

'I did not speak at all,' replied Jaguar with a grin. 'I swayed a little when the guards questioned me and I looked at them as though I was simple in the head. Then, when they pointed their spears at me, I rolled my eyes upwards and collapsed upon the ground like one of the tainted ones,' Jaguar said, referring to the people who were touched by spirits. Some became healers or seers, but there were some, the tainted ones, who never recovered and often fell in the street, frothing at the mouth or shouting at the demon voices in their heads. In Tenochtitlan such people could not be harmed, so, Jaguar had hoped, it would be the same here.

'What happened next?'

'They discussed what to do with me for a long time, but eventually they brought me before their tlatoani, a thin old man without any teeth whom our Lord Moctezuma could blow over with a fart.'

Everyone laughed at that except Two Sign.

'When the old man questioned me I rolled my eyes and barked like a dog.'

Tlacaelel looked puzzled, so Jaguar explained.

'I wanted it to look as though I was cooperating, you know… trying to answer but the wrong thing was coming out. Anyway, it did not go well.

'The tlatoani decided that I was possessed by an evil spirit. He said I should be taken to the temple and sacrificed, but the clansmen disagreed. They were scared that if I died, the evil spirit would escape its earthly vessel and attack the people of Zongolica. The high priest snapped at them both. He said that they were both wrong and that I was the spirit of Caimatlacatl, the god of the forest, who had taken a human shape to come among the people and judge them.' Jaguar paused. 'Lord Tlacaelel, perhaps I should just cut to the facts? I did a rough count of the houses and got a good look at their warriors.'

'In time, Jaguar,' insisted the general, waving him on. 'We must know how you escaped.'

'Alright. They paraded me through the town until we reached the far side of the village. By this time, there were five or six hundred townsfolk following the high priest. There, leaning against an enormous boulder, was a house made of sticks and palm fronds with wisps of smoke rising from the thatch. Two small dogs ran out to meet us, barking as though to raise the dead. Remembering my part, I barked in response.' Jaguar grinned at the memory. 'Hearing the commotion, an old man came out. He only had a few scraps of hair and he was so bent over that his gaze was mostly on the earth in front of him. The high priest and the tlatoani called him Teozonteotl, but the people of the town revered him as the spirit of the woods and none dared speak when he emerged.

'The high priest spoke to the old man and told him what had happened and dragged me over to him. He was so stooped with age he could not look directly at me but had to turn his head sideways to look me up and down. He complained that I was too tall, so one of the tlatoani's guards grabbed my hair, kicked the back of my knees and forced me to kneel down. Then the old man reached out and took my hand and cut it with a knife.' Jaguar held up one of his hands, which was bandaged.

'What happened then?' said Tlacaelel.

'He summoned another of the tlatoani's guard of honour and cut his hand too. He told us to hold our hands in front of us so the dogs could come and smell the blood. I understood what he wanted, but I pretended not to, so he grabbed my hand and held it where the dogs could come and sniff it. The guard knelt down as they came near, but the dogs shied away. When they came close to me, one of them licked the blood on my hand and the other started barking and tried to lick my face.'

Everyone in Tlacaelel's tent started talking at the same time, excited and arguing about what the sign could mean. Tlacaelel cut across them all and motioned for Jaguar to continue.

'At first, they didn't seem to know what to do, but then the tlatoani spoke sharply to the old man and then told his guard to approach the dogs again, but this time, when he moved forward they began to growl and whimper. The guard looked at me just then and I caught a look of fear in his eye. The old man jabbered something and pointed his knife at the guard. That was when everyone turned on him.'

'What?' Two Sign looked incredulous.

'The next thing I knew, everyone was dragging the guard away, to the temple to sacrifice him, while I was left alone with the old man. He told me to wait while he disappeared inside his hut. When he came out, he gave me this cloth to place over my hand and told me to go. "Be on your way. You have enough troubles of your own, young man," he said. Then he added, "He who is mighty will be laid low when the flower makes way for the crocodile. All that he has will be taken. When it is dark, look to the water and there will you find hope."'

'Pfff!' Tlacaelel scratched his head. 'What in the name of the Creator Pair did he mean by that?'

'I do not know, My Lord. I could not very well speak and ask him to explain or he would have known the depth of my lie. I shrugged my shoulders and he just winked at me before heading back to his little hut. The dogs looked at me, one with its head on one side, and then followed him inside. I ran for the trees and got as far away as I could before any of the townsfolk could return. I circled back round to the other side of the town where my men were. They had been about to leave, thinking that the screams they'd heard from the temple top had been mine.'

The tent erupted into a heated debate about what the sorcerer had said. Everyone had a different interpretation. Most of them thought that the reference to the flower and the crocodile meant the date Fifteen Cipactli, which was in thirteen days' time. Xipil said that it was a mythical date in the future, when Tlaloc was supposed to rise from the river and take over the land. No one could come up with any suggestions for the bit about looking to the water. With some difficulty, Tlacaelel managed to reestablish order and Jaguar told them all how big the town of Zongolica was, the whereabouts of the tlatoani's modest residence and the routes into the jungle that the townsfolk would take in the event that they were attacked. The information confirmed reports from a trade delegation from Texcoco that had visited the place nearly a year ago.

Tlacaelel looked pleased and then turned his attention to the other warriors who had been out scouting. Everyone told similar tales of towns and villages with rudimentary buildings and few defences. Some settlements took advantage of natural features such as rivers or ravines to protect themselves and a few had staked perimeters, but the majority had nothing.

'These people are too trusting,' observed Tlacaelel. 'They settle feuds with skirmishes and punitive expeditions with no thought of conquest. The little expansion carried out by Ahuilizapan is temporary, any gains soon lost to raiders from the north.

'For those of you who do not already know, Lord Moctezuma will visit us here in ten or eleven days' time. He arrives with one hundred and eighty more knights and one thousand porters bringing fresh supplies of food and weapons. Imixquitl, the ruler of Ahuilizapan,has been persuaded to put on a grand show.' Tlacaelel gave a wicked grin. 'I may have given him the impression that his life depended on pleasing our tlatoani.'

Everyone chuckled.

'Very well, once the tlatoani gets here with reinforcements we can move on Ixtlahuacan. It's too big and too far away to tackle until then, so in the meantime, we will focus on Zongolica. Heart of the Jaguar will lead the army. I will accompany the expedition in an advisory capacity. We leave in seven days' time, make an overnight stop a little over halfway there and strike the town on the evening of the following day. Two Sign, you will remain here in charge of Ahuilizapan.' The general nodded at the commander of the Eagle Knights. 'Go now and pick two hundred of the best men: the safest, most trustworthy fighters. Everyone else will go to Zongolica. I want the young and inexperienced or overweight near the front. This will be good training for them; not too hard but not easy either. Last Medicine, those five men we caught mistreating the locals?'

'Yes, Lord Tlacaelel. They are felling trees right now to help provide lumber for the townsfolk.'

'Recall them,' said Tlacaelel. 'I want them to be first into Zongolica. If they survive that, they can go back to chopping wood.'

Everyone began to file out of the tent, but Tlacaelel had a final request.

'Oh, and I want weapons drills and mock combat daily, not just alternate days.' He nodded his dismissal but caught Jaguar's eye, indicating that he should stay.

'How do you do it?' laughed the general when they were alone. 'I wager you will escape from the World of the Dead soon after Mictlan takes you.'

Jaguar laughed with Tlacaelel. 'I don't know what you mean.'

'Don't be modest, Jaguar. There was that escape from Chalco several years ago and then, just last year, you and two others managed to break free after a Tarascan war party took you captive. A man must sing of his exploits. They are the path to the afterlife.'

'Perhaps, Lord Tlacaelel,' acknowledged Jaguar. 'Although I may leave the singing to others; my voice is atrocious.'

'Yes. Two Sign warned me about that as I recall.' Tlacaelel smiled and then adopted a more businesslike expression. 'Listen, I am worried about the tlatoani's visit.'

Jaguar frowned. 'Have you explained to him that it's not safe?'

'I did,' growled Tlacaelel. 'I sent several messengers to him begging him to reconsider.'

'And?'

'You know what he's like. He dismissed the local threat and says he will have his own bodyguards with him anyway.'

'The Grey Privy Knights?'

'Yes.'

'Well, he should be well protected.'

Tlacaelel made a face. 'That would be true if his sons weren't coming with him.'

'What?' Jaguar sagged, horrified at the idea of being responsible for the entire male line of the Colhua dynasty wandering about deep inside enemy territory.

'You see!' exclaimed Tlacaelel. 'It wouldn't matter so much if they were all sticking together. Two dozen of the tlatoani's bodyguard would be more than enough to keep them all safe. The problem is that the tlatoani wants his sons to act as trade ambassadors. They and a number of our merchants are supposed to meet with local dignitaries to help them see the benefits of trading with royalty.'

'That will spread the bodyguards a bit thinly.'

Tlacaelel clasped Jaguar's shoulder. 'Exactly! That's why I want you to look after his sons.'

Jaguar worked to keep his dismay from showing. 'You want the commander of the Jaguar Knights to be their wet-nurse?'

'Who better? The tlatoani will be reassured when he sees that my top man is protecting his heirs.'

'You honour me,' said Jaguar, wondering what he had done to merit such an ignoble task. He wanted to be with his warriors, seizing towns and villages for the glory of the Mexica Empire.

'Come on, Jaguar,' coaxed the general. 'It's only for a short time. It will be many moons, or even years, before we reach the coast with many more fights along the way, but opportunities like this don't come along very often. My brother will doubtless reward you well for keeping his family safe. I will make sure that he does and it will mean honour and riches for your family.'

'What about Two Sign?' Jaguar made one last bid to extricate himself.

Tlacaelel patted Jaguar's shoulder. 'Come on! Two Sign is a fighting machine and a legend. He'd be my first choice if I wanted someone to defeat the God of War in single-handed combat, but this job requires more tact, more skill with people. Iquehuacatzin is difficult at the best of times, arrogant and demanding...out here, there's no telling what he'll get up to. Will you do this for me?'

Jaguar sighed, suddenly missing home and the warmth of Precious Flower's embrace. It had been more than two moons since he had seen her. Even then, he had only been back in Tenochtitlan for seven days after returning from a campaign to the north keeping the Tarascan threat at bay. Precious Flower was trying to be brave, but Jaguar knew it was hard for her.

'Lord Tlacaelel, I cannot watch over them day and night. I will need help.'

'By night, Iquehuacatzin and Mahchimaleh will be under the same roof as their father and therefore under the protection of the Grey Privy Knights. You will only need to keep watch over them during the daytime. For that, you can pick two of your Jaguar Knights. If I need you for some urgent task, you can hand over to Xipil, but other than that, they are your responsibility, understand?'

'Yes, My Lord. Of course. I shall not let you down.' Jaguar had an idea. Some good might yet come of this scheme. 'Lord Tlacaelel?'

'Yes, Jaguar.'

'Perhaps I could escort them home once they are done. That way I can see my family briefly before returning here. My wife is expecting...'

Tlacaelel winked. 'You see? Quick thinking turns the situation to your advantage. I knew you'd come round. An excellent suggestion. I don't know why I didn't think of it myself.'

Jaguar left Tlacaelel's tent, glad to get away from the gentle drumroll of the rain on cloth. Tlacaelel was right: protecting the tlatoani's family was an honour. It just wasn't what he'd thought he'd be doing in Totonaca. Still, at least this way he'd be home soon to see his second child. She would be born any day now. Precious Flower had assured him that she was due in Xochitl, the trecena of flowers, which was two days away.

Chapter 6 – Tenochtitlan

A raddled old priest wearing nothing but a black loincloth and sash stepped up to the funeral pyre and spoke the words of final dedication.

'O Great Lord of the ever-present,
Accept another soul
Into your blessed arms.
Keep watch on the spirit of this warrior
On the paths of the ever-night
And see it safe into the always-after.'

The priest lowered the pitch-pine torch to the oil-soaked logs and stepped back as the flames leapt up around the shrouded body of Quauhtlatoa, the erstwhile ruler of Tlatelolco. Night shrank back before the exuberant light of the bonfire, illuminating a crowd of dignitaries assembled respectfully at the top of the small temple. The deceased's son, Moquihuix, looked suitably humble in simple robes of mourning. Leaping fire glinted in the tear tracks on his cheeks.

Axayacatl sheltered from the incandescent fury of the pyre behind his father. Tezozomoc seemed untroubled by the heat. Axayacatl's grandfather, Moctezuma, had come with his sons from adjacent Tenochtitlan to pay their respects to the king of the Tepanecs. The great man's head was bowed, but Iquehuacatzin and Mahchimaleh looked bored, staring around disrespectfully. Iquehuacatzin was tall, wiry and good-looking with a youthful spring in his step. His brother, Mahchimaleh, was solidly built though only a whisker shorter. His jaw was wider than his forehead where a thick, continuous line of eyebrow brooded, giving him a slightly puzzled expression. It seemed hard to believe they were his cousins. Axayacatl wasn't quick to judge people, but everything these two did encouraged his innate loathing of them.

Nezahualcoyotl was there too. The ruler of Texcoco stood to one side so that his noble profile glowed a fierce orange against the night sky. He looked as though he was meditating, perhaps in silent communication with his own gods. Axayacatl had nothing but admiration for the man. This small temple to Tezcatlipoca was the site where his wise old teacher had been tortured and executed on the orders of the Tepanecs who had ruled the whole valley not so long ago. Worse than that, he had witnessed the execution of his own father by the same people, aided by the fathers and grandfathers of many of the people who stood around the fire.

The breeze changed direction and a shower of sparks caressed the standing figures on the temple top. Several brushed at the stinging embers. Nezahualcoyotl stood firm. Here he was, reflected Axayacatl, among the descendants of his own ancestor's greatest enemies, playing the part of the great statesman and working hard to keep the Triple Alliance together.

Axayacatl didn't think he was capable of such forgiveness. He had been schooled well. His tutors in the Calmecac had been at pains to make him aware of his royal ancestry. His grandfather, Itzcoatl, had reigned as tlatoani before Moctezuma, yet now his own family were being pushed inexorably away from the centre of power. The fact that Axayacatl's mother was Moctezuma's daughter meant nothing. The tlatoani and his closest advisors were grooming Moctezuma's own sons for the throne. None of this would have mattered much except for the fact that Moctezuma's sons wasted no opportunity to belittle Axayacatl and comment on the decline of his family's social standing.

The conflagration had reached its peak and when the flames began to dwindle, the assembled rulers and noblemen took their cue, descending the temple steps to join the celebrations that had been organised to usher in the new ruler of Tlatelolco. Axayacatl didn't feel in the mood for celebration, but he smiled at his little brother, Tizoc, and took his hand.

'Come on. There will be mountains of food to eat.'

'Sweet cakes?' asked Tizoc, eagerly.

'Yes,' laughed Axayacatl, leading patiently. 'More than even you can eat.' The temple steps were tall for a ten year old.

They had just reached the bottom step when a big hand clasped Axayacatl's shoulder.

'Look at these two strong warriors,' came a deep, melodious voice. It was the ruler of Texcoco.

'My Lord Nezahualcoyotl.' Axayacatl bowed politely and tugged suggestively at Tizoc's arm until he followed suit. They both looked in awe at Nezahualcoyotl. He had a comfortingly rugged face with an aquiline nose and flowing black locks set atop a pair of broad shoulders.

'Axayacatl, I hear good things of you.'

'Then I must challenge your sources, My Lord. They must be misinformed.' Axayacatl was genuinely puzzled. 'Instead of fighting with our army, my parents insist I remain in the city and work on our social obligations.'

'Don't underestimate the importance of diplomacy. I heard glowing reports of you from your time in Calmecac. It would be a shame to lose qualities such as yours to a moment of inattention on the battlefield.'

'You are kind, Lord Nezahualcoyotl, but my teachers were always disappointed with me.'

Nezahualcoyotl laughed, a warm and easy sound. 'I thought my teachers hated me too. I always believed those trips to the shrine on Iztacihuatl were a punishment. How well I recall my lonely pilgrimages through the frigid night with nothing but the moon and the stars to guide me. The priests insisted that I went naked, to teach me humility, and when I reached the blessed image of the White Lady, I had to cut both ears so that when I leaned forward to kiss her, the crimson drops stained her pale feet.'

The man spoke in a measured, lilting voice that was mesmerising. They had never exchanged more than the briefest of pleasantries before. 'Yes, I remember those times!' exclaimed Axayacatl. 'Why don't they make the other students do the midnight vigil?'

'They make me do it,' piped up Tizoc. 'I was scared the first time, but I'm not anymore.'

'It is a little scary the first time, isn't it?' agreed the ruler of Texcoco. 'Of course they make the other boys do night-time vigils, my friend,' he added. 'They just do it less often than you or I, for we are born of kings.'

'What good does it do, My Lord?'

Nezahualcoyotl assumed a paternal expression. 'One day, Axayacatl, you may rise to the post of tlatoani yourself, and if you do, you will have been well prepared for routine and loneliness. Come,' he added. 'We must follow the others or there will be no food left.'

Axayacatl was surprised to hear the Lord of Texcoco talk of loneliness. His court was a thrilling place, renowned for art, song and poetry. There were many parties and many new ideas were said to come from the lively discussions that took place there. He had accompanied his father, Tezozomoc, there last year and marvelled at the non-stop entertainment. Two courtyards outside the palace were home to musicians and artists, plying their trade and vying for the attention of the noblemen and members of the royal family who regularly came in search of new talent.

They caught up with the rest of the party in a courtyard not far from the temple. Slaves from Moquihuix's household walked around with large wooden trays offering the guests succulent cooked meats and piles of fruit. Tezozomoc was waiting for them. He bowed to Nezahualcoyotl. Tizoc darted off, unable to postpone the temptation of food any longer.

'What are you three scheming?' he joked.

'Tezozomoc, My Lord. Your eldest is a credit to your family. You should be proud of him. I think he will make a great leader one day.'

'Leader of what?' sneered Iquehuacatzin who had sidled up to the group unnoticed.

Axayacatl ground his teeth. The man's arrogance was so typical of that side of the family. Iquehuacatzin was a thinner version of his father, although his hooked nose was slightly less pronounced. He was slender and the generous lips gave his chiseled features the air of someone who's discovered a dung heap blocking the door to his house. His hair was tied tightly in a queue ending in an immaculately trimmed end at the level of his waist. The gold ear plugs were overtly large but not beyond the bounds of current fashion. Axayacatl hated that Iquehuacatzin was so handsome, but the thing that enraged him beyond any reason was the man's strutting walk.

Tezozomoc gave no answer save a face of silent scorn, so it was left to Nezahualcoyotl to bring the young man down to earth.

'Prince Iquehuacatzin, we are honoured! Pray speak to us awhile of the things that will come to pass.' Then, in a heavy aside, Nezahualcoyotl addressed Tezozomoc. 'I do so love it when the youth demonstrate that wisdom springs from purity of mind, rather than length and breadth of experience.'

Axayacatl enjoyed the sour look that Iquehuacatzin gave the ruler of Texcoco. Moctezuma's son was clever enough to understand the insult. Nezahualcoyotl's insult would have been lost on Mahchimaleh, so it was just as well that he was off somewhere, probably stuffing his face.

'What do you mean, old man? I'm not a soothsayer. Have the delights of your court addled your mind?' He laughed carelessly.

Nezahualcoyotl took it all in his stride. Axayacatl saw no sign that he'd taken any offence.

'Oh, pardon me. I must have misheard you. I thought you were predicting Axayacatl's future.'

Iquehuacatzin gave him a withering look. 'Of course I don't know,' he said and then waved dismissively at Axayacatl. 'But there can only be one royal lineage in Tenochtitlan.'

It was outrageously impolite and even Nezahualcoyotl, poet and master statesman, was lost for words.

'What of you, *cousin?*' continued Iquehuacatzin, using the word like it was a curse. 'I'm heading for Ahuilizapan to fight with our warriors. Will you be joining us? What's your tally of captives now? Is it still just two?'

'No, he will not,' Tezozomoc cut in.

'My Lord,' said Axayacatl, addressing his father and trying to hide his shame. 'I want to go.'

'Your mother and I have discussed this as you well know and the decision was made. Besides, I have other duties for you, my son.'

'My Lord, I'm twenty-four years old. Iquehuacatzin is right. I have fallen behind my peers. At this rate I will never make a name for myself!'

'You will have plenty of opportunity. There will be fighting for many years.'

'Too bad.' Iquehuacatzin smirked. 'Mummy says you can't go.'

Nezahualcoyotl had recovered his composure and rejoined the conversation. He caught the prince's attention. 'Your father told me that the purpose of your trip to the west was to help the pochteca establish links with the local noblemen.'

'That's true,' conceded Iquehuacatzin.' Our first duty is to lend some regal gravitas to our long-distance merchants, but we will get a chance to join the fighting too.'

'Which merchant are you working with?'

'Our uncle Lord Xiconoc has kindly made a space for me and my brother in his caravan. We leave in a few days' time.'

Axayacatl simmered while the two talked and his father listened, but the conversation didn't last long. Soon Iquehuacatzin prowled off, evidently happy with the affront he had caused.

'Why is he like that?'

Tezozomoc shook his head, but Nezahualcoyotl ventured his opinion.

'Iquehuacatzin and Mahchimaleh crave power, but the long life of your grandfather leaves them bitter. They see no end to his reign.'

'They can't both be tlatoani at the same time.'

Nezahualcoyotl laughed again and turned to Tezozomoc. 'You see! Your son is a clever man. He predicts trouble and I believe he is right.'

Tezozomoc raised one eyebrow. 'A wise man told me that when two eagle chicks are born, one pushes the other out of the nest as soon as it is strong enough.'

'I have heard that tale as well,' said the ruler of Texcoco. 'Maybe we should place bets on which of our eagle chicks here will push the other.'

The comment drew a wry smile from Axayacatl's father. Nezahualcoyotl excused himself on the grounds that he had a number of other people to talk with before his trip back across the lake.

Alone with his father, Axayacatl tried to reason with him, but Tezozomoc was adamant; there were too many duties to attend to, one of which was a ceremony for Tizoc's achievements in Calmecac. It seemed his little brother was more adept at school than he was.

Chapter 7 – Tenochtitlan

The Master of Learning carefully gathered the scroll up and handed it to an apprentice who crossed the room to return it to its place in a wooden framework of cubicles that stretched the length of the library.

'Now it's your turn,' said Hunter. He was one of only five men in the rank below high priest and younger than the others by a decade or more. He was a lean, earnest-looking man with a pockmarked face. All priests grew their hair long after their graduating from their years as acolytes. Hunter did not. He was the only senior priest with his hair shaved close to his skull, which showed off his ragged ears, ravaged by a thousand self-inflicted sacrificial cuts.

'What story would you have me tell?' asked Clawfoot who would rather have skipped his regular session with Hunter. He was having trouble concentrating. Scribing had never interested him much.

'Let's see if you can draw Tezcatlipoca creating the Fourth World. Here is a fresh parchment and here is some ink.'

'Just black?'

'Just black… until I've seen what you can do.' Hunter gave an encouraging smile and rubbed at one cratered cheek. 'Coloured inks are hard to come by. There's no sense wasting them on your feeble scratching. I'll come back in a while and see how you've progressed.'

The Master of Learning left to check on the other priests who were practising their skills with quill and ink. There were half a dozen young men hunched over their work wearing worried expressions. Clawfoot was about to start work when he noticed something on the floor. It looked like a scorched twig. When he picked it up, he realised that it was a wooden tube sealed at each end with a blob of wax. The exterior of the tube had been carved with exquisite care to give the appearance of a squatting skeleton, holding bony hands up to frame its screaming skull. The indentations had been charred black to make the skeleton stand out in sharp relief. It was a work of art. It must have been dropped by the Master of Learning. Glancing around to make sure he wasn't being observed, Clawfoot prised the wax plug from one end. Inside was a miniature roll of parchment. Opened out, it appeared to show one priest casting someone from a temple. The exile was clothed in rags or perhaps the decomposing skin of a sacrificial victim. If the parchment told a parable, Clawfoot didn't recognise it, but what he did appreciate was the skill that had gone into painting the scene. He decided to keep it. He carefully replaced the wax seal and stowed the tube in a pouch sewn into his loincloth.

Inspired by his acquisition, Clawfoot dipped his reed quill into the small earthenware pot of ink and began to sketch the outline of a lightning bolt. He carefully left a gap which he filled with the hand of Tlaloc before moving down to the God of Rain's tunic and shield. A shadow fell across his parchment just as he was trying to ink two perfect circles for eyes. Angry Lizard was standing over him with three of his half-trained monkeys at his shoulder. He was a thick-set man with a large wooden lip plug and a snout like a tapir. His poor grasp of the complexities of religious ceremony had condemned him to a life as a warrior priest and he carried a wealth of ugly scars that demonstrated either his valour or his lack of skill in that department, Clawfoot couldn't decide which.

'You must be lost,' said Clawfoot. 'This is the Hall of Knowledge.'

'He's a funny worm, isn't he?' Angry Lizard said to his followers who snickered obligingly. He pointed to one of them, a tall man with dead eyes, filthy loincloth and a heavy club over his shoulder. 'You... go and tell the other priests that they need a break from scratching at tree bark.'

The enforcer slouched over to the nearest man who immediately got the message, gathered up a few possessions and beat a hasty retreat. Clawfoot assumed the remainder would follow his example, so he looked up at Angry Lizard with what he hoped was an innocent smile.

'I suppose you thought it would be amusing for me to sleep on a bed of shit, eh worm?'

'I heard you shit your bed all the time,' said Clawfoot. 'What has that to do with me?'

Angry Lizard scowled. 'That trick with the entrails was your last mistake. You're from the gutter... worse than scum. I don't care how many tutors you win over by letting them fuck you, you'll never amount to anything; you know that, don't you?'

Clawfoot renewed his interest in the picture he was working on. Tlaloc's flamboyant headdress was next. He went to reload the quill, but Angry Lizard leant across the table and knocked the ink pot over.

'Oops!'

Clawfoot watched a river of blackness engulf his parchment.

'You don't understand, do you?' he said.

'What don't I understand?'

'Anything really.' Clawfoot shook his head sadly and pointed his reed at a small island on the parchment that wasn't flooded. He had been quite pleased with his depiction of Tlaloc's face; distinctly frog-like and unmistakable.

When Angry Lizard bent to peer at the spot, Clawfoot slammed his face into the stone table. Something cracked and the burly priest sagged, his fingers clutching feebly at the stone table and then he pitched over backwards, his forehead black with ink.

'I was raised on the streets.' Clawfoot's voice was calm as the first of Angry Lizard's accomplices came at him round the edge of the table. 'I was learning to fight while your fat mother was stuffing your inbred faces with fancy treats.'

He let the first man grab his arm and then threw himself against the corner of the table. He felt a snap and whirled away, leaving the attacker kneeling on the floor and clutching at a broken arm. These were the priesthood's finest fighting men. Clawfoot laughed aloud. While they had been training with fancy great swords for use in honourable combat, he had been gauging eyes and biting the fingers off his attackers just to stay alive in the filthiest alleys in the city. Dirty fighting at close quarters was how he liked it.

The next man had more of the look of a warrior about him. His long hair was swept back into a tight queue and a necklace of human finger bones hung around his neck. Clawfoot remembered his name: Third Arrow. Despite his arrogant expression, he slid round the table with the poise and caution of a jaguar entering an unfamiliar clearing. At his shoulder was the tall one with the club. This would be more interesting.

'Time you two had a go, don't you think?' Clawfoot grinned. He flicked his eyes from side to side to keep the one with the club in sight. Having emptied the room of witnesses, he was returning to the fray, swinging his club around his head. Slowly, Clawfoot backed towards the rack of parchments and pulled out the thin, translucent brown dagger that he had used to disembowel the sacrificial victim. He never went anywhere without it. 'I'm just beginning to enjoy myself.'

Third Arrow pulled his own knife, a rough, wooden-handled thing that looked very business-like. He lunged, but it was nothing more than a test of his opponent's reactions. Clawfoot stepped nimbly out of reach but realised he had run out of space. His back was against the rack of parchments and he had been herded closer to the one with the club. He would need to take the initiative or he would leave himself open to a combined attack, the outcome of which would be far less predictable. Thinking quickly, Clawfoot edged left again, bringing himself in range of the attacker with the club. He stepped away from the wall and made a short thrust, hoping to provoke a reaction, but the man with the club didn't rise to the bait at first. Clawfoot retreated a step moving left again and now the man with the club moved in, thinking that Clawfoot was readying to dash for the exit. This put him between Clawfoot and Third Arrow. Now Clawfoot lunged again, looking committed. He was low with his head down, reaching for belly flesh when the club swung, but Clawfoot's move was a pretence. He righted himself in a flash and danced left again, hoping to jab his opponent in the ribs... nothing fatal, just a nasty warning, but he hadn't reckoned on the speed of the defensive swipe that the priest made with his club. It struck Clawfoot's forearm so hard that the blade flew from his hand. The agony that followed, spearing up his right arm, made him cry out. His left hand instinctively reached to cradle the injury. Sensing victory, the tall priest grinned and swung his club in a high arc that would crack Clawfoot's skull open if it connected with his head. Although fast, it was a big open move that gave Clawfoot a fraction of a heartbeat to react. There was no way to get out of reach of the club in time, so he stepped in, crouching under the descending arm. The club sailed harmlessly over his head so that his opponent now had him in an unwilling and awkward embrace. It didn't stay that way for long. The lanky priest soon held both ends of the club and pulled Clawfoot tight against his chest. Clawfoot would have head-butted his opponent or bitten his nose off, but staring at the man's throat, he realised that he was too short and time was running out. Out of the corner of his eye, Clawfoot could see the priest with the finger-bone necklace had moved in beside them.

'Not so cocky now, are you?' his captor sneered, breathing hotly into Clawfoot's face.

'Perhaps you're in the right place after all.'

'Eh?'

'The Hall of Knowledge,' Clawfoot wheezed, 'is for learning.' He squirmed a little within the tight embrace. There wasn't much room, but there was just enough.

'So?'

'Learn this!' Clawfoot brought his knee up into his captor's groin as hard as he could. They were too close together for it to be a crushing blow, but it had the intended effect. The man's knees buckled and the two of them toppled over still locked together.

Clawfoot heard himself say 'Ooof!' as the lanky priest fell on top of him. They grappled for a moment, Clawfoot trying to use his opponent as a shield from the other man. They crashed into one of the racks against the wall and a shower of parchments rained down on them. Just when he thought things couldn't get worse, Clawfoot heard Angry Lizard's voice.

'Get out of my way! Get off him, East Light.'

Clawfoot hindered the process of disentanglement as much as he could. As undignified as it was, grappling on the floor was preferable to a return to facing three enemies and possibly four if the man with the broken arm was prepared to help out. It only brought a few breaths' respite, not enough to come up with a winning strategy, especially without a weapon, so Clawfoot stood up and dusted his robe down as though he'd taken an unexpected tumble on the way to the market.

Angry Lizard was a mess. He was all black ink, pale blotches, watering eyes and blood-soaked teeth and clothes. His nose was still dripping blood and mucus, but his general demeanour was unmistakeably one of murderous intent. His voice was low and menacing.

'You're going to have a nasty accident now.'

'Oh dear,' said Clawfoot. 'There was nothing predicted in my calendar today.'

'So unreliable, aren't they? Especially if your parents abandon you without so much as a birth date.' Angry Lizard strutted round behind Clawfoot. 'Knowing you as I do, I don't blame them.' With that, he kicked the back of Clawfoot's knees, sending him to the floor again.

Clawfoot readied himself for the onslaught, but instead he heard a shout from the other end of the hall and saw his attackers freeze. Voices could be heard drawing near. Clawfoot got to his feet and saw two priests approaching, one of whom was the Master of Learning, Hunter, and the other was Feathered Darkness. They were accompanied by one of the scribes who had been driven from the room earlier and a dozen more warrior priests all carrying clubs at the ready. Angry Lizard shot a venomous look.

There was silence as the newcomers surveyed the damage and the perpetrators tried to gauge the high priest's mood. Hunter looked furious at the destruction that had been wrought in his normally serene empire. Feathered Darkness' expression was unreadable. He turned his head slowly one way and then the other before sizing up Clawfoot and taking a long look at Angry Lizard's blood- and ink-stained face.

'Angry Lizard?' Feathered Darkness raised one eyebrow.

'I came to the Hall of Knowledge peacefully and he insulted me, Venerable Father.' Angry Lizard spoke thickly through his clogged nose.

'He insulted you?'

'Ah... yes, Venerable Father. Then he attacked me.'

Feathered Darkness nodded slowly, as if trying to assimilate a complex problem. 'These others were with you?' He glanced at the other three priests who were staring firmly at the floor. 'A vicious attack. He must have caught you by surprise to have caused so much damage.'

Clawfoot struggled to suppress a smile of grim satisfaction, but the high priest turned on him.

'Is this true? Did you insult Angry Lizard?'

It was Clawfoot's turn to look embarrassed. 'Yes, Venerable Father.'

'And then you attacked him.'

'I...' Clawfoot hesitated. Though it had only been moments ago, his memory was hazy about how it had actually begun. Hadn't Angry Lizard started the fight? Then Clawfoot remembered. 'Yes, Venerable Father. I did.'

'Very well. It seems you are innocent, Angry Lizard. You and your friends may leave.' Feathered Darkness waved them away. 'I will deal with the offender.'

Angry Lizard and his three accomplices gave thanks politely and slunk away.

'You have already been warned about starting fights.'

'Yes, Venerable Father, but—'

'But nothing! You think I don't know that they came here looking for trouble? The last time that idiot Angry Lizard was in the Hall of Knowledge was when he was shown around the temple precinct in his first days as an acolyte. I am not stupid. You blame him for sabotaging your ceremony so you came up with some way to take revenge on him and then he comes looking for you to even the score. No!' Feathered Darkness held up a hand to silence Clawfoot who had been about to protest. 'I don't want to know. Whatever you've done this time though, it really has upset

Angry Lizard. He couldn't wait until you were somewhere less conspicuous to pick a fight.'

'If you know it was him—'Clawfoot began.

'Enough!' barked Feathered Darkness. 'I don't care to follow the chain of events back five years to determine who first did what to whom. I blame you because, of the two, you're the only one clever enough to understand what I'm saying and take notice... at least that's what I thought. I also blame you because you are arrogant and disrespectful and because of that, trouble follows you wherever you go. Angry Lizard is only one of a long list of priests who you've upset. Are you aware that, aside from Eternal Flame and Hunter, the other elders have all called for you to be thrown out of the order?'

'I... I know they don't approve of me, Venerable Father.'

'A few lone voices have pleaded to keep your head off the skull rack. Only your aptitude and your thirst for knowledge have kept you alive so far. When we last spoke, I warned you about keeping your anger in check and you failed me...the very next day!'

Clawfoot winced. There was nothing he could say to placate Feathered Darkness. He had never seen the high priest this angry before.

Feathered Darkness laid a hand on Hunter's shoulder and took a deep breath. 'Clawfoot should stay here until this mess is cleaned up.'

Hunter cleared his throat. 'Ah... I'd rather he didn't, Venerable Father. He's covered in blood and ink. I don't want any of that getting on our parchments. I'll have some of my more experienced priests take care of this, but I thank you all the same.'

This seemed to fuel the high priest's temper. 'Very well, leave now, but be at the top of the steps of the Great Temple on the dawn of One Mazātl in six days' time. You have betrayed my trust and you will know the cost.'

Clawfoot kept his voice calm and level, but his head was full of the memories of other priests who had fallen foul of the order. 'Yes, Venerable Father. I will, but...' He hesitated, not sure if he should mention the business with Xiconoc. In the end, he decided there was little to lose. 'What of the task you wanted me to do?'

Feathered Darkness stared at him for a long time. 'You will know your path in six days' time. Until then, reflect on your disobedience. Now go!'

Clawfoot bowed his head. This time it really looked as though he had undone the years of patient work he'd put in to secure his place in the priesthood. For a long time after becoming an acolyte, everything he had done had been wrong and every day brought a new round of punishment. Beatings, punitive starvations and public humiliations had been a normal facet of everyday life. Eventually, the beatings and other tortures had grown less frequent. Clawfoot was a quick learner; there was no way to survive the harsh streets of Tenochtitlan without a certain degree of adaptability. Aside from a handful of reprimands for fighting, Clawfoot had grown accustomed to the privileges that came with success and progression through the ranks. He cursed himself silently and began to wish he had just allowed Angry Lizard to threaten him. Perhaps it would never have gone beyond bluster. Now the high priest had summoned him to the temple top and it seemed just about possible that Clawfoot might be the next offering.

'One more thing, Clawfoot,' came the older priest's voice as Clawfoot made to leave. 'From now on I want you to avoid Angry Lizard. No discussion, no arguments and no more brawling. Is that understood?'

'Avoid Angry Lizard and no fights.'

The high priest glared and then turned his back.

It was hard to imagine Angry Lizard leaving him alone, thought Clawfoot. He briefly contemplated leaving the city. There was nothing to stop him walking out of the temple precinct. He could walk through one of the gates in the Serpent Wall and keep on going, across one of the causeways until he was among the hills. A small settlement somewhere would have need of a priest. He would have to pretend to be a minister of Tlaloc or Quetzalcoatl. Villagers preferred priests who espoused the gentler nature of these gods to the fearsome Huitzilopochtli. Even as he considered the plan, he knew he wouldn't see it through. Clawfoot understood as never before that the order of Huitzilopochtli meant everything to him. Half a year passed when escape was the single thought that had possessed him. He had longed to go back to his old life, but gradually, Clawfoot had changed. He began to understand his place in the fabric of the universe and he saw that the gods had given him a chance to rise above the poverty of his early years. He never lost his anger, but now it was suffused with righteousness. Feathered Darkness had been right: this was his home. He was a servant of Huitzilopochtli, the power that sustained the universe, and he had more of a right to it than any of the other dim-witted priests. He would go and face Feathered Darkness on the temple, even if the high priest had decided on the ultimate punishment. This was his life, and he realised, if it was to be his death, he would meet it head on.

Chapter 8 – Tenochtitlan

'Are you ready to go?' Little Beetle called through the curtain.

Precious Flower was in the bedroom that she and Jaguar shared with Musical Reed. Musical Reed had risen at dawn to prepare food for the family and to give her daughter-in-law some privacy in the morning rituals. She claimed she didn't sleep much since her husband had died. Precious Flower wasn't sleeping much either, but that was down to her huge round belly. She couldn't sit or lie anywhere and feel comfortable for long. She put her hand on the taut skin and grimaced.

'Coming,' she called. Her sister-by-marriage was losing patience, but Precious Flower wasn't in the mood to hurry. She felt so ungainly. She ran her hand over her distended stomach, feeling for her baby. 'Let's go for a walk, not-so-little one,' she whispered. Using one hand to steady herself against the wall, she levered herself upright, reached for a shawl and draped it over her shoulders. Little Beetle waited on the other side of the woven sheet that served as the door to the family room. Precious Flower waddled towards her.

'Maybe you should stay at home this time,' said Little Beetle.

'Oh no! It's so boring just sitting around. Arrow One won't even allow me to help in the workshop anymore.'

'Alright, but let me know if you get tired and we'll come straight home.'

'I wish we could go to the market at Tlatelolco. I haven't been for weeks.' Precious Flower swept her long hair back and deftly tied it with a strip of red cloth.

'Tlatelolco is so busy and the people there are so ill-mannered,' complained Little Beetle as she stepped out into the street. 'Jaguar would never forgive us if we let anything happen to you. For now, you'll have to make do with visiting the weavers.'

The morning was well advanced, so Harbour Street was busy with porters coming up from the lake with baskets and bundles heading for the workshops and stalls all across the city. Precious Flower let the shorter woman carve a route through the throng.

'Where are the children?'

'They already went down to the lake to watch the fishermen come in,' Little Beetle called over her shoulder. 'Oh, and Fire Eagle wanted to try out the boat that he made.'

'Blade has been desperate to see that too,' said Precious Flower. They kept to the edges of the thoroughfare so as not to slow the crowds on urgent business. 'He really looks up to your son, you know,' she added. 'Fire Eagle is like a brother to him.'

In truth, Precious Flower was a little worried about her four-year-old son and Little Beetle's boy, who was only a year older, going down the harbour on their own. It seemed such a dangerous environment for children, but they loved it so much and Little Beetle was so relaxed about them playing around deep water, knives, heavy baskets of provisions and surly men that she had to tell herself she was worrying unnecessarily. Only bad weather deterred the boys from exploring the nets, paddles and upturned canoes under repair that made the waterside such an exciting haunt. Precious Flower had gone with them on one of their adventures, anxious to see the route they took and who they spoke to. Although they had teetered dangerously close to the edge of the water on several occasions and made her stomach lurch, they had not fallen in. Furthermore, everyone seemed to greet the children cheerfully, as though they were a vital part of the goings-on. On one of the many wooden jetties that pointed, like creaky fingers, across the lake to Texcoco, they'd found an older boy fishing. He had shown them his most recent catch: a fat, silver-bright fish that flapped when they poked it so that Blade and Rain Flower, Little Beetle's young daughter, squealed with a mixture of horror and delight.

Precious Flower was brought back to the present day by Little Beetle's incessant chatter. She had asked about Jaguar. 'I don't know when he's going to be back,' she replied, 'but it's not going to be soon.'

Precious Flower felt Little Beetle hold her arm affectionately. 'He's not been at home much lately, has he?'

'No, but he's doing an important job. I'm so pleased for him. He's the youngest ever commander of the Jaguar Knights. Our new child will be walking before he gets back,' joked Precious Flower.

'It's probably just as well,' laughed Little Beetle, trying to make the best of it. 'Men are hopeless when it comes to babies. You'd have thought that warriors would be able to handle a bit of blood. You know Paw? The one whose husband makes shoes for the tlatoani? Yes, well, she told me that her husband was present when their child was born and apparently he went as white as snow and passed out... just toppled over and would have been burned if the midwife hadn't rolled him off the hearth.'

Precious Flower couldn't help smiling. It was great to be part of Little Beetle's family. If any of them remembered that she had joined them as a slave, they showed no sign of it.

'You miss him, don't you?' said Little Beetle quietly.

'Yes, I'm worried,' said Precious Flower and felt Little Beetle squeezing her arm tighter.

'It will be alright. Jaguar is fast and he's one of the best.'

Precious Flower made a brave face. She remembered when Jaguar and Little Beetle's father hadn't returned from battle. It had taken a great many visits from the family priest and the astrologer and the passage of many years to dispel the sorrow.

'He can't stay in the workshop if the army needs him,' continued Little Beetle, as if reading Precious Flower's mind. 'He brings great honour to us. You must be so proud of him... one of Tlacaelel's closest advisors. You know, our best customers only know us because they have heard of Jaguar's prowess.'

Trade was brisk in the Street of the Weavers when the two women arrived. It was a wide street by the standards of Tenochtitlan, but the stalls that the weavers set out in front of their workshops constricted the flow of buyers and other, less interested pedestrians trying to make their way from one end to the other. Precious Flower loved the Street of the Weavers. There was no place in the city where the various strata of society mingled so freely. Noblewomen dressed in beautiful clothes rubbed shoulders with mayeques in grubby loincloths. Weavers haggled noisily with traders bringing bundles of raw materials in to keep the looms busy. One shop sold nothing but rough maguey cloth for sacking and construction work, while across the street another traded only bolts of the softest cotton from Cuernavaca.

Precious Flower was examining the handiwork of an embroiderer when she felt something wet against her feet. At first she thought that she had knocked over a pot of dye or water – there were many that littered the street between the stalls – but it felt too warm and had reached too far up her leg. Her confusion was momentary. When she glanced down at the ground, she could see no obvious source and the pool of fluid that darkened the dust around her feet was still growing.

'Little Beetle,' said Precious Flower, gripping Jaguar's sister's arm. 'My waters have broken.'

'Here?'

'Yes, here! Of course here!' *What a stupid question*, thought Precious Flower.

Little Beetle looked down and her eyes widened. 'Come on. We need to get you home.'

'What about this? Shouldn't we cover it up?'

'Forget the puddle! The street's filthy. Who's going to notice another stain or a smear? Come on.' With that, Little Beetle took the lead and shouldered her way back in the direction they had come.

Precious Flower's contractions started before the pair made it home. She sank to her knees on the flagstones and groaned. It was an unrecognisable animal noise from deep inside her. The whole of her abdomen clenched, as though she was vomiting from her arm-pits down to her thighs. A crowd gathered and made a concerned murmuring noise. Two neighbours helped her to her feet when the pain subsided and Little Beetle directed them home. Precious Flower made it back to her bed without help and lay there dreading the next wave of agony. She wished Jaguar was home. Little Beetle went and fetched Musical Reed and Jaguar's mother looked after her while Little Beetle went to find the midwife.

Everyone had told Precious Flower that the second child would be easier, but they had lied to her. It wasn't until the sun began to set that the contractions merged into an uninterrupted wall of agony. Babbling voices offered her advice, or so she assumed. She didn't really listen to them. She knew what to do. She grunted, as though in assent, and ground her teeth against the shredding pain. She cursed Jaguar for not being with her and she railed at the midwife who was brought in halfway through, accusing her of taking her time. After what seemed like an eternity, the dull fog of endurance ended with a rousing cheer and a degree of weeping from the three women who had spent the day with her. At last her body had stopped trying to turn itself inside out. She heard a hiccup and a brief mewling sound from her baby, signifying all was well. Someone placed a small bundle in her arms that scowled up at her with a puckered grey and brown face still covered in mucus. Precious Flower found enough energy to smile back at it before exhaustion claimed her.

Much later, when the tonalpouque arrived, Precious Flower was breastfeeding her baby girl. Arrow One had made the arrangements as Jaguar wasn't at home and now everyone was eager to see what birth signs the astrologer would ascribe to the child. Even Blade, who was sitting by the hearth whittling a piece of wood with a small obsidian knife that his father had made for him, stopped to hear what was in store for his little sister.

The tonalpouque, Silent Smoke, was well known to the family. He was a rotund man, as wide as he was short, with tiny sparkling eyes and a cheerful demeanour that was anything but silent. Precious Flower could only put up with him for short periods of time. In addition to his astrological work, he handled minor ceremonies that the priests saw as beneath them, such as the blessing of the extension to the workshop, which everyone had been concerned about because it had been completed on a day linked with the fire spirit, Xiutecuhtli.

Musical Reed held out a bowl of ashes.

'So good to see you following the traditional ways,' boomed Silent Smoke as he scooped up a handful and dusted his knees. 'I visited a neighbour of yours just yesterday who had replaced the ash with ground-up bone. This is some new idea that's commonplace now, although I cannot see how that will keep a newborn infant free from illnesses. Bone is a healing elemental as everyone knows, while ash prevents illness in the first place.'

The tonalpouque shuffled apologetically into the room. He was pleased to hear that the family had kept the spirit guide alight since the child had been born and instantly set about cross-examining the man of the house so as to better understand the context of the birth. Precious Flower was forced to listen until such time as the tonalpouque felt ready to speak to her. It seemed to her that Silent Smoke mostly just wanted to catch up on gossip, but he did eventually come round to more pertinent matters.

'A girl, is it not?' Silent Smoke already knew the answer because he ploughed on. 'And born today, let me see... today is Ehēcatl, the third day in the trecena of Xochitl.'

He turned to Precious Flower.

'Xochitl means your girl will be playful and creative, perhaps an artist like her mother.' He cast an admiring look at Precious Flower. 'I can tell you that in my examination of the heavens last night I was able to see the star of Tezcatlipoca chasing the lustrous beauty of Xochiquetzal towards her bed in the east. From this you can be sure that your girl will be beautiful or she will know great beauty in her time.'

Here the astrologer clapped his hands in glee, as though he had personally arranged for the heavens to be so aligned.

'At first glance this is an excellent conjunction. True, a day later would have put her in the day sign of House, which would have been even better for the lady of such a prominent household. Would you be interested in moving the official birth date to tomorrow?' This last was addressed to Arrow One who directed the astrologer's gaze back to Precious Flower.

'No, thank you, Silent Smoke. I recall a conversation with you from when Blade was born. Please correct me if I am wrong, but I think you said that Ehēcatl, the wind, in some interpretations or conjunctions, is tied with good fortune.'

'My dear, your memory serves you very well! Were you not so tied up with your family business here I should fear competition for my own post.' Silent Smoke squeezed his eyes shut tight and shuddered at the enormity of his own joke. 'Be warned though,' he continued, 'Ehēcatl is also capricious and presages the storm.

'Now I think it's time I took a look at this child. Have you chosen a name? If not, I have many excellent suggestions. Everyone around here loves the names I pick for their children.'

Precious Flower had no intention of letting someone outside the family choose the name of her child. The baby was making small contented sounds, so Precious Flower gently detached it from her breast. The little face that had been so grey and wrinkled that morning was now glowing a healthy brown colour. The little girl already had a good fuzz of black hair, long lashes and tiny, puckered pink lips. Precious Flower passed the bundle to the astrologer.

'Graceful Bird,' she said. 'She will be Graceful Bird.'

Silent Smoke took the baby and smiled weakly, failing to hide his disappointment. He handled the child with all the care that was expected of an official in his position, which was good to see. There had been an occasion last year when a priest had dropped the child of a wealthy merchant from the Cuepopan district. The infant had survived with no lasting injury, but as a punishment, the unlucky priest had been made to climb the tall pole left over after the Festival of Xocotlhuetzi and hurl himself off. He had been lucky. He had survived but with two smashed legs and a broken arm. Precious Flower wondered what had happened to him after that.

The tonalpouque gazed at the child in his arms. Precious Flower fervently hoped that the astrologer wouldn't spot anything untoward that might act as a malign influence on her child. An oddly placed mole could mean that evil spirits watched over the child or misshapen ears could be a warning that troublesome years lay ahead.

Everyone held their breath as they waited for the tonalpouque to speak. Musical Reed wrung her hands anxiously. Arrow One waited stoically with his arm around Little Beetle. Their children had been dispatched to spend the morning with a neighbour so as not to disrupt the proceedings. Blade was there, but he had lost interest. He was inspecting the twine on his toy bow.

'The signs that govern this child's future are mixed.' The tonalpouque had adopted a formal tone. 'The wind and the flower make an uneasy combination. Overall, the portents are good, so I will not recommend a change to this girl's birth date, but you should watch for signs of instability as she matures. Has the afterbirth been disposed of?'

'No, My Lord,' replied Precious Flower. 'I was hoping that Jaguar might return any day now. He was to have taken it for burial where the girl's grandfather fell in battle.'

Silent Smoke looked alarmed. 'No, my dear! You mustn't wait to complete this task. The risk to the child now is too great to ignore. Besides, there is no need for such an elaborate ceremony for a girl. I recommend you cast it into the lake from Snake Point. Throw in some flowers too and a handful of maize kernels.'

'Yes, of course,' said Arrow One.

'We will not!'

Everyone looked in surprise at Precious Flower.

'Jaguar will take the afterbirth to the place that his father died in battle. He made me promise that we wouldn't dispose of it before he returned.'

'But, Precious Flower, we have no idea when he'll be back,' said Musical Reed.

'It's dreadfully bad luck to delay,' insisted Silent Smoke.

'Bad luck that should be countered by the benefits of burying the afterbirth near Jaguar's father.' Precious Flower was determined to fulfil her promise. 'Are there any protective spells you could cast?'

'Well, I'm not sure...' began the astrologer.

'We should fetch a priest to help with the magic,' exclaimed Musical Reed tremulously.

'No!' Silent Smoke jumped up, bristling at the suggestion. 'No. There is no time to waste. We cannot wait for a priest, nor do we need to wait for one. I know the spells and the special offerings we must make.'

'How much will this special offering cost?' asked Arrow One sceptically.

'This is no trivial matter, My Lord,' the astrologer warned. 'No simple charm or amulet from a street seller will suffice,' he added as he pulled a folded parchment from a pocket in his cloak.

Arrow One haggled so aggressively that Precious Flower began to worry that he would offend the tonalpouque, but after a while the two men struck a deal. Musical Reed and Little Beetle were charged with fetching some ingredients for a poultice and Blade was dispatched to find a spider that was ground up and added to the mixture when it was nearing completion. Precious Flower was allowed to hold Graceful Bird so that the infant's chest was exposed. Silent Smoke sat beside her and began a melancholy song. His voice was high and quavered like that of a girl. The song was an allegory telling the story of a child, lost in the forest, of the dark shadows that pursued it and of an eagle sent by Ehēcatl to fly high above the forest to guide the child out.

As he sang, Silent Smoke took a fire-blackened stick, purified by flame, and used it to apply the poultice to the centre of the infant's chest. When the simple ceremony was over, he looked straight into Precious Flower's eyes. His expression was sad.

'I'm sorry,' said the astrologer. 'I cannot be sure how long the magic will hold, one cycle of the moon or perhaps two if the weather does not become too hot. We may need to repeat the spell if your husband does not return in that time.'

'I'm sure he will be back soon, but if he is not, we'd very much like your assistance again,' said Precious Flower.

As Arrow One handed over the payment, the astrologer spoke again.

'My lady, it's vital that the afterbirth is returned to the Creator Pair. If Jaguar is... further delayed, you must make the offering yourself. There is a shadow that prevents me from seeing her future clearly, but I sense...pain and sorrow.'

'I thought we just paid you for protection,' said Arrow One sharply.

The tonalpouque bristled. 'No one can make spells to ward a person for a lifespan, My Lord. Not even the priests and the most powerful sorcerers among the Huastecs have the power to make such magic. All I have done tonight is given you a few days' respite and even this takes great skill. This insistence on waiting until the father's return is very unusual, but you can be certain that you have bought her the best help that there is in all of Tenochtitlan.' Here Silent Smoke bowed to Musical Reed and to Beetle, then once more to Precious Flower before he turned and left.

There was a shocked silence in the wake of the astrologer's departure. Musical Reed and Beetle were dismayed by the dark future that had been foretold. Precious Flower could sense that Arrow One was also upset, but he was doing his best to cover it up with his usual degree of cynicism.

'Come here, Blade,' she beckoned to her son. 'Come and hold your little sister. She needs our support. We will make daily offerings and pray for your father's safe return.' Precious Flower tucked the infant back into the blanket, which went some way towards masking the pungent aroma of the poultice. Blade sat down beside his mother and tenderly took his sister in his arms. Precious Flower showed him how to support the baby's head and kept one hand at the boy's lap just in case he should let go suddenly.

'Mama, will she be alright?'

'Of course she will, son,' exclaimed Precious Flower. 'With her brave brother at her side, how can it be otherwise?'

Blade beamed from ear to ear, but Precious Flower could see that the rest of the family were upset at her decision. She could only hope Jaguar returned quickly and put their worries to rest.

Chapter 9
The Jungles of Totonaca

Jaguar got his sword up in time, but the heavy impact jarred his arm and set his teeth rattling. He spun away, instinctively parrying low to catch Two Sign's next attack and only just managed to block the vicious swipe that followed. He stepped back again to buy himself more room, only to find there was none. The wall of the makeshift armoury was right behind him and a ring of onlookers blocked his escape. A fight between the commanders of the two great orders of knights was bound to attract a great deal of excitement. Warriors from the Eagle and Jaguar Knights jostled for spaces near the front where they could cheer their leaders on.

Two Sign snarled triumphantly and advanced again. He was fifteen summers older than Jaguar, but age only seemed to have given him a ruthless edge. They were using practice swords that lacked the sharp, shiny obsidian blades set into the edges at regular intervals, but Jaguar knew that Two Sign would have no problem killing him, even with this toothless weapon. He watched his opponent raise the sword and judged the moment. He lunged forward reaching his own sword out far to the right. As he'd hoped, Two Sign switched direction in order to block on his left-hand side. With his opponent now committed, Jaguar planted one foot firmly in front of Two Sign and dived past him on the other side, pulling his sword arm behind him. Jaguar rolled, fetched up against the legs of the warriors encircling them and sprang up. Two Sign had already spun round with deadly speed that belied his size and age.

To his own men, he might be The Falling Claw for his ferocity in battle, but if that was the case, why did these practice sessions frighten him so much? Two Sign's reputation was impossible to ignore. It was said that the tribal elders of the Tarascan people had put a bounty on his head and emissaries brought back tales from Oaxaca that the women warned their children about the Tenocha devil, Two Sign, who would come for them if they misbehaved. No, there was no doubt that Two Sign was the greatest warrior of his age and this was why it was so important to take every opportunity to spar with him.

The veterans who taught fighting skills at telpochcalli began every lesson with the same warning: 'Complacency is your greatest enemy.' Jaguar had a feeling he was going to get another lesson in humility today. Two Sign was angry. It was obvious from the savagery of his attack. Blows rarely had much follow through in practice sessions, but Two Sign wasn't holding back at all today. Jaguar's mouth was dry and the hair on the back of his neck prickled.

His deft move had drawn a cheer from the crowd, but there was no time to enjoy the moment. Two Sign jabbed again, testing Jaguar's defences. He blocked and parried furiously, retreating once again as the crowd behind him flexed around the fighters. None of the other warriors were sparring anymore; they had all stopped to watch this contest. Jaguar probed for an opening in Two Sign's defences, but there was no way around the furious onslaught. Perhaps this was what it would be like to fight Huitzilopochtli, the God of War himself.

Two Sign stepped forward again, his face like a grave. He thrust his sword out at head height and Jaguar only just managed to swat it aside from his face. Unbalanced now, he saw Two Sign draw his arm back to aim a crushing blow at his head. He raised his sword to intercept and braced his arm. The shock rattled his whole body and hurt his teeth. It was only the steep angle that he had set his weapon that deflected the strike and saved Jaguar from serious injury.

The crowd sensed that something was up. Jaguar could hear it in the way they gasped. What was Two Sign playing at? The Eagle Knight tried to capitalise on Jaguar's weak position by swapping his sword hand, but Jaguar reacted quickly. He swept the weak backhand up and over his head and then rammed the blunt end of his sword into Two Sign's thigh. Bigger men were less nimble and usually stood planted firmly to the spot, taking longer to shift their legs, however strong and powerful they were from the waist up.

Two Sign staggered, but his face barely registered the hit. Jaguar had fought him many times in training and had never once felled the commander of the Eagle Knights; some said it was impossible. It was even rumoured that he was impervious to pain. Many years ago, when Two Sign had been a young warrior, his commander had drawn his attention to his hand after a particularly fierce battle. Two Sign had looked at the gap where the middle two fingers of his right hand had been, grimaced once and then crudely bandaged the wound in readiness for the trip home. He had never mentioned the wound again.

Jaguar pressed home the momentary advantage he had with a flurry of short swipes, trying to match the ferocity of his opponent. For a moment, it seemed to work. Two Sign retreated a pace and then one more, the crowd behind him flowing away to avoid getting caught up in the fight. Jaguar followed, trying to find a weak spot. The big man really was having more trouble in defence than in the attack. He leaned into the blows, trying to bludgeon Two Sign into the ground. Two Sign dropped to one knee. Jaguar struck again, but still the Eagle Knight held out. He stepped in closer to bring more downward force to bear, trying to knock the sword out of Two Sign's hand but without success.

Two Sign leaned back, as though to move out of range. Jaguar took another step forward and then it was all over. Two Sign had been waiting for this moment. He hooked the toes of his front foot behind Jaguar's heel and tugged back hard. Jaguar lost purchase in the loose soil and his leg flew out from under him. In an instant, Two Sign was on him, snarling and with the edge of his wooden sword pressed into Jaguar's throat.

Another one lost, thought Jaguar as he tried to draw breath through his constricted windpipe.

Slowly, the demonic face above him relaxed and Two Sign eased the pressure on Jaguar's throat. The eerie silence that reigned over the practice ground ruptured into cheers and howls of delight as Jaguar allowed his opponent to haul him to his feet. He wiped the sweat from his face with the back of his hand and fought to regain control over his ragged breathing. It was good to see Two Sign bent over with his hands on his knees and breathing hard. That was a rare thing. Xipil thumped Jaguar's back and one of Jaguar's best captains, Holds the Sun, congratulated him on lasting so long before taking the practice sword from him. At last Jaguar remembered a promise he had made and began to walk away.

'Where are you going?' asked Two Sign.

Jaguar turned back. 'I'm going to see the men who were wounded in the fight for Ahuilizapan.' Two dozen warriors were in such a bad way they could not be moved and had not been able to join the last supply convoy on its return trip to Tenochtitlan. They were housed in one of the community buildings on the out-skirts of Ahuilizapan. Here they were being tended to by healers who travelled with the army.

Two Sign made a face. 'Is that necessary?'

'Yes, Two Sign. You should come too. Some of them are your men.'

Two Sign scowled. 'Useless now.'

'You don't know that. Some of them may even fight again and they'll be much cheered by a visit from their commander.' Jaguar tried to sound upbeat, but he knew that Two Sign was right to be sceptical. The recovery rate of these men was never good and out here in the region of Totonaca, it was unac-countably worse than in all the other campaigns Jaguar had been on. The sizeable burial ground in a field just outside the town bore testimony to the losses.

'OK. I'll come with you,' conceded Two Sign. The two men extricated themselves from the approving handshakes and con-gratulations of their fellow warriors and set off. A short while later, when they were negotiating one of the muddy, narrow streets that were common in Ahuilizapan, Jaguar turned to Two Sign.

'Back there…what was that about?!'

'Eh?'

'You nearly killed me!'

Two Sign shrugged. 'You were being careless.'

Jaguar wiped at the sweat that was still pouring from his face. The cursed heat of the jungle didn't help.' No. You're angry, really angry. The last time I saw you like this was after...'

'Yes?'

'After Crocodile was taken.'

Two Sign said nothing. As one of the foremost warriors in the land, he'd never married and had children of his own, so he had formed a strong bond with a boy he had found in the ruins of a burnt out village, the only survivor of a raiding party. The judiciary of Tenochtitlan had granted him permission to adopt Obsidian Crocodile and, as was the custom in such cases, he had been enrolled in military school where he had first met Jaguar. After a difficult start, the two had become firm friends, so when Crocodile was taken in battle by the Chalca, Jaguar persuaded Two Sign to join him on a rescue mission, but by the time they got to Crocodile, he had already chosen to meet his fate head on. The priests of Chalco sacrificed him to appease Tlaloc, the god of rain. Two Sign had taken it badly. Already a prodigious fighter, his ferocity redoubled. For two years he had volunteered for the riskiest missions and although he still took more captives than anyone else, his butchery on the field of battle was what people noticed. Since then he had calmed down, becoming more like the man Jaguar had first met.

'I thought you'd put that behind you.'

'You know nothing of what I feel!' spat Two Sign. Then more softly, he added, 'My son has joined the hummingbirds in the halls of Huitzilopochtli. He died with honour and is at peace. I do not worry for him.'

'So what is it then?' Jaguar pushed. 'Have I offended you?'

'No.'

'What then?'

Two Sign sighed and ran his big hands over his face, the gesture looking strange because of the missing fingers on his right hand.' Bah! I don't know. Why is Tlacaelel leaving me in Ahuilizapan while the real men go out to fight?'

'Is that not an honour?'

'No, it is not!' snapped Two Sign. 'I'm the commander of the Eagle Knights, the advance guard of the Mexica Empire. I'm not a captain of the city watch!'

They rounded a corner into a small quadrangle, surprising a group of tough-looking local men who fell silent when they saw the Mexica warriors. Jaguar saw the mutinous looks and instinctively reached for the blade he carried at his waist. Two Sign could not have appeared more casual as he sauntered past them, offering a greeting as he went. Jaguar followed in his wake, keeping a watchful eye on the men. Three Mexica warriors had been caught alone and murdered in vengeful attacks by the people of Ahuilizapan. It was petty, low-level stuff, but it paid to be vigilant. Conquered towns had been known to rise up in rebellion, although the notable examples seemed to have been out to the west where the people were more warlike than these jungle-dwellers.

'You want to lead the expedition to Zongolica instead of me?' Jaguar said when they were back in the lanes. He had made the offer without giving it much thought and immediately regretted it.

Two Sign tutted angrily. 'Not instead of you. Xipe Totec's rotting hide, you've earned your place out there! No, why didn't Tlacaelel put Last Medicine in charge of this dump?'

Jaguar didn't have an answer for that. Last Medicine's days of charging into battle were certainly long past, but perhaps troublemakers in Ahuilizapan would sense that too and see an opportunity. With the tlatoani's imminent arrival, Tlacaelel wouldn't want to take any chances. Jaguar remembered the task he'd been charged with. He smiled and clapped Two Sign on the shoulder. 'You are not the only one who has been handed an unwelcome task,' he said. 'When the tlatoani gets here, all I'll be doing is keeping his heirs out of trouble.'

Two Sign's mouth gaped. 'Are you joking?'

'No,' laughed Jaguar. 'It's not as bad as it sounds. Lord Tlacaelel promised me I could escort them back to Tenochtitlan, so I will get to see my family.'

'Are you mad? Do you know what those two are like?'

'I expect they'll be a little difficult, but I'm sure I can handle it.'

'Difficult?!' exclaimed Two Sign and shook his head. 'You have no idea, do you?'

Jaguar shrugged. 'I've never had to deal with them.'

'Mahchimaleh shouldn't be too much trouble on his own; he's little more than a thug. It's his brother you have to watch out for. He struts about as though he's already the tlatoani, oh, and don't bend over and show him your pert little backside, eh? If you believe the rumours, he's fishing for Tlazolteotl.'

Jaguar smiled. 'Thanks for the advice. I'll be sure to avoid jokes about the Goddess of Excrement too in case he thinks I'm accusing him of anything. Look, we're here,' he added as they arrived at the building that served as a treatment centre for wounded Mexica warriors. He was about to duck inside when Two Sign grabbed his arm.

'Jaguar, before you go in there, I need to ask for your help.'

'You need my help, oh Grey and Venerable one?' Jaguar made a show of mock humility.

Two Sign laughed at last. 'Ha! When it comes to warfare, you'll always be my apprentice, whatever Tlacaelel thinks, but this is different. I have a temporary problem with funds. Can you lend me some cacao beans?'

Jaguar winked. 'Lost a few too many bets with Last Medicine, have you? How much is it this time?'

'No,' replied Two Sign dismissively. 'I won't have any problems paying him.'

Jaguar waited, but Two Sign showed no sign of volunteering more information. It was interesting that the debt to Last Medicine hadn't yet been repaid, thought Jaguar. That suggested he had bigger debts to service.

'How much do you need?'

'Two hundred.'

Jaguar whistled in surprise. It was a vast sum.

'Come on,' said Two Sign, bristled suddenly. 'You were only telling us all yesterday how well the jade-carving business is going.'

'Who do you need to repay?'

Two Sign shook his head. 'You don't need to know.'

'It might help. Obviously I don't have that much with me here, but if you need to pay someone back home, I could send word to Arrow One to pay on your behalf. If your debt is due here, I can arrange for it to be sent, but it will take time.' Two Sign was a proud man and the fact that he had even broached the issue was worrying.

'No, don't worry about it,' said Two Sign, suddenly appearing to lose interest. 'It's going to be too much trouble.'

'It's no trouble, it's just that it will take a bit of time. So the person you need to repay is here then?'

'No. Tenochtitlan.'

Jaguar frowned. 'If you tell me who it is, I can get it sent directly to them. It doesn't make any sense risking that kind of package on the journey here just to carry it all the way back again.'

'Forget it,' said Two Sign. 'Come on. Are we going to visit these poor people or are we going to stand here making idle gossip all day?' He ducked inside the hospice.

Jaguar followed, shaking his head. He prayed that the stench emanating from the doorway wasn't an indication of the general health of the building's occupants, but in his heart he knew it could only be a bad sign.

Chapter 10
The Jungles of Totonaca

Tlaloc confounded the predictions of the local weather experts and liberally doused the waiting army with rain. The evening cloudburst didn't last long though and Shield of Gold watched as tendrils of mist pulled back from sodden treetops. Six hundred Mexica warriors occupied an expanse of sloping ground where the jungle had been cleared for planting. Tender shoots of maize lay trampled in the mud. The trees began again where the ground levelled out and rose towards a softly rolling ridge beyond which lay the town of Zongolica that Jaguar and his party of scouts had reconnoitred twelve days earlier.

Shield of Gold tried to come to terms with the uncomfortable sensation in the pit of his stomach. He had never witnessed a battle before, let alone taken part. He was carrying a light shield that he could run with a short sword with only two cutting blades on each side. They looked like toys beside the weapons carried by the other men. There were over a hundred Eagle Knights with their beaked and feathered cowls and twice as many Jaguar Knights looking equally ferocious in their spotted skins.

Jaguar had passed by a short while ago on his way to meet up with Tlacaelel who was at the front of the expeditionary force. Shield of Gold had felt the hairs on the back of his neck rise. It was the first time he had seen Jaguar in his full regalia as commander of the most feared fighters in the land. His mentor's face emerged from the spotted, gaping maw of the regal cat whose name he bore. It was unnerving to be watched by two pairs of eyes and somehow the dead pair seemed even more penetrating than the wearer's eyes. Sleek pelt covered his neck and draped his shoulders. Underneath it, Jaguar wore a vest of brown quilted cotton sown with small overlapping tongues of leather that didn't conceal his sculpted stomach muscles. A sash made from more jaguar skin was wrapped around his waist so that two paws hung in front of his loincloth, leaving his powerful legs free for running and for close quarters combat. Greaves of boiled deer hide sewn over with more spotted skin were tied beneath his knees to protect his calves and shins, while bracelets of savage, yellowing teeth decorated his upper arms. This sturdy outfit and the long sword, set with four, close-fitting rectangular obsidian blades on either side made Jaguar look like a giant. Knights of both orders greeted him with reverence.

The thin stream of pee that Shield of Gold had been directing onto a sad-looking plant had dried up altogether as Jaguar and the dead cat on his head grinned at him. Shield of Gold realised that his mouth was hanging open. He closed it and tucked himself back into his loincloth. He felt distinctly underdressed now. Like the other warriors from the clans he had only a simple padded tunic for protection.

'Don't worry. You'll get used to that,' Jaguar had said. His voice seemed deeper and more gravelly than usual, but it was hard to see how the headdress could have that effect. He had indicated several other men who were relieving themselves. 'Everyone gets a little nervous.'

Once he'd been made aware of it, Shield of Gold couldn't help but notice the constant stream of warriors ambling off and loosening their loincloths in the direction of the already damp foliage. The men at the rear of the war party were, for the most part, older or stouter or both and there were two with pronounced limps. They were all trusted veterans with numerous campaigns between them but just not fast enough to be in the vanguard with their younger, nimbler brothers.

'Tlacaelel told me to tell you he's heading back this way. He will hang back at the entrance to the town. You'll wait with him in case he needs you to carry a message to me or one of the other captains fighting inside Zongolica.'

'You don't want me in there?' Shield of Gold had squeaked. He cleared his throat and added, 'What if you need to get a message out?'

'Don't worry, I have a couple of fast runners amongst my knights who I can rely on. Besides, your place is with Lord Tlacaelel.'

That exchange had been a short while ago. Jaguar had left them to take his place at the head of the army and the tension had risen since then. Shield of Gold could sense the men around him getting edgy. It reminded him of the atmosphere when street gangs went to war in a battle over territory, except this was a thousand times worse. Today, many people would die.

'What are we waiting for?' grumbled a seasoned veteran whose face was writhing with tattoos and whose lip hung down with the weight of a glistening black lip plug. He was one of the portly ones, about as wide as he was tall. His loincloth was the colours of a summer sky with a grey border. He had a short but solid-looking spear and a shield that looked as though it had been hewn as a section through a tree trunk. He wore a light grey tunic that was armoured with tough wooden pegs sewn across the shoulders and strung with rows of azure beads across the chest.

'It will be dark soon,' complained another clansman, looking up from an inspection of the feathers on his shield. 'It's bad luck to begin an attack at dusk. We don't know what evil spirits stalk this place after nightfall.'

Shield of Gold kept quiet. He knew that the attack had been timed for the late afternoon because of the information Jaguar had brought back from the town, but he doubted these seasoned warriors would listen to him. Tattoo-face caught him looking at them.

'Does your mother know you're here?'

The one who had been checking his shield laughed. 'Lizard didn't bring his skirt, so you won't have anything to hide behind.'

Lizard's patchwork face scowled at the other man, then turned back to Shield of Gold. 'Are you hoping to take any captives today?'

'No,' croaked Shield of Gold. 'I'm Lord Tlacaelel's runner.' He cursed his unreliable voice for letting him down again, just when he needed to give the appearance of being older than he was so he could fit in.

The one called Lizard laughed as well and a third man, who had been listening, joined in too. 'Wind of Darkness, did you step on a frog? Upon the rotting flesh of Xipe Totec, I swear that I just heard a frog.'

The three of them laughed even harder. Shield of Gold smiled nervously and stared towards the vanguard of the army, trying to avoid being drawn into the conversation. He knew they meant him no harm, but he certainly didn't feel welcome.

Lizard put his dark painted face close to Shield of Gold. 'Stay away from me, understand?' he hissed. 'My sword has a long reach, so you'd best remember that. I don't need frogs or children getting in the way.'

'Yeah, just try to stay alive for now!' jeered the shield man. 'Maybe you'd better go to the back.'

Shield of Gold thought it best not to point out that they already were at the back. He was spared any further humiliation when, at an unseen signal, the front of the army began to move forward. As the men began to advance, Tlacaelel walked back down the line with a bodyguard of four Jaguar Knights. They too looked majestic in spotted pelt cowl, shoulder-piece and leggings and each of them carried a long sword. The general was giving orders for each warrior to allow the one in front to get far enough ahead so that they would have enough room to charge when they broke cover of the trees on the other side. Tlacaelel reached the rear of the party, fell into step with Shield of Gold and put a hand on his shoulder.

'Are you alright?'

'Yes, My Lord.'

'Stay close to me, understand? We're going in to the town last. I may need you to run ahead and carry a message to the men at the front.'

Shield of Gold nodded.

'Don't worry though. It will be easier than if I had split the invasion force into two or more groups. A single, all-out attack from one direction will be enough to overpower this settlement, so the route to men at the front will be thick with our own warriors. Use them for cover.'

'Yes, Lord Tlacaelel.'

The long line of warriors headed into the wooded ridge, a glistening brown snake of men sliding into the greenery. Shield of Gold and Tlacaelel were amongst the last into the cover of trees. The general's two bodyguards easily kept pace with the less sprightly warriors around them. They trotted uphill and over the crest; above them the cracked canopy was black against the purple sky. Shield of Gold swatted a broad leaf out of his way and hopped over a rotting log, then suddenly he was out into the open and onto an expanse of cleared ground that Jaguar had described. Men at the front were running now, in a hurry to get to the town before the alarm was raised. Jaguar instructed a rearguard of thirty or so men to hang back.

'Our first duty is to protect the general.'

Five hundred strides ahead the lead warriors were already pouring into Zongolica. Screams could be heard and there was a clatter that might have been the clash of weapons, but Jaguar would be first among them. It didn't look as if the locals were putting up much resistance. Shield of Gold was grateful for his lightweight sword. The shield was also specially constructed with a small yet strong boss that would protect the wearer's arm, while the frame and outer panels were more for show. Even with these compromises, the combined weight still slowed him down in the dash from the treeline. Halfway across the open ground he had only pulled a dozen paces ahead of the lagging warriors.

A stone statue the height of two men kept resolute watch just outside the edge of the town. It was carved with a leering face that might have been Tlaloc or, Shield of Gold suspected, a former ruler of this town. Tlacaelel called a halt to his men here and climbed up onto the broad base that supported the statue. He shielded his eyes with the flat of one hand and scanned the surroundings.

'Wait here,' he cried out to the men who were bringing up the rear. Lizard and Wind of Darkness were among them. 'There's something wrong.'

'What's the matter, My Lord?' asked one of the knights guarding Tlacaelel.

A ragged cheer rang out from the town centre.

'It sounds like we've got their tlatoani,' said the knight.

'That was easy,' said Wind of Darkness, ruefully. Shield of Gold could see that he and Lizard and the dozen others who had stopped on Tlacaelel's order were disappointed not to have made it into Zongolica. They had missed out on the opportunity of taking captives.

Tlacaelel was still keeping an eagle-eye out from his vantage point. He glanced behind at the outlying huts and the temple that rose above the taller houses of the local nobility and then scanned the tree line once again.

'That was too easy,' he muttered. 'They should have put up more of a fight than that.'

'You think it's some kind of trick?' said the Jaguar Knight.

'It's possible the warriors are out on a raid of their own, but I doubt it. They have their own spies. They know we're in the area. They would not have left their own town so lightly defended.'

Tlacaelel was just about to jump down from the plinth when he straightened up and pointed at the jungle to the south. Shield of Gold followed the line and watched as the wall of greenery that marked the edge of the jungle shook and then disgorged about a hundred warriors who charged across the cleared ground, making straight for them brandishing spears, red shields and glass-edged war clubs. Somehow this tidal wave of butchery was all the more terrifying because of its ghastly silence.

'They mean to cut us off before we reach the town,' said Tlacaelel, calm as a mountain pond on a crisp winter's morning. 'Now I need your help, Shield of Gold.' The general fixed him with his icy grey eyes. If the general felt any sense of urgency, it was well contained. 'See our men at the edge of the town?'

Shield of Gold looked. Three warriors stood just inside the main entrance to the town, watching whatever was unfolding within, alert for townsfolk trying to escape, oblivious to the new menace.

'Run. Run as fast as you can and when you get close, if they haven't seen you or that lot...' Tlacaelel pointed one stubby finger at the enemy hurtling towards them.' ...shout. Shout as loud as you can to attract their attention. When they see you, they will see the enemy and your job is done. We will follow as fast as we can with the rest of these men. Give me your weapons, go now.'

Shield of Gold wasted no time. He thrust his sword and shield at the general and sprinted off as though the host of Mictlantecuhtli's hellish demons were at his heels. It was at least two hundred long strides to the outermost huts. Shield of Gold ran as hard as he had ever run, arms and legs pumping. When he was halfway there, he shouted at the warriors gathered in the entrance to the town, but the events unfolding inside were too interesting. Shield of Gold shouted again and this time they finally heard him. He pointed to his right and saw them start in surprise. Two ran into the town, presumably to fetch help. Shield of Gold reached the remaining man and tried to speak, but all that came out was a hoarse squeak.

'It's alright,' said the warrior. His expression was far from reassuring. 'Reinforcements are being rounded up.'

But far too slowly, thought Shield of Gold. The Mexica warriors would be too busy congratulating themselves on their lightning swift victory to comprehend the threat outside the walls. Tlacaelel and the stragglers would be intercepted before they reached the town. Shield of Gold dug the balls of his feet into the damp earth and set off the way he had come, breath sawing in and out of his lungs. If he didn't throw up first, he might just make it back to Tlacaelel before the hoard descended on them. He was nearly there when the enemy began to loose arrows. One glanced off Tlacaelel's shield and another thrummed harmlessly into the ground in front of Shield of Gold. All the other missiles plunged into the earth or bit into raised shields. Half a dozen spears followed in behind, but they were not well aimed. A return volley from the Mexica brought three of the attackers to a tumbling halt and then the maelstrom struck.

Tlacaelel stabbed one finger at the ground. 'Your weapons are there,' he cried as the first wave crashed against their defences. 'Get behind Yellow Dog and be careful!'

Yellow Dog was one of the men with a limp. He was sandwiched between Lizard and Wind of Darkness. They had taken up a position on the left and none of them noticed Shield of Gold as seven fighting braves from the town of Zongolica crashed into them. Lizard was instantly knocked over, but Yellow Dog slashed his glass-edged sword in a wide protective arc that had the enemy jumping back. Lizard scrambled to his feet unscathed, but Yellow Dog paid dearly for leaving his side exposed to the enemy. Someone lunged with a spear and caught him in the ribs.

Shield of Gold had only ever been this terrified once before, when he and Clawfoot and the gang they had been in had been ambushed by priests as they scavenged Tenochtitlan for food when they'd been young. To his right was Tlacaelel protected by three of the Jaguar Knights who were parrying a furious onslaught from another half-dozen local men. The knights appeared to have the upper hand and weren't allowing any of the attackers to get close to the general. Beyond them, their colleague was moving lightly on his feet, darting about and wreaking havoc on anyone who got close to him. He was calling out, issuing orders and trying to organise the tiny group against the onslaught, but there was little that could be done; the band of Mexica were already fully occupied just trying to stay alive.

The ranks of the attackers from Zongolica swelled as the first wave of the attackers was joined by the rest. The local men had the upper hand now. They forced the thin line of Mexica back and finally engulfed them. Tlacaelel called everyone to draw in tight. Shield of Gold saw a Jaguar Knight fall with a spear through his neck and Lizard was overrun on the left-hand side as he tried to pull back to the centre. The men from Zongolica were too numerous and where Shield of Gold had been safe behind knights, he now found himself face-to-face with death. One of the enemy who had circled round behind them rushed in, an ugly man with red paint on his face and arms, his armoured tunic decorated with a tatty spray of red feathers. Instinctively, Shield of Gold threw his left arm up protectively, but he had no time to swing his puny sword. The red-faced man from Zongolica crashed into him and bowled him over. Fortunately for Shield of Gold, the man had been expecting a more robust defence and was caught off balance. He crashed into the dirt behind Shield of Gold where he received a vicious sword cut to the back of his neck from Tlacaelel. Shield of Gold sprang up, hot with embarrassment that he hadn't managed to stand his ground, ashamed that his own weakness had put Tlacaelel in danger. He had no time to dwell on it though. Wind of Darkness was trying to hold the spot where Shield of Gold had fallen, a gap that needed two men. Shield of Gold took his place again and instantly another local man was on him, hacking down, his sword a glittering black arc. Again, Shield of Gold raised his shield. The shock of the impact was an explosive spike of lightning, penetrating his left shoulder and lancing across his chest. He fell to one knee, blinded by a blizzard of wood fragments. A small corner of his mind registered that his flimsy shield had disintegrated and then something smashed into his face and sent him reeling to the floor again, stars bursting across his vision.

At first, Shield of Gold thought he had died, but the pain and grit and dust said otherwise. He couldn't see properly and his mouth was filled with blood and sharp bits that didn't belong there. There was also a persistent din in his left ear. He tried to get up and was surprised when no one tried to stop him; his attacker was nowhere to be seen. Two bodies lay on the ground beside him and two more ahead where he could just make out Wind of Darkness and two others who were still standing their ground. Tlacaelel was behind him, which meant that Shield of Gold was safe for the moment. It might have been his first real fight, but he could tell they were in trouble. His left arm hung uselessly and any attempt to move it provoked such agony it brought tears to his already watering eyes. He reached down with his right arm and picked up his sword, blinked once and spat roughly, then staggered to the general's side. Tlacaelel was holding two men at bay. The one closest to Shield of Gold swung, his whole attention focused on his target. With all the strength he could muster, Shield of Gold hacked at the man's outstretched arm and felt the shards of his weapon bite into unprotected flesh. There was a howl of pain, but Shield of Gold had no time to follow up as he caught a movement in the corner of his eye. Another man came at him. Shield of Gold swung his sword arm back up and over his head, grunting with the effort. He deflected the strike, lowered his good shoulder and rammed into his attacker who stumbled over one of the bodies on the ground. Shield of Gold followed behind the man and chopped down on his exposed back, chopping again at a thigh as the helpless warrior writhed. Blood splashed Shield of Gold in the eyes and blinded him again. Barely able to see, he hacked at the dim shadow of a figure, then one of his feet slid out from under him and he fell once more.

This time, Shield of Gold couldn't get up. The pain in his shoulder and chest was excruciating and his breath came in ragged, heaving sobs. A dark shadow stood over him and this time Shield of Gold could do nothing about it. He tensed, waiting for the final blow, but then realised that something had changed. Through the roaring din that filled his head he sensed that the chop and crack of swords on shields were gone, replaced by cheering that was growing in intensity. Hands pulled him to his feet, heedless of the pain it caused him.

'Are you alright?' said a voice he didn't recognise.

'Yes,' replied Shield of Gold. 'No. I think my arm is broken.' His lips were swollen on one side and his mouth felt strange as he spoke. Probing with his tongue, he found a gap where a tooth had snapped off. He stood still while the same man wiped his eyes and when he opened them he saw that it was Yellow Dog, the man who had taken a spear in the chest. Shield of Gold hadn't expected to see him again. The veteran had taken his padded tunic off and was standing stiffly while another man prepared a bandage from a strip of fabric. There was a lot of blood down his side where the spear had glanced off his ribs and gouged a flap of flesh loose.

Shield of Gold blinked, trying to clear the dust and debris of battle from his watering eyes. When he could see properly, it was clear that a large number of Mexica warriors had reached them, spilling from the town to protect Tlacaelel.

'Look!' Yellow Dog pointed. 'Only ten or eleven of the scum left and they're running for the jungle.' Some Mexica were in hot pursuit.

'That's a shame. I haven't caught any.'

'No one has. We were too busy trying to stay alive. Is this your first fight?'

Shield of Gold nodded.

The man who was treating Yellow Dog finished bandaging his chest and approached Shield of Gold.

'Your arm is hurt?'

Shield of Gold reached up to touch his shoulder. The man ran an experienced hand over the affected area and his fingers quickly settled over the shoulder joint.

'Not broken,' he said. 'It's out of the socket. One of the healers will be able to put that back in for you, but your fighting is over for a couple of weeks.'

Shield of Gold wasn't sure whether to be delighted or disappointed. He had seen the gleam in some men's eyes when they spoke of the fights they had lived through. He didn't think he would ever look back on this carnage fondly. Just then, he noticed Jaguar talking to Tlacaelel. One side of his body was spattered with blood, the other was covered in mud and bits of grass. They had a short exchange, after which Jaguar went and checked the bodies of the fallen Jaguar Knights.

'You're hurt,' he said when he caught sight of Shield of Gold.

'But alive.'

'True. You did well to survive that. It looked bad. I'm sorry I didn't get back in time to help.'

'But you took Zongolica,' said Shield of Gold. He was exhausted and had begun to shiver, even though the night air was warm.

'Yes, we took the town. By tomorrow morning we may have as many as four hundred captives to send back to Tenochtitlan, and,' added Jaguar, 'thanks to your efforts Tlacaelel is safe.'

'Not your men though,' said Shield of Gold, glancing across at the dead who lay scattered like discarded sacks.

'No, they didn't make it, but don't blame yourself.' Tlacaelel had joined them. 'They fought like demented dogs and earned their place among the gods.' The general looked at the ground for a moment and then addressed Jaguar. 'Did we lose many more within the city?'

'Small losses for such a town, Lord Tlacaelel. One knight and fourteen macehualtin, perhaps a dozen wounded.'

The general nodded. 'Let's get everyone back into the town. It's nearly dark.' He turned to another Jaguar Knight who stood nearby. Shield of Gold recognised him as one of Jaguar's captains. 'Holds the Sun, get our fallen warriors into the town. We'll bury them tomorrow.'

'Yes, Lord Tlacaelel. What about the others?'

Tlacaelel made a sour face. 'The elders can send out their own people or leave them out here if they prefer, I don't care. Come on, let's go and see what kind of food the people of Zongolica have.'

When they reached the town they were greeted by the rest of the men and they were in good cheer. Warriors called out to Yellow Dog who was well known and asked him what had happened. Shield of Gold had to stop people from patting his injured shoulder. The friendly faces escorted them to the centre of the town where a group of Jaguar Knights held the local tlatoani and key members of the nobility. When they came to a halt, Tlacaelel asked for silence so he could give a brief account. He praised several of the group by name including the Jaguar Knights who had died defending him, Yellow Dog and he even mentioned Shield of Gold.

'He told me you fought courageously,' Jaguar whispered.

'Not really. I fell over a lot.'

'You didn't have to go back, you know. You're a messenger, not a warrior. You could have waited for the others.'

Shield of Gold shrugged. 'I...I thought they needed help. I don't know what I was thinking.'

'No, you did the right thing,' said Jaguar. 'Sometimes one man among a hundred may tip the balance.'

They listened as Tlacaelel, through his interpreter, made a formal demand to the ruler of Zongolica, whose name was Guardian Lord Above, to surrender, which he duly did. The Mexica conquerors cheered, while the townsfolk who had been rounded up stood by unhappily. When the cheers died down, Tlacaelel told Guardian Lord Above to command his people to light fires and lay on a great feast, standing over him with his sword so that he would understand the consequences should they disobey.

Shield of Gold watched the preparations commence. The nobility of Zongolica busied themselves on behalf of their ruler. Jaguar issued instructions to his men.

'Double sentry duties until first light,' Jaguar barked. 'We don't know how many more of their cowardly men are hiding in the jungle.' He looked at Shield of Gold. 'Come on. We need to get one of the healers to look at your arm.'

Chapter II – Tenochtitlan

Pre-dawn on the day One Mazātl saw Clawfoot crossing the square before the Great Temple. A sliver of moon cast a baleful light on the towering steps and a thin mist covered the ground, making the skull rack look as though it was floating silently upon a river of ghosts. Ten thousand bony grimaces in a stack eight deep, eye sockets stark in shadow, stared fixedly across the courtyard at the silent ball court, as though waiting, in rapt concentration, for the next game to commence. A crowd was gathering at the bottom of the steps: noblemen and key administrative figures from the city clans who regularly attended the most important sacrificial ceremonies. Torches were being lit around the square.

Clawfoot stopped and tried to breathe evenly. Swirls of damp mist eddied around his chilled feet. The pounding of his heart was a sharp pain in his chest and an unwelcome reminder of his destination. He didn't think that Feathered Darkness intended to sacrifice him. After all, hadn't the high priest chosen him for this business with Xiconoc because he was expendable? Surely it would make more sense for the high priest to send him on this mission and deal with him on his return, if he returned at all. Clawfoot seized the moment of tranquillity and moved one foot in front of the other. Twenty strides and he had pushed through the gathering throng and was climbing the newly enlarged base of the temple that was rising daily, entombing the old one in its own inexorable climb towards the heavens. A few more days and the new shrine of Huitzilopochtli would be completed on the left-hand side and then the construction team would switch to the right-hand side, raising Tlaloc's new shrine above the old.

All of Clawfoot's fragile certainty evaporated the moment that he reached the platform and saw how many priests had assembled for the morning's dedication. It could only mean one thing: Feathered Darkness himself was going to conduct the ceremony and word had got around to everyone except for Clawfoot. Three figures detached themselves from the gloom: warrior priests. They had been waiting for him. Two of them took a firm hold of his arms and steered him to a place near the entrance to the shrine, while the third stood nearby in case of trouble. Clawfoot swallowed hard. Soft orange light flickered inside the shrine.

There was a considerable delay while the formalities were checked and rechecked. The first day of each new sign was too important to leave anything to chance. Clawfoot aged a hundred years waiting for the moment when he would be summoned. Eventually Feathered Darkness emerged from the shrine and made his way towards the black slab of the altar at the top of the temple steps.

'Bring the offering,' boomed the high priest.

Clawfoot felt the two men beside him tighten their grip. He twitched, unable to contain his body's natural reaction to danger. This was it. He hadn't really believed that it was possible. His throat was dry and the warm light from the doorway pulsed and swam before his eyes. He tried to take a step forward, determined not to disgrace himself, but his legs wouldn't work. Then he realised why. The two men at his side were holding him back while another man was being led out from the shrine and herded towards the altar.

The ceremony passed by with all the surrealism of a dream. The men guarding Clawfoot let go of him once the real offering was held down on the altar. He stood with his arms hanging slackly at his sides. Once, he caught himself swaying slightly, as though he was about to pass out. The words of dedication that he knew so well were just a roaring in his ears.

The assembled priests began to disperse as soon as the ceremony ended. Clawfoot's guards remained with him, not restraining him but making it obvious by their presence that he was not allowed to leave. He waited, glad of the opportunity to clear his head. The light of the sun kissed the tops of the cordilleras to the west and lowered its warm embrace down broad flanks of the mountain range, and still Clawfoot waited. Feathered Darkness and several of the elders had descended the temple steps to welcome those who had watched the proceedings from below. A gang of young priests busied themselves around the altar and the chacmool and then departed. Waiting in the shadow of Tlaloc's shrine, Clawfoot shivered. Finally he saw the high priest clear the platform once again, accompanied as usual by the Silent Watch, eight stern men with short swords and sombre, charcoal-coloured cloaks. At a signal from the high priest, Clawfoot's own escort nudged him forward. They met beside the altar that was drying, now that the sun had cleared the top of Tlaloc's shrine. Excitable flies crowded the remnants of the morning's sacrifice and dozens circled Feathered Darkness, scenting the blood that had soaked into his robes.

'Good morning, Brother Clawfoot. Another cycle smoothly underway. Another faultless dawn in the playground of the gods. Did you appreciate the ceremony?' The high priest allowed himself a small but supercilious smile and waved languidly at the insistent flies.

'It... made a big impression on me, Venerable Father.'

'Good. I hoped it would. You still seem to think that the priesthood is here for you. It is not. It is the reverse. You are here to serve me and, through the priesthood, serve Huitzilopochtli.'

Clawfoot opened his mouth to say something suitably contrite, but the high priest cut him off.

'And...by serving Huitzilopochtli, you serve the people. Do you see, Clawfoot? Do you understand the magnitude of your arrogance?'

Clawfoot nodded.

'Sadly, I do not believe you do. Nevertheless, let us discuss your mission.'

'Is it still on?'

'The mission was never in doubt, Brother Clawfoot. It was only your participation that was in jeopardy. Do you know how many priests there are in our order, Brother Clawfoot?'

'In Tenochtitlan, nine hundred or so, Venerable Father. If you mean to include all of your people across the Mexica Empire, I do not know for sure, but I have heard it said that the number is near two thousand.'

The high priest nodded. 'Can you imagine, Brother Clawfoot, the kind of chaos that would exist if I allowed all these priests to brawl and draw knives on each other?'

'I...I have been justly punished, My Lord,' said Clawfoot. He brushed his face to chase a fly away. 'There will be no more fights.' It sounded like an empty promise as soon as he had spoken the words. What would he do if Angry Lizard or one of the other spoiled sons of some minor nobleman tried to vent their frustration on him for their own shortcomings?

'Oh, Brother Clawfoot,' resumed the high priest. 'This morning's show was not punishment. It was merely a demonstration, a warning if you will. Your punishment still awaits.'

As if on cue, two figures topped the platform behind the chacmool. It was Angry Lizard and one of his sidekicks, Third Arrow, the sharp one with the blade who hadn't succeeded in tangling with Clawfoot in the Hall of Knowledge. Angry Lizard's nose still looked swollen and there was bruising under his eyes. Both of them had swords slung over their backs and carried vicious-looking spears. They looked at Clawfoot with ill-concealed hate.

Feathered Darkness checked to make sure no one was close by. 'I promised Lord Xiconoc that I would send three men to Totonaca to help with his plan,' he said.

Clawfoot goggled as the realisation hit home.

'That's right, Brother Clawfoot.' Feathered Darkness smiled. 'I knew you'd understand. I need to send three people on a mission, three people with a natural inclination to violence, three people who I can afford to lose. I did not spend long deciding who.'

It was so outrageous that Clawfoot burst out laughing. Even Angry Lizard looked shocked. So, he thought, they hadn't known the reason for their summons.

'This amuses you?' asked Feathered Darkness.

'I'm sorry, Venerable Father. The idea just caught me by surprise. It... it's not what I expected. You're asking these two to take orders from me?'

As he said the words, the two warrior priests started to complain until the high priest cut them off.

'Be quiet! Yes. Angry Lizard and Third Arrow will accompany you to Totonaca. Anyone who wishes to know your business will be told that you are helping with the Ray of Truth, the Lord-High Spiritual Assessor's task to spread the word of Huitzilopochtli to the local people. The jungle savages mostly revere Tlaloc and other lesser deities. The Lord-High Spiritual Assessor will not be expecting your assistance though. Instead you will meet Xiconoc's man in Ahuilizapan and learn of his plans to assassinate the tlatoani. You will do whatever he asks of you unless it becomes clear that Xiconoc's plot will fail. If that happens, you will turn on the assassins and become the tlatoani's saviour.'

'I won't take orders from Clawfoot,' spat Angry Lizard.

Clawfoot watched, transfixed as Feathered Darkness lifted his hand and gently cupped the warrior priest's cheek. Dried blood from the morning's sacrifice caked the high priest's fingernails and wrists. Angry Lizard stared straight ahead, unsure how to react to the tender caress.

'You will take orders from him.'

'He's just a boy.' Angry Lizard's voice was a croak.

The high priest ran his thumb over the bruising that underscored Angry Lizard's eye.

'Or you could stay here and help me with my investigations.'

'Investigations?'

'The Master Curator assures me that a man can live for many days without flesh on his face and head.' Feathered Darkness moved his hand up to run it through Angry Lizard's hair. 'I haven't seen it yet. Can you imagine the thrill of the crowds at the prospect of seeing a living skull walk among them?'

Clawfoot's fascination was at odds with his stomach, which lurched uncomfortably.

Feathered Darkness allowed his hand to drop. 'You think you're fit to take command? Is that it?'

'Well...' began Angry Lizard uncertainly.

'Tell me, Brother Angry Lizard... what do the omens hold?'

'I'm sorry, Venerable Father?'

'You heard me. You have studied the tonalpohualli and use of the heavenly cycles for divine prognostication... so, tell me my horoscope!'

Angry Lizard looked down at his feet.

'No? Nothing? Perhaps Brother Clawfoot will oblige me.' Feathered Darkness held an open hand out, inviting Clawfoot to speak up.

Clawfoot had been busy revelling in Angry Lizard's failure and had to think quickly to gather an answer together. 'Today is Miquiztli who is death. Death in the trecena of the Flower means change and the start of something new and more beautiful than before, Venerable Father,' he recited. 'Elemental spirits lay down the many paths for us, but in the end, there is only one path we must tread into the halls of the dead. This is a hallowed time to seek new opportunities, Venerable Father.'

The high priest pursed his lips and turned to Angry Lizard. 'You see? This young man already knows more than you will ever learn. This is why he is progressing up the ranks of the priesthood and it is why you will progress no further, so this is why you *will* follow Brother Clawfoot and do as he says and bring him safely back to me. Consider this your punishment for your part in the disturbance that caused so much damage in the Hall of Knowledge. I command you to work together and fight alongside each other for the common cause. If you must satisfy your need to kill someone then make sure it's the tlatoani. Is that clear?'

Angry Lizard jabbed a finger at Clawfoot, some of his natural belligerence returning. 'What if we can't protect him? Anything could happen if we get mixed up in an attack on the tlatoani.'

'I'll make it simple for you,' said Feathered Darkness. 'If you make it back alive without Clawfoot, I'll have you killed.' He looked at Clawfoot. 'And if you fail in this mission, I'll offer all three of you up to the Master Curator and we'll find out which one of you really is the toughest, eh? I doubt that any of you will last three days with the skin flayed from your skulls.'

All three men murmured in agreement.

'I don't understand,' said Third Arrow, speaking up for the first time. 'I thought you said we were supposed to save the tlatoani.'

'That's the starting point,' replied Clawfoot, glad of an opportunity to demonstrate his command and show Feathered Darkness that his trust was well placed. 'Xiconoc and Moctezuma dance a fatal step in opposition to each other. Only one can win and when it becomes clear who that winner is, we must be seen to have helped the winning side.'

'Just so,' agreed the high priest. 'Xiconoc has arranged for an attempt on the tlatoani's life and you three are my contribution to his cause. He is content knowing that I am sending you to aide his men and that is what you will do. If the assassination goes poorly or is uncovered, you will switch sides and ensure that the tlatoani knows your part in safeguarding his life.'

'It sounds like we should play it cautiously.'

'That would be wise. If the tlatoani dies, whether you play a central role or not, Xiconoc will believe that we helped him, but if the attack fails, you must not allow yourselves to be associated with it. Make no mistake: I have plans in place to distance myself and the Order of Huitzilopochtli from you should you fail in this regard.'

'Plans?' said Angry Lizard, blankly.

'If the tlatoani parades any of you before me and questions my allegiance, I shall get down on my knees and beg him to release you to me so that the Master Curator can have his way.'

Clawfoot wondered whether the other two understood how deeply they were ensnared in the high priest's plans. *Exile will be the only option if we fail,* he decided. There was one thing he still didn't understand.

'Venerable Father,' he said. 'Why do we need to get involved at all? Can't we wait on the sidelines and rejoice with whoever is in charge when everything settles down?'

'And when it is all over... what will you say to the new ruler when he comes to see you, demanding to know what you did to support his cause, eh? What placatory words will you offer to the tlatoani who has narrowly escaped death when he asks why you did not intercede to save his life?'

'I see,' said Clawfoot.

'Understand this, Brother Clawfoot: politics has nothing to do with where one stands, but it has everything to do with where your enemies *think* you stand.'

Third Arrow spoke again. 'So we need everyone to think that we side with them?'

'Almost,' said Feathered Darkness. 'They must all think we side *exclusively* with them.'

'Don't you favour anyone, Venerable Father?' Clawfoot asked.

'I favour the gods, Younger Brother: Huitzilopochtli, Tezcatlipoca, Quetzalcoatl and the others. Arrogant, strutting mortals mean little to me. This is where my predecessor went wrong. He did not trust the almighty gods to do their work and took matters into his own hands, putting the entire priesthood at risk. Whatever petty squabbles break out around the throne, we must protect our order at all costs. We cannot risk another setback for the priesthood. Do you understand?'

Third Arrow looked shocked. 'But Lord Moctezuma is the incarnation of Huitzilopochtli!'

'Maybe he is now, Younger Brother, but once he was a snotty little child with an irritating cry who pissed the blankets that he lay in. The future is not clear to me, but Moctezuma is not getting any younger. His sons are spoilt, self-centred and vain. I dread to think what kind of chaos would befall our people if one of them took their father's place. There is no trust between them. Xiconoc is little better, but he is a greedy fool and greedy fools can be useful if used carefully.'

'So it makes no difference who sits on the throne?'

'Of course it does!' snapped Feathered Darkness. 'But you speak as though they represent causes that we must choose between, when, in fact, we are the cause and it is they who will support us to a greater or lesser extent.' There was a pause and then he added, 'And we certainly won't be able to count on much patronage if we're not seen to be enthusiastically behind our tlatoani!'

'I thought our position was more secure than that. Don't the gods look after their priests?'

Feathered Darkness gave Third Arrow a sympathetic look, then lowered his voice so that it wouldn't carry to the men of the

Silent Watch standing nearby. 'Let me explain this to you three since you haven't worked it out for yourselves,' he said. 'Our gods are monstrous and cruel, demons for the most part, capricious and vain. They barely know that we exist and they certainly won't help the weak or the lazy. Why do you think you are made to work so hard to become a priest? Every day we must remind the gods that we are here, demonstrate to them that we are strong and utterly determined.' The high priest shook his head.

Clawfoot understood. It was exactly like being back on the street where only strength and cunning prevailed. That a deity would respect this made perfect sense.

'Do you have any questions?'

'Yes,' said Clawfoot. 'How do we find Xiconoc's man when we arrive in Totonaca?'

'Ah, yes. You will travel with one of Xiconoc's trading caravans that is heading for the coast. It leaves just after dawn on the day after tomorrow from the Place of Flowers in the Cuepopan district. Xiconoc will meet you there and explain how you make contact with his people.'

'One more thing,' said the high priest. 'Watch out for one of Tlacaelel's men, a Jaguar Knight, himself called Heart of the Jaguar.'

'A Jaguar Knight called Jaguar. That shouldn't be hard to remember. Is he a problem?'

'Could be,' replied Feathered Darkness. 'He is loyal to the tlatoani and has been... obstructive in the past.'

'Are you sure that he is with the army, Venerable Father?' said Angry Lizard. 'Only a small army has been sent out to Ahuilizapan. I heard that Tlacaelel was worried that the people of Tlaxcala might be waiting for an opportunity like this when the city's defences are at their lowest.'

Feathered Darkness shook his head. 'No. I haven't any recent information on his whereabouts.'

Clawfoot had an idea. 'Venerable Father, if he is still in Tenochtitlan, would he be less likely to rejoin the army if he fears for the safety of his family?'

'Pah! I don't think one man will cause much trouble,' Angry Lizard cut in.

'Do not be complacent. Like his namesake, this man is cunning and surprisingly resourceful.' The high priest squinted into the rising sun momentarily and then looked at Clawfoot with something approaching approval in his eyes. 'Do it,' he said at last. 'You'll have to go tomorrow before you leave for Totonaca. His home is in Harbour Street. I don't want any accusations being made against the priesthood, so you'd better dress like mayeques before you go. You look too rough and bedraggled to pass as anything but peasants. Make a bit of a mess, steal some things, you know...maybe rough up his family a little if he's not around. If he knows we are watching him, he may be minded to stay here and keep watch over his family.'

Angry Lizard shrugged. 'If he's there, why don't we just kill him and get him out of the way?'

'No!' barked Feathered Darkness, even startling the men of the Silent Watch who stood a dozen paces away. 'Is that your answer to everything? You and Brother Clawfoot are like feeble-minded brothers. I'm surprised you have such trouble getting along with each other. No. You most definitely will not kill him or anyone else before you reach Ahuilizapan. Is that understood? A murder in the city will attract too much attention and jeopardise everything.

'Is everything clear?' said Feathered Darkness in a tone that demanded the affirmative. 'Oh, and one more thing, Brother Clawfoot...I believe this is yours?' The priest's black-clad arm reached out.

Clawfoot opened his hand and felt the familiar weight of his dagger drop into it.

'If I see it inside the Serpent Walls again, it really will be your turn on that altar.'

Clawfoot was about to reply, but the high priest was already halfway to the top of the steps.

Chapter 12 – Tenochtitlan

Gentle rain cloaked the city in a gauzy veil. Beast-like shadows loomed out of the mist and suddenly morphed into ordinary passers-by, trudging past with dripping cloaks and moisture beading on their faces. Precious Flower was grateful that the new workshop was adjacent to the family home so she could take the baby with her. Graceful Bird was sleeping comfortably on her chest in a sling, swaddled against the drizzle. Musical Reed and Beetle had decided to brave the weather to replenish their food supplies, taking Blade with them, so she was visiting the new workshop, determined to see the copper-smelting process that Arrow One was so excited about. For two years he'd been trying to persuade Jaguar that they should expand into metalwork. For two years, Jaguar had steadfastly refused, until the day Arrow One brought home a beautiful brooch of finely wrought copper, explained how much easier it was to carve wax than jade and proposed combining the lustrous metal and jade together. Precious Flower recognised the gleam in her husband's eyes and had held her tongue, knowing it was not her place to question the decision of the men of the household. The process seemed so complicated compared to carving jade; so many steps to go wrong.

Visibility inside the workshop was worse than outside because of the smoke and heat of the charcoal fire that was needed to fabricate the new jewellery. Soot and the dry air made Precious Flower cough. Arrow One was stooped under a low section at the back of the building, deep in conversation with a wizened, pot-bellied man with unruly hair and a filthy leather apron that was the only thing he was wearing other than his loincloth. Arrow One was bare-chested, having dispensed with his cloak, and the short skirt he was wearing was more appropriate for the suffocating heat in the workshop than Precious Flower's long dress. Xotatl, the craftsman, bobbed and nodded enthusiastically in response to Arrow One's request for him to demonstrate the process.

'Yes, yes! You do good timing,' he spluttered through gums only nominally populated with teeth. 'New piece ready to try.' His Nahuatl was poor, the accent sounding Huastec. 'You two!' He shouted suddenly at a stocky lad of no more than twelve and a severe-looking youth. 'What are you gawking at? Pumping bellows or copper will never melt!'

Precious Flower didn't like Xotatl much. He was arrogant and pugnacious, but she had to admit that he was enthusiastic and utterly dedicated to his work. She watched in awe as the craftsman took a carved wax figure the size of a man's thumb and held it upside down in an earthenware pot of sand, which he proceeded to tamp very gently around it until it was entirely hidden, all save its base. All the while, his indentured labourer and the sullen apprentice worked a pair of leather bags in the scorching confines of the new room. Precious Flower didn't believe she'd ever seen anyone sweat as much as these two lads. She made a note to fetch drinking water for them after the demonstration. When Xotatl was finished poking at the sand, the craftsman took to examining the pot nestling at the centre of the fire that was now sending so many sparks whirling up into the rafters of the workshop that Precious Flower was convinced the whole place would soon be alight. The heat was so intense it seared her throat and made her fear for her newborn child. She stroked the child's cheek briefly through the folds of fabric, relieved to see it make attempts to suckle.

After a good deal of squinting and muttering at his assistants, the toothless man reached into a bucket of water and pulled out what appeared to be two long fire-blackened sticks, joined at one end with hemp. He gingerly clamped them around the tiny pot and then slowly upended the contents into the urn full of sand where he had made a conical indentation around the base of the wax figure. Precious Flower was entranced by the fiery orange liquid that smoked and burped as it sank into the sand. *If the gods bleed*, she thought, *this is what their blood would look like.*

'Where has the metal gone?' Precious Flower asked Arrow One, her voice scratchy from the fumes.

'Its heat has melted the wax, which has run into the sand so the molten copper takes its place.'

'But why doesn't the metal just run into the sand like the wax?'

Arrow One didn't know. He looked apologetic and just shrugged. Although he'd persuaded the Huastec craftsman to join their jade-carving business, it was obvious to Precious Flower that the craft itself would always be beyond him. She sighed, realising that with Jaguar away so much of the time, she would have to work to understand this new art so it could be incorporated into the jewellery they made. Arrow One had seen the potential, a fusion of jade and copper, but he was an organiser and a businessman, not a craftsman. Precious Flower wished Jaguar was here. He should have been looking after this side of the business and working with the coppersmith to design new artefacts. Their new partner would never listen to a woman.

Precious Flower and Arrow One watched the craftsman pour water over the sand until it hissed and billowed clouds of steam and when those had died down a little, he used a thin stick to explore the sand where the wax carving had been. A moment later he held a small, amorphous clump of sand up triumphantly. Precious Flower was unimpressed. She looked to Arrow One.

'There's a lot of sand clinging to it. It just needs a good clean.'

The craftsman scowled.

Precious Flower realised how poorly she'd hidden her disappointment and silently cursed herself. She'd have to do better if she was going to win the coppersmith over. She crossed to a bench where half a dozen similar pieces lay in various states of completion. One looked like the wax piece they had just seen converted into metal. She realised now that it was a likeness of Ehēcatl, God of the Wind, a stout figure with his tongue sticking out from a broad pouting mouth. It had been brushed free of sand and the copper had been burnished to a lustrous glow that looked like reddish gold. It seemed alive in a way Precious Flower's own jade pieces never seemed to achieve. Her delight must have been evident.

'You like this, yes?' said the craftsman, his hands clasped contentedly over his pot-belly.

'It's beautiful,' breathed Precious Flower.

'You wait. I make moving.'

'You'll make what?'

Arrow One stepped in. 'He's promised to show us a piece with moving parts. I've seen one that he brought to Tenochtitlan with him before he sold it in the marketplace.'

'Your tlatoani buy,' said the craftsman with a smug expression.

'He did,' vouched Arrow One. 'It was a snake. It had a forked tongue that stuck out when you pushed its tail. Moctezuma summoned him to the palace and bought that piece as a gift for his wife.'

Precious Flower thought it was an unnecessary feature in a work of art, but she knew that jewellery and gimmicky toys like this were popular with the nobility and she had the sense to keep her thoughts to herself. Arrow One had been doing well as a senior clerk in Tenochtitlan's planning and civil administration and had resented giving up his post to run business that he'd married into, but soon after Beetle had persuaded him, it had become apparent to everyone that he had a gift. Everyone in the family agreed that the recent growth of the jade-carving business was almost entirely due to his organisational skills and far-sightedness.

Graceful Bird stirred at her chest and Precious Flower knew she would have to feed her soon. The stinging atmosphere in the room also made her keen to get her baby out. She turned to go, but Arrow One reached out.

'I've been meaning to ask you...'

'Yes?'

Arrow One looked embarrassed. 'Do you think you've done the right thing?'

'This is about burying the afterbirth, isn't it? Did Beetle ask you to speak to me?'

'Yes.'

'I made a promise to Jaguar. He wants to bury it where his father fell. I cannot go back on my word, we've already talked about this.'

'The tonalpouque's protection—'

'...is good for a long time yet,' interrupted Precious Flower. 'Don't worry. If Jaguar is not home at the end of the next trecena of Acatl, we will send for Silent Smoke and have him repeat the spell.'

'What if he cannot? He said it was not an easy one to work.'

Precious Flower touched Arrow One's arm. 'In that case, we will go out to the fields near Xochimilco and you and Beetle can help me bury it.'

Arrow One looked relieved. 'Thank you, Precious Flower. You know that Beetle and I care for you greatly. Would you like me to see you back to the house now?' he added, reaching for the door.

Precious Flower laughed. 'It's a dozen paces away! No, you seem to be making great progress here,' she added. 'Jaguar will be amazed when he gets back and sees what you've accomplished.'

She was still smiling on the short walk back to her home, but it died on her lips when she walked through the entrance. Three filthy-looking men were smashing the whole place up. Two of them swung rough clubs, crushing pottery and destroying the family shrine, while the other one, a very young man, was shredding all the clothing and fabric he could find with what looked like a fish-gutting knife. The excruciating noise woke Graceful Bird, who began to cry. All Precious Flower could do was wonder what it was they were looking for. There was nothing worth stealing. They looked as though they might be thieves or brigands, but what had brought them to this house and where were they from? The approaches to Tenochtitlan were well guarded.

One of the brutes with a club noticed her and stopped, causing the others to pause and see her standing by the door. She turned to run, but the youth was too close. He darted forward and grabbed her arm. Although he was shorter and thinner than she was, she could not pull free and her first thought was to protect Graceful Bird. There was a sinister intensity in his face as he drew her closer.

'Who are you?' he snarled.

'Precious Flower.'

'Where is Jaguar?'

'What?' said Precious Flower, baffled by the question. Who were these people and why did they know her husband?

The young man glanced down at the noise coming from the sling, annoyed. He twisted her arm cruelly until she was forced to her knees. Graceful Bird heard the noise and must have sensed her distress because her cries became all the more shrill.

'I said, where is Jaguar? We know he lives here.'

'He's the commander of the Jaguar Knights,' replied Precious Flower, her outrage beginning to foster some defiance. 'If he comes back and catches you here he'll kill you.'

Precious Flower gasped as the pain in her arm redoubled. The young thug was pushing her to the floor. She was in tears now, mostly because of Graceful Bird's terrified shrieks.

'Are you his bitch?'

'Wife.'

'Same thing. This his baby?' The man looked at the bundle in her arms.

'Noisy little maggot, isn't it?' growled one of the club wielders. 'Maybe you should cut it? Let's see if it bleeds maguey juice, eh?'

'No! Please,' cried Precious Flower.

'Tell me where her father is and we might just spare the child,' said the man holding Precious Flower. Now that the other one had spoken up, he seemed more reasonable than he had a moment ago. 'He's not here, is he? He's with the army, isn't that right?'

Precious Flower didn't know what answer to give. Would they leave if she told them the truth or was she safer pretending that he was nearby? Something in their manner told her they weren't worried about a confrontation with him. She was so terrified that they might hurt Graceful Bird that she had no choice.

'Yes,' she gasped. 'Yes. He went with the army nearly three moons ago.'

The young man glared down at her malevolently for a few heartbeats, as though he was trying to decide what to do and then he thrust her aside. Precious Flower fell awkwardly, trying to protect her baby. To her surprise, all three men started to leave. At the door, the burlier of the three stopped.

'If Jaguar comes back, make sure he knows that we'll be back again. Maybe you can get a message to him, eh?'

Then they were gone and Precious Flower was left trying to comfort Graceful Bird.

Chapter 13
The Jungles of Totonaca

'You did well for a part-timer!' Iquehuacatzin grinned, giving Jaguar a friendly pat on the shoulder as they left the ballcourt, his hand lingering fractionally.

'Thank you, Lord Iquehuacatzin.' The heat of the other man's hand unsettled Jaguar.

'I've already told you,' the tlatoani's son shouted over the din of the crowd, wagging a finger. 'There's no need for the formalities. They will become tedious if we are to share each other's company for the next few days. Besides, we are all brothers here on the ball court.'

Jaguar didn't like dealing with the nobility. Every conversation had to be guarded and constructed to the exacting standards of politeness that custom dictated. Because he had risen through the ranks from common stock, he had received special training in etiquette. He had excelled during the tests and subsequently proved himself in liaison roles, but he still didn't enjoy the nuances of the game. It was easy enough to concentrate and remember all the rules during a brief exchange with a member of the pipiltin, but it was going to be tough to avoid a slip during the many days he would have to spend with Moctezuma's sons, so Iquehuacatzin's easy manner had been a surprise. Now the overly familiar touch reminded Jaguar of Two Sign's warning. Iquehuacatzin was a handful of summers older than Jaguar. He was lithe and moved gracefully, even when racing across the ball court. A pair of showy gold earplugs stretched his otherwise tiny ear lobes. He had high cheekbones and full lips that turned down at the corners giving him a supercilious look, but when he smiled, his whole face lit up in a show of natural radiance. It was no wonder he was popular with the high-born women…and some of the young men, if Two Sign was right.

Mahchimaleh lurched alongside as they followed the other players from the court. In contrast to his brother, Mahchimaleh was a brutal slab of a man. His thick arms and big shoulders hung from a broad chest that made his legs look short and spindly. He had a thin gash for a mouth and a permanent frown, but he was undeniably fast around the court. Mahchimaleh had scored more points than any of the other players and had been instrumental in their victory.

'My brother told me you were good,' he grunted. 'I didn't believe him, but he was right.'

It was the longest speech Jaguar had heard from Mahchimaleh since they'd arrived in Ahuilizapan. He bowed respectfully.

'My thanks, Lord Mahchimaleh. I hope I didn't let you down. I don't get much time to practise these days. Anyway, without you, we would not have won that game.'

'Everyone put in a reasonable performance,' said Iquehuacatzin dismissively. 'It would have been better with the threat of sacrifice hanging over our heads. No one works as hard as they can in these demonstration matches.'

Mahchimaleh grimaced. 'I didn't like the court. No proper sides on it.'

'You are right, brother. There are a lot of things these savages need to learn from us.' Iquehuacatzin tugged at the edges of the cloth structure that spanned the end of the court. Inside, they each accepted a cup of water from priests. Jaguar slaked his thirst and handed the cup back. Octli was also on offer. Moctezuma's sons gulped back a cup, but Jaguar shook his head at the acolyte who held one out for him. Mahchimaleh snatched it before the boy could turn away. He upended and drained it in one practised movement. He wiped the spillage from his chin with the back of his hand.

'Not thirsty, Jaguar?'

'No. Lord Tlacaelel made it very clear that I was to look after you two. He will hack open my chest himself if he finds me getting drunk while I'm supposed to be on protection duty.'

'Ha-ha,' Iquehuacatzin laughed. 'I doubt it. Our uncle thinks very highly of you. The day he appointed you as commander of the Jaguar Knights, he told me that you were the youngest ever to be appointed.'

Jaguar took one of the wet cloths on offer and used it to towel off the worst of the sweat and mud. Ullamaliztli was more of a dusty game back home, but here, the rains that seemed to boil up every evening ensured that the surface of the court was almost always a treacherous slurry. As the three men emerged from the pavilion, two of Jaguar's men appeared beside them. They were dressed in common garb. Just above their plain loincloths they wore leather belts from which hung a small pouch and a short stabbing sword made of a single, thick slice of obsidian wedged and tied into a wooden handle. Their attire may not have been striking, but there was no mistaking Creeping Night and Holds the Sun for anything other than warriors. The way they stood, alert and scanning the surroundings for danger, filled Jaguar with pride.

'Come on!' growled Mahchimaleh. 'Let's get something to eat.'

'Yes,' replied his brother. 'Let's see what passes for food in this dreadful place.'

'I regret, my lords, that the banquets will have to wait a while longer. First we have the pleasure of witnessing the ceremony of the bird men.'

Mahchimaleh kicked at the dust. 'What's that then?'

Jaguar pointed at the throng of people all streaming from the ball court. 'We need to follow them. They're heading for the main square. I'll explain while we walk.'

The two warriors led the way. Iquehuacatzin and Mahchimaleh walked behind them, while Jaguar brought up the rear, talking over the shoulders of his charges. He was relieved that Tlacaelel had persuaded his nephews to dress plainly so that they would not stand out. In the end, they had embraced the idea, believing it all to be an exciting game. Even their titles had been shortened when the official had introduced them. The local people would see them as minor nobility, nothing more.

'When the local ruler, Imixquitl, saw Lord Tlacaelel's generosity, sparing his people from the bloodshed he feared the Mexica would bring—'

'Wait!' Iquehuacatzin interrupted. 'Tlacaelel told me that we killed thirty noblemen, five of whom were children or grandchildren of his.'

'Yes, that's true,' conceded Jaguar. 'But it was still fewer than he had expected. Everyone believes the stories that we Mexica slaughter all the men and any woman too old to breed. So, he promised a banquet in your uncle's honour and before it, a show like nothing he had ever seen before: men flying like birds!' Jaguar was genuinely curious about a spectacle he had heard about since coming to the region but hadn't yet seen. His excitement didn't seem to have caught the brothers' imagination. They hadn't moved on from the treatment of the people of Ahuilizapan.

Iquehuacatzin spat. 'It's true. Tlacaelel is too sentimental.'

'Too merciful,' rumbled Mahchimaleh. 'The greater the fear, the greater the cooperation.' It sounded as though he was repeating another's view on the subject.

Iquehuacatzin looked over his shoulder. 'Tlacaelel thinks he can buy long-term cooperation with mercy. What do you think, Jaguar?'

Jaguar was taken aback. He hadn't expected members of the royal family to consult him on anything. He opened his mouth to speak and then closed it, realising that he had been about to praise Tlacaelel for his wisdom. These two seemed less enthusiastic and he didn't want to cause offence. An afternoon spent gambling with the Lord of Death would be less tricky. He blew out a deep breath.

'I suppose it depends on whether you want to squeeze as much tribute as possible now or cultivate a longer-lasting relationship.'

Mahchimaleh grunted, disgust etched upon his face, but Iquehuacatzin roared with laughter.

'Well spoken. Are you a member of the council? Perhaps you should be.'

They were in the main square now. The crowds were gathering around a large circle that had been painted around its centre.

No one set foot inside the circle. Instead, they stared in awe. Jaguar joined them, craning his neck up at the nauseatingly high pole that rose from a hole in the middle. If it had been hewn from a single tree, it must have been the tallest tree in the jungle, decided Jaguar. Stout ropes fanned out from a spot one-third of the way up, descending to anchor points around the makeshift arena. At the top was a capstan, a strange mechanism of four spools and ropes, all topped off by a tiny platform.

Iquehuacatzin spoke again, but his voice was drowned out by the sound of horns. Jaguar cupped a hand to his ear, but the noise was too great. Instead, Iquehuacatzin pointed to one side where a viewing platform had been erected. Jaguar instructed his men to head for it. Creeping Night and Holds the Sun were skilled warriors, but they also understood subtlety. Without exciting any attention, they steered a path through the crowd until they reached the steps behind the platform. Half a dozen of Moctezuma's personal guard blocked the way but stepped aside when they recognised his sons. Jaguar followed Iquehuacatzin and Mahchimaleh up onto the wooden structure, leaving his men to wait below.

'Look,' said Mahchimaleh as Jaguar reached the top. 'Moquihuix has made it all the way out here.'

'Really!' exclaimed Iquehuacatzin. 'I'd have thought he'd have more important things to do back in Tlatelolco. His old man's death left the place in total chaos.'

The young man was deep in conversation with Tlacaelel, Last Medicine and the guardian of Xochimilco. One of Nezahualcoyotl's cousins stood nearby with several young men of noble birth, all anxious to bring honour to their families in the conquest of distant lands.

'It looks as though my father is determined to intimidate the locals,' observed Iquehuacatzin.

Jaguar followed his gaze. Moctezuma's outfit was magnificent. He wore a fanning headdress made from iridescent green and black quetzal feathers bound onto a wide frame with gold filigree that radiated power and warmth. He was carrying a staff that Jaguar had never seen him with before. This one was carved from a wood so black that it defied the sun's attempts to illuminate it. At its head was a single, prodigious green emerald that shone like the eye of a swamp demon in the dead of night. Beside him, Imixquitl, the ruler of Ahuilizapan, looked inconsequential. He wore his own ceremonial robes, but they were dull by comparison and his entourage numbered just two: his wife and one advisor, both wearing pained expressions.

Eight more Grey Privy Knights stood around the edges of the raised enclosure, gazing out mistrustfully at the sea of faces below them. Jaguar joined one at the wooden handrail and surveyed the square. Eagle and Jaguar Knights had been positioned all around it. They were reinforced by nearly four hundred Mexica warriors, commoners drafted from Tenochtitlan, Azcapotzalco and Tlatelolco. In spite of this show of strength, the conquerers were massively outnumbered by the people of Ahuilizapan who had all turned out to watch the 'Ceremony of the Birds'.

Iquehuacatzin appeared next to Jaguar and followed his gaze. 'They'll put on a good show for us while we're here,' he said, 'but it always turns out the same way in the end. They smile and nod and entertain us. They agree to send tribute of gold and seashells, rich cloaks, wild animals, slaves and exotic feathers, but once our army has gone... pffshuut!' He made a slicing motion across his throat. 'They'll kill our tax collectors, stuff their flayed skins with rotting fruit and send them back to us.'

Jaguar couldn't deny the truth of Iquehuacatzin's words. In the last year, he had been on two punitive expeditions to re-conquer troublesome towns. He was going to concede the point when the drums started up. At the base of the pole, five men had gathered, four of them wearing feathered costumes, complete with a small pair of wings strapped to their backs. The fifth man had a headdress like the crest of a cockatoo and a belt that held several reed flutes. Slowly, he withdrew one of the flutes from his belt and waited, perfectly motionless. When the drums fell silent, he lifted the flute to his lips and a mournful, tremulous tune drifted across the expectant crowd. Jaguar closed his eyes and let the music carry him away. The plaintive sound made him think of snow-capped mountains of Popocatepetl with its mystic shroud of smoke that danced and changed shape like a living wraith. Suddenly, the music stopped. Jaguar opened his eyes to see the musician stow his flute and begin his ascent of the pole. The four bird-men were already high above him, climbing hand-over-hand up the regularly spaced pegs as they made their way to the structure high above them. The drums began again.

Mahchimaleh edged closer. 'Why don't they want to be part of our empire?' he whispered, reviving the earlier conversation.

Jaguar was wondering what to say when Iquehuacatzin spoke up.

'Because they get nothing from us in return.'

'They get our protection,' insisted Mahchimaleh.

'From who? The people they most need protection from are us,' snorted Iquehuacatzin.

Jaguar decided it would be safest to stay out of the conversation. Iquehuacatzin had a point, but it wasn't one the warriors ever discussed. The Mexica Empire, with the burgeoning city-states of Lake Texcoco at its heart, was hungry for trade in food and merchandise, but it needed it on its own terms. Towns like Ahuilizapan controlled the flow of commerce from the lowlands and distributed it as they saw fit, even trading with Tlaxcala. That made Jaguar think again. Maybe Ahuilizapan was too far south to suffer from the banditry of Tarascan raiders here, but what if the Tlaxcala states awoke to the strategic value of this area? No, Tlacaelel's push for the coast and subjugation of the lands along the way was right. Any other course of action was weakness that their enemies would exploit. Still Jaguar held back from rejoining the conversation. It was loose talk between members of the tlatoani's family and however affable Mahchimaleh and Iquehuacatzin might seem, his own opinion was irrelevant. Tlacaelel might seek Jaguar's advice from time to time, but that wasn't the same as contributing to idle banter. Luckily, neither of the brothers pursued the matter further. The perilous height of the climbers had everyone staring in disbelief.

The four bird-men had reached the top of the poles. Here they began positioning themselves on the four bars of the capstan, while the musician climbed the final pegs to the seat at its centre.

They each picked up a rope that had been wound around the bars of the capstan and attached around their waists. One of them wobbled, waving an arm to steady himself. The people on the ground cried out in horror. There was a brief pause and then the musician called out across the town from his vertiginous perch that was even higher than the top of the nearby temple. So high up was he that his words were indistinct as they floated down to the spectators far below and even Jaguar, whose grasp of Totonacan was good, could not make out what the musician was saying.

After a while, Jaguar's neck hurt so much from craning back to watch the bird-men's antics that he decided to concentrate on scanning the throng for potential sources of trouble, which was, after all, his new role. At least the tlatoani looked well guarded with his regular bodyguards close at hand. In any case, no one was showing the slightest interest in the Mexica ruler; everyone was staring up. Jaguar scanned the crowds all around, searching for any sign that someone was paying an undue level of interest in the tlatoani's sons. There was nothing. Jaguar did not expect there to be any trouble at an event like this. The threat, if it came, would be somewhere more secluded and come from an unexpected quarter.

The clear, bright note of the flute was heard again and Jaguar heard the collective gasp as the spectators reacted to the men tumbling from their perches. He looked up just as their falls were interrupted by the ropes jerking taut around their waists. Suddenly, all four men were flying as the capstan at the top of the pole began to rotate, driven by the weight of the men pulling on the ropes that began to unwind from the central pole. The piper played as his companions circled in the sky below him and, bit by bit, they spiralled down towards the watching crowd. Jaguar was spellbound.

'Come on,' Mahchimaleh said when the bird-men reached the ground. 'I'm going to find out if Imixquitl's banquets are better than his entertainers.' He trudged down the steps where he was met by Jaguar's men.

'Didn't you enjoy that?' asked Jaguar when he caught up. 'It was much better than I had been led to believe. That pole...ugh!'

It seemed as though six or seven of those poles set one on top of the other would scrape the bottoms of the clouds. 'Too high! Far too high.'

'It was too slow.'

Iquehuacatzin frowned at his brother. 'Really?'

'Yes. I think it would have worked better if the bird-men had knives and had to try to cut each other's ropes.'

It was such an unexpected and outrageous suggestion that Jaguar burst out laughing. Iquehuacatzin joined him.

'Brother,' said Iquehuacatzin decidedly. 'I think you've hit on something. Perhaps the spectators might be allowed to hurl stones at the birds in the hope of knocking them off their perches.'

'Ah... I don't think that would work, Iquehuacatzin My Lord,' observed Jaguar. 'The spectators would be caught in a rain of their own projectiles.'

This comment set the usually dour Mahchimaleh laughing too. Soon Iquehuacatzin and Jaguar were in hysterics, miming idiotic spectators hurling stones straight up in the air and then realising their error and trying to run both ways simultaneously until the stone descended to knock them out where they stood.

Through tears of mirth, Jaguar noticed that the hilarity had attracted a lot of attention. The Mexica were used to Moctezuma's sons causing a stir, but the locals looked haughty, wondering what gods they had offended to be saddled with such indecorous overlords. Iquehuacatzin noticed and put a finger to his lips, calling for silence. It would have worked if he hadn't immediately snorted uncontrollably and gone into fresh paroxysms of laughter. It was childish, admitted Jaguar, but at least the evening with these two wasn't going to be as tedious as he had feared.

Chapter 14
The Jungles of Totonaca

Cursed fleapit! thought Clawfoot and swatted at another bloodthirsty insect that was trying to make a husk out of him. Ahuilizapan was a dump and nothing was going to change his mind. How was it possible to bring civilisation to a place where everyone sweated so much?

The journey from Tenochtitlan had been a revelation and a source of non-stop awe. With the exception of the occasional scavenging trips to Tlacopan with Little Maize and the rest of his gang, this was Clawfoot's first trip outside the city where he had been born. Since he had been captured by the priests, he had spent his entire time at worship or studying in the temple precinct, so everything on the journey had been fresh and exciting. The upland forests that flanked the towering slopes of Iztaccihuatl, the waterfalls and sheer escarpments that fell away towards the lowlands, the yawning ravines with their muddy torrents that swirled and thundered towards the distant, unseen coast, all these sights and sounds humbled Clawfoot. Praise be to the Creator Pair! Ometeotl and Omecuiatl had indeed wrought great wonders.

Ahuilizapan was another matter, decided Clawfoot. If the gods had sculpted the world in the likeness of a great warrior, as Clawfoot's tutor, Eternal Flame, insisted, and the valley of Texcoco was the chest with the strapping mountain ranges on either side as his arms, then Ahuilizapan was the arsehole. It was less than a third of the size of Tenochtitlan and the overwhelming impression was one of mud, as though it crept into the town from the surrounding countryside every night. It lacked the cool, sparkling canals that breathed life into Tenochtitlan. In contrast, Ahuilizapan felt oppressive with its two dirty rivers, unruly chaos of streets, and here, this older part of the city was decaying, abandoned after a spate of floods. The cloying heat and constant damp didn't help.

Dusk had faded to a sultry night and what little light that remained came from a patch of thin cloud, backlit by a shimmering crescent moon. Even the shadows seemed tired, failing to distinguish themselves convincingly from the wan patches of dirt that passed for a street in this part of the town.

'Are you sure this is the right place?' sneered Third Arrow, looking down at Clawfoot.

'I don't like it,' said Angry Lizard. His scarred face wrinkled in distaste. 'It stinks like a priest of Xipe Totec after the Feast of Skinning.'

'This is the place,' answered Clawfoot, his voice tight. 'The place where the rivers cross.' He scanned the mudflats and the profusion of reeds that intruded on the ill-kept dwellings.

'How do you know we're supposed to be on this side of the river?'

Clawfoot tried to contain his fury, but the relentless insolence of the two men Feathered Darkness had put him in charge of was grinding down his resistance. Angry Lizard had spent the entire journey belittling him, constantly referring to his youth and idly inquiring where his mother was and whether she would approve of the trip so far from home.

'Do you remember what Xiconoc told us?' asked Clawfoot patiently.

Angry Lizard waved a hand dismissively, as though it didn't matter.

'I thought not. Good thing I was paying attention then, isn't it? This is the old dock. The jetties are along this side.'

'There's not much of them left,' observed Third Arrow.

He was right. This part of Ahuilizapan had flooded so many times that it had been abandoned for ten years or more and the buildings were rotting back into the wetlands. All that was left of the jetties that had once been at the heart of a bustling riverside community were stumps of blackened wood squatting sullenly in the swirling river. The trading hub had shifted five hundred paces or so upriver where the ground was firmer and the banks higher.

Clawfoot stood and watched the silent waters eddy beneath the heedless moon and it was almost peaceful for a while. Inevitably, one of the other men started up, unable to let a moment pass without grinding their teeth upon the stone of their supposed injustice.

'You never told us how you managed to get promoted so quickly through the ranks,' said Third Arrow. 'Youngest priest ever to attain level two, isn't that right?'

'I already told you,' replied Angry Lizard. 'He's Feathered Darkness' pretty boy. He drops his loincloth whenever the high priest is near.'

'You must be right, brother,' said Third Arrow. 'Although it's hard to see why anyone would find Brother Clawfoot pretty.'

Clawfoot ignored them. He'd had enough practice on the trip to Ahuilizapan and his time on the streets of Tenochtitlan had taught him that words were cheap. It was only action that mattered. They could not be allowed to continue though. Disrespect fed itself and would only grow if left unchecked, but now was not the time for action. Angry Lizard and Third Arrow would be wary, watching for some kind of reaction after their last encounter in the Hall of Knowledge. There had been no opportunity for him to exercise his authority while they were simply travelling as part of the baggage train, so the two men had grown bolder. They'd thought of a hundred different ways to get under his skin, mostly by speculating on why he had no parents, which was an appalling and shameful prospect to members of the nobility such as these two. He knew that it was a mistake to let them continue. All his instincts screamed at him to hurt one of them, or perhaps both, to remind them what he was capable of, but Feathered Darkness had made his feelings clear about Clawfoot's habit of resorting to violence. He would bide his time and see how things turned out.

Clawfoot was just wondering whether Xiconoc's man would put in an appearance when a tired voice spoke from the doorway of a deserted house behind him.

'Is this it? Two part-time warriors and a boy?'

'Who is that?' demanded Clawfoot, reaching for his blade. He was pleased to see that the two warrior priests had moved to take defensive positions on either side of him. He hadn't expected that, although he realised that it was probably more to do with self-preservation and where they had been standing than any real desire to protect him. As though the newcomer wielded demonic powers, the moon disappeared behind a swollen bank of roiling cloud and the night swallowed him up.

'Peace. I mean you no harm,' said the stranger. His voice was deep and he spoke slowly, as though the words were too precious to hurl one after another.

'Who are you?' repeated Clawfoot. 'We seek the one Twice Blessed.'

'You have found him,' answered the voice from the doorway. 'Born once, twice blessed, three lives.'

It was the secret phrase Xiconoc had told them to expect.

'You are Clawfoot?'

'I am.'

'An unusual name.'

'It's the only thing my parents ever gave me,' said Clawfoot.

'That and your existence,' drawled the man in the shadows. 'Why?'

'Why what?'

'Why did they give you that name?'

'One of my feet was curled and twisted when I was born.' Clawfoot regretted answering as soon as the words left his mouth. Angry Lizard and Third Arrow would pick up on that theme later on.

'Looks like it healed well enough.'

'It did,' conceded Clawfoot, wondering if this was a man he could trust. 'What about yours, Twice Blessed?'

'It's not my name.'

The answer was abrupt and told Clawfoot he would get no further with that line of questioning. It was hard to tell from the voice alone, but the man sounded large and full of quiet confidence, a man content to meet three strangers in the dead of night on killing business. The smooth handle of Clawfoot's trusty glass blade felt reassuring in the palm of his hand.

'Wait,' whispered Third Arrow. 'How do you know this is the right man?'

'Because he said the words,' hissed Clawfoot.

'He could be anyone.'

Clawfoot gave up trying to hide the venom. 'A complete stranger in a deserted part of Ahuilizapan in the dead of night just happens to answer to a secret name, prearranged on the other side of Popocatepetl, eight days' journey away?' He waved dismissively at Third Arrow and turned his attention back to the shadow in the doorway of the abandoned hut. 'What's the plan?'

'Lord Moctezuma is planning a hunting party. He can't pass up the opportunity. He's a long way from Tenochtitlan and all his normal duties.'

'Won't he be heavily protected?'

'Much less than usual. Hunting is hard enough without an army of bodyguards trampling around and frightening off the wildlife. He'll have a few of his men with him, possibly several of Tlacaelel's warriors and one or two hand-picked local hunters who know where the quarry is.'

Clawfoot frowned. 'Still sounds like quite a large group.'

'Not if we do it properly. They won't be expecting any trouble.'

'I see,' replied Clawfoot. The rain was drumming down now. He wiped the heavy drops beading on his brow. 'When is this going to take place and how do we help?'

'Patience,' said the voice from the dark. 'I do not know. The date for the hunting trip has not been set, but it's almost certain to be before the moon wanes.'

Beside Clawfoot, Angry Lizard snorted. 'Who is this Twice Blessed? He has as much useful information as a coyote with a sun-baked brain. Let's just find the tlatoani and cut his throat.'

'Great!' called Twice Blessed from his hiding place. 'This is what the high priest of Huitzilopochtli sends?' Scorn slashed through the downpour.

There was no useful answer to the question. Clawfoot wondered whether this man could reject them and send word back to Xiconoc and through him to Feathered Darkness. The high priest's threats came back to Clawfoot with a visceral jolt. He could not allow them to fail.

'If you're in a hurry to die, go ahead,' continued the stranger, still talking to Angry Lizard. 'I can't see you now, priest, but before the clouds rolled in I watched the careless way you walked into this street that could have been a trap. The way you hold your weapon it looks as though you're going to grind maize with it. You warrior priests are all the same. You train for a few days a year, arrive last onto the field of battle to mop up any stragglers and call yourselves fighters.'

'This from the man who's hiding like a mouse,' scoffed Angry Lizard.

'Shut your mouth, Angry Lizard!' snapped Clawfoot. 'This is no game we're playing. If Twice Blessed is hiding, you can be sure it's not from us. The darkness may be hiding others, so let's get our business done and get out of here.'

For once, Angry Lizard was silenced by Clawfoot's warning and Twice Blessed continued.

'The tlatoani is heavily guarded both night and day. An assault on him here in Ahuilizapan would fail and would be certain death for anyone foolish enough to make an attempt. Let's do this job properly and live to never tell the tale.'

This was a man who was used to giving orders and being followed without question. Clawfoot had barely met the man, but he could see why Xiconoc had placed his faith in him. 'Alright,' he said in what he hoped was an authoritative tone. 'But how will you get a message to us when you have a plan?'

'I have seen you. I know what you look like and I know where to find you.'

A clatter sounded from the tumbledown houses behind them. Clawfoot and the two warrior priests spun round to face it, but the night was an impenetrable cloak. The broken outline of the crumbling buildings was picked out in faint luminescence, but all else was black. The sibilance of persistent rainfall could have masked a thousand stealthy footsteps. The three men watched, straining to make sense of the nightmare shadows, but the sound was not repeated and when they turned back, Twice Blessed had vanished. Clawfoot couldn't have described later how he knew that their contact had gone, but the quality of the darkness under the lintel in the empty house had changed.

'What the fuck was that?' hissed Third Arrow at no one in particular.

'I don't know, but we should get out of here.'

'I don't like this,' said Angry Lizard. 'We know nothing of this man or why he's doing this. How can we trust him?'

'Don't be an idiot.' Clawfoot had had enough of these two men. They were more like children than grown men. He wanted to get away from them and their constant needling. He wiped his face and shook his head to throw off the water droplets. 'If he had wanted to betray us, he would have brought the tlatoani's men down here. If he had wanted to kill us...' Clawfoot trailed off, unwilling to finish the sentence. His instincts told him that the warrior would have made light work of them and it made him uncomfortable. It upset his view of his own self-sufficiency and reminded him of the inadequacies of the two men the high priest had assigned him.

Clawfoot pushed past Angry Lizard and stalked off towards the centre of Ahuilizapan, hoping that a sinkhole would open up behind him and swallow Feathered Darkness' thugs without leaving a trace.

Chapter 15 – Tenochtitlan

With the celebration of young Tizoc's achievements at school finished, Axayacatl's evening was his own. He was still angry at his parents for denying him the opportunity to fight and was brooding on what to do when he noticed his mother leaving the house. It wasn't forbidden to her; after all, she was the tlatoani's daughter. There was no one who wouldn't open the door to her, even this late in the day, but it was frowned on for women to go out after dark and the nobility were expected to set an example.

Axayacatl's father, Tezozomoc, had left for the hills straight after Tizoc's party. He'd announced that he was going to check on his summer palace in the hills behind Naucalpan but would stop with a cousin in Azcapotzalco on the way as night was drawing in. Axayacatl wondered if the timing of his mother's outing was mere coincidence. He could see she was taking an escort with her, which would have been fine, except that it was another woman and one he recognised from her walk as his father's favourite concubine, Bright Garland. He decided to investigate and slipped out of the house in their wake.

It was late, but the crescent moon, low on the horizon, gave enough light to follow the two women at a distance without fear of being spotted. What, thought Axayacatl, was Atotoztli the Second, daughter of Moctezuma, Tezozomoc's wife, doing running an errand at this time of night? Ordinarily, he wouldn't have been interested, but the recent insults dealt to him by Iquehuacatzin still rankled. What was worse was that it was true: his mother did make many of the important decisions and Axayacatl was beginning to think his father was spineless.

Axayacatl trailed the women at a discreet distance until they came to a square that lay at the heart of the Atzacualco district.

A huge planter dominated the centre, palm trees black and proprietorial against the night sky. The leathery leaves moved in the light evening wind, whispering as though gossiping about the passers-by.

The women crossed the square to the opposite side, most of which was taken up by one of the grandest homes in Tenochtitlan. It was two storeys high and the far end sprouted a tower that commanded a grand view up and down Lake Texcoco. A pair of torches lit the arched entrance way between them. This was home to Xiconoc, Axayacatl's great-uncle, brother to the tlatoani and the wealthiest merchant in the land.

Axayacatl's mother and his father's concubine were met at the doorway, a guard most likely, and were ushered in. Now he was at a loss as to what to do. It was extremely disrespectful to spy on his mother like this, but it was also very bad form on his mother's part to be out at another man's house at this time of night. She would bring great shame on herself and Tezozomoc if it became common knowledge. Women had been tried, found guilty and put to death for less and her royal connections would count for nothing. Every boy who ever attended Calmecac knew this. Loyalty was a common theme in the respected works entitled *Duties of the Devoted*, a collection of drawings depicting honourable behaviour. The priests were tireless in their efforts to instil the virtues it extolled and the tlatoani's laws were ruthless in their adherence to its founding principles.

What could be so important that his mother would risk so much for? Perhaps he could confront her when she emerged, that would be safest. No. Axayacatl dismissed the notion. He knew his mother well enough to understand that she would be forced to protect herself. Whatever excuse she gave for being at Xiconoc's house in the dead of night, it would be a good one, and he would be made to look foolish. Having come this far, Axayacatl needed evidence, but sneaking through the front entrance would be impossible due to the guards.

A dog barked somewhere nearby and was answered by another, nearer the Great Temple. A third yapped and Axayacatl had to force their conversation from his head while he tried to think of what to do. There would be another entrance used by the servants and slaves of the household, but at this time it was most likely shut. Even if it wasn't, he was bound to run into someone and the alarm would be raised. He could own connection to his mother who was inside, but even if he was admitted, he would be brought before his mother and Xiconoc and they might not reveal the true purpose of the meeting.

Axayacatl remembered the layout of Xiconoc's large home from previous visits: the tiled central courtyard with a pond, the flowerbeds around the edges planted with chilli and avocado bushes, the two-storey atrium in the hall behind it and the lavishly furnished main rooms that led off it. If he could climb onto the narrow roof that surrounded the courtyard, he could jump down into the garden and from there he might be able to find a hiding place where he could eavesdrop on whatever his mother was scheming with her uncle.

The street was clear, allowing Axayacatl to scurry across and slide into the shadows next to Xiconoc's home. Halfway along, where he judged the courtyard to be, he surveyed the handholds. There was a firm-looking plank that protruded from the roofline of the building, just above head height. He jumped up and caught the plank, then pulled himself up onto the roof in one smooth movement. A quick check of the surroundings confirmed his location. He was on the flat roof abutting the courtyard. Axayacatl crawled on his stomach towards the edge and cautiously peered over the edge. Hopes that his mother would be in the courtyard, deep in conversation with one of Xiconoc's concubines, evaporated. It had never been likely, but then there's no harm in wishing for a thing, Axayacatl reminded himself.

He leaped nimbly down to the flagstones of the courtyard, bare feet making no sound at all. He was just congratulating himself for avoiding the friable clay tiles at the edge of the roof when he realised that the ground inside was lower than the street level outside. The height of the wall and the crumbling roof would make it impossible to get out the same route.

'Mictlan's bones,' he swore under his breath. He would have to find another way out.

The two-storey section of Xiconoc's house was to the right. The silhouette of the observation tower rose above that and punched a black hole in the tapestry of stars. Just below it, a feeble orange glow emanated from an opening high above the atrium. In the darkness, Axayacatl brushed past a flowering bush that immediately filled the air with its perfume. *The Tree of Forgetfulness*, thought Axayacatl and grimaced in the darkness. If things didn't go well tonight, some of that fabled forgetfulness might come in handy for him and for anyone that discovered him.

A small antechamber separated the courtyard from the atrium. It was empty, but voices were drifting through the open door. Axayacatl peered cautiously around the doorframe. Torches set into four pillars around the atrium lent a warm light to the room, but it meant that someone would be coming round soon to check on them. He would have to be quick. Exquisite drapes hung from floor to ceiling, softening the corners of the room. They looked as though they would make an excellent hiding place in case of an emergency. Axayacatl didn't know where his mother would be, but there was a low murmur of voices from nearby and it drew him on. The noise must be coming through one of the eight doorways leading from the atrium, but which one? Axayacatl tilted his head one way and then the other, listening for the sounds again, trying to get a bearing. Muffled laughter on the left. It sounded like one of the two rooms in the far corner, but it was impossible to be sure which one.

Looking through the doorways was going to be a problem. The interiors were all dark, which meant that, with the four torches flickering in the atrium, he would stand out in stark silhouette almost anywhere he stood and his shadow would sweep across the darkened rooms. *Lucky*, he thought. Only the fact that he had been standing still, listening for clues, had saved him from detection.

A noise from one of the rooms startled him. Someone was stirring and a shuffling sound moved closer. Alarmed, Axayacatl considered fleeing back the way he had come in, but in the next breath cursed himself for being a coward. He had come this far and would not leave until he got to the bottom of the mystery.

On an impulse, he sprinted across the hall and ducked inside the doorway next to the one he had heard the laughter coming from. He edged inside, terrified that he'd knock something over or trip over someone's bed.

Someone padded across the hall. Axayacatl supposed they'd gone out through the antechamber, probably to pee. He listened as the noise faded, leaving only the thundering of his own blood in his veins that sounded loud enough to wake everyone in the house. He wiped his forehead, suddenly beaded with perspiration. As his eyes began to adjust to the gloom, he realised to his horror that he was in a bedroom of some sort. There were beds: two close by and two more against the far wall. There were no telltale sounds of snoring or breathing, so Axayacatl approached the beds one after another until he was satisfied that he was alone in the room. *Not the room I'm looking for*, he thought. He was about to leave when he heard the voices again, this time close by. They sounded as though they were coming through the wall. He put his ear to it and discovered that the wall was covered by a large wall hanging. When he edged himself in behind it, he noticed four strange, glowing discs, no larger than his thumb, pinned to the wall about head height. The light they gave out was so faint that Axayacatl had trouble deciding whether they were real or some sort of artefact of his eyesight, perhaps left over from the torches in the hall. Intrigued, he moved closer to inspect them and found that they remained in a fixed position, which meant there was nothing wrong with his eyes. When he got up close he realised with a jolt that these were observation holes that let into the adjoining room.

A mixture of horror and fascination drew Axayacatl to look through one of the holes. For a while he struggled to work out what he was looking at. Only a portion of the room was visible through the aperture and the honey-coloured light from a tiny oil lamp in an alcove opposite was too feeble to allow easy recognition of what was taking place. Strange shapes hunched, their feebly illuminated edges highlighted against swathes of blackness. A grotesque shape moved in the centre of the darkness and resolved itself into the outline of a naked man with a large drooping girth.

Axayacatl knew that shape. It was Xiconoc. To one side, deeper into the gloom, was a raised platform, a bed, Axayacatl decided, unlike any he had seen before. It was huge and strewn with folds of fabrics edged with gold thread that glinted in the dark, but what marked it out as unusual were the sturdy posts at each corner. A second figure detached itself from the shadows with feline grace. Feminine curves flowed like molten amber and coalesced with Xiconoc's corpulent outline. Xiconoc's concubine, decided Axayacatl. Another woman with an achingly slim waist and young, proud breasts wrapped herself around the first two. A deep voice murmured, followed by a cascade of girlish laughter that Axayacatl recognised as Bright Garland, his father's concubine.

Axayacatl was shocked and not a little aroused. Bright Garland was the youngest of his father's concubines, possibly nineteen. There was something predatory about the way she had draped herself about Xiconoc. This was not the demure thing who greeted him politely in the corridors of their home! Axayacatl peered guiltily through the hole in the wall that he now realised had been made precisely for that purpose. This room had clearly been designed for the nobleman's pleasure so that he could watch others in the act or invite them to watch him. Axayacatl suppressed his own disgust and wondered where his mother had gone. Perhaps she was merely escorting the girl to Xiconoc as an offering. Meanwhile, Bright Garland wrapped herself tighter around Xiconoc, making a shape with a square back and a flaccid behind on one side and the graceful arch of the young woman's spine and full, round buttocks on the other. Axayacatl flushed, feeling hot and confused. How often had he dreamed of cornering this girl alone and risking an approach with more than just familial courtesy? Of course he had never acted, never taken that route of betrayal. Axayacatl sighed. One honest patolli player does not an honest game make, as the saying went. Whilst he was working hard to be honourable, others were... well, doing whatever they wanted, or so it seemed.

So this was why his mother was here. She was bringing one of her husband's women to pleasure someone else. Axayacatl fought his growing outrage. If it ever became widely known, his father would be the laughing stock of the city and the scandal might bring down the whole family. Whatever happened here tonight, he would have to confront his mother and force her to explain her actions. Where was she anyway while this was going on?

'Come on!' said a different voice, pleading. 'Stop teasing. I'm ready now.'

Axayacatl froze. There was a third woman in the room with Xiconoc, but the thing that shocked him was that it was his mother's voice. He peered again, squinting into the darkness, trying to interpret the shapes that the feeble orange lighting inscribed. Something moved on the bed, a knee perhaps, and then a corresponding movement near a post became a sturdy rope. At the far end, a head tried to lift, stopped as though by a restraint and Axayacatl could feel his eyes popping out of his head as he suddenly understood what was happening.

Bright Garland detached herself from Xiconoc's bulk, trailing a hand over his shoulder lovingly as she walked back to the bed and climbed on, her lithe shape poised on all fours over Axayacatl's mother. She dipped her head, eliciting a soft moan from the recumbent woman.

'Move aside, bitch,' said Xiconoc in a low voice.

With nausea blooming in his stomach, Axayacatl watched the merchant test a thin wooden switch or stiff leather thong, whipping it back and forth. It hissed, a thin, sharp noise that spoke of punishment and angry tutors in the Calmecac.

'It's time we taught this wayward girl a lesson, eh?'

Xiconoc moved to the bed and then the sibilant noise came again, measured and precise. Axayacatl's mother moaned again, a throaty howl from deep inside her that wasn't pain and wasn't pleasure, but something poised exquisitely between the two. Axayacatl didn't hear the end of it because he had moved away from the viewing hole, head spinning. Next thing he knew he was falling, tripped by the low bed. He crashed into a tall jar full of dried flowers. The noise was like thunder in the quiet house. There was no way he could remain hidden now. He had to make a dash for it.

Axayacatl crossed the atrium in six strides, still gathering speed as he shot through the doorway to the antechamber and crashed into someone, a woman, perhaps the person who'd come this way earlier. She squawked as he swatted her aside and sent her sprawling to the floor. *So much for a clean escape*, thought Axayacatl. He made it out into the courtyard, then remembered, too late, that there was no way out. The walls were too high and the roof too fragile to support his weight, even if he could reach it.

Someone had raised the alarm. Axayacatl could hear noises, cries and shouts from inside the house. There was no time to think. He sighted on the shrub in the far corner of Xiconoc's garden, the one he'd stumbled into on the way in. He ran and jumped, pushing off from the crown of the ornamental bush, but it was too frail to support his weight. He could feel branches snapping and the spindly trunk bending under the sole of his foot. His leap carried him high, but it wasn't high enough. He twisted in midair, willing his legs to roll up and over the elegant earthenware tiles. Axayacatl's body and one leg cleared the fragile edge, but his other leg did not. His knee slammed into tiles and a bonfire of lights exploded in his vision. He prayed that the splintering noise was not his bones.

Chapter 16 – Tenochtitlan

The sun was a fiery eye in the heart of the eagle's domain when the procession set off from the place that had been Little Maize's home for the last five years. The flagstone streets were baking to a dusty shimmer that had already sent the dogs in search of shade and the whitewashed walls of the narrow street were a harsh glare that did nothing to improve Mother's mood.

'I don't know why you look so sullen,' the old woman croaked.

Over the years, Little Maize had learned that the conversations Mother liked best were the ones in which she was the only participant. Besides, Little Maize was too uncomfortable under all the heavy new cotton dress and cloak. Although the clothing, a wedding gift from Lord Xiconoc, was the finest she had ever worn, it wasn't as soft as the threadbare pale blue smock she'd been wearing for most of the last year. The stiffness of the fabric and the heavy coral necklace and bracelets, also gifts from her husband-to-be, made her feel claustrophobic.

'You've always been an ungrateful bitch. All the years that I've looked after you and all you've ever done is cause me trouble. Really! You can be sure that I won't shed any tears at your departure. The least you can do is put a smile on your face and show some gratitude that Xiconoc chose you, though why he did is a complete mystery to me!'

Little Maize wanted to remind the old hag that the reason Xiconoc had chosen you was because she, of all the girls in the Sisters of Penitence, had been the only one wearing an old and threadbare dress, grey with unidentifiable stains. Little Maize's terror at the prospect of her impending marriage was mollified by the delight that White Moon's plan to deny her a new dress had spectacularly backfired. After taking part in lengthy cordialities and introductions to all the eligible maidens, Xiconoc had retired to confer with that sinister high priest of Huitzilopochtli and Mother. When they finally emerged, Mother's lips were tightly pursed together in a show of displeasure. She looked, Little Maize had decided, as full of joy as a dead dog's arse. It soon became clear why. Xiconoc began to explain pompously that he had been blessed with a great many things, so, at this stage of his life, he wanted to make a gesture of repayment towards the deities who had been so good to him. That gesture was to be one of humility and he had therefore decided to pick the lowliest-looking from among the eligible girls. Little Maize shuddered as she remembered the way he licked his lips when he looked at her and spoke her name.

'Xiconoc should have picked White Moon of course.' The old witch was still prattling on.' Although if he had, I would have been forced to intervene. She's the perfect First Maiden. I don't know what I'd do without her.' At this point, Mother plucked an immaculate white kerchief from her garb and snorted loudly into it. The pause was brief, allowing her a prompt resumption in her disparaging monologue. 'She certainly won't miss you. That girl has done everything in her power to help you since you came to us, while you go out of your way to make her life difficult.'

Little Maize stopped listening. She hoped the walk to Xiconoc's home was a brief one. Unfortunately, Mother's stooped frame and bird-like steps meant that progress would be slow.

The procession set off, led by a matchmaker who had been hastily commissioned to give the betrothal a more traditional feel. She was young for her profession but strode confidently ahead of the group, wrapped in a voluminous red and brown cloak, cleansing the air of evil spirits with a long-handled whisk with three slender willow tails. Behind her came two constables of the peace, on loan from the clan elders from the district of Atzacualco, retired warriors who supplemented their earnings with ceremonial duties. Little Maize gathered that the use of guardians was increasingly popular at marriages to prevent trouble, especially the kind of trouble posed by jilted suitors. For one crazy moment she imagined Clawfoot trying to disrupt the procession in order to carry her away and then shrugged it off, annoyed that she had allowed the thought to take hold. Behind her and Mother were other members of the procession including six members of Xiconoc's household slaves and two of his concubines who looked about as happy as if they'd been forced to eat a pitcher full of spiders. Bringing up the rear were two of Mother's Elder Maidens dressed in the purest white dresses with gilt-edged cotton sashes like the one Little Maize was wearing.

Although invited, White Moon had refused to come, which suited Mother because she didn't trust anyone else to look after her flock while she was away. It suited Little Maize too. She fervently prayed that she would never set eyes on her nemesis again. The night after Xiconoc's pronouncement, White Moon had come to Little Maize when all the other girls were asleep and had cried and begged her not to leave, insisting that she could turn Xiconoc down for any one of a number of reasons. Little Maize had immense misgivings about starting a life with a fat old merchant with a house full of concubines, but anything was better than another day with White Moon and the evil old harridan who everyone had to call Mother. When Little Maize had made this clear to White Moon in a determined whisper, White Moon had cursed her for a whore and had grabbed her, viciously digging thumbnails into Little Maize's upper arms. Little Maize had refused to give the older girl the satisfaction of crying out in pain, so White Moon had switched tactics, grabbing a handful of Little Maize's long hair in one hand and had tried to rake her face with sharp fingernails. Rage had come over Little Maize like a winter storm and without thinking, she had poked White Moon in one eye. The noise had been indescribable. Every girl in Little Maize's room woke up and together they had turned on the First Maiden, bundled her from the room and blocked the door, heedless of the repercussions that the morning might bring.

'Xiconoc is a wealthy man from a regal bloodline,' Mother droned on beside Little Maize as they followed in the matchmaker's footsteps. 'I am sure that he will be a benefactor to our good cause at the Sisters of Penitence. I'm counting on you to remind him of his obligation to us after all the nurturing and protection the Sisters of Penitence has provided you.'

Little Maize snapped. 'You mean imprisoning me and making me work like a slave.'

'You had better hold your tongue, you young wretch! If Xiconoc knew what an ungrateful toad you are, he'd call this whole thing off. Oh I don't know why I took you in!' Mother moaned and blew into her kerchief again. 'You were a street urchin when the priests brought you in. You were starved to death and you would never have made it past your twelfth birthday if it hadn't been for me. Really! I should have thrown you back out onto the street.'

The procession reached an intersection where the matchmaker sprinkled salt again to appease the capricious spirits that lurked at every corner. Her presence helped to clear a path through the swelling throng of gawkers. Little Maize kept her eyes fixed on the ground ahead, mortified that she was the centre of so much attention. Hundreds of people stopped to watch and word seemed to be spreading ahead so that their progress, already painfully slow, got slower with every step. Everyone was smiling and all the women clapped in delight as she drew level, but the celebrations didn't help to lift Little Maize's mood.

The crowds opened out on a large square that Little Maize recognised from her scavenging days. She and Clawfoot and the others had always found richer pickings where they blended in; here they had been too conspicuous amongst the wealthier citizens of Tenochtitlan. She saw Xiconoc then, standing outside his home on the other side of the square with a welcoming committee of family and friends. It was a daunting sight. There must have been a hundred people dressed in extravagant finery. The men wore two, or even three, richly embroidered mantles in defiance of the heat. The women were equally well clothed with colourful dresses or skirts and delicate shawls and almost everyone wore heavy necklaces, bracelets and broad anklets of beads and precious stones, some of them glittering gold. They all looked absurdly pleased at the prospect of the nobleman's marriage to a girl from the gutter, an orphaned vagabond with no lineage, worse than the lowliest mayeque. Little Maize had spent the last two days in a waking dream, or perhaps a nightmare, she couldn't be certain. Her life had taken on an unreal quality that she felt sure would shatter, landing her firmly back in the Sisters of Penitence again, where she would eventually be chosen as an offering to Huitzilopochtli or Tlaloc or any one of a number of hungry gods. That at least would have been some kind of release, dancing to the Great Temple with a reed flute and an armed guard of priests. Little Maize felt sad for the other girls who she had left behind, many of whom would make that fatal journey. She didn't know if it was that thought or her own plight, but now, with her bowels turned to water and struggling to draw breath as she faced the reality of her new captivity, Little Maize's granite facade slipped and a single tear rolled down her cheek.

The bridal party halted before Xiconoc's family and guests. Xiconoc himself greeted the matchmaker with a commendably low bow.

'Blessings, Most Esteemed Mother.'

'May the radiant sun forever warm your countenance, My Lord,' replied the matchmaker. 'I bear glad tidings. The gods have favoured you with a flower to cherish, a daughter of Nahua tradition.'

Little Maize heard Mother's snort of derision but refused to give the old woman the satisfaction of seeing her react. She knew her narrow face marked her parents out as foreign and, to the older generation that Mother belonged to, there were few worse crimes.

The formal exchange between Xiconoc and the matchmaker was lengthy, perhaps because the woman was keen to make up for her lack of involvement in bringing the couple together. Her speech was full of admonitions to Xiconoc to provide for his wife and treat her with respect. By contrast, she exhorted Little Maize to keep an orderly house and fill it with children. Little Maize grew hotter. She could feel lines of sweat running down her spine. At last the matchmaker's monologue came to an end and she stepped back. Xiconoc snapped his fingers and a youth brought him a carved wooden box inlaid with shiny rectangles of stone or shell. The merchant offered it to Mother. Whatever was in the box, it was bound to be a far larger gift to the Sisters of Penitence than any offered by the priests when they took one of the girls as an offering. The hungry look in the old woman's eyes made Little Maize feel sad. Whatever riches were in that box would make no improvement to the lives of those she had left behind.

At last the formalities of the greeting were over and Xiconoc waved everyone inside his palatial home. Little Maize was swept up by her cortege and herded in the big merchant's direction. She placed her arm in the crook of Xiconoc's elbow as the matchmaker had instructed and allowed herself to be towed inside.

Xiconoc was all smiles as he paraded his prize through his residence, greeting his guests with infectious good humour. Not once did he look at Little Maize, even when he was explaining the function of the rooms they passed. Little Maize hardly cared. Only when they passed into a fragrant courtyard did she suddenly wake up and take notice of her surroundings. The municipal gardens in Tenochtitlan were no match for the beauty of this oasis. Two paths, paved with dusky blue cobbles, curved away around a large bed of elegant, lime-coloured grasses with fluffy white heads. A stand of early flowering jasmine trees guarded the centre of the bed. As she followed in Xiconoc's wake, the area between the path and the left-hand wall revealed a crystal-clear pond with white and silver fish patrolling lazily beneath red-bottomed lily leaves. Just beyond the water feature, Little Maize noticed a bush with white flowers standing against the wall. It was the only imperfect feature she had seen. It looked as though something heavy had been dropped on it or perhaps, she thought, it had been clumsily pruned.

The path converged with its opposite number in front of a raised, flagged patio bedecked with a myriad of plant pots sporting a profusion of variegated plants with purple and pink trumpet-shaped flowers. The guests, standing expectantly around this low platform, parted, clearing a path onto it and toward a wide throne at its centre. At last Xiconoc turned to Little Maize. Even in the sweltering heat of the day, amplified by the courtyard, Little Maize felt a cold shiver run down her back when she saw him drinking her in.

'My Lady,' he bowed. 'You are more beautiful than I remember. You have the noble features of the people of Teotihuacan.'

The compliment caught Little Maize off guard. No one had ever said anything like that to her before. She cast her eyes downwards. Xiconoc put one finger underneath her chin and lifted her face up. Her eyes brimmed with tears. She hated herself for being weak and thought that this nobleman, the tlatoani's brother, would despise her for it too.

'See,' he said, smiling at the onlookers. 'My wife-to-be is chaste and demure.' He complimented Mother on the comeliness and good manners of her charge, adding, 'The Sisters of Penitence may be of low breeding and poor circumstance, but Mother has shown that they can be raised to a civilised life.'

There were cheers and cries of assent to which Xiconoc led Little Maize onto the patio where he bade her sit upon the seat. She did as she was instructed, whereupon the matchmaker stepped forward to thread a brilliant blue sash through the ties in each of their garments to bind them together. Then the matchmaker stepped back and spoke the words that Little Maize was dreading: the words that made two people as one. Everyone was smiling except her. Suddenly, she was wife to the tlatoani's brother and reality began to unravel. She heard the words that the matchmaker spoke, but none of them made sense.

'May the eyes of the Great One, Huitzilopochtli, see all and bless this union.

May the ears of Tezcatlipoca hear all and bless this union.

May the hands of Tlaloc hold them and never let them fall.

May the blood of Quetzalcoatl grant them wisdom and a fruitful union.

May the Dark One, Mictlantecuhtli, avert his gaze until their teeth are long and their eyes are cloudy.'

'May they know peace and contentment,' rejoined the assembled guests.

Three girls in yellow dresses, all about seven years old, rushed up. Two of them placed garlands around the necks of the newly wedded couple and the third handed a bunch of flowers to Little Maize, a simple act that finally broke through her defences.

She burst into tears. Great fat drops rolled down her cheeks and her chest shuddered as she fought to breathe. No one seemed in the least perturbed; in fact, she could hear more cheers and suddenly, everyone in the courtyard was talking and laughing at the same time. People came up and congratulated Xiconoc, some even prostrated themselves upon the floor, chattering their delight at his good fortune. Then Little Maize felt a slender arm around her shoulders.

'Here,' said a soft voice. 'Drink this. It will make you feel better.'

A cup was pushed into Little Maize's hands. She tried to focus on the kindly face beside her.

'I am Coszcatl, Lord Xiconoc's first concubine and now your sister.'

A shapely woman with lustrous black hair was sitting next to her. Large, liquid eyes looked at her from under impossibly long eyelashes, but it was Coszcatl's full red lips that held Little Maize's attention. She could not look away as the beautiful woman shaped the next words.

'Go on, drink. You will feel warm inside.'

Little Maize took a sip. The liquid was sweet and soothing like honey on the tongue, but as she swallowed it, it traced a line of viscous fire down her throat and into her stomach. She coughed once out of surprise.

'You see?'

'Is this octli?'

'Yes, my dear, but don't worry,' Coszcatl breathed conspiratorially. 'It is permitted on special occasions.'

Little Maize took another drink of the heady wine and marvelled as a mellow feeling began to take hold of her.

'Here, take this,' said Coszcatl, proffering an embroidered kerchief.

Little Maize accepted it gratefully and dried her eyes. Coszcatl tucked the scrap of cloth back inside her elegant blue gown, the shoulders and neck of which were trimmed with white down. Just then, Xiconoc turned to them and bade them stand.

'Come,' he said. 'We must speak to our guests.'

Little Maize was forced to stand very close to her husband because they were still tethered together. Coszcatl, she noticed, had taken up a position on Xiconoc's other arm as all three stepped from the patio and approached the guests. She moved with grace and poise, exuding femininity. All the men and most of the women watched Coszcatl, like the famished coyote watches the rabbit, thought Little Maize. No one was looking at her.

The afternoon wore on into evening as the numberless guests paid their respects to Xiconoc and chatted animatedly with his concubine. Little Maize's head began to hurt, so she was glad that she was required to do no more than smile and nod when anyone tried to bring her into the conversation. Xiconoc firmly answered all the questions on her behalf. For a time, Coszcatl stood beside Little Maize and pointed out the more noteworthy members of Mexica society, describing their relationship to the noble families or offering snippets of gossip. Little Maize smiled at Xiconoc's concubine, grateful that the woman was making an attempt to make her feel at home, though she was so tired she was barely listening. In truth she was surprised at how friendly Coszcatl was being. Shouldn't a concubine feel displaced when a husband takes a wife?

The sun dipped over Toluca and the heat of the day began to recede. People began to trickle out, some of them a little unsteady on their feet. Mother had retired a long time ago, citing pains in her feet. By then everyone had grown weary of the old woman, alternately fawning over them and grumbling about them in a whisper that could be heard clear across the other side of the garden. The end of what had been a very trying day would have been welcome to Little Maize except for the dread of what was to come. Sure enough, the courtyard was nearly empty when Xiconoc's sister, Flowering Star, caught up with them.

'Come now, brother,' she said with a smile. 'I hope you have not had too much octli. We have all been waiting for this day for too long for you to mess it up.' She winked at Little Maize. 'Coszcatl tells me that my brother falls asleep too quickly when he's had a few cups and snores as if to bring the roof down.' She laughed at the absurd image.

Xiconoc looked less amused, but he allowed Flowering Star and Coszcatl to lead him from the courtyard. Others joined them, including the matchmaker whose last duty was to see the curtain closed on the newlyweds' bedchamber. They were half pushed and half pulled along the corridors to an atrium with a vaulted ceiling. From there they were herded through a curtained doorway into a sumptuously appointed room. The throng stood politely outside, grinning like simpletons.

'You may leave now,' said Xiconoc, waving his hand.

Coszcatl lingered at the doorway until the others had gone.

'Xiconoc, dearest.'

'Yes, Coszcatl, flower of my heart.' Xiconoc untied the cloth that bound him to Little Maize and threw it on the floor.

'Go easy on her.' She looked at Little Maize. 'Your new wife is tired and—'

'Out,' said Xiconoc, pointing at the door.

Coszcatl was not so easily deterred. '...and very young,' she added before sliding from view.

Little Maize looked around the room, unsure what to do next. There was a low frame of dark wood covered with quilted cloths. It was so wide that it took a while for her to realise that this was a bed. She looked away, embarrassed. There were windows on two of the walls and deer skins on the floor. Several oil lamps had been lit; their dancing light struggled fitfully against the gathering night. Her husband stood with his stout legs apart, arms crossed over the wealth of his belly. His sunken eyes stared at her from behind his fleshy nose.

'Do you like your new home?'

Little Maize understood the tone of Xiconoc's voice. He wanted her to be impressed; he wanted her to be grateful that he had rescued her from the Sisters of Penitence. She tried to conjure an appropriate response, but the words wouldn't come. She was overwhelmed.

'I understand. You're frightened. You needn't be. Look, come and sit here.' Xiconoc strode over to the bed and bent down to pat the corner, where he wanted her to sit.

Little Maize did as she was told. Her heart was pounding so hard it hurt inside her ribcage. The bed was very low. Xiconoc towered over her. His head looked small atop his jowls and well-fed stomach. She looked down, close to tears again. She felt a hand reach down and expertly release the band that held her hair in place, then Xiconoc was running both hands through it. She knew it was supposed to feel nice, but it just choked her up and made it hard to breathe. He sat beside her on the bed and undid the knot that held her dress over her shoulder. It slid down around her so that she was naked from the waist up, apart from her hair that fell around her shoulders. Beside her, Xiconoc made a noise, but it wasn't clear what it meant. She felt his hand reach out and gently cup one tiny breast.

'You poor thing,' said Xiconoc. 'Mother didn't feed you very well, did she? There's not much meat on your bones.'

Little Maize shook her head. She knew that he was trying to be gentle, but all she wanted to do was scream and kick and run away.

'You'll have no shortage of food here. You'll see. Life will be better for you now.'

The smell of his hot breath was nauseating and for all his kind words, Little Maize knew what was coming. He was no different to White Moon who had just wanted to possess her, make her a plaything.

'Lie down.'

Little Maize shook her head again.

Xiconoc grabbed her throat and pushed her back on the bed. '*Lie down!*' he commanded.

Little Maize swallowed hard and closed her eyes. She felt the dress being pulled from her hips and then the bed lurched as Xiconoc was back at her side. A hot hand moved over her neck and breasts, teasing her nipples before shifting their attention to her stomach and then lower. An image came to mind of the farm she always imagined living on with Clawfoot, except that this time, she couldn't see him in the picture anymore. She let out a sob and felt the tears well up again.

Chapter 17
The Jungles of Totonaca

Shield of Gold was enjoying his last day of freedom from duties. After the fight to take Zongolica, a healer had fixed him up, twisting and pushing his arm until it clicked back into his shoulder. He had never known such agony. Afterwards, Tlacaelel had told him to rest and report for duty when he felt better. Bored after only two days, Shield of Gold had asked to return to service, only to be denied. Since then he had returned every morning to ask the same question, only to be turned away. This morning the general had finally given consent for him to return to his post on the following morning. Shield of Gold had nearly jumped for joy.

The sun was shining and for once it hadn't rained overnight. Jaguar had managed to delegate his duties for a day and had come to find Shield of Gold to suggest they go and watch the armorers at work. Twenty-two of Tenochtitlan's finest armorers had travelled to Ahuilizapan to help reequip the army and repair their weapons. The regular stallholders had been cleared from the broad street that led into the main plaza to make space for makeshift workshops, piles of logs, mountains of hemp that had been brought out to dry in the sun and a stockade where supplies of obsidian were kept under a constant watch. Smoke and the sweet, cloying smell of molten pitch billowed from two heavy-looking stone vats that sat in carefully tended nests of flames. Boys scurried with armfuls of wood to restock the hungry fires.

'What are they doing?' Shield of Gold asked Jaguar, pointing at three men who were sitting cross-legged on the ground, chanting while they mashed rounded granite stones into lumps of dark rock.

'They are releasing obsidian blades from the mother rock.'

'Releasing?'

'Yes.'

'You mean the blades are not made.'

Jaguar chided him. 'Of course they are made. They were made by the Creator Pair, Ometeotl and Omecuiatl, in the first days and left in the stone for us to find and use. The workmen are merely freeing the shapes that the gods have bound into the rocks. See the way they tap all around the mother stone?'

Shield of Gold nodded.

'They are listening for the shape.'

'What does that mean?'

Jaguar laughed. 'I have no idea. I hoped you wouldn't ask. It's something I heard…it sounded intriguing, but I never got around to asking.'

Over another fire, a toothless ancient was heating both sides of a sword, spinning it on its axis, waiting fractionally and then turning it again.

'I've seen that before,' said Shield of Gold. 'He's softening the pitch so the blades can be prised out.'

'Yes. That one's seen a lot of action.'

Shield of Gold looked again. The glassy black edges of the blades that were set at regular intervals along both edges were chipped and broken.

'Has your sword been fixed yet?' asked Jaguar.

Shield of Gold gave a rueful smile. 'It didn't need it. I think I only swung it once. I don't really remember. I need a new shield though. Mine was ruined.'

'Well, it surely gave your arm some protection.'

Shield of Gold found himself reflexively rotating his arm in its socket. 'I suppose it did.'

On the other side of the thoroughfare two men were sorting through bundles of saplings and branches to pick out the straightest ones to pare down to shafts for arrows or the spear shafts of atlatls.

They wandered all the way down to the entrance to the temple square, sometimes stopping to watch a process in the weapons

168

manufacture. There was a clear view of Ahuilizapan's small temple through the wide-set gateposts. Shield of Gold was surprised to see a lot of activity in the square. Then he caught sight of something so surprising that he missed his footing and stumbled against Jaguar. Standing at the base of the temple and apparently deep in discussion with two priests from Ahuilizapan was his erstwhile gang leader, Clawfoot. It was hard to be sure at this distance, but the way he was gesticulating at the other men, that brought back memories of his hot-headed ways.

'Are you alright?' asked Jaguar.

'Sorry,' replied Shield of Gold. 'I've just seen a ghost from my past.'

'Who's that?'

'Over there.' Shield of Gold pointed but was already beginning to have doubts. There was something deferential in the manner of the two older men who were with Clawfoot that made Shield of Gold think he might be mistaken. Whoever this person was, he was being accorded a great deal of respect that seemed out of keeping with someone Clawfoot's age.

'Someone from the gang?'

Shield of Gold nodded, still uncomfortable talking about his time on the street, even with Jaguar, who knew the whole story.

'You haven't seen him in all that time,' Jaguar guessed.

'No, and it looks like he's been very busy.'

'You'd better go and say hello. I'll be somewhere here trying to find a replacement for your shield.' Jaguar smiled broadly. 'No, no. Go ahead. I'm enjoying myself. This is the first time I've had to myself since Tlacaelel put me in charge of the tlatoani's pups.'

Shield of Gold set out across the plaza to reacquaint himself with his friend. He slowed his pace when he got closer, not wanting to cause a scene if he was wrong. No, from here he had a clear view; there was no mistaking the jutting chin and confident stance. Whatever he was now, a priest by the look of the long robes, Clawfoot had clearly gone up in the world. Shield of Gold thought back to that night, long ago, when Indigo had been caught by the priests and taken away. Perhaps the same had happened to Clawfoot. Questions swarmed to mind. Shield of

Gold understood that his new life was infinitely better than his time roaming the streets and stealing food to stay alive, but there was a pain in his chest that reminded him of the bonds they had all shared. More than anything, he wanted to talk to the boy who had ruled their small gang and helped to keep them alive.

'Clawfoot, is that you?'

The young man fixed Shield of Gold with a cold eye and then, very slowly, his eyes widened as though he was reaching for the memories.

'Shield of Gold?'

'Yes, Clawfoot, it's me,' laughed Shield of Gold. 'Mictlan's teeth! I knew it was you from the moment I set eyes on you.' He had a strong urge to throw his arms around Clawfoot, but the young man's priestly robes and the two stern-looking priests beside him proved a sobering deterrent. Shield of Gold noticed that they weren't ordinary priests; they wore the knee-length versions of the priestly robes, but they were armed as well. They looked about as friendly as a Tarascan border patrol.

Clawfoot seemed to thaw. 'Go on,' Clawfoot said to the warrior priests. 'I know this one. I'll find you back at our quarters.'

When the men had gone, Shield of Gold gestured at Clawfoot's long cloak and smiled. 'Look at you!' he exclaimed. 'You joined the priesthood.'

Clawfoot's response was not enthusiastic.' You abandoned us,' he snapped. 'What happened? Did you find rich pickings on your own and decide not to share them with the rest of us?'

'No,' replied Shield of Gold, shocked.' I was ill. I nearly died.'

'And then you got better, but you didn't think to come and find us.'

'No, Clawfoot. It wasn't like that.'

'You should address me with the proper respect for my position.'

The nascent joy that Shield of Gold had felt began to wane. This wasn't the boy he used to know. The old Clawfoot had detested the priests and any badges of authority.

'Venerable Father,' he said, gritting his teeth at the formality. 'You don't understand. A terrible illness swept through Moyotlan.

My father died and I was so weak afterwards that I could not walk for weeks. When I could finally stand and move about on my own, I had a debt to repay the woman who looked after me. I could not leave her and scour the streets for you and Little Maize. I gained an apprenticeship with a warrior whose family run a jade workshop.'

'Of course, I'm sure it was very hard for you.'

'And what were you doing while I was lying sick and vomiting blood?' said Shield of Gold, temper flaring at Clawfoot's dismissive manner. 'You knew I lived in the Village of Sticks. Did you ever think to look for me?'

Clawfoot appeared to mellow. 'No,' he said softly. He stared off into the distance for a time. 'We had no chance to come looking for you after we were captured.'

'You too?' said Shield of Gold, remembering the horror he had felt when Indigo was taken.

Clawfoot nodded. 'At first I thought I was going to be sold into slavery, but there was a priest who intervened on my behalf. He offered me a choice: a life of servitude in the western provinces or a life as a priest.'

'You chose to become a priest then. The training is long, isn't it?'

'My training is complete. The scholars have taught me everything they know.'

'Really? In five years?' Shield of Gold thought that the induction usually lasted from boyhood through to adulthood, but then, Clawfoot had always been a quick learner.' So what are you doing here in Ahuilizapan?'

Clawfoot frowned at Shield of Gold and then shrugged. 'We're doing what the priests always do after the local people have been conquered. We introduce them to the glory of Huitzilopochtli.'

'How can they not know of the God of War?'

'I have heard it said that they revere some deity of cipactli as their god of war.'

'And they have many of the other strange gods,' said Shield of Gold. He had been talking to many people during his convalescence, some of them locals.' They do worship Tlaloc and some of their other deities are various incarnations of Tezcatlipoca.'

Clawfoot's mouth twitched disdainfully. 'None of which will help them if they do not recognise the Guardian of the Skies and the First Avenger, Huitzilopochtli.' He paused as if waiting for Shield of Gold to dispute the point. 'The high priest is concerned about the lack of progress in the education of these savages. He asked me to come and help the Lord-High Spiritual Assessor.'

'So you're here to convert the local people?'

Clawfoot smiled thinly. 'We can only begin the work. It will take many years before they come to love him the way we do.'

Shield of Gold sensed that Clawfoot wasn't telling him something. The answer was too glib and disinterested. 'What happened to Indigo?' he asked, changing the subject.

'I don't know. We never saw him again after he was taken. Perhaps he was offered the same choice as I was and chose wrongly.'

'What about his sister then? Little Maize, is she alright?'

Clawfoot shrugged. He turned to go, but Shield of Gold grabbed his arm, heedless of the protocol. 'Where is she?'

A shadow passed over the priest's face.' She was taken to the Sisters of Penitence. She was well when I last saw her, but—'

'What?' Shield of Gold was horrified. 'Is she to be given up as an offering then?'

Clawfoot looked down at the hand that gripped his arm and then looked into Shield of Gold's eyes. 'If I understood correctly, she has been picked out by a nobleman. She may even be married by now.'

Shield of Gold saw doubt in Clawfoot, some regret or shame that the older boy was trying to suppress. Perhaps he really had cared for his gang and still felt responsible for the way it had all disintegrated. He relaxed his grip on the young priest's arm. 'Then perhaps she will be safe. At least she won't be doing the Flower Dance on the way to the altar.'

Clawfoot harrumphed in what might have been acquiescence and then knocked Shield of Gold's hand away brusquely. 'Enough of this. I don't have time to stand and make women's talk. I have to go.'

'Wait! I need to find out who Little Maize is marrying so I can find her.'

The priest didn't even look back. 'I don't know and I don't care.'

Shield of Gold watched Clawfoot until the young man cleared the far corner of the temple, then realised that his jaw was hanging open. He closed it with an audible snap and frowned. Priests were known for being aloof, but Clawfoot's behaviour was strange. Then again, the strictures and conventions of Tenochtitlan seemed to be less rigorously observed out here. There was no justification for such a hostile attitude, reflected Shield of Gold as he sloped back to where the armorers were working. He picked his way along the street until he spied Jaguar standing by a rack of shields. He was admiring one that was decorated with yellow feathers that fanned out from the hub.

'Look what I found!' said Jaguar with a smile. 'A golden shield for Shield of Gold.' He held it out. 'This is a yaochimalli,' he added. 'Tougher than the style you had before.'

Shield of Gold tried to look impressed, turning it over to inspect the straps behind it. It was certainly heavier than the previous one. His shoulder twinged, still unhappy at the prospect of carrying any weight. He couldn't admit to Jaguar that the thought of going into battle again filled him with horror. Just the thought of screaming men, hell-bent on hacking one-another to pieces and the stench of blood and urine was enough to make him feel sick.

'It's…wonderful.' Shield of Gold smiled and handed it back to Jaguar.

'It's yours. I explained that you are Tlacaelel's messenger. This man said he'd make sure it was waiting for you when we go to our next battle.' Jaguar returned the shield to the armorer who nodded and placed it back in the rack. 'How was your friend? I guessed that it was him from the time you two spent talking to each other.'

Shield of Gold described the encounter, leaving out nothing of Clawfoot's unfriendly response.

'That is odd,' admitted Jaguar, 'but you know what these priests are like. They turn even the smallest crisis into a full-blown catastrophe.'

173

'I can't understand it. After all we went through together.'

'People change.'

'Hmm...' Shield of Gold felt certain there was more to it. Even the passing of the many years and Clawfoot's position in the priesthood couldn't explain his hostility. 'It's hard to believe it's the same person. He looked after us, you know, and we all looked up to him.'

'So he's here to establish the ministry of Huitzilopochtli?'

'That's what he said. Working with the Lord-High Assessor.'

'Oh, I know him,' said Jaguar. 'That's the old priest Gathers the Dawn,' said Jaguar. 'Yes, he's been tasked with getting the local people to adopt Huitzilopochtli, but it isn't going very smoothly. He told me that the local people aren't very enthusiastic.'

'You know him then?'

'Who, Clawfoot?'

'Yes.'

'No, I don't. I've never seen him before.' Jaguar frowned. 'Now that I think of it, that is odd. I don't remember seeing him on the journey from Tenochtitlan. The Lord-High Spiritual Assessor blessed our army before we left Tenochtitlan and after we took Ahuilizapan and I don't recall seeing Clawfoot on either occasion.'

'Maybe he arrived later when the priests here realised that things weren't going as smoothly as they hoped.'

'Yes, perhaps your old friend has some special skills that they needed.'

Chapter 18
The Jungles of Totonaca

It was the sounds of the jungle that Jaguar found most disconcerting. Cawing birds and calling monkeys, mysterious rustling sounds and the occasional report as of a cracking branch, as though some stealthy predator stalked them just beyond the curtain of foliage that surrounded them.

Two Sign had explained that, for the most part, creatures scattered long before they could be trodden on or accidentally dislodged from overhanging vines. Some did stay stock still though, hoping to remain undetected, like the ixtlicoatl, a tiny snake with a fearsome reputation entirely disproportionate to its size. Jaguar glanced nervously at the shiny green fronds that draped the path, more worried for his royal charges than for his own safety. Behind him, Iquehuacatzin and Mahchimaleh strode along the narrow paths through the greenery as though on a gentle stroll along the North Canal back home. Creeping Night and Holds the Sun brought up the rear, continually scanning the undergrowth up and down the path.

'This way,' called their guide, a wiry runt of a man with a withered arm and a bone through his nose.

Jaguar tried to suppress his irritation at the presence of Moctezuma's sons on what was supposed to be a reconnoitring trip into enemy-held territory. It was an absurd and unnecessary risk, but Tlacaelel had dismissed Jaguar out of hand when he'd objected to the idea.

'They are warriors, Jaguar, just like you,' he had said. 'You cannot deny them their right to lead. What would the people say if they discovered their rulers were at home with the women instead of out earning glory, eh?'

Two Sign hadn't been sympathetic either. He was still smarting because he'd been put in charge of the garrison at Ahuilizapan. He and Jaguar had barely spoken since the tlatoani and his sons had arrived from Tenochtitlan.

'At least you've got young blood to look after,' the Eagle Knight had said on one of the rare occasions they'd crossed paths. Tlacaelel had made Two Sign responsible for Moctezuma's safety. 'Being with the tlatoani's entourage is as much fun as a funeral. We all scrape and grovel and there are no jokes for fear of offending him.'

Jaguar swiped disconsolately at the press of vegetation with his sword, while the two brothers joked and laughed behind him. Perhaps Two Sign had been right. *They're not bad company*, he reminded himself, *just not very disciplined*. As if to illustrate the point, Mahchimaleh threw a stick high above his head, trying to hit the lowest branches of the vast and implacably green canopy that stretched away in all directions. He didn't succeed, but the clatter of the stick against a tree trunk set a pair of macaws flapping away towards a distant sanctuary.

Jaguar rounded on them. 'Stop it!' he hissed, dropping the usual formalities. 'We must not alert the enemy to our presence.'

'Pfff,' said Mahchimaleh with a shrug. 'There's no one here. What are you afraid of?'

'These are their hunting grounds,' replied Jaguar.

'We're the ones doing the hunting now.' Mahchimaleh held his spear aloft and let out a war cry.

Iquehuacatzin put a hand on his brother's arm, forcing Mahchimaleh to lower the spear. 'We should do as he says. Jaguar is renowned...one of Tlacaelel's finest.' He nodded at Jaguar to reassure him, but his brother just frowned.

'Are you worried about something, Jaguar?'

'I'm worried about many things,' said Jaguar and laughed, trying to make light of his own sense of unease. 'I don't like the weather here. The jungle is too full of snakes. I don't like the fact that we're endangering your lives needlessly when others could come and check this village, but most of all, I don't like the fact that the tlatoani is going on a hunting trip.' Jaguar didn't mention that Two Sign was acting strangely. He didn't want to get his friend into trouble.

'Is that all?'

'I also think that the high priest, Feathered Darkness, is up to something.'

It was Iquehuacatzin's turn to laugh. 'That slippery snake is always up to something!' he exclaimed. 'That man's influence continues to grow at the expense of the other high priests. I'd be a great deal more troubled if you told me he wasn't up to anything.'

'You have a point,' acknowledged Jaguar, hacking at a plant with vicious thorns that drooped across the path.

'What is it this time?'

Jaguar paused. There was no reason spread his own fears. He had nothing to go on except gut feeling, but he needed someone else to make that point and put his mind at ease. 'He's got one of his acolytes or a young priest over here who claims to be part of our mission to spread the word of Huitzilopochtli.'

'Nothing unusual about that,' said Iquehuacatzin. 'There are more than a hundred of them here. Even the shit-eaters sent one of their priests.'

'Yes, you're right. I'm sure it's nothing.'

'But you feel otherwise.'

Jaguar glanced over his shoulder and shrugged at Iquehuacatzin who opened out his hands in a conciliatory gesture.

'Maybe we should go and see Tlacaelel.'

'What, about the priest?'

'No, Jaguar, not unless you have a story that looks less shaky than a family of fat people in a child's canoe. I mean, see him about your concerns for my father. Tlacaelel trusts you. That's why he's got you running around after my brother and me. I think we should accompany him on this hunting trip of his. The more of us there are, the safer he'll be.'

Jaguar nearly bumped into their guide. He had stopped and was pointing his spindled arm to their left where the tree trunks were silhouetted against a pale sky, as though the world and the jungle had been sheared in half. 'We must stay away from the cliff edge. From there the escarpment runs down towards the town of Chicanazca from where they would have a clear view of us. Also, we follow a hunting trail that is often used, so we must stay alert.'

'This way is very long,' complained Mahchimaleh. 'It would have been more direct to go down the valley.'

'We need to cut around to the back,' explained Jaguar. 'This end of the valley is well guarded. They are less likely to see us if we approach from the east.'

'Let's go then,' snapped Mahchimaleh, unused to being told what to do. He swept past the guide but was held up as the skinny man grasped his arm and brought him to a halt. 'What—?!' began Mahchimaleh, but his outburst was cut short.

'There are many caves and holes in this area.' The guide fixed the nobleman with a stony stare. 'Spirits inhabit this part of the jungle and not all of them are good. People disappear here without a trace. You may lead if you do not value your life.'

The guide used Mahchimaleh's momentary indecision to scuttle off up the slope that led to the top of the escarpment. He kept away from the edge and was moving a lot slower now, taking greater care with each footstep. Jaguar saw Iquehuacatzin's look of mock alarm and was unable to suppress a smile as the prince rolled his eyes dramatically. After a short while the group crested a rise to find a small break in the emerald canopy. The clearing was caused by a stony depression in the forest floor at the centre of which stood a hole nearly ten paces across. There was no vegetation in the rocky bowl save for one gnarled tree that stood guard at the edge of the gaping maw like a watchful sentinel.

'This is not a good place,' said the guide as the others drew level. 'We go around.' He made the gesture of a large detour.

'What is it?' asked Holds the Sun.

'Holy place. One of Tlaloc's places.'

'What are you talking about, old man?' said Iquehuacatzin. 'Tlaloc is no force for evil. He is the bringer of life, the one who feeds the corn and makes it grow.'

'Then you do not know Tlaloc like the people of Totonaca know him. Tlaloc brings floods every year, some very bad.'

'And this?' Jaguar pointed at the circular opening in the ground.

'The people of Chicanazca bring tribute here before the rainy season, every year. Much food, many gifts and one child.'

'They put children in there?'

'Usually a girl, unless there is a boy with some special mark.'

'Do they kill the child first?'

'No!' replied the guide, evidently shocked. 'What use is a dead child to Tlaloc? They tie a stone around its neck.'

'And this appeases Tlaloc?' asked Mahchimaleh.

'Not always.' The old man shuddered.' But in return, Tlaloc offers a warning when the year is going to be bad. This way, the people of Chicanazca know they must prepare for floods.'

'Really? What sign?' Iquehuacatzin butted in, suddenly interested.

'If it is a bad year Tlaloc rejects the child. The body appears below.' The guide pointed to the cliff edge and the town that lay in the valley below. 'Sometimes the child is seen in the river, but one time, the young girl was found sitting in the jungle on the path below the cliff.'

'Alive?'

'Of course not,' scoffed the guide.

'I'm having a look.' Mahchimaleh pushed passed the old man and picked his way down the slope to the hole in the middle. Iquehuacatzin followed, while the guide hopped from foot to foot in agitation.

'Go around to the far side,' Jaguar commanded the old man. 'We'll meet you there. You two,' he added, pointing at the two Jaguar Knights, 'stay with him.'

Holds the Sun nodded. Both men understood. Their guide was a local man, coerced into helping the Mexica. Jaguar did not want him running off like the two men they'd been relying on at Zongolica.

Jaguar joined the brothers near the rent in the ground just as Mahchimaleh lobbed a stone into the void. It was a thoughtless move that even had his brother gasp in horror. Jaguar said nothing; he and Iquehuacatzin were too intent straining their ears to hear the stone's fate. It was a couple of heartbeats before they were rewarded by the faint sound of a splash and an even fainter echo.

'That's a deep hole,' said Jaguar.

'Huge,' agreed Iquehuacatzin. 'The Great Hall in the palace echoes like that when it's empty.'

Mahchimaleh edged closer. Jaguar tried to call him back, but the big man wasn't listening. He moved closer, angry that he had allowed them to get distracted from their mission. He had to get Moctezuma's son to see reason.

'My Lord, Mahchimaleh, we must go. We have a task to do.'

Mahchimaleh ignored him and stepped on a large flat rock near the edge to peer over the ledge. There was a rasping sound and the big man flailed his arms as the stone beneath him tipped and then disappeared from view. Driven by pure instinct, Jaguar's hand shot out as Mahchimaleh dropped. He registered the nobleman's face, wide-eyed with shock, and the hand crushing his wrist before he was wrenched over. He slammed into the broken ground, just managing to jam his other hand into a crevice before Mahchimaleh's weight began to drag him into the abyss. Pain speared through Jaguar where the sharp rocks ground into his hip and chest and his shoulder muscles screamed in protest at the load on his arm, but these signals were drowned out by the fear that took hold of him as he gazed beyond Mahchimaleh's desperate face into the vault where the black water glittered far below.

'Help!' Mahchimaleh roared at last as a shower of loose screed and pebbles rattled into the hole, raining down around him.

Jaguar hissed something through his teeth, unable to draw breath because the sharp ledge was biting into his ribs. He watched, transfixed as detritus hit the blackness far below and set off a myriad of interlocking silver-dark ripples. His left hand was losing purchase.

'I've got you!' cried Iquehuacatzin and clamped two hands on Jaguar's wrist.

'Get your brother!' Jaguar hissed through clenched teeth.

It took Iquehuacatzin a moment to work out what Jaguar was asking him to do.

'You want me to let go of you?'

'Yes. Get a stick or a vine... something! Just don't go near the edge.'

Stretched out on his front with a mouthful of dust, staring down into the cavern, Jaguar couldn't see Iquehuacatzin but figured he'd understood. The man let go and returned soon after with a branch that he lowered over the edge. Creeping Night was there. He tossed one end of a hastily chopped vine into the hole. Jaguar grunted as the weight on his arm shifted. Mahchimaleh was testing his weight on the vine. Then Jaguar's wrist was released and Mahchimaleh was being pulled up, one hand wrapped around the vine and the other on the branch. A few moments later, he was hauled over the lip and sagged to the ground. His face was white. Iquehuacatzin was first to speak.

'You should have been strangled at birth, you useless piece of shit! You could have got us all killed.'

'Ah stop your flapping, brother. No harm's been done. Typical of you to turn a little scare into a full-blown crisis!'

'Little scare?' scoffed Iquehuacatzin. 'Don't make me laugh. You look as though you've stared into the pockmarked face of Mictlantecuhtli.'

Jaguar joined in, needing an outlet for the nervous tension. He was angry with the brothers for their irresponsible behaviour. 'I've never seen anyone so terrified. I'll bet you crapped yourself so badly that you could have stepped to safety on the mountain of your own dung.'

There was a short silence as the brothers digested this insolence. They looked at one another and then burst out laughing. Iquehuacatzin squatted down, blew with his lips and made a gesture with his hand to simulate copious defecation. The brothers guffawed until both Creeping Night and Jaguar joined in. They were still wiping tears of mirth when a shrill voice cut across the clearing.

'What have you done?'

It was their guide who had witnessed the incident from the far side of the depression where he and Holds the Sun were waiting. The man was shaking his stick at them. It was difficult to understand what he was saying. Anger had shifted his speech towards native Totonacan invective. Jaguar caught some of it.

'You have defiled this sacred place! I told you to stay away and now you have disturbed the spirits.'

'Shut up, old man!' Iquehuacatzin called out to him. 'We are all safe and there's no harm done.'

The three men picked themselves up and negotiated the shallow incline to rejoin the guide, but he was still angry. Jaguar tried to calm him down and was surprised when the guide rounded on him.

'You are the worst offender!' The spindly man shook with suppressed rage. 'Tlaloc claimed another soul, but you denied him. You should not have interfered. You trespassed on a holy shrine and should have paid the price.'

The guide grew more and more agitated and there was nothing they could do to calm him down. Eventually he seemed to come to a decision. He looked straight at Jaguar, raised his staff and cracked him on the head, then sprang away. Holds the Sun set off after him, but Mahchimaleh was quicker. He tugged his sword from the loop over his back and launched it at the fugitive. It struck with enough force to bowl the old man over with a squawk. Mahchimaleh brushed past Holds the Sun, marched up to his victim and pulled him upright by his hair with one hand, collecting his sword with the other hand.

'Tlaloc wants tribute, is that it?' Mahchimaleh snarled.

'Argh! Argh, yes!'

'And you think that should have been me?'

'Ow!' shrieked the guide, clutching at Mahchimaleh's hands with his good arm, trying to prevent his hair being pulled out at the roots.

'Well then, I think I can fix that,' Mahchimaleh said grimly and strode back towards the hole, dragging his captive along behind him. Jaguar and Iquehuacatzin suddenly realised what he intended to do and both of them shouted at him to stop.

They might as well have asked the sun to stand still in its path. Creeping Night tried to stand in his way but was forced to stand aside. He dared not interfere with the tlatoani's son.

'You can go in my place. Tell Tlaloc I'm not ready yet!' said Mahchimaleh and gave the old man a shove. The guide disappeared into the cavern, his mournful wail lasting another heartbeat longer.

Chapter 19 – Tenochtitlan

The luminous smiles of the staff greeting guests at the entrance to Moctezuma's palace did nothing to alleviate the angry silence that enveloped Little Maize and Xiconoc. They joined a queue of eager partygoers who were gabbling excitedly.

'Greetings, my lords, greetings, my ladies,' interrupted an obsequious young man. 'Blessings to you all on the Feast of Coatlicue, Earth Goddess and mother to the great Huitzilopochtli! Our Lord, Ilhuicamina Moctezuma, Guardian of the Light and father of all Mexica, sends his apologies for his absence. Urgent matters of state have called him away to the war against the savages in the east, but he bids you all enjoy the hospitality of his house.' He bowed low and ushered the guests through the great wooden doors.

Eight members of the tlatoani's bodyguard lined the antechamber, their eyes flicking briefly over the guests as they passed through. Extravagantly plumed cloaks hung on display. An iridescent green one held pride of place, the centrepiece of the collection.

'It belonged to Quetzalcoatl,' said the lady beside Little Maize who guessed where she was looking.

Little Maize gave a polite smile and looked away, unwilling to get drawn into a conversation. It was going to be a long and tedious evening and she was determined that Xiconoc would suffer for it. She hadn't wanted to come at all, but her new husband had threatened to return her to the Sisters of Penitence if she did not agree to be at his side. She was tempted to call his bluff. Mother would be incensed at the shame it would visit on the Sisters of Penitence. She might even insist that the priests take her for the next fatal ceremony. The prospect of being sacrificed would have been preferable to spending another night with

184

Xiconoc but for the small spark of hope that Little Maize held that she might yet find a way to escape her current predicament. Life on the streets had imprinted her with a fierce spirit of resilience that refused to be extinguished. For his part, Xiconoc was furious with her impassivity in the bedchamber. Little Maize was beginning to understand that her husband had an unquenchable appetite for sex, but the one thing he clearly hated was a woman who played dead. If grim satisfaction at his anger was the best she could expect, then she would live for that until something better turned up.

They passed through the inner entrance to the Great Hall where stone pillars stood resolute across the room like giant sentinels, silently holding aloft the vast beams on which the distant ceiling rested. Here, the very best of Tenochtitlan's society held court. Well-dressed men and women in the finest clothes and jewellery mingled, talking and laughing as though the night belonged to them. Little Maize could hardly have felt more out of place if she had been naked.

Xiconoc was casting his eyes about the cavernous hall when a dumpy little man with watery eyes and wispy hair sprang from the crowd. A svelte goddess of a woman, a head taller than him and many years his junior, trailed respectfully in his wake. She was clad in a shimmering golden gown that put Little Maize's simple outfit to shame. Xiconoc had told her that it was necessary to remind his peers of the altruism of his marriage, but she knew that he was taking revenge on her for her lack of cooperation in the bedroom.

'Stooping Eagle and Radiant Dawn.' Xiconoc inclined his head respectfully. 'May I present my wife, Little Maize, recently rescued from the Sisters of Penitence.'

Little Maize could tell that it was costing Xiconoc a huge effort to maintain a civil appearance. Stooping Eagle and Radiant Dawn favoured her with watery smiles, but neither could think of anything to say to her beyond a few platitudes. Radiant Dawn's attention was soon latched onto Xiconoc.

'Dear Lord Xiconoc, what a stroke of luck! You have plucked your new bride from harm's way in the nick of time.'

185

'What do you mean?' he replied.

'Why, my dear Xiconoc, haven't you heard? The priests have just chosen three girls for the Feast of Tlaloc that takes place in a little more than ten days from now.'

'Where from?'

'From the Sisters of Penitence, of course.'

Xiconoc shot Little Maize a meaningful glance. 'You see, My Lady?' he said in his most gracious voice. 'You have such a great deal to be thankful for.'

Radiant Dawn cooed her assent, while Stooping Eagle nodded, but Little Maize had already stopped listening. She was too busy wondering which of the girls had been selected, remembering the times she'd witnessed the preparations. On the morning a girl was handed over to the priests she was woken early by Mother. She would wash and, if she could eat, take a small meal before being led to a room where she was encouraged to pray. Then, when the others were awake, she was allowed to distribute any meagre possessions she might have amongst her friends and hug them one last time before being escorted away.

The little man and his wife conversed with Xiconoc for a while. With the congratulations out of the way, they remarked on how busy Tenochtitlan was and complained about how it was impossible to go anywhere in the city directly these days because of the detours necessitated as a result of all the building work.

'If only all these developments moved as swiftly as work on the Great Temple,' said Stooping Eagle. 'They'd all be over in a matter of days.'

'That's part of the problem,' remarked Xiconoc. 'All the skilled labourers have been soaked up by work in the temple precinct, so the rest of us must make do with a second-rate workforce.'

'Can't you have a word with your brother?'

Xiconoc shook his head. 'I've tried, but he is consumed with two projects at present: conquest of the eastern lands and construction of a temple to rival Teotihuacan.'

'So he's with the high priest on this.'

'Yes, but I don't think it's out of any great love between them. Each of them believes the temple is for their own benefit.'

The conversation moved on to gossip, mostly stories or rumours of goings on in the noble families. Apparently the new ruler of Tlatelolco, Moquihuix, was betrothed to a cousin of his from Azcapotzalco, a contemptuous match, according to Radiant Dawn. There was also a scandal surrounding a young nobleman from one of the lesser houses who had been caught in an indecent act in the steam baths with the son of one of the clan elders. Little Maize stopped listening. A short while later, the couple made way for a succession of well-fed people in expensive-looking clothes. They all ran out of questions quickly and even Xiconoc began to look bored, so when the last of the well-wishers had moved on, he told her to stay put while he went to speak some people about certain business matters.

'What am I going to do?' complained Little Maize. It was bad enough being dragged here against her will, but now she was being abandoned.

'I don't care,' Xiconoc snapped. 'Oh look, there's some food arriving. Why don't you eat something. That's all you've done since arriving in my house,' he added as he stalked off.

With nothing else to do, Little Maize turned her attention to the two slaves carrying trays of food. She wasn't particularly hungry, but she accepted what was on offer. It was half a seashell of a kind she'd not seen before containing a few elegantly arranged slices of avocado dipped in honey and shredded chillies. It was hotter than she expected, but it tasted delicious and it took the edge off her black mood. She handed the empty shell to a palace slave who was passing by with a basket on her hip and she was trying to locate a second portion when a distinguished-looking man approached, a statesman perhaps judging by his finery. He had a lean face from which papery jowls sagged, lending him a lugubrious expression. Little Maize gave a stiff bow as the newcomer introduced himself as Lord Tezozomoc.

'How are you finding life outside the Sisters of Penitence, young lady? I have been told these refuges offer a very frugal existence.'

There was no telling who this Tezozomoc was, so Little Maize kept her answer guarded. 'The girls are adequately provided for.'

Tezozomoc's eyebrows danced up and down. 'Hmm...and now you are married into the most powerful bloodline of the Mexica people. I hope your new circumstances are rather more than just adequate.'

Little Maize couldn't answer truthfully and didn't feel strong enough to lie convincingly. Her silence was just about to become awkwardly long when a beautiful woman arrived and took hold of Tezozomoc's arm. Although she was well into her child-bearing years, she possessed a regal grace that held Little Maize spellbound. Her large brown eyes transfixed Little Maize until she realised she was being impolite. She cast her eyes downward.

'Is this the young lady everyone has been talking about?'

'Yes, my dear. Allow me to introduce Little Maize. My Lady.' Tezozomoc bowed again to Little Maize. 'This is my wife, Atotoztli.'

No upbringing in Tenochtitlan could be so sheltered as to hide someone from that name. Little Maize's sharp intake of breath made her hiccup painfully. This was the tlatoani's eldest daughter. She stared even more intently at the floor, as though by force of will she could make up for staring so brazenly into Atotoztli's face.

'It's an honour, My Lady.'

Little Maize felt the woman's hand on her shoulder.

'Please. You needn't go through all that. You're married to my uncle so we're practically sisters now.'

Little Maize looked up and was bathed in warm smiles. For the first time today, she didn't feel like dirt.

'What were you two talking about before I arrived?' Atotoztli asked her husband.

'I was asking the young lady whether your uncle's hospitality was an improvement over the Sisters of Penitence.'

'And what did she answer, dear Tezo?'

'I had the feeling she would rather not answer, so I was about to change the subject.'

'A good idea,' replied Atotoztli with a concerned expression. 'Who are we to say she wasn't happy at the refuge, or...' She paused and it seemed that she was boring deep into Little Maize's soul. '...perhaps she's just exchanged one form of captivity with another.'

Little Maize felt her stomach swoop. How could the woman say such a thing unless she knew what Xiconoc was like? Surely that wasn't possible...and yet, he was her uncle. Little Maize wanted to say something. She wanted to make a connection with this older, wiser woman and lean on her for help, but she didn't know how to begin. Atotoztli was a princess, the daughter of the most powerful man in the world, practically a deity. Little Maize was a nobody. Her marriage into the same blood was nothing but a twisted joke. She would never be their equal. She realised that she hadn't said anything to these people who were simply trying to be kind.

'We are all captives in one way or another,' she said with a sad smile.

There was a moment of stunned silence and then Tezozomoc laughed. A moment later, Atotoztli joined in. Little Maize wondered if they were laughing at her.

'Such wisdom in such a young woman,' said Atotoztli.

'Aye,' said her husband. 'We are all in the thrall of the gods.' He bowed to Little Maize. 'It's so nice to hear someone speak what's on their mind for once. The nobility always say the right thing. It's so dull and predictable.' He nudged his wife. 'This one is a spirited woman, too clever to allow herself to be pushed around.'

'Good. It's time Xiconoc stopped getting things all his own way,' said Atotoztli. She held her hands out. 'I hope we can be friends.'

'My Lady, My Lord,' replied Little Maize in a quiet voice. 'Life has not been generous to me with friends. I hope you will forgive me if I seem...defensive.' She reached out and allowed Atotoztli to take her hands. They felt warm and reassuring.

'Of course, my dear,' said Atotoztli. 'At least reassure us that you are settling in. Are you comfortable in my uncle's home?'

'I am, My Lady. Lord Xiconoc's home is wonderful and full of so many interesting artefacts that he has collected from across the land. The only problem is that now I have inspected all of the ones on display, I don't know what to do with my time. In the Sisters of Penitence my days were busy with cleaning and cooking or taking lessons.' Of course, Xiconoc was so busy during the day that Little Maize rarely saw him until the sun had gone down, but that wasn't something she wanted to change.

'Hasn't Coszcatl spoken to you?' Atotoztli looked puzzled. 'I'm certain she always has many things to do: shopping for fabrics and clothes, deciding on meals with the cooks and making sure the household staff are doing their chores. She ought to be glad to have someone to help out.'

'If you're bored, you could go and see how Xiconoc's garden is turning out,' suggested Tezozomoc.

Little Maize's jaw dropped.

'Of course,' laughed Tezozomoc, seeing her astonishment,' he doesn't do any digging or planting. He has an army of labourers for that. It's true though. He acquired one of the largest fields between here and Xochimilco and it's a poorly kept secret that he plans to create a paradise of plants and birds out in the chinampa to rival the tlatoani's gardens.'

'I know nothing of it.'

'I'm sure you will see it soon,' said Tezozomoc. 'From what I heard, it's only just being planted up. It was just a large strip of mud until the beginning of the year.'

Little Maize nodded, knowing she would never be interested in any of Xiconoc's projects. Unbidden, an image formed in her head. She saw it clearly, even though her eyes were open and staring across the Great Hall. It was a picture of Xiconoc, kneeling on a patch of tilled earth with rows of planted maize on one side and a field of immature amaranth bushes on the other. Xiconoc's face was turned to one side, mouth open in a soundless scream, while one hand groped behind his back to reach the hilt of a knife. Little Maize shuddered and shook her head to clear it. Tezozomoc was still talking.

'Excuse me, My Lord,' she interrupted.

'Yes?'

'Do you believe in premonitions?'

'Of course, My Lady. The priests often have visions. Some use special potions to help them cross into the spirit world.'

'What about ordinary people?'

'It's not unheard of. My wife once claimed to have been visited by Coatlicue who begged her for some peyotl to relieve the pain of childbirth and one need only stroll through the markets to be accosted by countless mayeques offering to heal you with their powers or foretell the future.' The statesman stopped and peered at Little Maize more closely. 'Are you alright, My Lady?'

'Yes, why do you ask?'

'You look very pale and... I think you have a nosebleed.'

Little Maize touched a finger to her top lip and it came away red. It was a sign. She wasn't sure exactly what it meant, but she was convinced that it was linked with what she had just seen. Perhaps the gods were punishing her for entertaining such dark thoughts. The room around her wobbled unpleasantly. Motes of light winked in and out of existence at the periphery of her vision and Tezozomoc's voice sounded muffled. Little Maize felt herself pitching backwards and was powerless to do anything about it. The last thing she saw were the stone beams that held the palace roof aloft so that it seemed to her that she had been swallowed by a giant beast and was looking up at the inside of its ribcage.

Chapter 20 – Tenochtitlan

Precious Flower looked around the room and smoothed the wild ends of her hair back into place. Beetle gave her an exasperated look.

'Come on, come on! There's nothing else. You've checked twenty times.'

'I know, I know. I just wish Jaguar was here.'

Beetle scoffed. 'Huh! He wouldn't be much help. You'd still have to be the one to remember everything. Anyway, there really isn't much that you need to take with you.'

'You're right. I'm done here. Blade must be getting bored waiting. Will you be alright without me?'

'I'll be fine. You're the one who's in danger. Those men weren't after me.' Beetle picked up a small bag that held several clean swaddling cloths for the baby and handed it to Precious Flower. 'You need to get out of the city until Jaguar gets back.'

Precious Flower took the bag and slung a good quality deer-hide water bag across her back. The two women stepped out onto the street and surveyed the scene. A dozen adults from four neighbouring families had congregated close by with as many children larking about, excited at the prospect of a trip to the countryside. Eight slaves, three of them purchased specifically for the trip, stood by, surrounded by bundles and baskets of supplies that would make the journey with them.

'You'll be safe in Xalatlaco,' said Beetle.

'Do we have a house in Xalatlaco?' asked Blade who appeared without warning at Precious Flower's side.

'Yes, we do, my little man,' replied Precious Flower. 'It sits on the edge of two hundred poles of land that was a gift from Moctezuma to your father and your grandfather.'

192

Blade stuck his chest out proudly. 'Because my father is a brave warrior and my grandfather was a brave warrior who sips nectar in the halls of the gods.'

'That's right, Blade,' added Beetle. 'Now it's your turn to be a brave warrior and look after your mother for a while.'

'I will.' Blade frowned. 'I'm not afraid of a few dirty ruffians.'

'Shush-shush-shush,' said Precious Flower quickly and glanced around, terrified that her attackers might be nearby, watching. She reached down, pressed a finger to her son's lips and smiled. 'Keep your fighting talk to yourself until we're outside the city.'

Before the boy could reply they were interrupted by Fast Rabbit, a veteran of the wars with Chalco. He had a rolling gait as the result of a deep wound to his thigh sustained in battle, but he had a ready smile and gave no sign that he missed his days as a warrior.

'Are you ready to go?' asked the veteran.

'Yes,' replied Precious Flower. 'It's kind of you to accompany us.'

'It's no trouble. It's time I paid a visit to my own holdings in Xalatlaco. I have been using the feeble excuse of my old wound for too long. Do you have everything?'

'Yes, Fast Rabbit, all except my daughter.'

Fast Rabbit laughed and pushed his mop of black hair out of his eyes. 'You needn't worry on that account. I think my wife has fallen in love with your little girl. If you're lucky, she'll carry her all the way to Xalatlaco for you, but I can't be sure you'll get her back afterwards.'

Precious Flower laughed with Fast Rabbit. 'I think she may change her mind when she finds out how little Graceful Bird sleeps at night.'

'Oh dear!' Fast Rabbit feigned chagrin. 'I'd better warn her. Our own four are bad enough as it is.' His expression switched abruptly and he began again in a more businesslike manner. 'We should set out now. You must be long gone from the city when those criminals return. The day is passing and Xalatlaco is still no closer.' He turned and instructed the slaves to pick up their loads.

'Goodbye, Little Beetle,' said Precious Flower. They hugged briefly. 'Will you be alright?'

'Of course! Arrow One doesn't take much looking after. He's so excited now that the new brooches are coming out well.' Little Beetle smiled. 'We will manage fine in the workshop. Hopefully Jaguar will be home soon and we'll send him out to the farm to get you.'

The two women hugged again and Precious Flower called out to Blade as the procession set out for the farmlands.

Progress was slow and by midday the travellers had only cleared the southwest corner of the lake. The town of Coyoacan was behind them but only just. It wasn't Fast Rabbit's limp that was slowing them down but the children, of whom there were thirteen, and their incessant demands for water and stops to relieve themselves. They were all from the same district in Teopan, which meant that they were all getting along well, so Precious Flower was able to relax. Ever since their home had been violated she had been trying not to allow Blade to see how worried she was. Just then her son trotted over.

'What day is it, Mother?'

'Seventeen, Calli in Acatl,' replied his mother.

'Why does the day have two names?'

'It doesn't my dear,' replied Precious Flower. 'Calli is the name of the day. Acatl is the thirteen-day period. Do you recall the two calendars? Tonalpohualli is the religious calendar and xuihalpohualli is the calendar that describes the passing seasons of the year.'

'Why are there two calendars, Mother?'

'One tells us when the seasons are coming and the other one helps us to talk to the gods.'

Precious Flower was pleased with her answer, but Blade wasn't listening anymore.

'I like this adventure,' he announced, beaming widely. 'Have I visited our fields before?'

Precious Flower smiled back at him. 'No, my dear. The carving business has been so busy since you were born that we haven't had a chance.'

'Ah, here you are,' said Fast Rabbit as he drew level with Blade. He put his hand on the boy's shoulder. 'I've got an important job for you, young man. Do you want to help the expedition?'

'Yes, please, Fast Rabbit, My Lord!'

'Excellent! I want you to walk at the front and keep an eye out for snakes. Are you afraid of snakes?'

'No!'

'Well you should be,' said Fast Rabbit, bending down to look into the boy's face. 'When I was a warrior, I knew three strong and brave men who fought and took many captives while they were alive and all three of them died because they got careless and were bitten by snakes.

'If you see one, don't go near it,' the retired warrior warned. 'Take this stick and strike the ground with it. Snakes are very sensitive to vibrations in the ground. They will slide off the path if you make enough noise.'

'Alright, I'll be careful. Can I hit the snakes?' asked Blade earnestly.

Fast Rabbit levered himself down onto one knee so that he was at the same height as Blade and fixed him with a serious expression. 'Never, ever hit the snake. For a start, without the proper blessings of one of the priests of Coatlicue you will anger the gods. Secondly, there is no need. Like I said, if you frighten the creature it will slip away. Thirdly, I saw someone try that once and by mistake, they got the stick hooked in the snake's coils and hurled it backwards over their head and into a crowd that had gathered to watch.'

'Ooh! What happened?'

'Nothing on that occasion, but several people nearly died of fright!'

Blade laughed and bobbed up and down in excitement.

'If you have to, you can use this end of the stick here to pin the snake's head down on the ground.' Fast Rabbit demonstrated using the forked end of the stick. 'Whatever you do, make sure you reach out with the stick, eh? Keep your legs away from the snake and wait for me to come and deal with it.'

'I will,' promised the young boy and ran off to join the head of the march where he could survey the track they were taking.

'Will he be alright?'

Fast Rabbit levered himself upright on his cane. 'It will be fine. The snakes come out to warm themselves when the sun comes up, but it's too hot for them now. They're either off hunting through the undergrowth or sheltering underground. They aren't likely to be on the main path.'

'Oh,' said Precious Flower, reassured by the veteran's words.

'He's a good boy, that one. He'll grow up to be just like his father.' Fast Rabbit had a faraway look in his eyes as he spoke. Precious Flower imagined that he was thinking of the army and wishing he was fighting on the frontline. 'Is Jaguar well? Have you heard from him?'

Precious Flower replied that she had not. The army took many runners with them, slaves mostly, who could earn enough money in one year carrying messages between the Mexica army and the valley of Texcoco to buy themselves out of servitude. Many supplemented their income carrying personal messages along with the ones the empire entrusted them with.

'He will be fine,' the veteran said. 'I know your husband. I have fought alongside him. He will return home to you.'

'Thank you,' said Precious Flower. 'I tell myself he will be back, but it's good to hear those words coming from someone else.'

'Yes, I'm sure it's hard. My own wife was pleased when I took my injury.' He smiled. 'It took me a lot longer to see it for the blessing it really is. Without it I'd either be traipsing about distant corners of the land or maybe even dead. Instead I got to spend some time with my children before they left home.' Fast Rabbit pointed up the road. 'Look, you see… I'm slowing you down. The convoy is getting ahead of us. It's a good job the crops can't move about or I'd be useless in the fields as well.'

Precious Flower kept pace with Fast Rabbit's rolling gait, which was more pronounced now that he was working to close the gap. He swayed and dipped his head on one side to swing his damaged leg forward. It looked uncomfortable, but he never once complained. As they walked, they discussed planting and speculated about the year's harvest. Eventually they caught up with the rest of the travellers and Precious Flower took her daughter back from

196

Fast Rabbit's wife. She was pleased to have someone to share the burden with. The pregnancy had given her back pains that still hadn't subsided.

There was only a light breeze giving respite from the heat of the spring day and Graceful Bird was getting fretful. With the sling securely fastened, Precious Flower slipped one arm from her dress and allowed her child to suckle while they walked. What with the back trouble and caring for Graceful Bird, she wondered how much help she would be with the planting.

As though the woman could read Precious Flower's thoughts, Fast Rabbit's wife spoke. 'As soon as we've got most of our planting done we'll send our two slaves over to help you. You shouldn't be working so hard. You've just given birth.'

'You are very kind,' said Precious Flower. 'I will be very grateful for the help, but please don't send anyone until you're sure you can spare them.'

The conversation continued for a while on the business of farming. Much of it was alien to Precious Flower who had grown up in the jade workshop. Holdings had to be protected by rebuilding cairns that marked the edges, there were irrigation channels to dig and pests to frighten off, such as the rabbits that ate the young maize shoots and birds that ravaged the ripening cobs. After a while the road forked. Precious Flower remembered that the right-hand road lead to Toluca and the left to Xalatlaco where their smallholdings lay, but she was still caught unawares by the change in the landscape.

'Look at that!' she exclaimed. 'I hardly recognise the place. The last time I was here, this place was so thick with trees and undergrowth we had to cut our way through parts of it. Look at it now!' Her face was a mask of dismay. 'It's just open fields.'

'This whole area is farmed now,' explained Fast Rabbit. 'Tenochtitlan is growing and with it, the need for food.'

'It was cleared for firewood first,' added his wife. 'The wood gatherers are having to range further and further afield to collect firewood. I heard one man at the market joking that he would have to steal into the royal gardens of Chalco to gather his next load to sell.'

The group took the left-hand track that was less trampled than the route to Toluca. It was strewn with gnarled rocks of all shapes and sizes, some large enough to have emaciated juniper bushes eking out a meagre existence on top. From here the land rose slightly, forming a set of wooded hills that the convoy would have to negotiate in order to catch a sight of Xalatlaco in the valley beyond. They hadn't gone far when there was a scream from up ahead that drained the colour from Precious Flower's face. Blade's shriek was unmistakable. Fast Rabbit set off at an awkward lope, but Precious Flower left him behind as she charged towards the sound, holding her baby tight to her chest.

Chapter 21
The Jungles of Totonaca

'I'm not taking orders from you anymore!' growled Angry Lizard.

It was late afternoon and it had rained again. Clawfoot was standing in a puddle outside the Long House, a communal building used as an administrative centre by the local council of elders and religious leaders that had been commandeered by the various orders of priests from Tenochtitlan as their centre of operations. Clawfoot was standing with his back at the door where the tightly jointed blocks of stone met the relief carvings that ran around the doorway. Water dripped down his neck from the mildewed thatch of leaves and the smell of mould was tickling his nose. He and the two warrior priests had just left a meeting of holy men. The priests from Tenochtitlan had commanded their local counterparts attend in an attempt to spread the message of Huitzilopochtli's supremacy. It had not gone well. The discussions were heated right from the outset and had very quickly turned rancorous. The town needed local men to staff and run Huitzilopochtli's mission. Appointing them had not been particularly contentious, but as always it was the subjugation of the lesser priesthoods to the Sun God's rule that caused outrage. Calm only returned thanks to the intercession of elders on both sides who called for a break in the proceedings.

'What did you say?' said Clawfoot.

'I said that I'm through taking orders from you. Why, in the name of Tlazolteotl, did you make us sit through that? What possible benefit can there be to listening to those old farts arguing over who sits in which shrine when and who has to kiss whose arse?'

Clawfoot stilled the surge of anger in his veins. 'I already explained on the way to Ahuilizapan that we need cover stories for our presence here. We need people to see us and remember us taking part in Huitzilopochtli's conversion of these heathens.'

They all stopped as two local women walked by, eyes downcast to avoid any interaction with the foreigners. An old man passed in the opposite direction, treading carefully between the many puddles.

'Well, I say we just wasted an entire afternoon listening to a bunch of ragged grey wits who won't even remember where they put their cocks this morning, let alone recall three strangers from the back of this meeting.' Spittle flew from Angry Lizard's lips and he shook his fist at Clawfoot.

'We can't talk here,' said Clawfoot. 'We're going to draw attention to ourselves for all the wrong reasons. Over here…'

He pointed to a narrow alleyway bordered by a row of dismal huts on one side and a high wall that surrounded the palace compound. To his surprise the two warrior priests followed his lead.

'You have no idea what you're doing,' said Clawfoot when they were fifty paces in. There was less chance of them being observed here. The alley was strewn with broken pottery and piles of rotting wood, speckled with yellow fungus. Clawfoot's stomach felt as though it was filled with ice. This confrontation was long overdue. He stilled himself in preparation for what was to come.

'I've had enough of traipsing around after a child.' Angry Lizard looked at Third Arrow for support and Clawfoot noticed the curt nod. 'Feathered Darkness told me not to kill you, but he didn't forbid me from taking over the mission. I'll tell him that I did it to keep you safe and he'll thank me for it. Third Arrow and I will get this done. Stay out of our way. Flap your lips with wizened old priests or stare at the stars for all I care. This work is for men, not boys.'

All along, Clawfoot had known it would come to this. He had hoped to find a clever way out of the predicament, deferring any hard decisions in the hope of inspiration. The approach had failed. No bright ideas had materialised and now that it had come to this he felt pleased. Now they would finish the fight that began in the Hall of Knowledge. He hung his head.

'Ha!' triumphed Angry Lizard. 'I knew it. Our Venerable Father, Feathered Darkness' favourite is a weakling. Go and offer to help Gathers the Dawn in his pointless attempt to train these narrow-minded yokels. We'll go and meet with Twice Blessed, then go and finish the job. If you behave yourself we'll tell Feathered Darkness what a good lad you've been.'

'You'll need this then.' Clawfoot pulled out the small wooden tube that he'd picked up in the Hall of Knowledge all those days ago. Unwilling to part with the tiny scroll carrier, he had kept it with him ever since. He saw the warrior priests' eyes narrow as they tried to work out what it was and used the opportunity to grasp his blade.

'What's that?'

'It's an official request from Feathered Darkness and it carries the seal of Huitzilopochtli. His protection for you if you get caught.' The lie came easily.

'Give it to me.' Angry Lizard held his hand out.

Clawfoot held the prize down low, forcing Angry Lizard to stoop to take hold of it. It wasn't much, but it brought him within reach. As Angry Lizard's fingers closed on the tube, Clawfoot calmly extended his knife-arm and slid the blade into the warrior priest's exposed neck. For a moment, Angry Lizard wasn't sure what had happened. His eyes flicked up at Clawfoot. He dropped the wooden tube and he moved his hands to his throat just as Clawfoot pulled the glassy shard away. Angry Lizard gave a pained look as he touched the wound. He breathed in and coughed, bright red blood gushing from his mouth and nose. Then, slowly, he fell to his knees.

Third Arrow glanced down at his foot, staring in disbelief at the blood that splashed across his foot, and then at Angry Lizard who was still trying to stem the flow from the gash in his neck.

'You see,' Clawfoot began, 'Feathered Darkness made you promise to get me back safely, but he never made me promise the same for you.'

Angry Lizard made a wet gurgling sound and reached out for Clawfoot. The light in his eyes was already fading. He would know now that he was doomed. Clawfoot stepped away, keeping

Third Arrow at bay with his outstretched knife. There was no telling how the man would react, so Clawfoot decided to steer him, before he made his own mind up.

'Want to side with a dead man?' he said, forcing his voice as low and menacing as he could manage. 'The high priest chose me for a reason,' he continued. 'He chose me.' Clawfoot had to step back again because Angry Lizard was still moving towards him on his hands and knees, but his strength had gone, leaked into the puddles that pockmarked the muddy backstreet. The warrior priest made one more lunge at Clawfoot's leg and collapsed face-first into the soupy earth.

Finally, Third Arrow found his voice. 'What have you done?' He was shaking.

'What's the matter? You never seen anyone killed before?' Clawfoot picked up the wooden tube, pleased at how useful it had been. He wondered why he'd ever disputed the importance of scribing with the Master of Learning. 'I've killed a traitor and if you decide to run... well, that will just mean I have another traitor to deal with, won't it?'

'I won't help you.'

'We were given a job to do, remember? I intend to see it through and when I get back to Tenochtitlan, I'll be sure to report on your performance.' Clawfoot could see that his words were having the desired effect. He cleaned his dagger on the hem of his robe and sheathed it. 'You know, your head is an interesting shape, all pointy at the top. I wonder what the bone underneath it will look like once the Master Curator has peeled it.'

The man's mouth worked soundlessly for a moment. He glanced down at the now lifeless corpse between them and then raised his hands. 'Fine! This wasn't my idea. I'm with you. Angry Lizard was a fool, always trying to make trouble.'

'Good. Now help me strip this idiot and hide his body before anyone comes along.'

They hefted Angry Lizard's body against the wall and covered it with a stack of rotting logs. Clawfoot rolled the priest's bag and short sword up in his cloak, planning to toss them in the river. He glanced around to make sure they had missed nothing and used his foot to stir up the mud in one puddle, diluting the blood. Clawfoot shivered, but it wasn't the damp that gave him gooseflesh. He suddenly understood what it was to wield power. Angry Lizard had tried to wrest that from him and he had refused to let it happen.

'Come on,' he said. 'Let's get away from here.'

'What do we do now?' asked Third Arrow as they eased between two huts and stepped onto one of the main thoroughfares that criss-crossed the workers district. 'Do we wait some more?' He sounded miserable.

'We have to wait. Twice Blessed is the one who must act. Our task is to go along with what he says.'

'It's been ten days since we spoke to him. Do you think something has happened to him?'

Clawfoot shook his head. He pulled his robe tight around his shoulders. The recent downpour must have chilled the air; it couldn't be a reaction to killing Angry Lizard.

The two men walked down the street. Hardly anyone was about. The wet weather had chased away all but the hardiest of buyers. A few men and women haggled with the traders who had set their wares out beneath awnings of dried palm leaves. There were neat stacks of squash and baskets full of beans, cages of coati and a dozen chachalacas tethered by their necks to their owner's shop front. There was no shortage of produce, but the oppressive nature of the sky lent a desultory feel to the commerce. Third Arrow was silent, likely still shocked at what had just taken place. The lack of conversation suited Clawfoot who was still feeling the aftereffects. His spirit soared triumphantly above the queasy wreckage of his bowels.

The two men had just reached the hut they shared with the visiting priests of Huitzilopochtli when they were accosted by a boy with a raggedly shaved head and yellowing loincloth.

'You must go to meet Twice Blessed,' he blurted out, chest puffed out with pride in his mission.

'What, now?'

'Yes.'

Clawfoot frowned. 'Alright, but where?'

'He said you would know.' The boy bobbed up and down impatiently and then noticed something. 'There are supposed to be three of you.'

'Our friend was taken ill,' said Clawfoot. That seemed to satisfy the boy who bobbed his head and scurried off.

The ruined wharf looked more forlorn in the lambent daylight. A pair of mangy dogs with miserable expressions and soaked fur slunk off, tails low, ceding their territory to the intruders.

'In here,' called the gruff voice that Clawfoot remembered from the last meeting. A slab of a man beckoned to them from the remains of a fisherman's house across the street from where they had met Twice Blessed last time. It was a dilapidated husk right on the edge of the river, half of which had already been washed away. Clawfoot nodded at Third Arrow. They had no option but to put their trust in this man. They ducked inside and were pleased to see that the walls and roof of the house that had not already been claimed by the river were doing a fair job of keeping the earthen floor dry. On their left, the swollen river rushed past the open end of the building.

Standing in a relaxed posture in the centre of the room was the man who had beckoned to them, a warrior by his stature, his square jaw, broken nose and the two fingers missing from his right hand. The front of his head was shaved, while the remains, dark but streaked with grey, were tightly scraped back into a long warrior's queue. His easy poise and tree-trunk chest matched the image Clawfoot had formed based on the deep voice they had heard before.

Third Arrow looked uncertain. 'Two Sign,' he said, dipping his head with guarded respect. 'Lord Commander of the Eagle Knights.'

Clawfoot had heard of the man but would never have recognised him. He had spent the last five years learning about the gods and how the world had come into being. He had practised the art of capturing the ancient stories on parchment and studying the movement of the heavens. He knew how to prepare offerings for the God of War and how to carve a man's heart from his chest, but when it came to the nobility, the council or the workings of the empire's military machine, he knew nothing. Third Arrow, like so many of the priests, came from noble stock and would have spent the early years of his childhood surrounded by chatter about the upper echelons of society and famous warriors.

'If either of you calls me by that name again, it will be the last thing you ever do,' warned Two Sign, his voice like a distant landslide. 'Where is the stout one with the bad attitude?'

'He didn't want to cooperate, so I had to silence him. He wanted to take control, so I showed him how ill-suited for the role he was.'

'In what way is he ill-suited?'

'Right now, his least helpful trait is that he's dead.'

'I see,' said Two Sign.

'Do you have news?' asked Clawfoot, silently wondering how Xiconoc had managed to corrupt someone so close to Tlacaelel.

'I do,' said the Eagle Knight. He put his hands behind his back. 'In seven days' time, Tlacaelel makes war on the town of Ixtlahuacan. Instead of going to witness his great army at work, the tlatoani plans to go on a hunt.'

A loud clonk from the direction of the river made Clawfoot jump. Third Arrow whirled round and the Eagle Knight reached up behind him for the sword that was slung over his back. Outside, a half-submerged tree trunk swirled past the jagged post that was all that remained of a once sturdy jetty, one branch outstretched towards the sky, like a drowning man with twisted fingers, imploring the world to come to his assistance. As the three men watched, it made a lazy pirouette and then was swept away on the torrent.

'So this is the opportunity you mentioned,' said Clawfoot when they had settled down.

'Yes, and it's as I hoped.'

'He'll be less well protected than usual?'

'Only ten knights from the royal household.'

'Grey Knights,' scoffed Third Arrow. 'Old men. Warriors retired from active service and grown fat on crumbs from the tlatoani's table.'

Clawfoot saw the flash of irritation on Two Sign's face. Just as he held the warrior priests in contempt, the warrior priests derided the men of the Grey Privy Knights, veterans retired to a cushy number. The Grey Privy Knights did nothing but stand about the palace and look unfriendly and they, for their part, believed themselves to be elite and looked down on everyone else.

'Underestimate them at your own peril,' said the big man softly. 'I fought with three of these men against the tyrant Maxtla. They may be long in the tooth, but they taught me everything I know and probably held some back.'

'Where is the hunt taking place?' asked Clawfoot, ignoring the dispute.

'There is a place south of Ixtlahuacan where the water slows and the valley widens into a swamp with many small channels cut through it. The locals say that there are crocodiles there.'

'Is the plan to make the tlatoani's death look like an accident?'

Two Sign frowned. 'I hadn't thought of that. You mean, make it look as though he's been taken by one of the creatures?'

'Why not?'

'It might work. I'll give it some thought.'

'So we have to ambush them in the swamp?' asked Clawfoot.

'There is no need to ambush them. We all go with the hunting party. My people have already been selected and one priest is to be allowed for prayers and blessings on the endeavour, one priest with two acolytes, although it looks like he will have to make do with one now.'

'How many of your people are there?'

'Five. The tlatoani is travelling light this time. One of the guides is with us and four porters. All local men with a grudge to bear and personally vetted by me.' Two Sign gave a savage grin.

'Five!' exclaimed Third Arrow. 'I thought you commanded the Eagle Knights—'

'The knights are loyal to the tlatoani,' Two Sign cut in. 'I might as well kill myself as to try to recruit from among them. Anyway, you're contributing only two.'

'So there are seven of us, but we have the element of surprise,' said Clawfoot.

'It's not enough!' complained Third Arrow.

'I thought you priests were more than a match for these old greybeard warriors,' rejoined Two Sign.

Third Arrow scowled.

'Why are you doing this?' Clawfoot asked the knight. 'If the rest of your men are so loyal to our ruler, what happened to you?'

Two Sign stared at Clawfoot, silent for a long while before he spoke. 'My life and everything that I ever had has been given in the service of the tlatoani. Do not presume to judge me. Circumstances change. When my turn comes to stand before the gods and make my reckoning, I will tell my story and remind them of what has come to pass.'

'And Xiconoc, you think he belongs on the throne?'

'What do you care what I think?'

'I like to know what motivates the people whose lives I depend on, especially when I'm about to go into a fight to the death alongside them. I want to survive this.'

'For one so young you seem to know a great deal about survival.'

Clawfoot said nothing. His instincts told him that Two Sign would be deadly once the fighting started, but anyone who had turned traitor once could do so again. Instead he asked where they were supposed to meet up with the hunt.

'The day is set. We will assemble in the main square on the morning of Five Ozomahtli. Be prepared, young priest. The tlatoani expects a lengthy blessing on the hunt. He has long dreamed of capturing a crocodile. Make sure you get the expedition off to a good start and put him at ease, eh?'

'Five Ozomahtli,' repeated Clawfoot. 'A special blessing on the hunt.'

The Eagle Knight gave the two warrior priests one last look before prowling from the tumbledown building. Clawfoot and Third Arrow followed, but the street was already as deserted as the ghost city of Teotihuacan.

Chapter 22
The Jungles of Totonaca

'Do you think he's got the message?' Holds the Sun asked Jaguar.

'Who, Imixquitl?'

'Yes. One entire xiquipilli is garrisoned in and around his city.'

Jaguar's gaze swept across the square. There was no doubt that the might of the Mexica army was on display. The units that had been sent south and those that had pushed northwards to close the gap with the forces of Texcoco had all been recalled to meet up in preparation for the assault on Ixtlahuacan. Just over half of those eight thousand men had managed to cram themselves into the town's main square to hear Tlacaelel give them a send-off. Moctezuma's hunting party had already left for the lowlands, entrusting his half-brother with the morale-boosting speech.

'Impressive, isn't it? Especially when you recall that we took this place with just one quarter of this force.'

'Was it your idea to have the Jaguar Knights and Eagle Knights occupy the centre of the square?'

Jaguar nodded. The pelts stood ranked upon the left-hand side and beaked cowls, although there were fewer of them, made an impressive spectacle on the right. The regular warriors, the clansmen, were ranged around the sides.' Lord Tlacaelel agreed that we should ram the message home. The ruler of Ahuilizapan might be a bit provincial, but I don't think he's stupid,' replied Jaguar.

'You're right,' agreed Holds the Sun. 'He'd be a fool to start a rebellion while we're away in Ixtlahuacan. If he tried anything, we'd slaughter him on our return.'

Jaguar paused with one foot on the ladder to the makeshift platform from which Tlacaelel would give his address. Iquehuacatzin was trying to catch his attention.

'I will come with you,' said the prince when he'd got close enough for Jaguar to hear what he was saying. 'Tlacaelel is my uncle, he will listen to me.'

'No, Lord Iquehuacatzin. He is still angry about what happened to the guide.'

'*I* didn't throw him into the hole!'

'I know, My Lord, but your brother's actions are somehow yours as well.' Jaguar glanced across at Mahchimaleh who was now conversing easily with Holds the Sun. Even under his father's withering criticism he had refused to recognise that he'd done anything wrong by hurling their guide into the sinkhole.

Iquehuacatzin patted Jaguar on the shoulder. 'Alright. I'll wait here and make sure my brother doesn't do anything else stupid.' He winked.

Jaguar scaled the short ladder two rungs at a time. The Jaguar Knights let him through. Tlacaelel was standing back from the edge of the platform, talking to Last Medicine. He didn't want to draw attention to himself until just before his speech.

'Lord Tlacaelel.'

'Come to listen to my speech, Jaguar?'

'Of course, but I must also speak to you about the tlatoani.'

'What about him?' demanded the general. 'He's gone off on his foolish expedition to catch a crocodile.'

'That's exactly what I'm worried about. I think he's in danger.'

The general's eye never left his warriors. He clearly wasn't giving his full attention to Jaguar.' I doubt they'll see a single one.'

'No, Lord Tlacaelel, I don't mean he's in danger from the crocodiles, although of course, he might be...I mean that something unusual is going on. Someone may use this opportunity to get to him.'

'He has Two Sign and a retinue of Grey Privy Knights to keep him safe.'

Jaguar breathed a sigh of relief. Two Sign was going. 'How many knights?'

'Ten of the tlatoani's best men.'

That was a surprise. It didn't seem enough. Even with Two Sign's formidable strength, ten good warriors could be over-whelmed by a large raiding party. 'My Lord, ten men is not enough. We are on enemy soil with only a few large towns under our control... many others only feigning friendship.'

'You think I don't know this?' Tlacaelel's voice was a low, warning rumble. 'The tlatoani is already angry with me. I wanted twenty warriors to go with him.'

'Twenty would have been better,' agreed Jaguar.' Let me join them, Lord Tlacaelel.'

'And what of the princes?'

'They would come too, along with two of my knights.'

'Out of the question, Jaguar! If you are correct and the tlatoani's life is in danger, the last thing I will allow is for his sons and heirs to join him. You need not fear though, Two Sign had a good idea. The hunting party must necessarily carry quantities of provisions, food and shelter. Two Sign has hand-picked four local men, good, strong warriors who have no love of Imixquitl. They will serve as porters and have vowed to protect the tlatoani.'

A seed of worry took root in the pit of Jaguar's stomach. 'Why did Two Sign pick local men when he could have selected from among his own men?'

'He did select warriors first. Later he came and told me he'd changed his mind. He said we needed all the Jaguar Knights and Eagle Knights for the attack on Ixtlahuacan. He is right, of course. Our forces are already stretched more thinly than I would like. Nearly seven hundred warriors keep watch along the route from Tenochtitlan to keep our supply and communication lines open. A hundred and twenty men keep watch at Zongolica and we must leave at least two thousand here to keep the peace while we take Ixtlahuacan. Two Sign talked me through it, the way he always used to, before...' Tlacaelel didn't finish the sentence. He gazed at the ranks of warriors arranged across the square.

Jaguar didn't need to ask. By the time Two Sign had recovered from the death of his son, Tlacaelel had already delegated some of his duties to other warriors in the Eagle Knights and was relying more on Jaguar for planning and logistics.

'And that was when he came up with the idea of using warriors from Ahuilizapan?'

The general tore his gaze away from the troops. 'Yes, but I do not think they are from here,' he said. 'They are from one of the towns nearby. They complained about the tribute being levied by Ahuilizapan.'

'Are you sure about them?'

'Of course,' snapped Tlacaelel. 'Two Sign vouches for them. Anyway,' he added, 'we've taken their families into our protection. They understand all too well what will happen to their loved ones if they allow the tlatoani to come to harm. Now, if you've finished, I have a speech to give.'

Tlacaelel stepped forward to give his address to the assembled warriors, but Jaguar took hold of his arm.

'Lord Tlacaelel,' he said, determined to continue, in spite of the general's angry look. 'Something's not right. Two Sign seems different of late, distant and angry. Suddenly, when he's worried about the tlatoani's safety, he picks four unknown warriors to help him, outsiders whose loyalty isn't proven.'

'Jaguar, I will not tell you a second time,' warned Tlacaelel. 'Let go! Your behaviour is disrespectful. I will not tolerate it. Two Sign is an excellent warrior with an unblemished record. His loyalty is beyond question and I am delighted that he is taking an active interest again. He reminds me of the man I used to know, but now I find myself questioning your motives for interfering. I suggest you do your duty and take care of your charges.' He shrugged Jaguar off and stepped to the front of the platform.

The crowd was roaring its approval of the general as Jaguar climbed down from the platform.

'No luck then,' said Iquehuacatzin who had guessed the outcome from the look on Jaguar's face.

'No. He will not bend. Firstly, your father is already angry that the hunting party has grown so large. He thinks they will scare the animals away. Secondly, Lord Tlacaelel doesn't want the tlatoani and two of his heirs together in a dangerous swamp, a long, long way from help.'

Iquehuacatzin curled his lip like a snarling coyote. 'Maybe there is more to it than that, Jaguar.'

'What do you mean?'

'Perhaps this has all been arranged by my uncle in the hope that the tlatoani will have a nasty accident, thereby leaving him free to take the throne.'

Jaguar looked at Iquehuacatzin, disbelief writ large across his face. 'That's ridiculous!'

'Is it? Listen to him speak. See what you think.'

At that moment, four men lifted gilded conch shells to their lips and blew a sonorous blast that rumbled across the plaza. Tlacaelel raised his arms for silence and a hush fell over the multitude.

'*Can you smell it?*' the general roared. He waited, a dozen heartbeats, and called again. '*Can you smell it?*' There was another pause as he scanned the sea of upturned faces.

Four thousand fighting men waited, as silent as the deepest, driest cave.

'Our scouts have seen the ocean…and I swear to you that sometimes, when the wind blows from the east, I can smell it too. The ocean is our destination, but it is much more than that…the ocean is our destiny.'

The crowd murmured its assent.

'Today we march on Ixtlahuacan and when we take it, the Mexica people will be one step closer to that destiny, because once we take this coast, we can turn our attention to the west. We will follow the path of the sun and forge a mighty empire that stretches from one coast in the east to the beaches in the west. With that conquest will come peace and prosperity for all. Bountiful supplies transported all across the world along secure trade routes. All people will be brothers and bow down to the one tlatoani, worship the same gods. Those who would be our enemies today will one day be our brothers. When they travel to our valley and see our wondrous city on the lake, they will comprehend the wonders we can bring to them.'

Now the warriors cheered and shouted their approval until Tlacaelel quieted them with a wave of one hand.

'So, in a few days' time, when we draw up outside Ixtlahuacan and brave warriors stream out to meet us, think not of pain and death. Think not of suffering or of tears. Remember that these people do not know Huitzilopochtli; we must take his name to them. They are not trained in warfare like we are; we must show them what we know. That does not mean it will be easy...in the heat and press of the battle, some of you will feel as though you stand at the gates of hell itself, Mictlantecuhtli waiting to welcome you with open arms. Do not be afraid. Glory awaits you, be it triumph in this life or be it immortality and heavenly paradise in the next. But...I believe the battle will be swift. These lowland people are no match for us. I am already proud of what you will achieve because I know what you are capable of. Also, I know that in the next few days, many heroes will arise and many legends will be born. These next few days will make us, and in the coming years the poets and the song makers will tell our story, so our children will recall our valour. Believe in your own strength and our victory is assured.'

More cheers rang out, but Tlacaelel wasn't finished.

'A few of you will make the ultimate sacrifice and pass into the lands of darkness, so as you stare into the eyes of the Lord of the Dead, bare your teeth and snarl.' The general raised his clenched fist high. 'Snarl your raw defiance and shout my name for you are the hand of Tlacaelel!'

'*Tlacaelel!*' The warriors' cries rang out and they crashed their spears and swords against their shields.

Iquehuacatzin looked at Jaguar when the noise had died down. 'Well?'

'Well what?'

'Don't you think he's been working on his oratory skills?'

'I've never heard him speak for so long...or so well,' admitted Jaguar. 'He usually leaves the big speeches to Moctezuma.'

'He bids the warriors call his own name,' said Iquehuacatzin, pointedly.

213

Jaguar rubbed his chin thoughtfully, replaying the speech in his head. It was all standard rhetoric, except the last part, the rally to his name.

'I'm not convinced.'

Iquehuacatzin waved dismissively. 'Pfff! Maybe you are right, but you know my uncle is very clever. Everything he does is planned in exquisite detail. You won't find any evidence to incriminate him. You'll have to rely on subtle clues, small signs that he is moving out from under his brother's shadow.'

'There is something else that's not right.'

'What's that?'

'Two Sign is accompanying your father on the hunting trip and he's taking local people with him instead of our own people.'

'Guides?' volunteered Iquehuacatzin.

'No,' replied Jaguar. 'Well, yes. Obviously they know the area, but he said they are warriors, for the tlatoani's protection.'

Iquehuacatzin frowned. 'That does sound unusual. We should follow them.'

Jaguar shook his head. 'Lord Tlacaelel has forbidden it.'

'Not true. Tlacaelel has forbidden *you* from joining them. My brother and I may come and go as we please; only our father may deny us.'

Jaguar opened his mouth, but Iquehuacatzin cut him short.

'And Tlacaelel commanded you to stay close to us at all times, did he not, Heart of the Jaguar?'

'He did, My Lord.'

'Excellent!' Iquehuacatzin's smile would have charmed the birds down from the trees had there been any close by.' In that case, we will march out with Tlacaelel's army and then, when we reach the lowlands, we will head south, seek out my father and see that he comes to no harm.'

Chapter 23 – Tenochtitlan

Several days had passed since his last nocturnal visit to Xiconoc's home, enough, Axayacatl hoped, that the household would have returned to normal, allowing him to sneak in once again. This time the night was cloudy and a stiff wind was whipping dust from the dry streets. He half-closed his eyes to keep the grit out and worked his way down the side of the house by memory.

Since his last visit he had been unable to pluck up the courage to confront his mother about her betrayal. It had been gnawing away at his insides while he tried to work out what to do. At last Axayacatl had decided that the neatest solution would be to break back into Xiconoc's home and find something he could use against the man. One of the many rumours that circulated among the nobility concerned Xiconoc's vast trading empire. It was said that demonic magic was the reason for his enduring success, some even going so far as to claim that Xiconoc's home hid a shrine, complete with altar on which all manner of scandalous and illegal sacrificial ceremonies were conducted. Axayacatl had decided that it was worth investigating. If there were evidence that Lord Xiconoc was talking to the spirit world without the presence of priests, that sacrilege would give him the leverage he needed. Failing that, Xiconoc often boasted around court that his success was due to the meticulous notes he and his scribes kept of his business dealings. If that was so and there was even a shred of truth to the rumours, there would be records and, reasoned Axayacatl, in those records there might be something he could use against the merchant.

Axayacatl had even made a rudimentary plan for how he would use the information he hoped to find. He saw himself confronting Xiconoc, forcing a confession from him and then getting him to promise that he would never again see Atotoztli except in public. The scandal would ruin both of them, but Xiconoc had more to lose, much more. He would see sense and call off the affair. It was a simple plan. Axayacatl hoped its execution would be straightforward too once he had dealt with the tricky matter of raiding the merchant's home in the dead of night.

Axayacatl got into the house over the courtyard roof as on the previous occasion. This time he was a little more prepared and left a rope secured to one of the joists so that he could slip quietly away. This excursion was later than the previous one. Axayacatl reasoned that there would be less chance of discovery early in the morning. Whatever Xiconoc might get up to in the evenings, it would surely be over by now.

The downside to breaking in this late was that the torches had all gone out, so Axayacatl had to negotiate the merchant's house by feel alone. He crept past a room that smelled like the kitchen. The embers of yesterday's fire could still be seen smouldering in the hearth. In the dim glow, it was just possible to make out a rack of unlit torches and a sack of dried grass to use as kindling. Axayacatl cursed his feeble plan, wondering how he was going to search the place if he couldn't see. What little light there was outside under the overcast sky was all but useless through the small windows in Xiconoc's house. It would be hard to find anything, let alone work out whether it was useful. Annoyed, he resolved to continue his search anyway. Perhaps he could return and light a torch if he found anything that looked promising and the way remained clear.

After a lot more tip-toeing around, Axayacatl was sure he had found the room that served as the nerve centre of Xiconoc's trading empire and, miracle of miracles, there was an unlit oil lamp standing on the monstrosity of a stone table that squatted in the middle of the room. A hasty round trip to the kitchen allowed Axayacatl to relight the lamp with which he could explore properly. Shadows lurched about the room as Axayacatl moved from one item to another, not sure what he was looking for. Piles of neatly folded cloth stood in one corner of the room, while the other appeared to be a dumping ground for dozens of rods that might have been used for measuring land holdings. The rear wall of Xiconoc's workroom was stacked to the ceiling with parchments; that seemed like a good place to start.

Years of watching his father's meticulous treatment of parchments came into its own as Axayacatl set about searching through the racks of information. He had to stop a couple of times when he thought he heard noises in the corridor but eventually worked his way through everything obvious. There were a lot of dry, factual records relating to the movement of goods around the empire; nothing that looked incriminating. Axayacatl moved around the table and began looking at the other objects around the room. It was then that he noticed a waist-high, nondescript earthenware pot brooding in the corner. He reached into the pot up to his armpit and pulled out several scrolls that were covered with sketchy pictograms. Unrolling them on the table beside the lamp, Axayacatl was disappointed to discover that they looked like the others. Numerous rows indicated payment for goods, each split into two boxes. The left-hand one showed a picture representing what had been bought, along with a count, while the right-hand one showed what had been traded in exchange, also with a number. Sometimes, the left- or the right-hand indicated a payment in gold rather than goods. The one he was looking at now was such a one: gold on the right and a strange glyph that Axayacatl couldn't understand in the left-hand box. It looked like back-to-back twins along with their names, but another interpretation could be 'he who looks both ways' or... Axayacatl shook his head and put it to one side. Probably one of Xiconoc's extensive network of traders or maybe a spy in a far-flung part of the empire.

At last Axayacatl came to a more interesting set of papers with what looked like the names of some of the members of the Calpullicalli and donations to them or the clans they represented. Whatever these documents were, it was clear that large gifts of cloths, timber, copper and some gold had been made to Azcapotzalco and Xochimilco. Axayacatl understood the workings of the Grand Council enough to know that both were troublesome partners in the Mexica alliance, one arrogant because of its heritage and the other far enough removed from the centre that they felt safe. This information was consistent with someone trying to buy loyalty or perhaps votes from those clans who ruled. Axayacatl's breath quickened. He could hardly believe his luck. It seemed that his crazy plan might actually pay off.

He was just rolling up the parchments when he heard voices outside, this time for real. His eyes darted about, looking for a hiding place, and lit upon the measurement rods. He just had time to ease himself behind them before two figures stepped through the door. The first was lumbering and wrapped in a voluminous evening cloak, the second was graceful and dressed in a shift of gauzy cotton, the like of which Axayacatl had never seen before.

Xiconoc was complaining to his concubine. 'I don't care if she's crying again. Marrying that girl was a terrible mistake. I don't care how well the whole thing has been received; nothing can compensate me for being lumbered with a broken woman.' He stopped and gave the lamp a strange look.

Axayacatl's heart leapt into his throat. The lamp! He hadn't had time to extinguish it.

'Coszcatl, My Light, My Path,' said Xiconoc. 'Have you been in this room this evening?'

'No, My Lord.'

'Has anyone else been in here?'

'I'm not sure, My Lord. Your clerk often slips in without my noticing. I don't like him. He looks like a ghost and moves like one too.'

Xiconoc laughed. 'That's because he spends his whole life scribbling in darkened rooms. Don't worry about him. He will be loyal to me until the end because he has no choice.'

'Is he the one who stole the rabbits from the market?'

'His son,' corrected the merchant. 'I will have to speak to him. He could set the whole place on fire leaving a lamp on like this.'

'Little Maize will change in time,' said Coszcatl, returning to the previous subject. She flowed through the feeble lamplight like liquid gold and her diaphanous gown left nothing of her figure to the imagination. Her voice was full of warmth and concern for Xiconoc.

Axayacatl swallowed hard and tried to shut out the memory of this woman, in bed with his mother. At least the subject of the lamp seemed to be behind them.

'I don't understand,' said Xiconoc. He began searching through the stack of scrolls. 'Why is she so ungrateful? She had nothing. If she had stayed at the Sisters of Penitence, sooner or later she would have been...'

'Taken to be the bride of Huitzilopochtli,' finished Coszcatl. 'You know, I have been speaking to her. She had a rough time there. Mother is not as caring as she would have her benefactors believe.'

'All the more reason for her to show some gratitude!' barked Xiconoc, real anger in his voice.

'The point I'm trying to make is that Little Maize will surely come to appreciate her change of circumstance, my dear.' Coszcatl wrapped her arms around Xiconoc's stout neck and stood on tiptoe to rub noses with her lord. 'Let her have the run of the house for a few moons before you return to her bed. She just needs a bit more time.'

Xiconoc rubbed his face. 'Perhaps you're right. She is young.'

'And frightened,' added Coszcatl.

Xiconoc nodded.

'Why are we here anyway?' asked the concubine.

'I need to do some work,' replied Xiconoc, gently removing Coszcatl's arms from around him.

'Aiee,' cried Coszcatl. 'This is no time for work. Come to bed with me. I will show you how a good wife should behave.' She looked at Xiconoc through her long lashes and pouted extravagantly.

Xiconoc smiled wanly.

'What is it, My Lord? You're not still worried about the intruder, are you?'

Axayacatl started and nearly kicked the poles that hid him from view.

'No, I'm not,' said Xiconoc, but the denial wasn't convincing. 'I expect it's one of Feathered Darkness' spies. He's like a damned spider at the centre of a huge web; it's disgusting.'

'I thought you said he was helping you?'

'I'd sooner trust a rattlesnake's kiss. That man promises one thing and when your back is turned he promises something completely different to someone else.'

'He sounds a bit like you, My Lord,' said Coszcatl playfully.

'Mmm…' said Xiconoc sounding unamused. 'And that boy he's entrusted with this mission, what's his name… Clawfoot, that's it. He's far too young. He must have hundreds of experienced men to call on for work like this.'

'Why would he choose someone he thinks might fail? Wouldn't that put him in danger?'

Axayacatl was impressed and made a mental note not to underestimate Coszcatl. Xiconoc's commercial acumen could not be doubted, but perhaps some of his success was down to this woman. She was certainly handy in a number of different ways.

'Would you like me to stay with you while you work?' Coszcatl asked when Xiconoc began to shuffle his papers in earnest.

'No, you go back to sleep, my devoted one,' replied Xiconoc, patting her rump lovingly. 'It would be terribly boring for you. All these dusty papers and boring facts about cotton imports and movements of maize from one storehouse to another.'

Coszcatl slunk from the room with a languorous wave, but Xiconoc had already turned his back on her. He checked parchments from the rack, holding them near the lamp and squinting at them for what seemed like an age. Once or twice he made a grunting sound, as though he had stumbled upon an important fact.

Axayacatl's buttocks were going numb, so he was pleased to see Xiconoc clearing up after his research. He had just convinced himself that the merchant would return to his concubine when Xiconoc went over to the stone jar. Axayacatl took fright a second time when he realised that the papers that he had plucked from their hiding place moments ago lay on the floor beside him. As soon as the merchant discovered that they were missing he would surely begin a search of the room. Axayacatl decided not to wait to be discovered. While Xiconoc's back was turned he tried to extricate himself from his hiding place. It was a clumsy move executed in haste. His foot caught one of the measuring rods and the whole stack crashed to the floor while he sprawled in the doorway.

Xiconoc spun. 'Mictlan's shrivelled cock! You scared me half to death,' he said. 'Another intruder! What in the name of the Creator Pair are you doing in my house?'

Axayacatl disentangled himself from the scattered poles and stood shakily, still clutching Xiconoc's scrolls in one hand. He was nearest the door. Escape was still possible if he went now, but something made him pause. Xiconoc had defiled his mother and defiance bloomed in Axayacatl's heart.

'You...you monster!'

Xiconoc peered at him. 'It was you here the other night, wasn't it?'

'It was me,' growled Axayacatl and, emboldened by the nobleman's passive response, he moved to the heavy stone table that separated them.

'By the gods, it's you, Axayacatl,' began Xiconoc. 'What are you doing here?'

'Protecting my family's honour.'

Xiconoc's laugh was explosive, but then, as if realising his mistake, he raised his hands and appealed for calm. 'I'm sorry,' he said. 'I... you looked so serious, so determined. Your parents would be proud of you if they knew what you were doing in their name.'

'Don't talk to me about my parents! You disgust me. I saw you... I saw what you were doing to my mother and my father's concubine.' Axayacatl advanced towards the table.

'You don't understand.'

'Oh, I understand all too well. You have corrupted her and dishonoured my father. If the tlatoani got to hear of this, you would surely be killed for an adulterer.' Axayacatl felt triumphant as Xiconoc's face fell.

'You may be right,' Xiconoc said softly, 'but your mother would also be put to death. I don't think you want that, do you? Your father would never recover.'

'I'm going to kill you,' croaked Axayacatl, his moment of elation gone. 'You're disgusting! How dare you mention my father as if you care for what he thinks! You're not fit to eat his excrement! I saw what you were doing.' Axayacatl felt tears of shame burning his cheeks and began to work his way around the edge of the stone table, not sure what he would do if he managed to catch hold of Xiconoc.

'You want to know the truth?' asked Xiconoc.

Axayacatl took another step around the table.

'I'll tell you anyway, boy!' said the merchant, defiance ringing in his voice. 'Your parents don't know how to look after their finances. They've been spending beyond their means: throwing parties, buying lavish gifts for every member of the nobility you care to name. I think they have some foolish notion to keep close to the centre of the Colhua dynasty. Your father is too willing to help his dear wife… who still thinks she has her father's coffers at her disposal.'

'You're a liar!' shouted Axayacatl, not wanting to listen anymore. 'I'm going to crush your skull, you filthy old man, and it will be a mercy! If Moctezuma hears of what you've done, he'll feed you to the crows! He'll flay your skin and paint your raw and bleeding flesh with salt and set the city dogs on you!'

'I don't think so,' said Xiconoc, stepping nimbly round the table to stay out of harm's way. 'You're not going to tell a soul and do you know why?'

'Shut up! I don't want to know.'

'Really? You would rather be ill-informed? You see your family's precious honour is propped up by my money. It's me who funds your elegant banquets and your mother is part of the bargain.'

'No,' cried Axayacatl.

'Yes, and it's a perfect deal. Your mother and I enjoy each other. She's a dirty woman who knows no boundaries, just the way I like them. As for your father, he's happy just as long as he has funds to entertain the nobility.'

With an inchoate roar Axayacatl lunged across the desk. Xiconoc promptly stepped back out of harm's way. Too late,

Axayacatl saw that the merchant had gathered up the figurine of Tlazalteotl from the table because the next moment it crashed into his face. He flinched so that it only caught him a glancing blow, but it was enough to send him sprawling into a stack of reed baskets.

Xiconoc bellowed for his guards. Equally enraged and aware that his time was running out, Axayacatl leapt to his feet and followed Xiconoc round the table again. Blood dripped from a gash on his forehead. He would have to go across the table.

'Gah!' Axayacatl shrieked at a sudden stabbing pain in the small of his back. He collapsed to the floor, writhing. Above him, clothed only in a savage grin was Coszcatl, clutching the spear that had so recently poked a hole in him. It seemed she'd beaten the guards to the protection of her master. Axayacatl's breath came in short, painful gasps. He could do nothing but watch as the naked woman reversed the spear in her hands and swung it at his head. A million stars exploded in his head.

Axayacatl surfaced groggily to hear more voices.

'Where have you idiots been?' Xiconoc was demanding. 'I could have been killed!'

The first guard struggled to explain. 'We... My Lord, both entrances to the building have been closed from the inside. No one has entered.'

'How do you explain this then?' Xiconoc gestured at Axayacatl who made no attempt to move. His ears were ringing and he was having difficulty focusing.

The guard looked crestfallen.

'Tie him up until I decide what to do with him. We can't kill him, he's Tezozomoc's brat, but that doesn't mean we have to treat him like a prince.'

From his place on the floor, Axayacatl watched Coszcatl hand the spear to Xiconoc. She was beautiful and alarmingly handy with weapons too. She slipped out of the room with a confident swagger and Axayacatl could only marvel at her. In spite of her state of undress she was as nonchalant as though she was off to the market.

The guards tied leather straps around Axayacatl's ankles.

'So, Axayacatl, how did you get in?' quizzed Xiconoc.

Axayacatl tried to reply, but his tongue didn't seem to work properly. Xiconoc rapped him smartly on the head with the blunt end of the spear.

'I didn't understand that. Try again. How did you get in?'

'Roof,' said Axayacatl, carefully forming the word. He wiped his bloody cheek on the bindings that held his wrists.

'Into the courtyard?'

Axayacatl nodded.

Xiconoc turned to the guards. 'I don't think anyone knows the boy is here. Maybe we can kill him after all.'

Axayacatl sniffed hard, trying to clear blood from his nose. 'Nezahualcoyotl knows I'm here.' It was a lie, but the situation was looking bleak. Anything was better than nothing, however flimsy.

'What?'

'You heard me.'

'What did you tell him?'

The corner of Axayacatl's mouth turned up. 'It doesn't matter what I told him.'

'Of course it matters,' shouted Xiconoc and struck Axayacatl again. 'What did you tell him?'

Axayacatl lay on his side and groaned. Perhaps Xiconoc wasn't so clever after all. 'He knows that I was coming here tonight.'

A shadow passed across Xiconoc's face as he looked down at Axayacatl. 'You couldn't tell him why you were here, could you?' he said. 'If you did, you would have had to explain that your mother's a faithless bitch and your father's too busy pleasuring the nobility to pleasure his wife. How well do you think that will reflect upon your family, eh?'

Axayacatl groaned again and tried to sit up, the ligatures round his ankles and wrists making it difficult. Xiconoc knelt down and manhandled him into a seated position, then glared into his face.

'If you ever tell anyone what you've seen here, you may get your vengeance on me, but it will come at such a price as it will break your life apart. Who do you think they will laugh and joke about on the streets once they know what your mother has been up to? Do you really want the whole of Tenochtitlan questioning your parentage?'

Axayacatl held Xiconoc's eyes and let his anger burn through the shame of his capture. *Stupid to get caught*, he thought, and Xiconoc might still decide to silence him.

'Guards, take our guest away and teach him some manners. It's not polite to break into other people's houses, is it, boys?'

The two men laughed.

'Make sure he doesn't die. I don't believe he has told Nezahualcoyotl, but it's not worth taking any chances.'

'Yes, My Lord,' the guards chorused. As they hauled him from the room, Axayacatl heard Xiconoc calling after him.

'Think about what's important to you, eh?'

Chapter 24 – Tenochtitlan

The thick stone wall of Xiconoc's home lent a chill to the air. Little Maize hugged her shawl tight around her shoulders and climbed into the window opening to sit in the early morning sun. She had to pull her knees up under her chin so that she could fit into the narrow space, but it didn't matter as long as she could turn her face up to the warmth.

Nine days had elapsed since Little Maize had passed out in Moctezuma's palace and had to be carried back to Xiconoc's home on a litter. The bruises across her back and buttocks were little more than yellow smudges now, a reminder of her husband's anger when he himself had returned from the tlatoani's palace. Little Maize's fainting fit and her nosebleed had caused a great deal of gossip that night and it hadn't been the kind of attention that Xiconoc had wanted. He had beaten her mercilessly with a cane until Coszcatl and another of his concubines had intervened. On the whole it had been a blessing. At least he hadn't wanted to sleep with her since that night. Blood and pus running from the ragged sores had rendered her too repulsive. Escape from the Sisters of Penitence and the clutches of White Moon had come at a heavy price. The triumph at her victory over Mother's cruel First Maiden had been very short-lived and now her heart felt heavy. From the jaws of cipactli into the coils of the mazacoatl, so went the saying!

This side of the house looked out onto the Street of Flowers, which the fishermen used as the main thoroughfare from the bustling harbour up to the market. Little Maize knew from her time on the streets that the shoreline along the Atzacualco quarter would already be swarming with leathery-looking men and their wiry sons bringing boat loads of fish ashore.

'Shall I fetch you your water now, My Lady?'

The voice belonged to Ninth Girl, the most junior of Xiconoc's slave girls who had been assigned to Little Maize. Although she was a year younger than Little Maize, the slave girl was taller by a hand and, thought Little Maize, rather plump. All signs that she had lived and worked in this wealthy household for some time.

'Yes,' said Little Maize hollowly, turning back to watch the street outside.

Ninth Girl, whose real name Little Maize had discovered was Industrious Bee, always kept her head bowed. Any spark that the girl might once have possessed had been effectively quashed by the training in Xiconoc's household. If she knew of Little Maize's humble background she had made no reference to it.

'Do you believe that our lives are preordained?'

'Yes, My Lady. Black Tezcatlipoca made the Fourth World and put us on the face of the Earth and decided how everything must be.'

'And yet Quetzalcoatl destroyed the Third World and everything in it, so whatever was preordained at the start was upset.'

'I don't understand,' said the girl in a small voice.

'What I'm trying to say is that the people or creatures, or whatever they were, who lived then believed that their lives were determined by Tezcatlipoca and yet it was all torn down and changed.'

'Yes, My Lady,' answered the girl, obviously uncomfortable with the conversation.' If you say so.'

'So perhaps we can also change our own destinies,' sighed Little Maize.

Ninth Child refused to be drawn any further.

Little Maize ground her teeth and after a while she spoke again, but this time it was to the open window. 'I wasn't made for this. I won't be used anymore. Not by Mother, not by White Moon or... or anyone else.' She didn't want to mention Xiconoc for fear the girl would convey a message back to him via one of his concubines. Xiconoc had been all smiles and reassurance from the moment they had first met, but that had all changed that evening at Moctezuma's palace. White Moon had been bad enough, but Xiconoc was a monster, plus he was fat and his breath stank. Little Maize had thought herself tough, but recently she seemed to have done a lot of crying and that familiar knot in her stomach was growing tighter again. She thought about the vision she had seen on the night she had collapsed, Xiconoc on his hands and knees with a knife stuck in his back. She tried to remember if there had been anyone else in the image, someone with murderous intent who had done the deed and then stepped back into the shadows. The thought that she had committed the crime was both appalling and thrilling in equal measure. Of course, she could never enact the scene in real life. Life on the street had toughened Little Maize up, but she knew that plunging a knife into someone's body, even Xiconoc's, was too horrific to contemplate and anyway, what would happen next? She would be apprehended and hanged or beheaded or, worse still, handed back to the priests. No, her only way out would be to escape, but how? She never went anywhere without Coszcatl or other members of the household acting as an escort. Her thoughts turned to Xiconoc's garden. Maybe if she could persuade him to take her there she could find somewhere to hide and then, when everyone was looking for her in the wrong place, she could make a break for the hills. Little Maize sighed. It all seemed like an impossible dream.

The slave girl must have sensed Little Maize's misery and tried to make conversation.

'My Lady, I heard who it was who broke in the other night.'

'What?' said Little Maize, pulling back from her own personal despair.

'You remember all that commotion a few nights ago?'

'Someone got into the house and attacked Xiconoc…'

'Yes, My Lady. Well, I don't know if you've heard, but the sergeant of the guard is courting Sleek Heron, one of the women who grinds the maize, and he told her that the young man who broke in was Lord Axayacatl!'

This last was exclaimed in shrill amazement as Ninth Child clapped her hands to her mouth, watching Little Maize for a reaction that never came.

'Come, My Lady,' said the slave girl. 'Have you not heard of Axayacatl? Lord Tezozomoc's boy?'

Realisation dawned. Little Maize's eyes opened wide. She had met Axayacatl's parents at the palace. What possible motive could he have for breaking into his great-uncle's home and trying to kill him? Maybe this was the mystery attacker from her vision.

'Did you hear that it was Coszcatl who came to the master's aid?'

'No,' replied Little Maize.

'I heard she ran him through with a spear.' The girl was wide-eyed with awe.

'Why did he attack Xiconoc?'

Ninth Girl suddenly developed a renewed interest in her chores. 'I don't know,' she said as she bent to collect clothes from the floor.

Little Maize could see she was lying but didn't think she'd part with the truth easily. Little Maize turned her face to the sun again and tried to draw strength from its warmth. Would Xiconoc ask her back to his room now that her wounds were healing or would he keep Coszcatl by his side? Little Maize marvelled at the thought of the concubine sticking an intruder with a spear.

The thought had no sooner formed in her head than there was a soft voice at the doorway and Coszcatl slunk in with feline grace bringing with her the scent of a sweet amaranth perfume. Her poise, confidence and womanly curves combined like the ingredients in a magic potion to weave a powerful spell everywhere she went. The concubine took in the surroundings as though seeing them for the first time. Her dress was short, excessively short, thought Little Maize. She gave the impression of being all dimpled knees and lustrous black hair. Coszcatl looked down her pert nose at Ninth Girl before shooing her from the room.

Since Little Maize had arrived at Xiconoc's house, Coszcatl had treated her with a polite but distant formality. It wasn't the outright malice that Little Maize had been used to from White Moon but was a long way from sisterly affection. Little Maize looked out at the bustling street to avoid eye contact.

'You look well, My Lady.'

Coszcatl was bound by protocol to address Little Maize as her superior.

'You mean better,' said Little Maize without turning. There was a commotion from down the street, but her line of sight was blocked. She would have to wait until it got nearer to her position.

'Of course. You look much better now. Your wounds have healed quickly.'

'Hmmm...'

Coszcatl paused, waiting to see if there was more. When it became clear that Little Maize had nothing to add she battled on. 'You aren't happy?' she purred.

Little Maize snorted in derision but again made no attempt to elaborate.

Coszcatl sidled across the room and picked up a jade ornament from a ledge on the far wall. It was the carving of a monkey, hands over its head and its mouth open, screaming at the ceiling with its eyes turned up and almost hidden beneath stretched eyelids. The concubine stroked the carving sensuously with a pensive look on her face. 'Xiconoc has noticed too, you know,' she said after a pause.

At last Little Maize did answer, her voice like a sack of ash. 'Well, that's two of you with razor insight.'

'What do you want?' asked Coszcatl.

'What?'

'I said, what do you want? This marriage wasn't your idea, so what were you dreaming of before Xiconoc showed up at the Sisters of Penitence?'

Little Maize didn't want to say anything. She didn't know this woman, couldn't fathom her motives and yet there was a directness about her approach that disarmed her. No one had ever asked her what she wanted, not even Clawfoot.

'I want to be free.'

'You are free, My Lady! You're not a slave.'

'I might as well be. I can't choose where I want to live.'

'And you don't want to live here, with us?'

Little Maize gave the smallest shake of her head. Coszcatl had been expecting that answer and it was obvious that the conversation was heading just where she wanted it to go. Little Maize knew she would have to be careful. The conversation would almost certainly be repeated to Xiconoc word for word. Then it dawned on her that perhaps the two of them had a common goal after all: that of returning the household to the state it had been before her arrival. Coszcatl would want to be rid of her. The problem would be avoiding any number of options that worked for Coszcatl but that might have unpleasant outcomes for Little Maize.

'Maybe I can help,' said Coszcatl, lowering her voice. She put down the jade monkey and drew close.

Little Maize looked into Coszcatl's face that was so much more beautiful than her own, so much prettier than the one she'd seen in the mirror she had found and kept hidden in the Sisters of Penitence. But White Moon had taught her that beauty went hand-in-hand with malice. 'Why would you do that?'

Coszcatl smiled. 'Xiconoc is my master and my life. There is nothing I wouldn't do for him. He will not be happy while his wife is miserable and you will be unhappy as long as he is your husband, am I right?'

'Yes.'

'We could find a way to share him if you stayed.' Coszcatl put her hand on Little Maize's arm and withdrew it quickly when Little Maize shuddered.

'I don't want any part of him.' The woman's easy proximity was unsettling.

Coszcatl looked her in the eyes for a moment and then she said, 'Then I will find a way to help you.'

Little Maize gave a wan smile, hoping it looked appreciative.

'He can apply to have the marriage cancelled if you refuse to lie with him.'

'But look what he did to me the last time I displeased him! He'll kill me if I refuse.'

'Perhaps not, if I am there to stop him.'

Little Maize didn't want Coszcatl to be in Xiconoc's bedchamber with her and she didn't believe that she would be able to stop Xiconoc if he flew into a rage like last time. Her scepticism must have been obvious to Coszcatl because she changed track.

'Do not worry, My Lady. I will think of some other way this might be accomplished. There will be something. A cousin of mine lives in Azcapotzalco. I can arrange for him to shelter you for a while if you decide to…take a break.'

So that was it. Coszcatl *was* encouraging her to run away. Well, whatever plan she came up with, there was no way Little Maize was going to share it with Xiconoc's concubine, but that reminded Little Maize of something Tezozomoc had said. 'My Lady?' She didn't need such politeness when addressing Coszcatl, who was, after all, of lower status now, but it was a habit born of five years of subservience in the refuge. 'I…I heard that Xiconoc has a garden.'

Coszcatl was already at the door. She turned. 'Yes. Halfway between here and Xochimilco.'

'I would like to see it.'

'Really?' Coszcatl gave Little Maize a strange look as though she might have guessed what she was thinking. 'Well, that should be easy enough. The first plantings are done, so Xiconoc is arranging a tour for some of the members of the Great Council.'

'I'll ask him if I can go.'

'Are you interested in gardening?'

'I planted flowers sometimes at the Sisters of Penitence, but I used to have a dream of owning a farm.'

Coszcatl nodded. 'He'll be pleased that you're taking an interest.'

Little Maize watched her leave the room and then looked back out at the street again where a dozen men were hauling and pushing a large block of pale stone along. Two boys were alternately running from the back of the stone with logs and inserting them back under the stone at the front. The men were a tangle of sinew and sweat as they worked up the slight incline, no doubt heading towards the Great Temple and the interminable works there. As she watched, a small dog ran at the crew and began yipping at them and the stone that was progressing monstrously up the Street of Flowers. A long while later, when they had passed from her line of sight, she climbed down from the window and found the bowl of water that Ninth Child had fetched. She stripped off her fine cotton shift and used a clean cloth to scrub herself thoroughly. When she was clean she decided to explore Xiconoc's home. There were still nooks and crannies that she hadn't looked into. The place was as large as all of the dwellings that made up the Sisters of Penitence.

The atrium had already been swept and fresh flowers placed in urns at each of the four central pillars. It was late morning and this section of the house was very quiet. Little Maize knew most of the rooms around the atrium. They belonged to Xiconoc's four concubines and one was occupied by an elderly uncle who never came out of his room. Little Maize was curious about the room next to the bedchamber she shared with Xiconoc, until the night he beat her, since when he'd moved out and was sleeping with one or other of his concubines. No one had told her what the room was for and it was always empty. She paused in the open doorway. It seemed odd that such a large room was unoccupied. Low beds occupied each corner of the room and the furnishings were too sparse to suggest anyone was using the room permanently. Little Maize decided that it must be a guest room. The only indulgence was a large tapestry, richly embroidered with scenes of village life, hanging on the wall adjoining her own room. A breeze from an unseen window set it moving gently and yet it was nowhere near the window. She reached out and pulled the tapestry away from the wall revealing the source of the mysterious breeze. There were air vents in the wall. Perhaps they had been made to keep the master bedchamber cool. Their presence probably explained why this room was unused because they allowed a clear view into the room next door. Little Maize let go of the wall hanging and returned to her search.

Little Maize looked into the darkened room that was supposed to be home to Xiconoc's reclusive uncle, but the sharp tang of unwashed sweat drove her away. Leaving the atrium, she crossed the antechamber and did a tour of the courtyard before heading into the servants' quarters. Several women were busy in the kitchen making tortillas and sweet cakes and another was cooking chillies over an open fire. Little Maize could tell they were surprised to see her. She had mostly kept to her quarters since the beating. She nodded mutely and pushed on through the clouds of stinging smoke to the entrance on the far side of the room. Through the opening was a small courtyard with high walls stacked with woven baskets. A latticework roof of rushes kept the worst of the sun off the produce. The Master of the Household was trying to eject an itinerant tradesman from the small archway that led out on to the Street of Flowers.

There was another exit from the narrow storage yard, but unusually, this one had a door. She looked around surreptitiously, wondering whether the Master of the Household would object if she decided to investigate. It was clear from the heated tone of his voice that his entire focus was on the uncooperative visitor. She slipped through the door and into the dark, promptly tumbling down a short run of steps to a dank floor. Little Maize emitted a street curse that would have made a warrior blush and rubbed at her tender ankle while her eyes adjusted to the surroundings. She was in a long corridor that ran underneath Xiconoc's household. It was cool and Little Maize felt sure there was water close by, as though a stream was running directly beneath the floor. Black openings on either side of the corridor convinced her that this was a storeroom for more perishable foods that would not survive in the courtyard outside. During her days as a street urchin, begging and stealing on the streets, finding this storeroom would have been like stumbling on a vast treasure hoard, but she had no need of it now. She was about to limp up the steps when she heard a noise.

'Hello?' called Little Maize, wondering if one of the slaves was already down here on an errand or perhaps a dog had somehow found its way into the cellar; the noise had seemed too small to have been made by a person.

There was an answering cough, so Little Maize moved cautiously into the dark. At first she could see nothing in the black recesses of the room, but then a movement on the floor drew her attention to a pair of legs, cruelly bound. The stench of urine and sweat was enough to make her wrinkle her nose. She moved out of the doorframe to allow a little more of the feeble light from the passageway to penetrate and at last she could see the figure of a man, curled up on the floor, hands tied behind his back. He was naked and caked in dirt. Little Maize couldn't make out his features and then realised it was because he had been beaten. His face had disappeared under a puffy mask of bruises and dried blood and he'd been gagged. This was an interesting development. Little Maize's pulse quickened. Nosing around Xiconoc's home – she couldn't think of it as her own – had given her a sense of independence that she hadn't felt for a long time.

Unsure why she was doing it, Little Maize untied the cloth and pulled it from between his teeth.

'Water, please!'

It was the voice of a young man and Little Maize suddenly remembered what the slave girl, Ninth Child, had told her about the attack on Xiconoc.

'Who are you?' she breathed, too scared to approach him.

'Axayacatl,' was the hoarse response.

It was the intruder and now Little Maize wished she had quizzed Ninth Child further.

'Please help. My father will offer you a huge reward.' Axayacatl winced at the effort. His lips cracked and he coughed feebly.

Still Little Maize held her distance. 'Why did you attack Lord Xiconoc?'

'He's a monster.'

'He's my husband.' The words were out before she even realised what she'd said. It had only been stated as a matter of fact, but it had sounded defensive.

Axayacatl moaned and his head slumped to the floor. Little Maize got to her knees and scraped the matted hair from Axayacatl's face. He had passed out. She sprang up again and went in search of water. There was a half-filled jug in the storage room next door. She brought it back to Axayacatl and propped his head up on her lap and dripped water onto his lips until he awoke. When he had drunk some of the water, she spoke softly to him.

'Why did you attack Xiconoc?'

Axayacatl hesitated, perhaps uncertain about speaking openly with her. 'He has brought shame on my family.'

'Why? What has he done?'

'Not just him...my mother as well.'

Little Maize waited. She could see that Axayacatl needed to tell someone.

'I followed her,' he continued. 'She leaves the house after dark and my father does nothing to stop her, so I followed her to this place. She was with another of my father's women and the guards let them in. I couldn't very well follow, so I climbed in over the roof.'

Axayacatl paused to take another drink of water but judged it poorly. It slopped over his chin and he must have breathed some in because he had a coughing attack. Eventually he recovered enough to continue.

'I didn't find them for a while, but when I did...she was tied down to the bed. Your new husband and one of his concubines were taking their pleasure.'

Little Maize heard the words, but a few heartbeats elapsed before she grasped what he had said. 'Wait!' she gasped. 'Your mother...she is Xiconoc's niece.'

'Yes.'

'I don't believe you.'

'I...wait!' He gripped her wrist tightly, trying to pull himself up to get a better look at her. 'You're the one he just married, the one from the refuge.'

'Yes, that's right.'

Axayacatl released Little Maize and slumped back, as though disappointed. 'You haven't known him for long then. You don't know what he's like.'

'I don't believe you,' repeated Little Maize. Xiconoc had abused her and beaten her and although she knew that was wrong, the possibility that he was sleeping with his niece, Tezozomoc's wife, was too implausible.

'You know what the worst of it is?' said Axayacatl, ignoring her protest. 'I think he gets people in to watch. Other depraved members of the merchant classes or the nobility.'

'How do you know that?'

'I found the room, next to his bedchamber, the one with the holes in the wall. That's how I saw them. Come on! Don't tell me you haven't seen them!'

Little Maize's hand flew to her mouth. That was what the holes were! She was appalled. It had never occurred to her that they were anything other than for ventilation. Perhaps Coszcatl and the other concubines had already watched her and Xiconoc together. Perhaps he had already invited some of his sick friends to watch him take her.

'You see?' said Axayacatl. 'You understand what I'm saying.'

'You saw it happen,' Little Maize blurted out. 'You could go before a tribunal or tell Lord Moctezuma. He would listen to you. You're of noble blood.' She imagined Xiconoc's punishment would be severe, perhaps even death. The judges would defer to Moctezuma in a case involving his family, but the tlatoani would not be lenient. It was by his decree that the death penalty for adultery had been introduced for the nobility, to set an example, so it was said.

'So you can see why I was so angry.'

'Yes,' breathed Little Maize. 'And you tried to kill him.'

'Yes.' Axayacatl was defiant. 'Yes, and I would do it again!'

'And Coszcatl would stick you with a spear again,' goaded Little Maize.

Axayacatl ignored the jibe. 'You have to help me escape.'

Escape! The word sounded like paradise. 'We'll go together. I don't want to stay here with Xiconoc. What do we do?'

'First, you're going to untie me,' said Axayacatl. 'Then you're going to help me kill him.'

It was at that moment that the door to the storehouse crashed open. Footsteps hurried along the passageway preceded by the light of a torch. Then Xiconoc's men surged in.

Chapter 25
The Jungles of Totonaca

Drizzle blanketed the jungle and a grey mist seeped between the tree trunks. Soft earth and leaf mulch oozed between Jaguar's toes as he paused to check in which direction they were headed. Moctezuma's sons were unusually quiet, but Jaguar supposed that had something to do with the apparent threat to their father's life. Jaguar shook his head to shed the droplets that beaded his face. The marsh where Moctezuma had gone hunting would be downriver. Holds the Sun beckoned to them from a clump of tall reeds. He had gone ahead to scout for firm ground.

'This way,' said Jaguar and set off at a steady trot. Iquehuacatzin and Mahchimaleh made no complaint; neither was very fit. Although they fought with the warriors in the most important and the ceremonial battles, they were not constantly at war or training like Jaguar. Creeping Night brought up the rear.

After a while, the ground became even softer underfoot and the five men found themselves splashing through more and more pools of water. Jaguar noticed the change in the trees too. Mighty, single-trunk behemoths soaring hundreds of feet into high canopy had given way to lush, lower-growing vegetation and fruit trees. They passed through a stand of tzapotl trees that were already heavy with the first crop of the year. Half-eaten fruits were scattered everywhere, evidence that a troop of monkeys had been feasting here recently. Jaguar twisted several of the fruit off as he passed by and shoved them into the loose cloth pouch that was slung over his shoulder. Beyond the tzapotl grove lay a carpet of lilies and thick water weed swamped the trunks of the shrubs and trees that lived at the edge of the swamp. Jaguar didn't need a guide to tell him that the water level was rising.

'How are we going to find the tlatoani in all this?' said Holds the Sun, looking across the expanse of water, tangled roots and dripping foliage.

'How do we know he's still here?' added Creeping Night.

'The group can't be far ahead of us,' answered Jaguar. 'We can travel faster than them. Also, we know that they're following the main watercourse.'

'Don't worry. He won't leave until he's caught a crocodile,' said Iquehuacatzin confidently.

Mahchimaleh shook his head.' This place is immense! We need a faster way to travel.'

'It would be quicker in a boat,' said his brother. Iquehuacatzin was scanning the reeds nervously. 'Safer too if the stories we've heard about this place are true.'

Jaguar laughed. 'We're making so much noise that even the crocodiles will steer clear of us. You're right though, we need a canoe.'

After a brief discussion they decided to continue in the same direction, hugging the riverbank where a village was more likely to be found and hopefully a canoe as well. The decision proved to be a good one. A short time later, they arrived at a settlement of forty or fifty dwellings and the villagers, who were even well disposed to strangers, engaged them in animated chatter about a wealthy ruler who had passed through the day before, requisitioning supplies and canoes until the village had been all but emptied out. The head man was pondering what to do with the pouch of gold, a heavy wooden statuette of Huitzilopochtli and half a dozen beautifully crafted swords when Jaguar, Iquehuacatzin, Mahchimaleh and the two Jaguar Knights were presented to him. Jaguar asked whether there was another boat they might borrow or purchase. The people here spoke an unfamiliar Mayan dialect, but Jaguar understood enough to work out that the only serviceable craft had already been taken. The headman then pointed further downstream and spoke of a fisherman who lived around the next bend of the river who might be able to help. Jaguar thanked him and the five men took their leave.

The narrow path through dense vegetation petered out and the way became more arduous, so it was growing dark by the time they located the fisherman's hut. The family's dwelling was a circular, one-room shack that looked on the verge of collapse. Its walls were made of decaying latticework reed panels plastered over with crumbling dried mud. Drunken-looking driftwood poles supported a thin, conical roof of palm leaves with strictly limited weatherproof properties. It looked as though a hearty sneeze would have toppled the whole sorry structure into the swollen river. The embankment of trampled mud on which the family had built their home included one other dilapidated structure that appeared to be a crude shelter for animals. It consisted of a single large frame of broad, brown leaves woven together that was canted over at an angle.

Jaguar managed to question the old man who had a better grasp of Nahuatl than his fellow villagers. He did have a boat but was in no mood to let it go, it being his livelihood.

'We should just take it,' grumbled Mahchimaleh. 'We're wasting time.' He didn't seem to care if the fisherman understood what he was saying.

'Shut up and let me talk,' snapped Jaguar, too angry to use the polite form of address. Mahchimaleh could not be allowed to do anything rash again. 'I do this kind of thing all the time. It's why I'm in Tlacaelel's service. We may need to come back this way and they won't take kindly to us if we harm them or steal their property.'

Mahchimaleh grunted irritably but left Jaguar to continue.

'These good noblemen are just looking for their father. He's here on a hunting trip, but we're worried for his safety. This is why we need to borrow your boat.' Jaguar paused to let the fisherman speak, but he was looking down at the floor, so Jaguar continued. 'We will pay you for the inconvenience...compensate you for lost catches. How does that sound?' Jaguar took out three coiled gold wires that he carried with him for such occasions and held them out. He caught the interest that flared in the fisherman's eyes and the way it was swiftly suppressed.

'It is a good boat, My Lord,' replied the fisherman. 'How can I be sure you return it? If you don't return, what do I do?'

'Are you suggesting we would steal it?' rasped Mahchimaleh.

'No, My Lord, but there is much danger on the river. Rapids, snakes, big crocodiles, if you have a problem...' He left the sentence unfinished and shrugged.

Iquehuacatzin stabbed a finger at the fisherman. 'Buy another one.'

'With what?' He pointed at the crumbling walls and leaky roof of his house. 'I am a humble fisherman. All my family owns is here for you to see. I could not buy a new boat.'

'What if we leave you enough so that you can buy a new one if we don't return?' said Jaguar. He offered up his last two strands of gold wire. 'If we bring your boat back, you give these back to me.'

'Your idea is acceptable, My Lord, but the amount is not. New canoes are not instantly available, especially if, as you say, there are none left in the village. I would need to feed my family for many days while a new one is built.'

Mahchimaleh towered over the fisherman, fists clenching and unclenching. 'You worthless son of pus-soaked dog! We will not tolerate your impudence any longer. You have no idea of your station—'

'Stop!' cried Jaguar and put a hand on Mahchimaleh's shoulder. He didn't want a repeat of the previous incident with the guide. The princes were used to getting their way and had almost certainly never had to negotiate to obtain anything they wanted. 'Lord Mahchimaleh, please have patience. Our host is simply trying to secure the best possible trade for the sake of his family. This is normal market-stall haggling, nothing more. We make another offer, we talk a little while longer and eventually we come to a mutually satisfactory arrangement.'

'Fine,' spat Mahchimaleh. He looked down at the fisherman. 'Understand that if we return and you are not here, or cannot repay us, I will hunt you down and pull your guts out while your children watch.'

The fisherman held his hands up. 'Please, My Lord...I meant no offence. Your friend is correct though. I only want what's fair for my family. That boat is our livelihood and their construction is a skilled business, conducted by craftsmen who are very much in demand. Be assured that my boat is yours to take but for a little additional security.'

Iquehuacatzin leaned forward. 'Well, Jaguar? What are you waiting for? Up your offer and we can finish the deal. I tire of this.'

'I cannot, Lord Iquehuacatzin. I have nothing more to offer him,' said Jaguar.

'What?!' exclaimed Iquehuacatzin and Mahchimaleh simultaneously.

'I'm a warrior, My Lord. I didn't come here equipped for trading.'

'What about your men?' Iquehuacatzin pointed at the Jaguar Knights.

'They brought nothing of value. I hold our emergency reserves and I have already offered them as the price of borrowing the canoe.'

Iquehuacatzin came over and stood face-to-face with Jaguar. He looked livid. 'What exactly are you planning to offer then?'

Jaguar's gaze was steady as he looked into Iquehuacatzin's eyes. 'It was your idea as much as mine to come here, Lord Iquehuacatzin. If we are to catch up with your father, I suggest you offer the man one of your ear plugs.'

Iquehuacatzin looked as though he'd been slapped in the face. 'You want me to offer up my personal property?'

'You will get it back when we bring the canoe back, My Lord.'

'I don't care!' Iquehuacatzin's tone was petulant. 'They are mine and I will not risk them.'

'Fine,' replied Jaguar. 'Then in the morning we will return to Ahuilizapan.'

'No.' It was Mahchimaleh. 'In the morning, we will take the boat and if anyone tries to stop us, we will kill them.'

'I cannot allow that, Lord Mahchimaleh.' Jaguar moved to put himself between the prince and the fisherman. 'It's dishonourable and it goes against all our training. Either we do a fair deal with this man or my men and I will stand with him.' Jaguar was keenly aware of how much stronger Mahchimaleh was. He was the same build as Two Sign but a little stouter around the middle. He had a good reputation on the battlefield too, but he was a nobleman. Jaguar had seen his kind before. They shouted and blustered, but they were never as quick with the sword as with their mouths; at least he had to hope so.

'Wait!' called Iquehuacatzin. He was angry with his brother and with Jaguar. 'Here.' He twisted the plug from one of his ears and slapped it into Jaguar's hand. 'Take it. Let's just end this and move on.' His change of heart was complete and with it, his interest in the dispute. He pointed at the fisherman. 'You! I trust this piece will secure your boat for our party. The finest gold from Oaxaca.'

The fisherman inspected the proffered payment and nodded his consent.

'And you!' Iquehuacatzin jabbed a finger at Jaguar. 'You will find a replacement for me if this man fails to return it. Now, if everyone is done squabbling I suggest we find somewhere to sleep. It's getting dark.'

'May we stay here for the night?' Jaguar asked the fisherman. 'We'll be gone first light.'

The man looked agitated. He knew his guests were of noble blood, at least some of them, and was worried about his meagre homestead.

'May we sleep there?' Jaguar asked the fisherman, pointing at the sloping thatch.

'It's for drying fish,' said the fisherman, looking puzzled.

'Doesn't matter,' said Jaguar. 'As long as it keeps the worst of the rain off.'

Iquehuacatzin grabbed Jaguar's arm. 'I'm not sleeping under that!'

'Why not? We all slept on the forest floor last night.'

'Last night we had no choice. Now there is a hut to sleep in.'

'But it belongs to the family, Lord Iquehuacatzin,' replied Jaguar.

Mahchimaleh leaned in. 'I say we kill them and take their filthy hut and their canoe.'

The fisherman looked scared. He moved in front of his wife.

Jaguar rounded on Mahchimaleh. 'We are not at war with these people! They are not fighters. Did you learn nothing from the warrior code school? Assaulting unarmed civilians, women and children is strictly forbidden.'

Before they could argue the point further, the fisherman pointed at his home and made it clear that his family would move out. Jaguar steadfastly refused, but Holds the Sun intervened and brokered a compromise with Iquehuacatzin's help. The princes would occupy one half of the hut, while the fisherman, his wife and daughter would take the other half. His two young sons would sleep outside with Jaguar and the two knights under the shelter for drying fish.

The fisherman appeared to have forgiven Mahchimaleh his threats because he insisted everyone share the evening meal with his family. A short while later, everyone sat cross-legged in the tiny dwelling, while the fisherman's wife produced a catfish stew that made a warming, if meagre, meal. Jaguar and his men contributed small strips of dried dog meat from their provisions to which Jaguar also added the fruit he had gathered earlier in the day. There was little talk until the fisherman brought out a pipe, which he lit and passed around for his guests.

When Iquehuacatzin passed the pipe to him, Jaguar took a shallow breath and let the smoke roll over his tongue before drawing it deep into his lungs. It was good tobacco, not like the stale stuff that was so common in Ahuilizapan. A cool sensation crept around Jaguar's chest and ran down his spine. He took another pull then passed the pipe on, marvelling as his limbs grew light, as though they wanted to drift away. Holds the Sun declined to partake, but Creeping Night sucked on the pipe so greedily he nearly set the contents ablaze. Mahchimaleh peered into the remnants to check there was enough left for him and then grunted his approval when he tried it. The fisherman smiled faintly. Iquehuacatzin, who had also inhaled deeply, had a broad grin on his face.

'This is an interesting blend, brother. We should find out where our friend gets his supply and corner it for ourselves, eh?

Maybe we can steal a march on our uncle's trading activities for once.'

'Will be popular in Tenochtitlan,' agreed Mahchimaleh from behind a curtain of blue smoke.

'Where does this come from?' asked Iquehuacatzin. 'And where did you learn to speak our language so well?'

The fisherman spread his hands. 'The tobacco comes from the hills to the north and as to your language, I travelled much before I...' The fisherman looked back at his family who were huddled in the corner behind him. His wife smiled. '...before I settled down. I lived in Texcoco for half a year and tried to make a living there, but it didn't work out.'

'What happened?'

'I did not know how to fish a big lake like that.' He shook his head sadly. 'It is craziness. Where to put the nets so fish swim into them? In a river, the fish run where the current suits and they rest where it is gentle. Understand the current and you know where to place the nets or wait with spear. The lake...' Here the fisherman made an expansive gesture with his arms and shook his head sadly.

'So you came back home,' said Jaguar.

'Yes. Also, Texcoco, too many people. Everyone move quickly and don't talk.' He refilled the pipe and said something in guttural words that Jaguar didn't understand. His daughter scurried outside and brought back a twig from the fire to relight the pipe. The fisherman tossed the twig through the open doorway; the fiery end looped a ribbon of orange through the darkness. 'I came back to where I grew up. Why did you come here?' he asked quietly.

'He already told you,' Iquehuacatzin pointed at Jaguar. 'We came in search of our father.'

'No. I mean, why did all of you come to this area? Your father didn't come all this way from Tenochtitlan for a day or two hunting.'

Jaguar glanced at Iquehuacatzin and Mahchimaleh. He wondered how the princes would react to this line of questioning. The last thing they needed was another argument now that they were all settled. There was nothing disrespectful about the fisherman's tone of voice, but Moctezuma's sons were unused to being questioned. He needn't have worried. The pipe smoke had soothed them all and Iquehuacatzin was smiling benignly at their host.

'The Mexica are destined to conquer this land.'

The fisherman made no reply. Instead he bent over the pipe, refilling it. When he was done, he lit it and passed it round again. Jaguar declined to partake, but when it had done the rounds, the fisherman took a deep drag on his pipe.

'Well,' he said, aiming a plume of smoke at the tatty roof over their heads. 'I'm honoured that you chose my home as your new palace.'

Iquehuacatzin looked at his brother for a moment and then burst out laughing. Mahchimaleh grinned too.

When he was sure that the mood of bonhomie was genuine and that the brothers would behave themselves, Jaguar left the confines of the shack to prepare a bed for himself under the crude shelter outside. It stank of fish but looked comfortable enough. Jaguar threw himself down on the freshly cut leaves set aside by the fisherman's wife. For a while, he listened to the murmur of voices from the hut, tensing every time a voice was raised or whenever there was an uncomfortably long silence that might signal the start of another dispute. The last thing he remembered were scuffling noises, which might have been others joining him under the shelter, but whether it was the two Jaguar Knights or the fisherman's sons, he could not have said.

Chapter 26
The Jungles of Totonaca

In the morning, the five men packed themselves into the fisherman's canoe. Jaguar watched the waterline rise dangerously high against the hull. He needn't have worried; the craft was very stable. Holds the Sun and Creeping Night paddled downriver in the direction that the villagers had reported Moctezuma's hunting party going. The river was roiling brown and had subsumed large portions of the surrounding jungle, massively increasing the search area. Several times, they were forced to paddle across the broad, turbulent flood to check out what looked like canoes on the opposite side, only to discover that it was yet more flotsam. By the middle of the afternoon, Jaguar had convinced himself that they would not locate Moctezuma's expedition, so he was more surprised than anyone when they did find it.

Jaguar and Mahchimaleh were taking a turn at paddling when they rounded a bend in the river and spotted a plume of smoke rising above the far bank. There they saw two members of Moctezuma's personal bodyguard standing watch. As the guards on the riverbank followed the progress of the canoe, a third figure emerged from the foliage behind them. Two things were immediately obvious to Jaguar; from his bulk and by the way he moved, the third man on the riverbank was unmistakeably Two Sign and it looked as though he was stalking the two guards. The scene didn't make sense, but natural instincts suppressed Jaguar's desire to call out a warning. He glanced over his shoulder and saw that Iquehuacatzin and Mahchimaleh were also watching the proceedings intently. Jaguar stopped paddling and allowed the river to carry them forwards. On the bank, Two Sign reached the first of Moctezuma's guards. The big warrior put his arm around the man's neck and gently lowered him to the ground. Two Sign had broken the guard's neck, but the second one must have caught a glimpse of it out of the corner of his eye. His shout carried across the water. He reached for his sword, but Two Sign pounced on him. The two men wrestled on the ground briefly, while Jaguar watched, utterly baffled.

'Is that Two Sign attacking the tlatoani's bodyguard?' asked Creeping Night.

'It…looks like that,' agreed Jaguar.

He watched the big warrior rise over the lifeless body of his opponent and look their way. Something in his pose struck fear into Jaguar's heart. Something was wrong and whatever it was, he knew he had to get there as quickly as possible. The canoe was in the middle of the river, its current already threatening to sweep them past the landing site and its paddles were not suited to propelling five grown men against such a torrent. Jaguar gauged their trajectory and made up his mind. He handed his paddle to Holds the Sun.

'Get this boat to the riverbank as fast as you can. I'm going after Two Sign. Come and find us, but make sure you keep these two safe, yes?'

Jaguar didn't wait for an answer. He stood up and hurled himself into the swirling muck and began swimming, long powerful strokes. He checked over his shoulder once and saw Mahchimaleh standing up, trying to rebalance the canoe. Ahead of him, Two Sign turned and ran into the trees. The current slowed as Jaguar neared the bank, but it still carried him two hundred paces downstream of where Two Sign had been standing before he could pull himself ashore. He'd had to leave his sword in the canoe for fear it would drown him, so he was forced to follow the edge of the river back to where Two Sign had murdered the tlatoani's men. There, he snatched up a sword from one of the fallen men and charged in the direction he'd seen Two Sign go. Throwing caution to the wind, he surged through the bushes and careened into a clearing where another incomprehensible scene met his eyes. Moctezuma and six of his Grey Privy Knights were backed up against a small copse and were trying to fend off a savage assault from Two Sign and three others. Four men lay dead and a fifth was set to join them shortly, crumpling as arterial spray surged from his ruined arm.

Moctezuma called out, his usually regal voice rent with urgency. 'Two Sign has gone mad! Stop him.'

The tlatoani was right. Three men fought beside Two Sign and they all looked equally intent on reaching him. Jaguar remembered his last practice bout with the Eagle Knight and recalled the ferocity with which Two Sign had set about him, but this was more than a test, more than just a practice session; this was an attack with deadly intent and it didn't make sense. Here was Two Sign, an Eagle Knight, sworn to protect the tlatoani and yet there could be no doubt that he would slay the ruler of the Mexica people if he could get close enough. Jaguar had no time to work out what was going on. The choice was between duty or friendship.

Between Jaguar and the skirmish lay the partially skinned carcass of a crocodile. It was the largest creature he had ever seen. The fighting must have broken out just as the monster was being unmade. Jaguar looked at the pale pink flesh and tracery of purple veins, picturing Moctezuma lying dead beside it, and in that instant he made his choice. To side with Two Sign was to side with chaos. Moctezuma was Huitzilopochtli's appointed ruler and all Mexica knights took an oath to protect him. Using the scaly tail of the crocodile as a springboard, he leapt for the protective circle that shielded the tlatoani and took his place alongside the Grey Privy Knights.

'Your sons are with me, Lord Moctezuma,' he called out.' They will be here shortly along with two Jaguar Knights.'

News of reinforcements did nothing to dent the enthusiasm of the attackers. A young man surged in with a spear, hoping to stab Jaguar in the guts. He turned the point aside, pushing it down with his sword and only noticed the young man's other hand slicing in towards his neck at the last moment, a dagger glinting in the sun. He caught the hand and pushed it up so that it just grazed his head. The young man let go of his spear and wrapped his fingers around Jaguar's wrist. Suddenly the two were locked together, face-to-face. Jaguar recognised the youth as the priest who Shield of Gold had gone to talk to: Clawfoot! The surprise distracted him and nearly cost him his life. His defensive hold weakened and Clawfoot pushed the thin blade to within a whisker of his throat. He stared into his attacker's cold black eyes and saw death.

Instinct kicked in, driven by the need to survive. The sick sensation he had felt at the thought of facing Two Sign faded as he focused on the task in hand. He used his strength to force Clawfoot away and kicked him in the stomach. Clawfoot tripped over the remains of the crocodile and sprawled backwards, but Jaguar had no time to follow up because another attacker leaped into the gap. Out of the corner of his eye, Jaguar saw Two Sign dash out the brains of one of Moctezuma's guards and his hopes began to fade. How many times had he watched Two Sign wade deep into the enemy lines, seemingly outnumbered and still emerge triumphant?' Savagery' did not capture the Eagle Knight's controlled style of fighting. It was too elegant for that word to do it justice, but in the end, there was no denying the butchery that it wrought.

Jaguar's second attacker was lithe. He had a necklace of finger bones that rattled as he leapt forward, chopping with a mid-length sword. Jaguar was forced back a pace and then another. He parried twice and blocked a third blow that twisted his wrist painfully, but there was no time to waste; giving ground had allowed the man with the necklace an opportunity to strike out at the unprotected flank of one of Moctezuma's men. Jaguar hurled himself forward and jabbed low. The blunt end of his sword caught the man in the stomach. The breath hissed between his teeth and he grimaced in pain but managed to stay upright. Jaguar repeated the movement again and when his opponent stepped back, Jaguar followed him in, hooked his foot behind the other man's ankle and pulled. The man hopped forward, trying to stay on his feet, but Jaguar was already alongside him, pushing past, the glass edge of his sword pressed against the man's stomach. He pulled the sword, wrenching it up and through his victim with a powerful roll of the shoulders. There was a grating sound as the finger-bone necklace was crushed beneath its falling owner. There was no need to check if he would stand again.

Now there was an opportunity for Jaguar to move closer to Moctezuma who was sheltering behind his last three men. It wasn't much of a defence against the frightening onslaught that was Two Sign. They were tough, experienced veterans, legends in their own right, but age was not on their side and whereas the commander of the Eagle Knights was fit from recent battles, the Grey Privy Knights' gruelling campaigns during the reign of Itzcoatl were a distant memory. They were tiring badly. Jaguar recognised the one nearest to him. He had seen him many times at the tlatoani's palace and his family lived in the Teopan quarter, not far from him.

'Coyotl!' bellowed Jaguar. 'Get the tlatoani to a canoe and get him out of here now! The rest of us will hold them here.'

The Grey Privy Knight checked over his shoulder and saw Moctezuma's pale face nod once. A moment later the pair of them dashed off. Jaguar saw movement out of the corner of his eye as Two Sign tried to cut off their escape. He moved to intercept, but another of the Grey Privy Knights beat him to it and charged into Two Sign, shoving him aside and bringing the big man to the ground. By the time Two Sign had disentangled himself, the last of the tlatoani's men had retreated to block off the trail that their ruler had taken. Pursuit through the surrounding jungle was impossible. Jaguar stood beside the last man.

'We hold this spot!' he shouted. 'No one gets past.'

They would not hold Two Sign and his remaining accomplice for long. Jaguar cursed his own Jaguar Knights, Holds the Sun and Creeping Night, wondering why they had not already arrived. They would have helped to even the score.

There was no time to speculate further. The young priest who Jaguar had knocked over was back. He had recovered a sword from one of the fallen men. Jaguar's irritation flared. He needed to watch Two Sign to prevent him breaking through and pursuing Moctezuma. He parried Clawfoot's new attack. Their blades met with a grinding screech. The young man's easy fluidity marked him out as a natural fighter, but it was obvious that the youth was unused to wielding the heavy sword of Mexica warriors. Jaguar rained a succession of blows down on him, forcing him back a little at a time until the young priest was up against a tree. Jaguar feinted right and went left, but Clawfoot saw the ruse and met the sword as it swept up and across; it smashed awkwardly into the pommel of Jaguar's weapon. The swords jarred violently and Jaguar's was torn from his grasp. Pain seared his hand where the weapon had been wrenched free, but it was clear that Clawfoot had also suffered from the blow. He hadn't dropped his sword, but he clutched it loosely in a lifeless hand, agony stretched across his face. To his right, Jaguar could see that the tlatoani's man was in trouble; he needed help and quickly. Jaguar scooped up a discarded spear and as his hand closed about its shaft, he realised that the little finger on his sword hand had been sheared off right down to the knuckle. *Nothing I can do about it now*, he thought and hurled the spear as hard as his damaged hand would allow. Clawfoot saw the danger. He ducked and threw his left hand up protectively. There was a solid thump as the spear embedded itself in the tree, firmly pinning Clawfoot's hand.

Jaguar turned just in time to see Two Sign cut down the last of the Grey Privy Knights. From beneath a blood-streaked face, the big man swept his gaze across the scene until his eyes met Jaguar's. The only two men standing. There was a moment's hesitation and Jaguar almost thought his old friend was going to speak, but instead, he spun around and set off in the direction that Moctezuma had fled. Clawfoot was struggling feebly to get free. There was no time to finish him off. Jaguar recovered his sword and set off after Two Sign. He could not be allowed to reach the tlatoani.

The pain in Jaguar's wounded hand blossomed like a flame in summer kindling. He glanced at the damage once as he sprinted off in pursuit. There was no stump. Clawfoot's blade had sheared through the first joint. The flow of blood hadn't been bad at first, but it was seeping steadily now. He would have to bandage it later, but there was no time now. Jaguar gritted his teeth and pumped his arms and legs harder, dodging between the trees, hurdling fallen branches and ducking under hanging vines. Suddenly, he burst out of the tree line and caught sight of Two Sign, who was standing looking out over the river. There was no indication that the big man had seen him.

'You lost, Two Sign,' Jaguar panted. 'Whatever your game was, he got away.'

Two Sign gazed out over the swirling brown current for what seemed like an eternity until at last he spoke, his gravelly voice already calm after the fight.

'He's not safe yet.'

'What in the name of Xipe Totec's festering flesh are you doing?'

Two Sign looked at Jaguar at last. His face was drawn and serious. 'He has to die...and so must you, Jaguar. I'm sorry, but I cannot allow you to tell of what you've seen.' The Eagle Knight climbed to the top of the riverbank and hefted his sword.

Jaguar was about to ask his old friend why, what had driven him to this, but beyond the Eagle Knight he saw Iquehuacatzin and Mahchimaleh loping along the shoreline coming from downstream. Finally! Their canoe must have been swept some distance downstream if it had taken this long for them to make their way back. Holds the Sun and Creeping Night were nowhere to be seen, so perhaps they'd come across the tlatoani and were helping him to safety, which just meant that his sons were in danger now.

'Watch out!' Jaguar called before they could get too close. 'This man attacked your father.' The brothers ignored his warning and drew closer and Jaguar began to hope again. The Eagle Knight was fearsome, but Moctezuma's sons were fresh. Mahchimaleh would be particularly handy. Jaguar remembered how he had picked up their guide and casually tossed him into the sinkhole. Working together, the three of them might even be able to overpower Two Sign and get him back alive.

'Why did you do it?' asked Jaguar, trying to buy time for the others to approach.

Two Sign had turned slightly, caught between Jaguar and Moctezuma's brothers. He spat. 'You wouldn't understand.'

'Tell me anyway.'

'I had no choice,' said Two Sign. His voice was flat. 'I got too heavily in debt.'

'Gambling?' asked Jaguar.

Two Sign nodded. 'Like a fool, I thought I was in control. I lost often, but many times I won and told myself that I could fix things, if only I could win one big bet...really high stakes. That dream fell apart at the ullamaliztli tournament last year.'

'I was there,' said Jaguar. 'We watched it together.' He remembered the game. It had been a thrilling end to a two-day festival. Two Sign had slunk off, leaving Jaguar to celebrate with Last Medicine and some of the other warriors.

'I lost everything that day and more besides. I borrowed heavily, certain that Katal's team would win. I owed three noble families after that. They sent the judges after me. Have you any idea what they would have done to me, Commander of the Eagle Knights?'

'Public humiliation, stripped of your rank, sold into servitude?' Jaguar shrugged. 'What happened then?'

Two Sign looked defeated. 'One of the judges took me aside and told me he knew someone who could help...someone who might cover my debts. If only I had known the price he would extract in payment.'

'Surely Tlacaelel would help. Come! Let's return to Ahuilizapan and speak with him.'

Two Sign gave a hollow laugh. 'It's far too late for that.'

'You don't want to fight the three of us,' said Jaguar. He shook his head. 'Come peacefully. There's been enough bloodshed today.'

'No,' growled the big man. 'There hasn't been enough.'

Iquehuacatzin and Mahchimaleh had come to a stop just out of range of the Eagle Knight.

'Look. You are caught—' Jaguar began but was immediately interrupted by Iquehuacatzin.

'Is it done, Two Sign?'

'No, My Lord, it is not. Your father escaped in a canoe.'

'He's still alive?' Iquehuacatzin's voice was incredulous. 'You let the tlatoani escape an attempt on his life and to make things worse, this idiot witnessed it!'

Jaguar listened to the exchange with growing disbelief and horror. The brothers knew of the assassination attempt. Worse, they may even have planned it! Now he was worried for Holds the Sun and Creeping Night. He recalled seeing Mahchimaleh standing over them in the canoe.

'You? You are part of this?' he exclaimed.

Iquehuacatzin just sneered.

'What have you done to my men?' said Jaguar.

'They are with Tlaloc now, in the belly of the river,' answered Mahchimaleh. 'We would have been here sooner,' he continued, explaining to Two Sign, 'but they put up something of a fight.'

Jaguar looked at Iquehuacatzin who he had joked with not so long ago about hurling stones at the bird-men. They had laughed together. The nobleman looked back at him and now his thoughts were clear. Jaguar turned on his heel and tore off into the jungle. Over his shoulder he could just hear Iquehuacatzin's roar.

'Kill him! Kill him now and then we go after the tlatoani!'

Jaguar ran as he had never run before. Terror lent him strength. He felt confident that he could outrun Two Sign. The Eagle Knight would be tired from the fight and his size would be a disadvantage in the jungle. Iquehuacatzin would be more dangerous; Jaguar had seen him on the ball court, so he knew how fit he was. Mahchimaleh was a veteran who had taken dozens of captives and he had a fresh pair of legs. Jaguar tried to keep the panic down so he could concentrate on threading his way through the thick vegetation and boggy ground at full speed.

Chapter 27 – Tenochtitlan

Axayacatl groaned and blinked at the grass stalks that tickled his eyes. His head hurt and his right arm was lifeless where he had been lying on it, pressing it into the dew-soaked grass. The acrid stench of vomit assailed his nostrils and he realised he was lying in a puddle of his own sick. He remembered Xiconoc's men forcing quantities of octli down his throat and now that he thought of it, he could smell that too, a rich, sweet smell. He rolled onto his back and stared up at the pale grey light that suffused the heavens. At least he could open his bruised eye now. Xiconoc could congratulate himself on having two very enthusiastic guards in his employ. They had worked him over very thoroughly and then had a second go at it once he had been discovered with the girl. Axayacatl groaned again. Perhaps the pain would go away if he lay with his eyes closed for a while longer.

What had they done with Little Maize? The guards had been cautious at first, aware that she was the mistress of the house, but when they realised that she had been in the process of untying the knots that bound him, they had taken a more belligerent tone. The master had been very specific about their 'guest'; he was to be made to look like a drunkard and dumped out in the chinampa somewhere far from the city centre. It was a warning; Axayacatl understood that. They could just as easily have dumped him somewhere where the city watch would have found him and then his punishment for unsanctioned consumption of octli would have been severe. The thought of the two thugs force-feeding him alcohol made him gag again.

Axayacatl was disappointed to find that his lying-down-and-waiting-until-it-all-went-away plan wasn't working; everything still hurt. He sat up and yelped as the wound in his back complained at the sudden movement. After a while the world stopped spinning, so he made his way down to the water's edge where he had a drink and cleaned himself up. The sun rose and canoes began to make their way along the canals. Axayacatl hitched a ride with one that was heading towards Cuepopan but changed his mind as they got in sight of the family home.

'Drop me here,' said Axayacatl to the oarsman. He couldn't stand the thought of facing his parents. He needed to speak to someone else. 'You go the rest of the way and take a message for me,' he said. 'My parents will repay you for your trouble. Let them know that Axayacatl is well. Tell them that I have gone hunting with my cousin Zolin from Texcoco and I will return in a day or two.'

One of his old teachers, a mentor from his days in Calmecac, would have listened patiently, then challenged Axayacatl to reason his own way out of his troubles. Sadly the old man had passed away and now the only other person he could think of was the ruler of Texcoco. Nezahualcoyotl was known for his wisdom and had spoken kindly to him on the night of Quauhtlatoa's funeral. The only problem would be getting an audience.

A short time later, Axayacatl found a ferryman who recognised him. The boatman was one of the many who worked the route between Tenochtitlan and Texcoco and proved to be a good source of gossip.

'Do you know if Nezahualcoyotl is in residence?' Axayacatl asked, trying to ignore the pounding in his head.

The ferryman confirmed that the tlatoani of Texcoco was at home in his palace and consented to take Axayacatl across the lake on the promise of future payment. The journey across the lake would have been recuperative but for the incessant chatter from the ferryman. Axayacatl tried to look interested and made what he hoped were appropriate noises at the succession of trivialities, but it proved hard to concentrate on anything but his fluttering stomach, the queasiness aggravated by the rocking of the boat. At last the canoe drew up at the broad steps that passengers to Texcoco used to disembark.

The Water Gate at the top of the steps was busy. Travellers were accosted by the dispossessed, selling painted stick animals, rough bags made of the coarsest maguey fibre and hastily carved effigies of dubious-looking deities. There were beggars too, mayeques who had been thrown off the land they worked and freed slaves who had nowhere to turn. They squatted or lay on the dusty steps beneath the arches and held their hands out in supplication. Axayacatl spotted several ex-warriors among them, one missing an arm, another most of his leg below the knee and a third who looked as though one side of his body was being consumed by rot. He shouldered his way through the central arch and wondered if Tlaloc's baleful stone eyes condemned him for his lack of charity. It couldn't be helped. He had nothing with him.

It was market day in Texcoco and the square beyond the gate was full of stalls and open patches of pavement set out with neat piles of fruit, fish laid out in rows by size, bats and unidentifiable bits of meat roasting on spits. Through the market was the outer courtyard where the lesser craftsmen showed their wares, entertainers and musicians wove their spells, hoping to be noticed and get an invitation to the inner courtyard where Nezahualcoyotl himself sometimes came down to inspect what was on offer.

In contrast to the regimented layout of Tenochtitlan, Texcoco's houses and state buildings sprawled joyfully across the city. Axayacatl negotiated the narrow streets of the old town until he came out onto the southern plaza that was dominated by the royal palace. Three pyramid temples hunched over the northern plaza, the tallest of which was now dwarfed by the ever expanding Great Temple in Tenochtitlan.

Nezahualcoyotl's palace was busy and Axayacatl's dishevelled appearance made it hard for him to persuade the dolorous clerk and indifferent guards of his heritage. Eventually, they were satisfied and allowed him to bypass the queue of commoners, waving him through to another hall that was about half the size but more lavishly decorated. Here, Axayacatl found himself among members of Texcoco's nobility and a quiet group of serious-looking men who might have been emissaries from a neighbouring state. There was no way for Axayacatl to jump this queue, so he took a seat in the corner and passed the time eating fruit and sweet cakes that were being offered round, asking himself what – in the name of Mictlan's bones – he was doing here. Discussing his family troubles with Nezahualcoyotl didn't seem like a good idea, but who else was there to turn to? Time ground by as one by one the people waiting were ushered into an audience with the ruler of Texcoco. It wasn't until mid-afternoon that the chief clerk signalled that it was Axayacatl's turn. He stood up, expecting to proceed into the audience chamber, instead of which Nezahualcoyotl swept out, dismissed his advisors and other administrative staff and guided him by the arm down a corridor and into a long room that housed his collection of art.

'You look terrible, cousin,' said Nezahualcoyotl.

Axayacatl marvelled at the man's easy manner. Where Iquehuacatzin sought to put distance between himself and others, Nezahualcoyotl went out of his way to bring people closer. They shared the same great-grandfather, Acamapichtli, the first ruler of Tenochtitlan, but even Axayacatl admitted that it was a tenuous connection.

'Have you been in a fight?'

'No, My Lord.' Axayacatl's voice echoed in the vaulted ceiling.

'Are you sure?' The ruler of Texcoco smiled, leading the way through a forest of stone pedestals on which sat a thousand stone carvings of the Mexica pantheon, some no larger than Axayacatl's thumb with the largest three times his height. 'Because I know how little love there is between you and Moctezuma's sons.'

'No. It is not them. They're with the army in Totonaca.'

'Of course,' said Nezahualcoyotl, nodding carefully. His bright eyes burned like fires against the darkness of the world. His cheeks, one slightly pockmarked, and his strong jaw were framed by his long hair, which he rarely tied back. Close up, Axayacatl noticed a scattering of grey at the man's temples that matched the silver-grey in the slender-fitting, armless tunic that he wore. His loincloth was the same colour, but its sash, which hung to his knees, was edged with rectangles of aquamarine cotton, stitched on with black embroider-work.

Nezahualcoyotl looked at the cuts and bruises on Axayacatl's face. 'It looks as though you have found someone to keep you on edge while Iquehuacatzin and Mahchimaleh are away.' The tone was faintly mocking, but the man's smile was warm. 'Seriously, you must face up to those two one day or you will never reach your full potential.'

'And what might that be?'

Nezahualcoyotl stopped next to a waist-high granite plinth that was painted black and covered with an assortment of finely wrought weapons, most of them set with precious stones and gold filigree. He looked at Axayacatl, genuinely surprised. 'Why, ruler of Tenochtitlan of course.'

'What about Moctezuma's sons?'

'You think one of them should rule after their father?'

'You mock me, My Lord. Is this some test?'

'Of course it's a test. Life itself is a test. The gods set up the game and place the challenges before us and we... we must rise and meet them, but no, I do not mock you.' The ruler of Texcoco picked up the plainest dagger from the dark tabletop. Its blade was milky translucent and sparkled with iridescent rainbow flaws. Its handle was carved in a simple style from a black wood that had an unusual, sensual lustre.

'So if this is a test, you want me to choose who will rule the cities across the lake after Moctezuma?' said Axayacatl, unable to take his eyes off the blade.

Nezahualcoyotl placed a hand on Axayacatl's shoulder and looked into his eyes, his gaze unwavering. 'Let us imagine that it is your choice to make, eh?'

'Choosing one's desired outcome isn't hard,' observed Axayacatl. 'Making it come to pass is the hard part, but alright...I believe I would do a better job than either of Moctezuma's sons.'

'Excellent! Now that you have made one choice, let me set you another test.'

Nezahualcoyotl turned the dagger over in one hand with a single, neat movement so that he was holding it by its beautiful see-through blade, handle ready to grasp.

As the dagger was presented, Axayacatl noticed a procession of delicate Mayan carvings that wound their way up its handle.

'From the coast,' explained the ruler of Texcoco and, still holding the blade, guided the point of the weapon up to his own throat. 'I think the blade came from a very deep cave. I've no idea what stone or gem it is made from, but it's very hard and almost as sharp as the best of our stone weapons. Maybe,' he went on, looking into Axayacatl's eyes,' you could return home a hero. How seriously would people take you if you killed the tlatoani of Texcoco? You might even go down in history as the man who unified two of the three cities in the Triple Alliance.'

Axayacatl was dumbfounded.

'Close your mouth, cousin. That's not a good look.'

'I… I'd never get out of here alive. Even if I did, your people would never accept me as their rightful ruler. They'd probably declare war on Tenochtitlan.'

'Oh I'm not sure it's as clear-cut as that.' Nezahualcoyotl shook his head. 'People like a strong leader and no one is stronger than the man who has just slain the previous strongest man. But, for what it's worth, I think you've just made your second wise decision of the day. The guards at the doors here would very likely cut you down.' He waggled the blade gently.

Axayacatl took the hint and let go.

'Since you have so graciously permitted me to live, perhaps I can repay your kindness by listening to your woes.' He replaced the knife among the other exhibits and moved off towards a plinth set with neat rows of jewellery.

'Xiconoc…' began Axayacatl and then changed track. 'No, my mother is the problem.'

'Your mother did this to you?'

'No. My mother is unfaithful to my father.' The words came out in a rush like a dying gust of wind and with it, Axayacatl felt relief. 'She steals out at night sometimes and… and dishonours my family in Xiconoc's bed.' When it became obvious that Nezahualcoyotl wasn't about to say anything, he continued. 'I broke into his house to avenge my father's honour.' He dropped his head. 'I wanted to kill him at first. Then I decided to get into his home and find some information or some evidence that I could use against him.'

'And you got caught.'

Axayacatl nodded. 'His guards roughed me up and locked me in a cellar. All the time, they told me that my father would be the laughing stock of the city if I breathed a word about any of this. I've been captive for a few days. Yesterday they filled me full of octli and threw me out.'

'Hmm... I thought I could smell something fruity. Are you sure of your mother's infidelity?'

'I saw her with my own eyes.' Axayacatl tried to keep his voice neutral, but his throat sounded taut with emotion.

'So what do you want?'

'I don't know who to turn to. I need help.'

'You don't need help,' replied Nezahualcoyotl with a stern look. 'What you need to do is come up with some ideas and make some choices.'

'Alright then, I'm going to kill Xiconoc.'

'That's one idea. Have you got any others?'

'You think it's a bad idea?'

'I didn't say that,' countered Nezahualcoyotl, 'but maybe you should try to understand the situation before you charge in. Try to think of other ways to deal with the matter. How about a trial?'

'Impossible!' exclaimed Axayacatl. 'My mother would be put to death and my father would die of shame. Xiconoc must die. With him dead, my mother will be forced to stop her games.'

'Hmm... I haven't got through to you yet, have I?' Nezahualcoyotl rubbed his forehead.

'You haven't given me any advice yet either.'

Nezahualcoyotl put his hand on Axayacatl's shoulder. 'I have discovered that the only counsel people really value is their own. As a result, it's always best to help people find their own solutions, but since you ask, I advise you not to kill Xiconoc. Do you have any idea how to accomplish the task in secret? No? Because if you are discovered, you will stand trial and what do you suppose the punishment is for someone who kills a member of the royal family, eh? Whatever happens to you, the trial would bring disgrace to your family and visitation of the shame that you so desperately want to avoid.'

Axayacatl's heart sank. 'My Lord, you tell me what I cannot do. Is there anything that I can do? Is there no help that you can offer me?'

'I certainly cannot help you in any plan to kill Xiconoc. He is Moctezuma's brother and one of the heirs to the Colhua dynasty. The Triple Alliance would not hold in the face of an accusation that the ruler of Texcoco had reached the hand of death across the lake. Our people would be at war and we already decided that was a bad idea.'

Axayacatl nodded morosely. He had never really believed that Nezahualcoyotl would offer him assistance, but hearing the refusal firsthand brought his position into sharp focus. He was alone. There was no one he could turn to for help.

'You are looking at this problem the wrong way,' continued the ruler of Texcoco. 'You are like a snake-catcher on his first day at work. You are afraid of the head because it bites, so you go for the tail instead, unaware that the snake will coil back on itself and strike you anyway. You need to go for the head of the problem.'

'Xiconoc is the head: poisonous and perfectly prepared to strike.'

Nezahualcoyotl made one of those disappointed expressions that made Axayacatl pause momentarily.

'Wait. Are you telling me my mother is the problem?' Suddenly Axayacatl was angry.

'That was what you first said to me, but that isn't the point that I'm trying to make. What I'm trying to tell you, Axayacatl, is that you really don't know what's going on, do you?' Nezahualcoyotl's voice was full of compassion. 'Your mother goes of her own free will, doesn't she? Perhaps your father knows about this. He's a shrewd man. Perhaps there is something going on that you don't understand and so yes, perhaps the head of the problem lies in your own family.'

Axayacatl shook with suppressed rage. 'No. I won't believe it.'

'Good. Continue with your scepticism until you know the facts, but go and find out what they are. You want advice so here it is. Go and speak to your mother, alone. Do not share anything with your father until you have heard your mother's point of view.

Maybe she is a dishonourable woman, as you suggest, but maybe desperate circumstances have brought her to this. You owe it to your parents to establish the truth before you act. You owe it to yourself as well.'

Axayacatl looked up. 'Suddenly everything is much more complicated.'

Nezahualcoyotl laughed gently. 'I remember when I was your age, the world seemed such a simple place. I know your father well. He would love to see you take the throne one day. You may throw away your own dreams, but think carefully before you put other people's hopes at risk.'

'This talk of thrones sounds like foolish hope to me.'

'Really?'

'Iquehuacatzin will be the tlatoani after his father.'

'That young man is an idiot and a dangerous one at that.' Nezahualcoyotl looked severe again. 'Trust me in this, he has more enemies than you do and I suspect they are a good deal more determined too.'

'Mahchimaleh then?'

The flash of anger in Nezahualcoyotl's eyes spoke volumes and Axayacatl suddenly understood that the ruler of Texcoco would do everything in his power to prevent Moctezuma's sons from acceding. He wondered what sort of influence the man could exert from his side of the lake, but he already knew the answer. Nezahualcoyotl was the master statesman. His own people knew his wisdom and loved him for it. Axayacatl's own father had a deep respect for the man and told of how even Moctezuma was in awe of him, jealous of his common touch, the easy grace with which he ruled his people.

'Speak to your mother about what you have seen. If this is some folly of her own, perhaps she'll realise that she has to stop. On the other hand, if this is some clever ruse, you'll develop a new appreciation for your parents.'

'Ay! That sounds like risky business,' said Axayacatl sadly. 'Perhaps the shame will kill her.'

Nezahualcoyotl shook his head. 'I don't share your low opinion of your mother or your father. Find out her reasons and then make up your mind. People usually have powerful motivations for the way they act.' Nezahualcoyotl clapped him on the shoulder. 'Rest here awhile until you've cleared your head. You can have a room in my palace for a few days. I'll have my healers visit you and send word to your father that you are well and that you are my guest. Leave when you are ready, but remember this... you cannot rule if you will only make the easy choices. Many decisions will leave you with a bitter aftertaste and steal your sleep at night, not because they were wrong, but because they were not entirely right.'

'Thank you, My Lord,' said Axayacatl. His voice sounded small in the vast room of treasures. He had been so sure of himself before he came here. Get help, kill Xiconoc. Now he didn't know what to do. For a moment, he thought of the girl, Little Maize, and remembered the unhappiness he'd seen in her eyes and wondered what she'd do.

Chapter 28 – Tenochtitlan

Chaos reigned in the Tezozomoc household on Axayacatl's return. His mother, Atotoztli II, daughter of the tlatoani and princess of the Mexica people, was harrying five members of the household staff who were engaged on some elaborate preparations. For once, she looked as though she had bitten off more than she could chew. The hallway was piled high with baskets of fresh flowers, so the only route from one doorway to another was along the increasingly narrow paths as porters kept bringing more. The scent of lilies was overpowering.

Slaves were carrying logs and heavy urns. Servants bustled, edging past each other on the disappearing floor, too few carrying away the mounting clutter. Others hovered near Axayacatl's mother, awaiting new instructions or clarifications on the last.

Axayacatl wanted to speak to his mother, strike while the idea of questioning her was fresh and his indignation was still hot. Just getting to her looked impossible. *Not the right moment*, he thought and began to retreat.

'Axayacatl my dear!' exclaimed his mother, catching sight of him and sweeping her helpers aside in her rush to embrace him. 'We were so worried about you!'

Axayacatl stood woodenly, unable to return her hug. 'So worried you decided to hold yet another party?' He cursed himself for being unable to keep the disdain from his voice, already angling for a fight. Nezahualcoyotl would have been disappointed.

'Don't be ridiculous, son. We received word from Texcoco that you were safe. Nezahualcoyotl's message said that you were using your time usefully. What was it he said now? Politics, diplomacy and the finer points of the law in Texcoco. I hope it was enjoyable. You've been gone for more than twelve days!'

Axayacatl's mother released him and stepped back. She was tall, as Colhua women were. Axayacatl had barely outgrown her and he was not short. Her hair reached down to the back of her knees and was bound by a series of red and gold bands of cloth. She had warm, brown eyes with only a few lines at the corners that spoke her true age, but it was her small nose and full lips that tricked many into believing her too young to have birthed three sons. The russet robe and copper-braided belt looked like the height of Tenochtitlan fashion and showed off her womanly figure in a way that reminded Axayacatl of the night he had spied on her and Xiconoc. He groaned.

'What is it, dear?'

'Mother, I need to speak with you about a difficult matter.' Axayacatl spoke determinedly and tugged at her sleeve, meaning to lead her towards a quieter part of the house.

'I can't leave, Axayacatl,' she insisted, pulling away. 'There's too much to prepare! These idiots will never get it right.' She gestured over her shoulder.

'Mother!' Axayacatl's voice was sharp and he was pleased to see the effect it had. 'I've been away for many days and you can't spare me a few moments?'

His mother looked at him in surprise. 'Alright, a few moments, but then I have to get back. We have important guests tonight.' She shooed away the gaggle of household staff who were standing a discreet distance away, awaiting orders, then turned to follow Axayacatl.

'Who have you invited this time?'

'Oh, you know... the usual crowd: nobility, my family, members of the Great Council and a number of prominent merchants from across the valley. Oh, and the new ruler of Tlatelolco, Moquihuix. I feel sorry for him. It's going to be years before he sorts out the mess his father left behind, you know.'

'Your family?' Axayacatl scowled at his mother as she led the way into the main reception room. One wall consisted of arches beyond which lay a terraced garden with a view over the neighbouring buildings. Servants were bringing in unfamiliar-looking cushions that must be on loan for the occasion. Others were arranging flowers or bringing in low wooden tables, which would be set with food. There would be no private conversation in here, but the walled garden looked deserted.

'Well, your grandfather is with the army in Ahuilizapan, of course, as is Tlacaelel, but many others are coming.'

'Have you invited Xiconoc?'

Axayacatl squinted in the midday sun that seared the terrace. The carved stone handrail that topped the low wall around the terrace was hot to touch and yet his mother grasped it, as if to steady her hands. She looked out across Texcoco, avoiding eye contact. He could hear his mother trying to breathe deeply. Just when it seemed she was about to speak, they heard a voice calling.

'My boy!' It was Tezozomoc. 'I'm so glad you are home.'

Axayacatl tried to hide his annoyance at the interruption.

'Where have you been? Surely not preying on Nezahualcoyotl's hospitality all this time. Is all well?'

'I'm fine, Father.' Axayacatl noted that his father had a casual air that suggested a low level of involvement in the preparations for the forthcoming event. He had a generous smile and the capacious cloak that swathed his slender frame made him look as though he was floating towards them.

'You look as though you've been prepared for the skull rack by a group of incompetent priests.'

'Really, I'm fine. I had an accident, that's all. I tripped and hit my head. It was stupid.'

'It sounds like you got drunk,' chided Axayacatl's mother.

Axayacatl looked to the heavens but made no reply.

'Did I interrupt something?' said Tezozomoc good-naturedly. 'You two looked as if you were deep in conversation.'

'Our son was asking who we've invited,' replied Atotoztli.

Tezozomoc draped his arm conspiratorially around his son. 'Don't worry about your odious cousins. They've left...'

'For Ahuilizapan. Yes, I know.'

'Actually,' Atotoztli chimed in, 'he was more interested in whether Xiconoc would be there, weren't you, my dear?'

'Really?' exclaimed Axayacatl's father. 'Have you some business proposition to put to him?'

Axayacatl's discomfort was complete. There was no way he could question his mother now. 'It's nothing. I didn't realise how busy you were. I'll come and find you later when this is all over.' He waved a hand in the general direction of the house, taking in the preparations. This time it was he who gazed out from the raised garden across Lake Texcoco and Xaltocan to the north. A heat haze shimmered over the tanning district of Atzacualco. A gentle breeze blowing in over the fisherman's wharves kept the temperature on the terrace bearable.

'If you have something that troubles you, son, you must speak of it.' Tezozomoc's lined face had a kindly smile.

Axayacatl was trapped. It had been hard enough plucking up the courage to broach the subject, but it was unthinkable with his father present. He tried to think of some other topic to bring up in front of his parents. Nothing came to mind.

'I wanted to discuss something with Mother, in private,' he tried again.

'Really! You're making such a show about this. Your father and I have no secrets, isn't that right, Tezo?'

Axayacatl's frustration got the better of him. 'It's about Xiconoc, Mother,' he blurted. Perhaps that name would give her reason to change the subject or ask Tezozomoc to give them some privacy. He immediately regretted the ploy but then noticed the look that passed between his parents. It was such a brief exchange that he might have missed it if he had blinked and suddenly it dawned on Axayacatl that his father might know of his wife's night-time excursions after all. Atotoztli held her husband's gaze and the moment stretched out, Axayacatl watching both, hoping for an insight. Eventually, Tezozomoc nodded at his wife. It was a small gesture that could have meant any number of things, but to Axayacatl, it seemed his father was agreeing to leave them to discuss the matter alone. His surprise was complete when his mother kissed him lightly on one cheek and walked back into the house.

Now it was Tezozomoc's turn to stare out across the lake. He let out a deep sigh. 'This is the finest view in the whole world.'

Axayacatl said nothing.

'The tlatoani's palace is grand,' Axayacatl's father continued, 'but we have the better position. We get the light from the sky and its reflection in the water here. I wouldn't swap it for a storehouse full of quetzal feathers.'

Axayacatl nodded pointlessly. His father was still looking out across the dazzling path of sunlight that stretched to the far bank of Lake Texcoco.

'How did you find out?' he asked at last.

'I followed her to Xiconoc's place.'

His father nodded.

'So you know about this?' Axayacatl's voice cracked.

'Yes, son. I do.'

'Why? How could you?'

Axayacatl's father turned his back on the view, finally looking him in the eye.

'You help me with the family business. You know how much money we take in.'

Axayacatl nodded.

'And do you have any idea of our outgoings?'

'No... not that part. Not really.' It was only half true. Axayacatl understood that his parents, like so many noble families, spent vast sums on the functions they arranged. He vaguely recalled his mother telling him how much they had paid the entertainers for their part in the Festival of the Dead, last year's most extravagant party. The show had been a tremendous success. The dance troupe had enacted a piece entitled *Eighteen Ways to Die* and everyone had cheered as the long-dead, arrogant Prince Ometeotl had been 'resurrected' time after time, only to suffer a new and often painful demise by fire or water or was cut down in epic combat. Fearsome jungle predators of one sort or another had put an end to him at least three times.

'This event...' Tezozomoc's arm swept over the house, taking in the preparations for the afternoon's party. '...is ruinously expensive.'

'I don't understand why that's relevant. If we cannot afford to throw such big parties, we should invite fewer guests, spend less on them or just stop altogether.'

'We can't do that. We're part of the royal family. You and I have Itzcoatl's blood running through our veins. You're Moctezuma's grandson. The nobility won't respect us unless we put on a show for them.'

'But how many events did we stage last year? Four? Couldn't we do three or two instead?'

'Ha! And allow ourselves to be outdone by lesser nobles?'

'Why does that matter?' insisted Axayacatl. 'Why do you need to put on such lavish events? You don't even like half of the people who you invite!'

Tezozomoc grasped Axayacatl's shoulders. 'You really don't get it?'

'No.'

'It's all for you, my boy. Your mother and I – your mother especially so – have high hopes for you. Your royal blood is strong and perhaps one day you might...'

'Might what?' Axayacatl could sense embarrassment.

'You might yet rise to the post of tlatoani?' Tezozomoc smiled apologetically.

'Have you been talking to Nezahualcoyotl?'

'We do talk occasionally,' said Axayacatl's father, defensively,' but you're the one who just got back from Texcoco, remember?'

'Yes,' replied Axayacatl, getting annoyed. 'He said the same thing to me.'

'Maybe it's because we both believe in you.'

'Alright,' said Axayacatl, shaking his head and trying to remember why they were on this topic. 'Never mind that. What's this got to do with my mother and Lord Xiconoc?'

'We needed the money and Xiconoc offered to help.'

'So you sold my mother to that monster?' Axayacatl was appalled. There was no keeping the outrage from his voice and he was past caring if his father thought it was disrespectful.

'No, it wasn't like that, not at first.' Tezozomoc's lean features stretched in anguish as he tried to explain. 'He said he wanted to help... said that he couldn't bear to see a once-proud family reduced to such desperate straits.'

'Didn't you think there would be any consequences?'

'I told him I would repay him when our family's good fortunes were restored.'

'Except they never were, were they?' said Axayacatl, voice thick with accusation.

'We have established some commerce with Oaxaca, you know this. Also, our family is the only supplier of quetzal feathers to the tlatoani.'

'But it wasn't enough, was it?'

'No, Axayacatl, it wasn't.'

Axayacatl was suddenly filled with loathing for his father. 'So how did the deal come about?' He didn't want to know, not really, but having come so far he had to understand.

'Xiconoc has had a thing for Atotoztli ever since they were young...'

'But she's his niece!'

Tezozomoc nodded but carried on regardless. 'But she always held him at bay. She's far cleverer than he is. Several years ago he renewed his request to her very forcibly, I doubt that you know that part, and she came and told me everything.' Tezozomoc sighed. 'Later, when Xiconoc saw that I was struggling to repay the debt, he came and spoke to me, offering to help us, asking...' Tezozomoc couldn't say the words. He swallowed and looked away, eyes staring towards Texcoco on the far shore. 'I was angry with him and sent him away too, but your mother heard me shouting. She'd listened in. She knew what it was about.'

'Are you telling me it was her idea?' Axayacatl was outraged.

'You mustn't blame your mother. She knew how bad our situation was.'

'So you let her go to him... you encouraged it. Xipe Totec's putrid breath! He's her uncle!'

'We had nothing left! Don't you see? Without his help, we would have had to leave this house and live in poverty.'

'You'd better pray the others don't learn of this.' Axayacatl doubted that his younger brothers would understand any of it. Tizoc and Ahuitzotl were too young, but their sister, Chalchiu, would be very upset. Axayacatl closed his eyes, trying unsuccessfully to shut out the memory of what he had seen in the half light in

Xiconoc's bedchamber.' Aren't you afraid of losing her?' he whispered when it became clear that his father had nothing to add.

'Yes,' Tezozomoc sighed. 'Yes, I am terrified. I am no fool. She has always been a lively woman with a great appetite for life. I… I cannot give her everything she needs. What I know is that her life revolves around her hopes for you. She lives in hope of securing the throne for you. This is why we spend so much on entertaining the lords and council members.'

Axayacatl felt numb. He sat down on the wall of a planter full of cacti, careful to avoid the sharp spines. 'I don't understand. How can this family ever claw its way back to the top? Too many people stand in our way. Moctezuma's sons, Tlacaelel and those are just the obvious ones. Even Xiconoc has a stronger claim to the throne.'

'Xiconoc has no designs on the throne, your mother is convinced.'

'Then he has deluded us all,' spat Axayacatl. 'There is no limit to that man's ambitions. He has not built his trading empire for nothing. With his riches, he could buy Huitzilopochtli down from the heavens and take his place.'

'Surely he cannot lay claim to the post of tlatoani? His family's next-in-line is Iquehuacatzin.'

'I don't know, but I have seen papers in his home that show he has been making large donations to Azcapotzalco and Xochimilco. Why would he do this unless he was trying to buy influence on the Great Council?'

'How did you come to see this information?' Axayacatl's father's tone was suspicious.

'Another day, Father, I'll tell you another day, but I saw it with my own eyes.'

'Perhaps they merely detailed some exchanges, trades his people have done with outlanders.'

Axayacatl shook his head. 'They were all one-sided. You taught me how to keep records for our family's trading activities. You showed me how both sides of the deal must always be represented.'

'True,' acknowledged Tezozomoc. 'It's the only way to avoid disagreements at a later stage. You didn't remove these papers from Xiconoc's house, did you?'

Axayacatl sensed hope in his father's voice. 'No, Father. It wasn't possible.' He watched his father's face, pinched tight, a mask of self-control and suddenly the man he thought he'd known was someone very different. His studious yet affable father, a man born to nobility with few cares in the world, instead was riven with quiet desperation. The lands they owned brought little revenue and the family's foray into trading with distant lands was little more than a costly sideline. All the while, Tenochtitlan's high society demanded a tribute of ever more ostentatious displays of wealth, events that Axayacatl's family could no longer support.

'I should kill him.'

'You'd never get away with it!' Axayacatl's father looked alarmed.

'Do you think I care about that?'

'Don't do it, please. Even if you succeed, you'll face the tlatoani's justice and the whole story will come out and our disgrace will be complete. Your noble sacrifice would have been for nothing.'

'Then you must stop these parties.'

'You don't understand,' said Tezozomoc. 'Your mother is utterly determined to keep the family... you and the boys especially, at the centre of it all.'

'I can't offer you gratitude for what you and Mother have done. Can you see why?'

Axayacatl's father nodded sadly.

'You must put an end to it. I don't know how, but you have to get her out of there!'

'Maybe we can do it.'

'Do what?'

'Repay our debts. If we could just secure a few more trading links, find some routes that have been overlooked...Will you help me?'

Axayacatl swallowed, trying to steady his voice. 'No, Father. I'm too angry right now. You need to fix this. I'll help later... when I get back.'

'Where are you going?'

'I'm going to do what I've wanted to do for a long time.' Axayacatl set his jaw determinedly. 'I'm going to Ahuilizapan to join our warriors. There's a convoy every three days that takes supplies to them. I don't know when the next one is, but I'll head out with them. I'm not sure I will be able to stop myself from murdering Xiconoc if I remain here in the city.'

'Your mother will be disappointed.'

'She's not the only one,' Axayacatl observed sourly.

Tezozomoc bowed his head, acknowledging defeat, and then reached forward, as if to embrace his son. Axayacatl took a step back.

'Be careful,' said his father. 'Come back to us.'

'I will, so you'd better sort out this mess, because if I come back and discover that these…' He waved his hands in the general direction of the party. 'If you don't find a way to curb our expenses, I will.' The words sounded good, but in his heart Axayacatl knew it was an empty threat. He had no idea what he would do. Perhaps a spell with the army would clear his head.

Chapter 29
The Jungles of Totonaca

It wasn't until he saw the cliff through the treetops ahead that Jaguar knew where he was. It meant two things: firstly, he had been running in approximately the right direction. The town of Chicanazca was off to the right somewhere. Secondly, it meant that he was trapped. He had hoped the escarpment here would allow a short scramble to the top of the ridge. Instead, it would be a long, dangerous climb, visible to his pursuers throughout. To change direction and head north now would be suicide. Two Sign and the other two were close; they would cut him off before he had gone four hundred strides. He had no choice but to head directly for the base of the craggy wall and hope there was a way up.

Jaguar could not believe his bad fortune. He had managed to put some distance between himself and the others before nightfall on the previous day and had even continued throughout most of the night. He had stopped once to tear off a strip of his loincloth to use as a bandage for his lacerated hand, carefully packing it with clean moss, and a second time to catch a few moments of rest, it being impossible to sleep. Progress was much slower at night because it was so hard to maintain a true heading, but still, Jaguar persevered, knowing that it would be certain death if the others caught up with him. So when dawn had slid a pale, dusty light into the canopy above, Jaguar nearly despaired when he discovered that he was too far south. Changing track had corrected most of that error but not enough.

The jungle came to an abrupt stop where the cliff began. Jaguar scaled the short slope of fallen detritus that lay piled against the rock face and looked for a way up. There were none.

Here and there, straggly bushes clung resolutely to the crumbling surfaces but not close enough together to serve as handholds on a continuous route. Such cracks as he could see were too far apart to be of any use and many of them looked lethally slippery with moss.

Jaguar stood still, trying to hear the sounds of pursuit. He fought to get his breathing under control and willed his heart to silence, but all he could hear was the sound of water somewhere. A rivulet, a small outlet, was disgorging from the solid stone nearby. Perhaps Two Sign, Iquehuacatzin and Mahchimaleh had turned aside, convinced that he would avoid this dead end. It was a miserable place to die, thought Jaguar; unremittingly damp and dark. The open plains and searing sky of the valley of Tenochtitlan would be a better place to make a last stand. He thought of the guide who had died not far from here, thrown into the sinkhole somewhere at the top of the cliffs. Then Jaguar remembered the story that the guide had told before Mahchimaleh cast him to his death. Something about the bodies being washed out when Tlaloc was displeased. Was it possible they came out somewhere near here, perhaps where that stream emerged?

Dashing the vegetation aside, Jaguar followed the line of the cliff until he found the source of the noise. In a narrow, rocky ravine overhung with vines and creepers ran a small watercourse that was fed from a cave set into the rock. Water cascaded from the base of the opening, which was about chest high, while the aperture itself was roughly twice Jaguar's height. Now he could hear the sounds in the jungle, even over the rushing water. There was no time to lose; it was this or death. Death itself was not so troubling to Jaguar; he had seen it many times in battle and he knew that he would give a good account of himself and Jaguar knew his cause was righteous. Protecting the tlatoani from the assassins was surely a feat that would earn him a place in the afterlife, but that was far from certain yet; he needed to get back to Ahuilizapan and warn Tlacaelel. Then there was his family. Jaguar had promised Precious Flower he would return home. He wanted to hold her in his arms and feel her warm skin mould itself to him once more. He wanted to press his face into her cascade of hair and breathe in her perfumed scent. He needed to see her laugh and more than anything, he had to see that look of all-embracing love that Precious Flower reserved for her family in the quiet moments. He wanted to play with Blade again and see their newborn child.

Quickly, Jaguar scaled the rock beside the outfall and eased himself into the flow of water that reached above his ankles. Choosing his footsteps carefully, he moved deeper into the maw of the cave. It resembled the throat of some fantastical creature, all fleshy folds and wrinkles in the wet, pale pink stone. The walls looked diseased in some places, bulging obscenely into the tunnel. Jaguar had expected the air to smell stale or foetid, but instead it was cool and damp with a mild, loamy quality. Half a dozen footsteps further and the darkness was almost tangible. A torch would have been useful.

The noise of pursuit was getting louder. Looking back, the opening of the cave was a bright circle of light set into a wall of darkness and it was hard to discern any detail in the pale jungle beyond. The pursuers must have guessed that Jaguar was making for the cave. Without torches of their own, they may not see him if he retreated deep into the cave. Jaguar breathed, trying to ease the tension in his stomach and pushed on into the gloom. He didn't like caves.

A little ahead, the tunnel opened out into a small chamber, flooded from one side to the other. It was this tiny underground lake that fed the stream. Ripples on the surface of the river scattered just enough light into the depths to confirm Jaguar's suspicions: there was no way out. It was a dead end. He crouched down to one side and waited, willing himself invisible. The sounds outside grew fainter and Jaguar's hopes began to rise. They had assumed he was looking for somewhere to climb. He waited for what seemed like an eternity and then, just when he thought he was safe, the unmistakable silhouette of Two Sign detached itself from the rough edges and took up a central position.

'Nowhere to go?'

'No,' acknowledged Jaguar.

'We have to finish this now, you know that.'

Jaguar shrugged his shoulders. The chill water sloshed around his ankles and made an animal, sucking noise. He sensed that Two Sign was out of breath from the chase and would be happy to talk for a while.

'You won't get away with this, you know that, don't you?'

'Yes, we will.'

'The tlatoani got away and the last of his men will see him to safety.'

Two Sign laughed, a deep confident sound that echoed from behind Jaguar. 'He won't. Iquehuacatzin and Mahchimaleh went after them. Their father won't suspect a thing until the two get up close and slit his throat.'

Jaguar considered this piece of news. 'And the young priest?'

'He's just outside.'

'Waiting for the stream to run red?'

Two Sign nodded.

'I thought we were friends.'

'Times change,' said the big man quietly. 'I was Tlacaelel's favourite once.'

'What are you talking about? You're the commander in chief of the Eagle Knights.'

'He doesn't listen to me anymore...doesn't care what I think.'

'He might, if you were less distracted than you've been of late.'

'Maybe, maybe not, but we will never know now.'

'What do you mean?' said Jaguar. 'Maybe there's still time to make everything right. Perhaps I can repay your debts. Who do I need to pay and how much?'

Two Sign laughed. 'It's far too late for that. You could never repay Lord Xiconoc all that I owe and anyway, the tlatoani saw me lead the attack. My life is forfeit unless I finish the job I started. Putting Lord Xiconoc on the throne is my only way out now.'

'All this is to make Moctezuma's brother the tlatoani?'

'Have you found him or are you talking to the spirits of the river?' came a voice from outside the tunnel. 'In the name of Mictlantecuhtli, just get on with it, will you? I'm fed up with this place.'

Two Sign raised his eyebrows. 'You see? I'm taking orders from boys now.' He took a step closer.

With sadness in his heart, Jaguar unslung the sword that hung across his back and held it at the ready, understanding that the big man had held back, waiting for him to prepare. Now that it was done, Two Sign came at him with predictable ferocity. The tunnel was an unsettling place to fight. The floor was uneven and a constant rush of cold water had rendered Jaguar's feet numb. As he and Two Sign traded the first blows, Jaguar sensed he was at a disadvantage. Whilst it was easy to see Two Sign's outline move against the light penetrating the mouth of the tunnel, stark contrast made the scene very flat. It was very hard to gauge the direction of Two Sign's movement. Pure instinct kept Jaguar alive in those first exchanges. If he had learned one thing during all the sparring he and Two Sign had done it was to keep calm. Two Sign was used to his opponents panicking.

Inside the narrow confines of the tunnel, the harsh clatter of obsidian blades was deafening. The sound reverberated, jarring Jaguar's senses. He switched to a two-handed grip to compensate for his severed finger and still struggled to contain Two Sign's brutal onslaught. The Eagle Knight had had twenty years to adjust to the loss of his middle two fingers. Every change of stance brought danger, so Jaguar stood firm, shifting his feet only a little at a time as Two Sign tried to batter him into submission. Fresh blood seeped from Jaguar's roughly bandaged hand causing his grip to fail. His sword shifted and a moment's inattention allowed Two Sign to get in under his guard. The heavy sword sliced into his exposed chest, gouging into ribs. Jaguar cried out and his knees nearly buckled under him. Somehow he managed to recover, fending off the next attack one-handed, praying that his diminished grip would hold.

Two Sign eased off, perhaps sensing that the fight was won. It was just enough to allow Jaguar to wipe the blood from his hand. The Eagle Knight moved back in, striking on one flank and then changing the direction of the attack. Jaguar held his own, clumsily, until the assault tailed off again. Two Sign seemed content to wear him down.

'You're not going soft on me, are you?' said Jaguar through gritted teeth.

'Just giving you a chance to warm up,' grunted Two Sign. 'I was hoping for more of a fight than this. Your men would be disappointed with The Falling Claw if they could see him now.'

'The slippery rock doesn't help.'

'Of course not. Doesn't suit your style of combat.'

No, it doesn't, thought Jaguar. His agility was one of the few advantages he had when he was sparring with Two Sign.

'Want to go outside to finish this off?' drawled the Eagle Knight.

'So the priest can stab me in the back while I'm keeping you at bay? No thanks,' said Jaguar. 'You'll have to do your own dirty work.'

'I didn't want it to end this way, Jaguar. If you'd only stayed away, we could have both been celebrating the accession of a new ruler.'

'Do you really think the new ruler would have let you live, knowing the secret of his rise to the throne?' While they were talking, Jaguar was exploring the tunnel floor with his frigid feet, trying to find purchase. He had only been trying to buy himself time to think up a way to gain the upper hand, but it was obvious that the question had given Two Sign pause for thought. Jaguar recalled their last encounter and had an idea. He shifted his weight to make it look as though he was about to dive past Two Sign,reproducing the move that had allowed him to get past the Eagle Knight in their mock combat. Startled that Jaguar had taken the initiative, Two Sign took the bait, believing that Jaguar was going to make a break for the exit. He began to turn. It wasn't much, the slenderest of chances, but Jaguar was committed. He ducked the other way, keeping his feet firmly planted in the notches they had found. Now Two Sign had to correct and tried to shift his bulky frame back again. This put him off balance, but it was the floor of the tunnel that was his undoing. His foot slipped and automatically he had to wave his arms to stay upright. Jaguar swept his sword up and under Two Sign's armpit, slicing through muscle and severing tendons.

Two Sign's sword fell from his grasp and was lost in the water. The big man staggered and slipped again, this time falling backwards. With one arm useless, he was unable to cushion the fall and the river wasn't deep enough to kill the speed of his descent. There was a sickening crack followed by a splash that swamped the walls of the tunnel.

Two Sign lay face up across the tunnel, unmoving in the darkness, water piling up against his side. Jaguar drew ragged breaths, waiting to see if he would get up. After a while, Clawfoot called from outside. He'd heard the noise and was trying to work out what had happened. The next thing Jaguar saw was the silhouette of the priest rising like a ghoul into the tunnel entrance, thin blade held out in front of him. Jaguar was tired and his ribs hurt. The cold and damp had seeped inside him, but defeating Clawfoot had to be possible. He was only a priest, young and inexperienced at that.

Just then, Two Sign stirred and coughed, then climbed resolutely to his feet. Somehow he had located his sword beneath the water, perhaps by falling on it, and was holding it left-handed. It was impossible to believe. If the man wasn't dying as the result of blood loss from his nearly-severed arm, the impact to his head should have killed him. The narrow confines of the tunnel would make it hard for both men to take him on at the same time, but Jaguar felt his chances of surviving fading.

Before he could decide what to do, Two Sign charged at him, but his movements were so awkward that all Jaguar had to do was raise his sword and invite his neck to slide onto its edge. The Eagle Knight crashed into Jaguar and bowled him backwards into the sump. There was a brief struggle, before Jaguar realised that his opponent was dead. He pushed the floating body aside and had waded to the side when he saw Clawfoot approaching, looking to take advantage while he clambered out.

Exhaustion and despair were overwhelming. There was nothing left to give. Jaguar's chest was agony and his right hand was numb from the hammering it had taken. Even if he hadn't lost the sword somewhere behind him, he knew he wouldn't be able to grip it.

'Impressive!' The sound of Clawfoot's voice echoed up the tunnel. 'I would have wagered my place in the priesthood that the old man was going to kill you.'

Jaguar took his time to reply. He was still out of breath. 'So what do you get out of all this? Two Sign had debts to repay.'

Clawfoot laughed, a thin voice. 'We all have debts to pay. Mine are to the gods.'

'And Feathered Darkness? What's his place in this?'

'Nothing to do with you, Heart of the Jaguar.'

Jaguar nodded.

'Don't worry about being tired,' said Clawfoot. 'You can rest all you like when you're dead.' The young man advanced, a thin blade twitching in his hand. 'What do you think of your tomb?'

Jaguar didn't like it. It filled him with sorrow. He would never see Precious Flower again, never feel her glossy hair caress his shoulders. He wouldn't get the chance to see his son, Blade, grow to be a man. Maybe by now Precious Flower had given birth to another son, a boy who would never know his father. It was the thought of a boy wrenched from his father before his time that caused Jaguar to remember the sinkhole in the cliff above them and the sacrificial offerings. There had to be a way through.

'How sad you look!' exclaimed the young priest. 'Are you thinking of your family? Good. Cooperate with me. Come quietly and I'll leave your family alone, eh? If not...if you make trouble, after I've done with you, I'll go and dispatch them to the afterlife as well. I know you have a woman and a baby, I visited them while you were away. I know where they live.'

'Why?' Jaguar cried out. 'Leave them alone. Your fight is with me.'

Clawfoot advanced cautiously. 'You hurt me.' He held up his hand. 'No one hurts me and gets away with it, but I'll make you a deal. If you come and kneel in front of me, I'll make yours a quick death and maybe then I'll leave your family alone.' Now he was close enough to see Jaguar in the poor light. 'Tsk, tsk,' said Clawfoot.' You may have bested the old man, but it looks like you've lost your weapon in the process.'

The young priest exuded confidence. Jaguar felt drained. It wouldn't be a long fight. He uttered a silent prayer to Tlaloc and Quetzalcoatl, who Precious Flower had always claimed watched over them. Then, without a word, he took a deep breath, turned and dived into the sump, hoping his instincts were correct. As his body slowed beneath the water, he felt the current that was the source of the water feeding the pool. He swam into it and began to panic when he sensed how strong it was. His left side hurt and the darkness made it impossible to tell if his lopsided stroke was making any progress. It was so black he couldn't even tell if he had his eyes open or closed. Already his lungs were burning. He cracked his head on a rock and the shock forced huge bubbles of precious air from his lungs. He thrashed his legs in earnest. Was the current lessening now? It seemed to be easier to swim, so much so that it almost felt lazy. Jaguar's chest convulsed trying to suck air in. He fought it, mouth clamped shut but wondering why it mattered. It was like a dream in which the more he fought, the less effect it had and there was no way of even telling which way was up. Immense calm settled over Jaguar. There was something firm under one hand, but it made no sense. The only thing he wanted to do was open his mouth and breathe; breathe air into his tortured, heaving lungs and so he did. Cool sweet water filled his mouth and his mind sank into a cavern of its own.

Chapter 30
The Jungles of Totonaca

The streets of Ahuilizapan were full of dancing people. Shield of Gold held hands with a local girl who had flowers in her hair. Her name was Gentle One and her yellow smock flew as she spun, her radiant smile and pretty white teeth shredding Shield of Gold's heart. Music played somewhere nearby and the whole town throbbed to the sound of enthusiastic drumming. The people of Ahuilizapan were handing out food and garlands, eager to swap the gloom of their recent subjugation for a joint celebration in the Mexica's capture of Ixtlahuacan. Their part had been a small one, but they had been encouraged to rejoice as well, to cement their place in the great empire. They had helped provision the Mexica army and fourscore of their own warrior elite had gone along, at Tlacaelel's request, as a gesture of their new and glorious unity. They had hardly been necessary. The people of Ixtlahuacan had raised a large army from the surrounding villages but had still been overwhelmed by Tlacaelel's force.

The girl twirled away from Shield of Gold and was swept into the arms of a seasoned Mexica warrior with strong arms, lightning tattoos and a mischievous grin. They stamped and shook their hands in carefree unison until they were lost in the crowd. Shield of Gold sighed and pushed through the excitement until he reached Tlacaelel's headquarters. Pandemonium reigned inside. He had only been gone long enough to get a bite to eat…and dance briefly with a pretty girl. Moctezuma's sons were being questioned by the general. There were no signs of jubilation over the capture of Ixtlahuacan in here. Shield of Gold had never seen Tlacaelel like this before; the general looked apoplectic. He sidled over to Last Medicine and asked him casually what was going on.

'The princes have just returned from the jungle,' rasped the veteran. 'They say that the tlatoani has been attacked and may have been abducted.'

Tlacaelel's face held the menace of an approaching storm. He barked at Xipil, a stocky, grizzled Eagle Knight with a scar that creased one side of his face from his temple to his jaw, narrowly missing his eye. 'You're in charge of the search parties, take anyone you need and get back out there!' he roared. 'Take canoes and search downstream. Search the riverbanks and all the villages. With these floods there's no telling where they could have ended up.'

Xipil rode the general's anger.' Yes, My Lord,' he said from the side of his mouth that worked properly. There was a spark in his eye and he looked enthusiastic at the prospect of going back out into the jungle, even though they had only just returned from the battle against Ixtlahuacan. He strode out taking four of his men with him.

Moctezuma's sons were tucking into bowls of fruit and roasted peccary. A serving girl was pouring them a round of chocolatl. Two dozen minor nobles clustered round them, waiting respectfully for the princes to finish eating and provide more detail.

'They don't look very worried, do they?' Shield of Gold whispered to Last Medicine.

The old warrior's lip twitched in agreement.

Tlacaelel rounded on Iquehuacatzin and Mahchimaleh, unconcerned that they were mid-mouthful.

'You are certain that the Eagle Knight Two Sign led the attack?' asked Tlacaelel.

'Yes, of course,' said Iquehuacatzin wiping his mouth with the back of his hand.

'And you claim that Heart of the Jaguar was part of this?'

'That is correct. He told us he was worried about the tlatoani, thought he might be in danger. His concern seemed genuine enough, so we agreed to go with him and two of his warriors. Then, when we found the tlatoani's hunting party, Jaguar dived from the canoe and capsized it. He swam for the shore leaving my brother and me trying to help his knights, but they were too burdened with their weapons and were taken from us.'

Mahchimaleh burped and then pointed a greasy finger at Tlacaelel. 'It was a treacherous part of the river; Iquehuacatzin and I were lucky to make it out alive.'

'Then what?' Tlacaelel's tone was caustic, his disbelief evident. 'Jaguar joined the attack on the tlatoani?'

Iquehuacatzin shrugged. 'He must have done. By the time we reached them, the tlatoani had managed to escape, all praise to Huitzilopochtli, and we found Two Sign and Heart of the Jaguar talking about what they would do next.'

'What happened then?'

'We ran,' said Iquehuacatzin. 'We thought we might be next.'

There were murmurs of support from the assembled noblemen. Shield of Gold coughed, unable to believe this version of events. Everyone looked at him and he was forced to make a show of his discomfort, raising his hand to his mouth and coughing again as though something was stuck in his throat. Last Medicine played along, cuffing him on the back. When attention had shifted back to the centre of the room, Last Medicine bent close.

'Let's hope they get back soon so they can give their own account, eh?'

Shield of Gold smiled at the veteran, grateful that he wasn't the only one sceptical of the brothers' account of what had happened.

Seeing his former commander with Shield of Gold, Tlacaelel appealed to him. 'I don't understand it! I would have entrusted those two with my own life. Why would they have done this?'

Last Medicine approached the general and laid a hand on his shoulder. 'Lord Tlacaelel, do not trouble yourself with these questions for now. I will see to it that they are questioned when they are captured or return of their own accord.'

Tlacaelel rubbed the bridge of his nose. 'It worries me that the tlatoani is still out there. Even if those two are innocent there are many dangers.' He turned to Moctezuma's sons. 'You idiots should never have gone out there. It was irresponsible to put yourselves in harm's way and Jaguar would never have gone if you had stayed here.'

Iquehuacatzin stood up, eyes blazing. 'How dare you talk to us like that? You may be our uncle, but you have no right to command us. Anyway, if my brother and I hadn't gone, you would have no idea what was happening out there. It was the obvious thing to do.'

Tlacaelel's gaze was like a shard of obsidian. 'Congratulations then. You took the most obvious course of action.'

The two men stared at each other oozing mutual dislike. The room was silent. No one wanted to be the focus of attention while the threat of violence crackled like lightning over a storm-lashed jungle. The standoff seemed to last forever but eventually was over-shadowed by an uproar outside. Shield of Gold heard shouting and cheering and, as he drew close to the exit, he slipped through and was one of the first to emerge onto the stone stairs outside. A crowd had gathered in the street. At its centre stood the recently dispatched search party who had made a protective cordon around Ilhuicamina Moctezuma, Lord Tlatoani of the Mexica, and a grim-faced Grey Privy Knight. They were covered with scratches and looked exhausted. The warriors were having a tough time pushing their way to the bottom of the steps. Eventually they made it and climbed the small flight of steps. There, Moctezuma came face-to-face with Tlacaelel who had come out to see what the commotion was about.

'You made it!' boomed the general, moving to embrace his half-brother.

'No thanks to you, Tlacaelel!' The accusation cut across the excited clamour like a thunderclap. The tlatoani's displeasure soured his face.

'My Lord, news of the attempt on your life has only just reached my ears. I had just dispatched Xipil to look for you and was about to send out more search parties to scour the land between here and the coast.'

'We need to speak inside.'

'A good idea,' replied Tlacaelel. 'Let's not spoil the mood out here.' He looked out across the expectant faces. 'Spread the word that the tlatoani is back with us and safe.'

There was a cheer, but the crowd showed no sign of dispersing, even as Shield of Gold followed Moctezuma, his hastily appointed bodyguard and Tlacaelel inside. The hall belonging to the former ruler of Ahuilizapan suddenly felt cramped again.

Iquehuacatzin and Mahchimaleh appeared magically within the protective circle of their father's bodyguard and went to embrace him, heedless of his anger.

'Father!' exclaimed Iquehuacatzin and then stepped back, sensing that he had overstepped the boundaries of etiquette with such a familiar gesture. 'My Lord, we have been so worried. Everyone has been out looking for you.'

Moctezuma regarded his sons momentarily. 'Of course,' he said drily. 'Where were you two searching, the palace?'

'No, My Lord,' answered Iquehuacatzin smoothly, ignoring the insult. 'Mahchimaleh and I were both there in the jungle when the assassins struck. We were there when the whole thing started, but we were not able to get to you in time to help. Our canoe capsized and by the time we made it ashore, you'd already gone.'

Moctezuma's surprise was evident. 'Then you will have seen the assassins.'

'Yes, Lord Moctezuma,' echoed his sons.

'Two Sign, commander of the Eagle Knights.' Moctezuma looked at Tlacaelel pointedly.

'So say your sons, My Lord. I can scarcely believe it. It's unthinkable.'

'He's your man, Tlacaelel,' emphasised the tlatoani. 'Your right-hand man.'

Shield of Gold had to watch the exchange through the press of bodies. He stood on tiptoe, but even then the view was partially obscured. Moctezuma was in a black mood. He spoke softly, but there was a deep undercurrent of menace in his voice. Nobility and warriors alike backed off to a respectful distance and lowered their eyes.

'Were the others your men too?'

Tlacaelel's response was guarded. 'My Lord, I know nothing of this madness, but I assure you that I will hunt down the people responsible. Describe them to us now. I will have them rooted out and then I shall kill them myself.'

The place where Iquehuacatzin and his brother had eaten was cleared and fresh food was brought out. The tlatoani lowered himself gingerly onto two plump red cushions. He was unaccustomed to walking, so the journey back to Ahuilizapan had left him footsore and stiff. Moctezuma ate in silence for a long time and everyone was forced to wait, staring at the floor. He described how they had caught a crocodile, eyes shining with excitement, and then explained that the two guides they had taken as porters and both priests had turned on the Grey Privy Knights just as they were skinning their catch.

'Two Sign said he was going to check on two of the men who were watching the riverbank. I thought we would be safe when he came back, but he joined in with them. If it hadn't been for Heart of the Jaguar, arriving when he did, we would have all perished.'

'So the commander of the Jaguar Knights defended you?' asked Tlacaelel.

'Yes, that's right,' replied Moctezuma. 'He joined my men and helped hold off the attack.'

Mahchimaleh shook his head and Iquehuacatzin spoke sadly. 'It was a trick, My Lord.'

'What?'

'As you know, Tlacaelel appointed him as our bodyguard so he was with us. We were surprised at how eager he was to find you, weren't we?' Iquehuacatzin turned to his brother.

'That's right. It was his idea—'

Tlacaelel interrupted. 'Jaguar is loyal to the core,' he protested. 'He is no traitor.'

'Like the commander of the Eagle Knights, Two Sign?' sneered Iquehuacatzin.

'No, he's right,' said Moctezuma. 'Jaguar fought alongside us. I saw him kill at least one of the assassins.'

Iquehuacatzin shook his head. 'It was a trick to gain your confidence. We saw him cut down at least one of the Grey Privy Knights once he was in behind you.'

'Wait,' said Tlacaelel.' You told us you were swept downstream when your canoe capsized and that the tlatoani was gone by the time you got back. How could you have seen them fighting?'

'Never said we saw nothing,' growled Mahchimaleh. 'We caught glimpses before we were swept round the bend in the river.'

Iquehuacatzin put a hand on his brother's shoulder, as if to calm him. 'Maybe we didn't see it clearly, but that's how it looked to us. Those two are known to be close. They often spar together. Would it not be safest to assume they are both dangerous until we find out more?'

Tlacaelel nodded. 'I will ensure they are both taken captive and questioned.'

Moctezuma pointed at his half-brother. 'You will have no part in the proceedings,' he warned, raising his voice for the first time. 'Someone else will question the traitor Two Sign and Heart of the Jaguar when they are found.'

'Brother, you cannot think I had something to do with this!'

'Right now I trust no one and the fact these are two of your closest advisors leaves me no choice. What would you do in my place?'

Shield of Gold could not believe what he was hearing. He moved a little to catch sight of the general's face. How could the man look so calm? Shield of Gold fought to contain his own anger. He knew all the hard work that the general had ploughed into this campaign in Totonaca. He had been running errands and messages for Tlacaelel for nearly a year as Tlacaelel had pulled the whole operation together, arranging supplies, sending out envoys to loyal garrison towns along the route to ensure the army's passage would be safe and well provisioned. All of that work and the recent conquests, secured by Tlacaelel in Moctezuma's name, meant nothing now.

Tlacaelel spoke again. 'My Lord, do not forget that I begged you not to come to Totonaca. I told you it might not be safe. I also tried to stop you going on the hunt. Why would I have done that if I had secretly been involved in a plot to take your life?'

'Maybe it was all said to hide your true intentions,' cried Iquehuacatzin. 'You know the tlatoani does as he pleases.'

'Yes,' added Mahchimaleh. 'Perhaps you even planned for Jaguar to take us there too, eh?'

'Imagine that!' breathed Iquehuacatzin. 'The entire Colhua family removed at a stroke. Answer me this, uncle? When the grieving people of Tenochtitlan wiped the tears from their eyes and cast around for a new ruler, was it your plan to volunteer yourself for the role?'

'Hush, Iquehuacatzin,' said Moctezuma. 'Enough! I will not hear any more speculation on this matter until we have more evidence. The two knights must be found!' His eyes blazed as he turned to the member of his own bodyguard who had accompanied him back from the jungle. 'Coyotl, I'm putting you in charge. Have someone fetch a cage for Tlacaelel. He stays in here, but put him in the corner and make sure he speaks to no one without my permission! Once he's secure, assemble search parties and find those men!'

The Grey Privy Knights moved to surround Tlacaelel, but his own warriors made a defensive circle around him. Last Medicine pushed through them all to stand with Tlacaelel and Shield of Gold slipped in after him. Perhaps not the smartest move, he thought, but it was too late because he'd made his choice.

Tlacaelel smiled warmly at the display of loyalty. 'You have my thanks, men, but you must stand aside. The tlatoani is your leader now. Do as he commands. I will be fine.'

Something in Tlacaelel's tone must have angered Moctezuma because suddenly the tlatoani was shouting.' I know that you have a long reach, brother,' snarled Moctezuma. 'The fighting men love and respect you and I have no doubt that you can reach out from this confinement, so know this. If Two Sign or Heart of the Jaguar are killed before they can be interrogated, it will go badly for you! Do you understand?'

'Yes, My Lord,' came Tlacaelel's cool response.

Over Moctezuma's shoulder, Shield of Gold caught the faintest flicker of a smile at the corner of Iquehuacatzin's mouth, a smug look that showed how pleased he was with the outcome.

'Last Medicine,' said Shield of Gold as Tlacaelel's hands were being bound.

'Yes?'

'We have to find Two Sign and Jaguar before the tlatoani's sons do.'

Chapter 31
The Jungles of Totonaca

It was the shivering that woke Jaguar. His body was trembling uncontrollably and the reason became obvious as he regained consciousness and took stock. It was dark and he was lying half in and half out of water. His first thought was that he had crossed over to the world of shadows. Mictlantechutli might be wending his way up from the lower levels right now to collect him. *Were those footsteps?* thought Jaguar. He listened more carefully and heard the irregular sound of droplets striking water, small musical drips interspersed with deeper, echoing plops. Perhaps he was still alive after all. He got to his feet shakily and immediately cracked his head on an overhanging rock causing him to cry out involuntarily. He cursed silently and held still, listening for any sign that Clawfoot might be nearby. Nothing happened, so he felt around in the dark until he established that he was standing at the edge of another pool of water under an overhang of rock that stretched out on either side. Somewhere above at an indeterminate height hovered a small, dark brown disk of unknown size. Jaguar explored his lacerated ribs gingerly and then flexed his muscles, testing to see if they would do as bidden and hoping to generate some warmth. What was that object hovering overhead? It was too dark to be the moon and was inscribed with unusual tracery. Jaguar felt along under the overhang to see where it led. The surface underfoot was horribly unpredictable; at times steeply shelving off into the water, at times it lay heaped into mounds that Jaguar was forced to scramble over, the ground lurched downwards, resulting in a wet slog to regain dry ground.

Thirst drove Jaguar to stoop down and test the water at his feet. It tasted clear and clean, so he drank from what he now realised was large enough to be a small lake. Faint from hunger, Jaguar rested for a while with his back propped against a smooth piece of wall. *Close my eyes for a bit*, he thought. Images flashed through his mind, burned into his memory like molten pitch on exposed flesh. Two Sign silhouetted in the tunnel mouth; Two Sign falling backwards into running water and the crack of his skull striking rock; Moctezuma and his one remaining knight fleeing into the jungle. Then Jaguar's thoughts drifted back to Tenochtitlan and Precious Flower grinding corn and then of Arrow One in the workshop, fussing over the installation of the granite slabs that would serve as the base of the furnace.

Jaguar woke with a start, aware that something had changed. The shape above was lighter, a pale pink, casting its meagre light into the vast cavern that he recognised as the one he and Moctezuma's sons had seen from above. Inside, the cave was the shape of a cone that narrowed to the opening high above. Tendrils sprouted from around the opening in the ceiling, great roots that reached down into the water far below, a handful of them just long enough to drink from the silent surface. They were the cause of the strange striations on the opening's disc. There was no way to climb the walls of the cavern to reach the skylight; maintaining a grip under that arching overhang would be impossible, especially with his damaged chest. If there was any hope, it lay in shinning up the roots.

There was no time to lose. *Getting weaker all the time*, thought Jaguar. Dawn was rising and now there was enough light streaming into the huge vault to contemplate the ascent, but the lake itself was impenetrably dark. He waded carefully into the water and began to swim out to the slender tangle of roots. Like everyone else growing up on the edge of Lake Texcoco, Jaguar was a strong swimmer, but in his weakened state he barely made it to the twisted roots that hung from the opening in the roof. He grasped at a bundle of weed or organic matter, thinking that it capped something solid, a submerged mound that he might be able to use to haul himself higher and get a good purchase on the roots. Cloth and something slimy came away in his hand. The bundle turned over and a misshapen face with flaccid skin stared up through brown water with its clouded eyes, flesh sloughing from the cheek bones. Jaguar gasped. The guide whom Mahchimaleh had thrown down the hole! Had he tried and failed to climb these roots?

Jaguar pushed the corpse away carefully, hoping he had not disturbed its spirit should it still be trapped inside, and reached an arm up to begin the ascent. The smaller tendrils broke in his grasp, but the main rope of roots held firm. He tried to raise his left arm, but the pain in his side made him cry out. Jaguar stopped for a moment, wondering whether he would be able to locate the submerged exit back to the tunnel. Clawfoot must have gone by now. The problem was that he had no idea where he had come in and would probably die of starvation or cold before he found it. The hole in the roof was the only way out. Gingerly, Jaguar tried a series of holds with his right hand. The roots fanned out where they hit the water into a thick mat, which Jaguar could clench between his thighs, but as soon as he hoisted his body above the water, there was only the main trunk of the root to hold and that afforded very little purchase. Jaguar was shivering again when he finally hit on a technique that worked. He hauled himself upwards one hand span at a time, first shifting his left hand up a fraction and then curling his body to clamp it tight between his thighs, then sliding his right hand fractionally up the root.

Water on Jaguar's hands rendered the climb slippery at first, but as he inched his way up, he began to dry out and his hold improved. It was cruel work though. It seemed as though an entire day had passed and Jaguar was no more than about halfway up when the cramp in his arms became unbearable. There were more roots around him now, reaching blindly downwards. Desperate, Jaguar took one in his teeth and swung free for a moment before twisting his legs into half a dozen finger-thick strands. When he felt secure, he let go with his right hand and hung there by his teeth and legs, trying to ease some life back into his arms.

Now that he was closer to his target, Jaguar could see that the roots were not trailing over the edge of the hole, instead they had broken through the thinner portions of the roof surrounding the opening. This meant he would have to rely on handholds in the rock, assuming there were any. Jaguar was suddenly concerned that reaching the ceiling of the cave would be the easy part. Perhaps the guide had climbed that far and fell back, exhausted and out of options. The next worry that struck him was the possibility that Clawfoot would be waiting for him at the top. Perhaps he had found a way up the cliff or had gone the long way round.

There could be no turning back and no more rest. Jaguar could feel his strength waning with every heartbeat. He took hold again and began the arduous ascent towards the overhanging rock. He was forced to rest again when he reached the ceiling. Every sinew felt like it was on fire. His forearms were trembling from the effort of gripping the roots. To his relief there was another snake-like tendril twisting its way down from the edge of the hole, but it was thin. Jaguar used his teeth again to steady himself and shifted his good arm to the new root. There was no possibility of continuing the climb with only one arm. With a low groan, he managed to raise his left arm as the damaged muscles along his ribs screamed white spikes of pain. By jamming his toes into small crevices in the rock and concentrating on the muscles in his forearm to grip the handholds, Jaguar reached the lip of the opening. His spirits sank lower as he surveyed the underside of the slab of rock that stood between him and freedom.

Escape was tantalisingly out of reach. Both of his legs were already stretched out wide, one foot jammed sideways into a crack and a toe on the other foot was hooked over a deformed twig protruding from the craggy stone ceiling. His breath hissed in and out through gritted teeth. The lake-induced cold was a distant memory, perhaps from days ago. Sweat poured from his body. Salty water dripped into his eyes, so he had to blink to see properly. It was time to move again before his strength failed him entirely or his fingers slipped.

Jaguar tested his footholds and then let go with one hand to reach up over the top of the slab. One toe began to scrape loose and Jaguar panicked. He cast about for a way out of the predicament, but there was none. A gecko might have circumnavigated the opening, looking for the easy route, but not a human. His toe-hold slipped completely and Jaguar did the only thing that he could think of: he launched himself upwards. The slab had a split down the middle and one half had slipped aside and turned slightly, leaving a tapered vertical crack that ended just above his head. He screamed and wrenched himself upwards with one last, desperate effort and jammed his head inside the crack, then howled as his body dropped into the void, wedging his head inside the fissure. An earlobe tore away from his head.

Jaguar fought down the panic that swelled from the possibility that he might be inextricably wedged in place and scrabbled desperately with his right arm, feeling for the top of the stone slab. It was there, he could feel it. He hooked the three remaining fingers on his right hand over the lip, but his feet were hanging in free space with nothing to push up from. Jaguar let out a sob. It had all been for nothing. When they held the next dedication to Tlaloc, or whatever accursed spirits they worshipped here, they would discover his corpse suspended in the opening.

Chapter 32 – Tenochtitlan

It was a grand convoy of brightly decorated canoes that navigated the chinampa and docked alongside Xiconoc's island garden. Little Maize was going to get to see her husband's grand project but not as a guest. She wasn't tied up, but she might as well have been with Xiconoc's two thugs flanking her, never more than an arm's reach away. Xiconoc had invited most of his household and a selection of Tenochtitlan's highest society had also turned up. Some forty people in all, none of whom knew that Little Maize was a prisoner.

The ferrymen manoeuvred their narrow craft in a delicately managed dance, there being too little room along the jetty for all the boats to moor up at the same time. The three canoes owned by Xiconoc would remain alongside. Some had been parked against the steep earthen bank beyond the jetty, while the rest would return later to collect their occupants.

Little Maize was terrified. Things had gone from bad to worse since she had been caught with Axayacatl. Xiconoc had had her tied up and beaten again. This time he had delegated the job to one of his men rather than trouble himself. Minimal food and water had been provided and whenever she asked what had become of Axayacatl, the guards had set about her back and legs with a cane. On Xiconoc's instructions they avoided her face and hands so he could bring her out in public without having to deal with any awkward questions. Yesterday was the first day she had been able to sit properly. She had learned her lesson well. Whatever had happened to Axayacatl, she was not going to find out from Xiconoc or any of his household. Anyway, she had more immediate concerns now. There had been something dangerously smug in Xiconoc's demeanour when he had come to her room to announce that she would be joining him at the opening of his spectacular new garden. He had provided no details.

Little Maize and her minders trailed a dozen extravagantly dressed people from the jetty. They were heading for a reception area that was fenced with slender, head-high poles. Ropes, stretching between the poles, had been decorated with many thousands of strips of coloured cloth that waved gently in the breeze. An archway into the area had been created using three saplings planted on either side of the path that had been bent and bound into position overhead. Inside, the welcoming committee included musicians playing a cheerful melody and six of the household slaves whose job it was to hand out refreshments.

'Have you seen it before?' someone said to Little Maize as they shuffled through the archway. It was an elderly man with a scholarly look and drooping skin beneath his watery eyes. 'Five years in the planning and I hear that your husband has had nearly a hundred people working on it at one time or another since the Feast of Toxcatl last year!'

'No, My Lord,' managed Little Maize. Her chest was tight and she could hardly breathe. 'This is my first visit.'

'Look at all those trees,' he said, pointing a wrinkled claw at the forest of saplings behind the enclosure. 'It's hard to believe this place was razed to the ground just over a year ago.'

Little Maize feigned interest as the old man babbled on enthusiastically about the possibility of bringing plants from the lowlands. He seemed to know something of the subject. 'They're hard to transport but surprisingly adaptable,' he said. 'The converse is true for the animals. The jungle creatures are, for the most part, easy to transport, but they dislike our climate and easily grow sick.'

The chatter helped distract Little Maize from her misery. She found a question to keep the conversation going. 'You've done this before?'

'Indeed, My Lady. My name is Temamecatl. I designed and built Lord Moctezuma's gardens and menagerie.'

'I'm so sorry, My Lord,' replied Little Maize demurely. 'Please excuse me. I should have known.'

'Not at all, My Lady. You are new to all this.' Temamecatl winked. 'But unlike the poor animals taken from the wild you will adapt, yes?'

No, thought Little Maize but nodded anyway. The answer hardly mattered because her minders were leading her away from the old man, towards the rear of the enclosure. Xiconoc wanted to keep her away from his guests. She wanted to call back to the old man and tell him that he was wrong and that she would never adapt. She didn't want to adapt. She thought the animals were right to fret and grow ill in captivity. It was nobler to rage against confinement than to cave in and become docile.

Those members of Xiconoc's household servants and slaves who weren't preparing refreshments were gathered in one corner. Coszcatl and the other three concubines were close by too. They were laughing at some private joke. If they had seen Little Maize's approach then they made no move to speak to her, which was fine because she had no desire to speak to them. The other guests stood about in small groups and Xiconoc was flitting between them like a bee in a meadow of summer flowers welcoming them all. His head gardener was following him about meekly and looking uncomfortable in a pristine new cloak that had obviously been forced on him for the occasion.

Anxiety as to what Xiconoc was planning gnawed at Little Maize's guts. She passed the time trying to work out an escape plan. If she could find a way to make peace with her husband just enough to be allowed to visit this garden of his, she'd be out of the city and a step closer to freedom. Boats plied these waters frequently and it might be possible to hitch a ride with one heading for Azcapotzalco or Xochimilco. From there she could head west or south until she found a village so small that no one would think to look for her there or a settlement sufficiently large to disappear into the crowd.

After a while, Xiconoc finished exchanging pleasantries with his guests and announced that there was to be a guided tour of the island, after which there would be food and more drink in plentiful quantities before the boats returned to collect them. Xiconoc would lead everyone around, explaining the layout and pointing out how the project would mature in future years.

'My head gardener will be on hand to answer difficult questions,' said Xiconoc.

'What sort of questions are those?' asked a voice from the assembled guests.

'Any question relating to plants or gardens,' replied Xiconoc with a smile. Everyone chuckled appreciatively as he led them all out through a second archway that let out into the heart of the garden.

Little Maize's guards materialised beside her and bade her join the tail of the group. Beyond the archway was an avenue of amatl trees so large it was too much to believe they had been planted here since the start of the year. The avenue met another one running perpendicular to it that crossed from one end of the island to the other. Together, these two arteries divided the garden into quadrants much like the roads emanating from the temple district in the city divided Tenochtitlan into its four quarters. At the head of the tour, Xiconoc was explaining that each of the four areas was themed. One represented agriculture, another was planted with trees from the lowland jungles. The third, on their left, even included a small hill heaped with vast boulders between which conifers emerged. The scent of pine needles was wonderful to Little Maize. She had only come across it once before in the market where a girl with almond eyes and peasant shawl had tried to sell her a pine-scented oil that she claimed had the power to banish evil spirits. On the right-hand side of the avenue lay the fourth garden. This one was also strewn with large boulders, but instead of trees, this one was dominated by huge cacti and desiccated grey and brown bushes. Xiconoc's guests were impressed. They chattered eagerly, pointing at features that caught their attention.

The tour continued across the island, the agricultural garden on their left and the jungle on their right. The jungle was the least impressive of the four areas. Little Maize thought the trees were too sparsely planted, they looked untidy and there was nothing but mud between them. Someone else commented on it and Xiconoc's gardener explained that the trees were still too young.

'When they are fully grown,' he explained, 'they will be taller than the Great Temple and their canopies will make a roof more beautiful than the royal palace.'

'Ahh!' said the guests in unison.

The avenue opened out onto the sparkling waters of the canal. Here, another wondrous creation was laid out for all to see. Where the jungle ended, it was bordered by palm trees and there, stretched out beneath the palm fronds that fluttered lightly in the breeze, lay a beach of golden sand.

'Impossible!' shouted one man, overcome by the spectacle. Everyone laughed at him.

Xiconoc looked very pleased as he and his gardener fielded many questions, most of which revolved around how they had managed to transport everything from the coast. Some people waded into the canal, laughing at the feel of the sand between their toes. Eventually, they were coaxed away and steered along the beach towards the northern end of the island. Little Maize decided to dabble her toes in the water. She ignored the glares of her minders who didn't want to fall behind the rest of the group. The water was cool and the sand felt delightfully soft. Reeds swayed on the far side of the canal and beyond, the cordilleras were a pale violet against a hazy blue sky. Little Maize sighed.

'Come now,' growled one of the guards. 'Enough.'

'Alright.'

Grains of sand clung to Little Maize's feet as she made her way up the slope. There did appear to be a limit to Xiconoc's funds because the beach ended after a hundred paces, giving way to a more conventional embankment planted with saplings with gnarled white bark, pendulous yellow twigs and spring green spears for leaves. By the time she rounded the end of the island where the arid garden took over from the dark green leaves of the jungle, the tour was nowhere in sight. No sooner had one of the guards taken hold of her arm to hurry her along than Little Maize stepped on a thorn. She yelped.

'What now?' said the guard, irritated by this new delay.

Little Maize ignored him and hopped over to a tussock of bunch grass and sat down so she could examine the damage. The guard tutted and walked over to where his colleague was scanning ahead to see where the others had got to. There was a brief exchange that ended when one of them set off to tell Xiconoc why they had fallen behind. Little Maize took her time. She picked at the broken tip of the thorn with her nails until she managed to pull it free and then hobbled down to the water's edge to clean the wound. When she was done she made a performance of putting weight on the injured foot. The remaining guard gave a contemptuous look but didn't seem inclined to hurry her along, so she returned to the tuft of grass and pretended to continue the treatment.

Little Maize was just beginning to relax when Xiconoc returned. The second guard wasn't with him. Her husband's face was a mask of rage. He gripped her arm painfully and hauled her to her feet.

'I don't know what game you're playing,' he snarled, 'but I'm glad of the opportunity to catch you on your own. I've got some news for you. You're leaving.' He glared at her, waiting for a reaction.

Little Maize blinked at him uncertainly. She didn't understand. Did he mean that she was to be escorted back to Xiconoc's home? Perhaps he meant that she was leaving the land of the living. 'Back to the Sisters of Penitence?' she managed at last, choosing an option between the two extremes that had first sprung to mind.

'Oh no,' snarled Xiconoc, twisting her arm tighter. 'That would bring far too much shame on me and it would be far better than you deserve. You're going far, far away.'

Little Maize could see he was watching her, hoping to see her distress, wanting to revel in his victory. She kept her face emotionless.

Disappointed, Xiconoc surged on. 'I have business contacts in many places. Some of them lie beyond the borders of our empire. Many of these places are rough and uncivilised, lacking the laws such as we have here in our great city. One of these towns lies at the northern extreme of Mexica territory and is constantly threatened by Tarascan raiding parties. It takes a certain kind of man to hold an outpost like this. Trading is good and so are the rewards, but it takes guile, ruthless determination and a great deal of unreasonable good luck to survive. Such men are not easy to come by and demand extraordinary recompense in exchange for their loyalty.'

Little Maize had a bad feeling. She felt sure she knew where it was headed.

'The man who I rely on in this town goes by the name of Grey Bones.' Xiconoc gave a nasty smile. 'He has a nasty reputation.'

'He sounds like just your type,' said Little Maize, allowing some of her old street gang attitude through the cracks.

Xiconoc pulled back his free arm and backhanded her across her face. The impact stung her nose and upper lip and she tasted blood.

'I'm through taking your insolence. You're a nobody. I checked with Mother. Many of the girls are taken into care by the Sisters of Penitence when their families can't afford to feed them or when both parents die. You don't even know who your parents were. You're a street rat. You're scum, no, you're worse than scum. Scum gets washed away by the winter rains.'

Stressed by the weight of the many years of abuse, Little Maize finally cracked. What little dignity she had fought back from deep inside her. 'I'd rather be honest scum than a disgusting pervert like you,' she shot back, hot tears springing to her eyes. 'You're a bloated, greedy leech.'

'And you're an ungrateful witch!' shrieked Xiconoc. 'By the time you realise how good I have been to you it will be too late. A few weeks in the company of Grey Bones and you'll be begging him to kill you!'

'Really?' said Little Maize, defiantly. She pulled away, trying to break Xiconoc's hold on her arm. The guard drew nearer to make himself useful in the event of a struggle. 'Perhaps I'm already praying for death.'

Xiconoc laughed then. 'You have no idea, do you? You will see me in a whole new light when you've been with Grey Bones for a few days. He likes his women and boys young, like you, but he once told me that people don't have enough orifices. Apparently he likes to cut new openings in them to enjoy. Sometimes his victims last many days.'

Little Maize stopped struggling. The blood drained from her face as she stared at her husband in disbelief. The world held more horrors than she had imagined. She had to try to gain control somehow. She had to find a way out of this nightmare.

'And what if I threaten to tell Tezozomoc that you're sleeping with his wife? Even though the tlatoani is your own brother, there's no way he will pardon you for defiling his daughter.'

Xiconoc turned purple in the blink of an eye. He wrenched Little Maize towards him, putting her off-balance. She toppled against his bulging stomach causing him to step back, except he must have tripped against a stone or uneven ground because he suddenly let go of her and flailed his arms. Little Maize lurched forward and fell on top of him as he toppled backwards. There was a sickening crack and she knew that he had hit his head on something hard. She rolled off his bulk and got up.

'What have you done?' exclaimed the guard in shock. He dithered, uncertain as to whether to grab her or look to his master. Xiconoc groaned and his eyes rolled back up into his head. The guard made up his mind. Instead of grabbing Little Maize, he bent down to help his master. For a moment, Little Maize was convinced Xiconoc would rise, but when the guard tried to pull the big man upright, blood poured from the back of his head onto the flinty path.

Little Maize suddenly knew what she had to do. She didn't want to become a plaything for some demented slave trader. If she was going to act, it had to be now. This was the moment she had seen back at the palace except there was no knife. Instead, Xiconoc had struck his head on a rock. Now all she needed to do was take care of the guard. He was distracted, still fretting over the man he was supposed to have protected. Little Maize reached down and picked up a rock. This was her chance to escape. She checked that no one else was coming back to find them and then swung at the guard's head with all her might. He must have sensed the movement because he turned towards her as the blow struck. The rock made an oddly wooden thump as it caught him above the ear and knocked him sideways so that he slumped over Xiconoc's body where he lay, unmoving. Little Maize looked down at the blunt weapon in her hand. *I've killed him*, she thought, surprised at how easy it had been and how devoid of emotion she felt.

Now all she had to do was swim across the canal and make her way by means of the various islands to the town of Coyoacan.

From there she would head to the hills and well, it was impossible to know, perhaps she could find a farm to live on. It would have to be a long way away from Tenochtitlan just in case search parties were dispatched to bring her back. Perhaps, if she could evade them for long enough, she would find somewhere to hide until the fuss had died down. If she was lucky, she might even find a smallholding prepared to take her in and give her work. *Ridiculous*, thought Little Maize and shook her head. I have to leave now. Lying at her feet was her husband, feet on the path and his head at the water's edge. His breathing was unsteady and something was making an intermittent clicking sound in his throat, his tongue perhaps. She knew she had to go, but there was a job that needed doing. The next thing she knew, she was hauling the guard clear of Xiconoc's body. She rolled her corpulent husband into the canal and held his head under water. It didn't take long. At the end, Xiconoc thrashed briefly, but it was too feeble to give Little Maize any trouble. She watched as the wound in the back of her husband's head leaked red coils into the water. The tendrils reached out, holding their structure momentarily before collapsing to a brown cloud that mingled with the churned up silt.

Little Maize couldn't think clearly. There was something she was supposed to do, but the memory of it was out of reach. She looked down, uncomprehending at the half-submerged body of her husband. A rotund fly landed on the floating platform of Xiconoc's corpse and began to inspect his wet clothing.

Laughter and shrieks from across the island brought Little Maize to her senses and she remembered what she had been about to do. It was time to flee. She looked up and scanned the bank of the island opposite; no one in sight. To her right, just out of hailing distance a canoe glided by on a perpendicular channel through the chinampa. Perhaps she would pick up a lift on the far side of the island opposite her. She couldn't wait here. She removed her cloak and rolled it up tightly, tying it into a bundle that she slung over her back. It would still get wet, but at least this way she could keep it out of the mud. Her underskirt and loose cotton top would dry again quickly enough. Two steps into the canal and she was out of her depth and swimming, with nothing in her mind except the opposite bank. When she reached it, she hauled herself out and looked back, keeping low so as to avoid being spotted. The pale smudge floating in the reeds was Xiconoc's body. Some distance away, several figures were coming back along the path to find him.

Little Maize pushed into a field of maize and struck out for the next canal. There would be more swimming to do before the day was over.

Chapter 33
The Jungles of Totonaca

Everything had turned to shit, reflected Shield of Gold sourly. Numerous victories of the Mexica armies throughout Totonaca could not make up for the appalling news that Jaguar and Two Sign had turned traitor – no one could say why – and had tried to kill Moctezuma. An absurd rumour was doing the rounds that the tlatoani's sons had arrived just in the nick of time to foil the assassination attempt. Shield of Gold had no doubts as to who had started *that* story. More troubling was one report that claimed the commanders of both the Eagle and Jaguar Knights were dead. Whatever the source of this information, it wasn't Iquehuacatzin or Mahchimaleh. Shield of Gold distinctly remembered them saying they had run from the two warriors. No one seriously believed this story, least of all the men under their command who still expected their leaders to show up at any moment and give their version of events. Notwithstanding, on Moctezuma's orders, the Jaguar Knights were operating a double shift under the watchful eye of the Grey Privy Knights, with orders to seize them on sight.

No one had any real understanding of what had happened, but Moctezuma didn't appear to be convinced that Tlacaelel was at the heart of the conspiracy because he was also vigorously pursuing the possibility that it was a locally hatched plot. Imixquitl, the tlatoani of Ahuilizapan, was now in a cage in his own residence, alongside Tlacaelel, something that his subjects were deeply upset about. Repercussions were being felt across the entire garrison. Pockets of trouble were springing up all over Ahuilizapan in protest and the Mexica had put a strict curfew in place to try to keep the peace. Already, five local men had received forty lashes for being out and about after dark and had been promised death on a second offence.

Shield of Gold was carrying a message from Tlacaelel. The general wasn't allowed to speak to anyone unless a member of the Grey Privy Knights was present, so he had given his instructions while one of the old guard listened in. Now Shield of Gold was trying to locate Last Medicine to remind him to arrange supplies for the convoy of wounded men who were heading back home tomorrow.

'Excuse me… your name, may it be Shield of Gold?'

A boy of no more than ten summers, dressed in a filthy scrap of loincloth, cocked his head but kept a respectful distance. He had a mop of unkempt hair and an unsavoury-looking bone through his nostril. He reminded Shield of Gold a little of himself when he lived on the street.

'Yes, lad. That's me.' Shield of Gold's voice didn't quaver for once and the sound came out very grown-up.

'I have a message,' continued the boy.

'Yes?' Shield of Gold was glad the boy wasn't speaking Totonacan. He understood most of what he heard in the language but in spite of many weeks in the region could only hold a simple conversation.

'The jaguar has sharp claws and teeth, but the tapir kills more often.' These words were spoken in halting Nahuatl, as though memorised.

A chill came over Shield of Gold. 'Say that again?'

The boy paused, evidently wondering if he'd got some part of the message wrong, but Shield of Gold knew that he had not. 'The jaguar has sharp teeth and claws, but the tapir kills more often.'

'Who gave you this message?'

'I cannot say,' said the child. 'But I take you. He told me you do not want come. He also told me warn you that it very dangerous if you seen with him.'

'Where is he?' Shield of Gold remembered the day he'd first heard those words, at the ceremony of the 'Marking with the Swords'. It could only be Jaguar.

'Not far, but he has wounds upon him and very weakness,' replied the boy.

Shield of Gold made a mental note to study the Totonaca dialect more closely. The boy's message was barely intelligible. If he was going to spend more time in the region as Tlacaelel's messenger, a firm grasp of the language would be invaluable. He wasted one heartbeat wondering whether he should trust Jaguar but instantly dismissed any concern. There was no one Shield of Gold trusted more than his mentor and there could be no possibility that he had tried to kill the tlatoani; it was unthinkable. Even if Jaguar had turned traitor, he would have a very good reason for doing so and Shield of Gold owed it to the man who had saved his life to hear what he had to say. If there was any danger, it was more likely to come from the boy. Other Mexica had been lured like this into traps set by the local people.

'Show me,' said Shield of Gold. The coded message had to be genuine.

The boy trotted off. The instant Shield of Gold went to follow he got a nasty feeling that they were being watched, but glancing up and down the street, all he could see was a porter, two women turning a corner in the distance and a pair of scabrous dogs tugging at a scrap of cloth. He had to jog to catch up with the boy.

Ahuilizapan was the largest town in the area, but it was nothing when compared with the size of Tenochtitlan, so it was only a short walk that led to a scruffy set of dwellings. The boy showed Shield of Gold to a dilapidated hut that was propped against the side of a circular building with a conical roof of palm leaves. A worried-looking Jaguar Knight stood in the doorway, apparently on guard. He was one of the many who Shield of Gold didn't know, but he must have known who to expect because he let them through. Inside, tall baskets fitted with tumplines were everywhere. A few of the upright ones were piled with round green nuts that the local people called Tax'Osh; others, mostly empty, lay on their sides where they had fallen.

'Is this one of the storerooms that were set aside for the Mexica?'

The boy nodded and then pointed towards the rear of the hut. There in the half-light, hidden from view among the baskets, lay Jaguar. His features were ashen and one mangled ear was held in place by a crusting scab. A dirty, threadbare sheet spread over a layer of leaves kept him off the mud floor and an equally grimy blanket was draped over his legs. His body was a mass of scratches and stank horribly, the source of which Shield of Gold quickly traced to a black poultice smeared down Jaguar's left side. One meagre bandage ran through the mess and round his chest.

'Mict-lan-tecuh-tli!' swore Shield of Gold as he knelt.

Jaguar smiled weakly. It looked like he had a fever. He raised a bandaged hand in a feeble salute. 'My man there, Tall Tree, told me that Moctezuma is safe.'

Shield of Gold picked up a cloth that lay next to the rough palliasse and carefully wiped Jaguar's forehead. 'Yes, but the whole place is in uproar. They're saying you tried to kill him, you and Two Sign.'

'Who said that? His sons?' Jaguar groaned and released his hold on Shield of Gold's arm. 'They're lying. Has the tlatoani forgotten that I was one of the ones who stood beside him?'

'Well, his sons have managed to weave a different cloth into that loom and now they've put everyone on alert. There are search parties looking all over the place for you.'

'That's why Tall Tree brought me here. He said I should wait, but I must go and speak to the tlatoani now and Tlacaelel too.'

'You can't,' said Shield of Gold. 'It's not as easy as that. Tall Tree was right to hide you here. Lord Tlacaelel has been imprisoned, but I can get a message to him. I'm still allowed to speak with him, although it will have to be in code. The tlatoani's bodyguards always listen in to what we're saying.'

'Wait, you say that Tlacaelel is in a cage?'

'Yes.'

'Why?'

'The tlatoani thinks that if you and Two Sign tried to kill him then he must be behind it all.'

'But if I go and speak to the tlatoani, he'll remember that I fought beside him.'

Shield of Gold remembered the strange look he'd seen on Iquehuacatzin. 'That may be dangerous. I think Iquehuacatzin is up to something.'

'Of course he's up to something. He and his brother are in this too.'

'That explains why he looked so pleased when the tlatoani said you and Two Sign had to be brought to him alive. If he and his brother find you first, they'll kill you and then it will look as though Lord Tlacaelel had you silenced to keep himself safe. Where is Two Sign anyway?'

Jaguar's voice was flat. 'He's dead.'

'How?' Shield of Gold was shocked. So that rumour had been true.

'I had no choice. He did this to me.' Jaguar indicated the wound on his ribcage.

Shield of Gold drew breath sharply. 'So Two Sign *was* involved! What in the name of Xipe Totec's rotting flesh happened?'

'I'll tell you. Ask the boy to bring me some more water.'

Shield of Gold held a pot out for the lad to fill and watched as Jaguar struggled to sit and lean his back against the wall. Clear pus oozed from underneath the compress on his ribs. When the pot was brought back, Shield of Gold instructed the boy to stand at the entrance and keep watch with the knight.

Jaguar's strength returned a little as he talked. He described the journey down to the swamp to locate the hunting party and how he and Moctezuma's sons had purchased a canoe from the fisherman. Pausing only to drink, Jaguar explained how he had witnessed Two Sign killing the watchmen on the riverbank and how he had dived overboard to avoid being swept downstream with the princes, Holds the Sun and Creeping Night. Whether it was his wound or the memory of that day that made Jaguar grimace, Shield of Gold couldn't tell. After a brief pause to sip more water, he resumed his tale, describing the pitched battle by the crocodile carcass, and recounted how Moctezuma had escaped with the last of his bodyguards. He told Shield of Gold about his flight through the jungle up until he became trapped in the cave and then repeated what Two Sign had said to him about working for Xiconoc.

'And then he went for you.'

'Yes.'

Shield of Gold whistled in astonishment. 'But instead you killed him! You beat Two Sign, the greatest warrior in the history of our people.'

'I got lucky. Anyway, I think he might have succeeded in taking me with him.' Jaguar peered at his wound.' This isn't good.'

'I'll find a healer.' Shield of Gold wrinkled his nose at the putrid smell. 'Are you sure that's medicine? It smells like dogshit. Who treated you with that?'

Jaguar nodded at the doorway. 'The boy's mother. Tall Tree said a local healer would be safer. No way to be certain that one of ours wouldn't go straight to the tlatoani.'

Shield of Gold thought that the risk was worthwhile. 'Are you sure? That salve looks more likely to finish you off than heal you.'

'No. I'll be alright. You need to get back to Tlacaelel and tell him what happened. He'll work out what must be done.' Jaguar's eyes burned into Shield of Gold. 'Promise me you will go to see him now.'

Shield of Gold was about to answer, but Jaguar cut him off.

'Oh wait, your old friend Clawfoot... he's part of it.'

'Part of what?'

'He was fighting alongside Two Sign, trying to kill the tlatoani.'

'Did you kill him too?' asked Shield of Gold.

'No. I should have killed him when I had the chance. He followed Two Sign into the cave and would have finished me off, but I managed to escape through a flooded tunnel.' Jaguar explained how he'd made the connection between the sinkhole into which Mahchimaleh had thrown the guide and the outfall at the base of the escarpment.

Shield of Gold listened as Jaguar described the impossible climb to the opening of the cave where he had got his head wedged into the great stone. He shook his head in awe. It was no wonder that Tlacaelel had entrusted Jaguar with command of the knights.

'Wait! How did you free yourself? Your head must have been jammed tight.'

Jaguar sighed. 'I couldn't at first. The more I struggled the weaker I got. After a while I stopped and thought.'

'Didn't your neck hurt?'

'Not as much as my ears.' Jaguar turned so that Shield of Gold could see the partially detached flap of skin on one side. 'The rock was too smooth to get a handhold, so I knew I had to find some other way to lift myself out.'

'Roots to get hold of?'

'There were a few flimsy ones I could reach with one foot, but nothing above me to grab, but then I remembered that Iquehuacatzin had fetched a branch to hoist his brother out of the hole. I felt around on top of the rock with one hand, but it wasn't there. Either it was out of reach or someone had passed by and moved it.'

'Maybe an animal.'

Jaguar nodded. 'Anyway, I couldn't give up on the idea. It was my only hope, so I hooked a scrap of root with one foot and pulled it up to where I could get hold of it. I tore it off and managed to fashion a hook from the top end where it forked.'

'And you fished for the branch over the top of the stone,' Shield of Gold said, laughing at the ingenuity.

'One of the gods looked after me, I don't know which. I got it on the third try, dragged it partway towards me before the root slipped off, but on the next throw I hooked it again and brought it within reach. From there it was easy enough to position it across the crack in the stone above my head. That way I could reach up inside the crack with one arm and grasp the branch—'

Shield of Gold cut in. '…giving you enough purchase to haul your head out. Astonishing,' he added. 'There's a story to delight your grandchildren with!'

Jaguar smiled weakly. The effort of telling the tale had weakened him again. Shield of Gold suddenly remembered something else.

'So hold on, if Clawfoot is involved, does that mean the priests want Lord Moctezuma dead too?'

'Maybe not all of them.' Jaguar groaned. 'Listen, the tlatoani is still in danger. He has to be warned.'

'Surely they wouldn't dare to act in full view of everyone else.'

'Perhaps not,' said Jaguar. 'It's not their style, but they will look for another opportunity. Listen, you have to get to Tlacaelel and tell him what happened. He's the only one you can trust. He will think of something.'

'I will. You need to rest here and stay out of sight. Lord Tlacaelel will need you to bear witness to what happened.'

Now Jaguar's head was lolling, as though he was about to pass out. 'Tell him I knew nothing of Two Sign's treachery. Two Sign was heavily in debt.' Jaguar's voice slurred. 'Started gambling after he lost his son...got in too deep to repay what he owed and from that moment, Xiconoc owned him outright.'

Tall Tree and the boy – who had been standing quietly in the doorway up until this point – both hissed a warning. 'Men coming!'

Shield of Gold leapt up and peered out. It was just what he had feared. Iquehuacatzin and five members of the nobility dressed for war were conducting a search. Mahchimaleh would probably be leading others on a sweep nearby.

Jaguar focused on Shield of Gold. 'Can you get out without being seen?'

'No. Too late for that, Jaguar.' Shield of Gold scanned the small storehouse. There were several empty baskets, but Jaguar was in no fit state to be helped into one, much less climb in on his own. 'You two, come here.' Shield of Gold surprised himself. His voice sounded deep and full of authority. Even the Jaguar Knight, Tall Tree, obeyed.

'What are you doing?' hissed Jaguar. 'They'll kill us all!'

'Only if they find you,' replied Shield of Gold. His voice was firm and for the first time in his life he was in control. Today it was his turn to save his mentor's life, or try to, and perhaps at last return the countless favours Jaguar had done for him. He had an idea, but there wasn't much time. Already, he could hear Iquehuacatzin's voice barking orders as the door-to-door search grew closer. He signalled to Tall Tree.

'You. Pass me your blade and then lift a basket onto the boy's back.'

The warrior took the knife that hung at his hip and passed it over. In one swift movement Shield of Gold upended one of the empty reed baskets, sliced the base off it and then lowered it over Jaguar's head. Jaguar understood what was required of him, tucking his knees in and tugging the basket down to his feet. Shield of Gold hefted another basket of the fruit to his shoulder and tipped it up into the top of the one that hid Jaguar. Meanwhile, the boy was adjusting the tumpline on his forehead and Tall Tree was adding more fruit to load on his back.

'What are you doing?'

Shield of Gold turned to see Iquehuacatzin strutting into the storeroom behind two fierce-looking warriors. They looked warily about them before pointing an unfriendly set of weapons at him. He put his most surprised look on.

'I said, what are you doing?' demanded Iquehuacatzin.

'I'm acting on orders, LordIquehuacatzin.' Shield of Gold indicated the baskets of wizened fruit. 'There's a caravan leaving tomorrow taking wounded men back to Tenochtitlan. I've been instructed to gather supplies for the journey.'

Iquehuacatzin kicked at one of the misshapen fruits that had escaped and was lying at his feet. Shield of Gold had to steady his breath as the three men made a show of peering at the contents of the containers nearest to them. Iquehuacatzin gripped the rim of the one that was hiding Jaguar. He picked a green fruit from the top and sniffed at it. Shield of Gold could tell that he'd scented the malodorous poultice.

'They smell bad.'

'Yes, My Lord,' agreed Shield of Gold. He stared the tlatoani's son straight in the eyes and continued in the most innocent voice he could manage.' A lot of them have. Everything seems to go rotten so quickly in this climate.'

Iquehuacatzin glared at him through narrowed eyes and then cast his gaze over the untidy storeroom. 'We're looking for the traitor, Heart of the Jaguar. Seen him?'

'No. Not for many days now. I heard he was dead, but I suppose you wouldn't be looking for him if that were true.'

'No, indeed, but if he is in Ahuilizapan we will find him and when we do, he will wish that he was dead.'

Shield of Gold decided that the only safe response was none at all. It didn't look as though he had been followed here. Iquehuacatzin's house-to-house search had happened across him by accident.

'If you see him, you'd better come straight to me, understand?'

'Yes, My Lord.'

'Good, because if I hear you've helped him to get away from us, I will personally light the pyre beneath your feet.' At this last, Iquehuacatzin smiled, genuinely satisfied with himself. He lifted another pod from the basket and made to bite into it, then appeared to remember that they were bad. He tossed it on the floor and stalked from the hut, sweeping his two noblemen in his wake.

Shield of Gold pretended to sort more fruit into a bowl. When he was certain that Iquehuacatzin would not return, he lifted the basket from Jaguar's head.

'We were very lucky. You have to get away from here. If they find us, we're both as good as dead.'

'I'll go to Tlacaelel now,' said Shield of Gold. 'You rest here and when I'm sure that no one is looking, I'll bring a healer and some more food.'

'I won't be here,' sighed Jaguar. 'I have to go.'

'Go where? You shouldn't be going anywhere in that state.'

'Home. I have to get back to my family. Clawfoot said he'd kill them.'

Chapter 34
The Jungles of Totonaca

The street was a river. Chocolate-coloured water sluiced between the buildings and joined the exuberant torrent that was making its way towards the river. Ahuilizapan was awash. Raindrops pummelled Axayacatl and turned into rivulets that streaked his body. He had been dry a dozen paces earlier, but now his thin tunic and loincloth were ringing wet.

'You need Moctezuma's blessing to join the order of Manifest Light,' Obsidian Snake explained through the clatter of rain.

'You think he'll see us now?' asked Axayacatl, sloshing through the muddy torrent. He glanced at the man his father had advised him to seek out. Obsidian Snake was a distant cousin who had already served three years with the elite company of fighting noblemen and had already gained an impressive reputation. Hunched against the weather, the man looked stockier than he was. Built to deal out damage, thought Axayacatl, yet the only evidence of his soldiering were the two missing front teeth. He had to be good.

Obsidian Snake shrugged, a small gesture in the downpour. 'It's impossible to predict when the tlatoani will grant an audience. We're not in Tenochtitlan now. Everything's a bit, well... chaotic. It's best to show up as often as possible without making a nuisance of yourself.' He turned a corner and headed for the local ruler's palace that Moctezuma had commandeered for his temporary home. It looked very basic.

'Have you fought much, Axayacatl?'

The question was discomfiting. Axayacatl knew that his cousin was perhaps a year younger than he was and yet had nine scalps to his name. Nine enemy combatants who he had captured in fighting for delivery to the priests at the Great Temple. Axayacatl hoped he could avoid divulging his own pitiful haul. 'A few years ago,' he said, deliberately vague. 'I have been too busy lately, helping my father with the family business.'

'Ah, I see. What changed?'

Axayacatl didn't like the line of questioning. He needed a way to close it out or before he knew it, Obsidian Snake would be onto the nasty details of his mother's infidelity.

'Well, this is a big campaign that Tlacaelel has organised. The biggest push towards the coast since Moctezuma Ilhuicamina took the throne. We're all required to do our duty, isn't that so?' It was bland enough to deter even the most zealous inquisitor. In truth, Axayacatl reflected, his parents had been in no position to object. Recent events had worked in his favour. In the end, they had been unable to look him in the eye, much less object to him joining the army.

At the mention of the general, Obsidian Snake shook his head. 'You will see Tlacaelel in the main hall. It's a sad sight, him in a cage.'

Axayacatl had learned of the attempt on Moctezuma's life on the journey to Ahuilizapan. His convoy of a hundred men, mostly warriors had met a similar number returning from the war, some of them grievously wounded. Those in no condition to walk lay in stretchers being pulled along or carried by less badly wounded comrades. The news of the failed assassination and the subsequent imprisonment of Tlacaelel had been shocking and galvanised the fresh troops onwards towards their destination. On his arrival in Ahuilizapan, Axayacatl had sought out friends and noblemen he knew to establish the truth of what had happened, but everyone had a different version of what had taken place. What they all agreed on was that it was an unprecedented, alarming turn of events and that at least one of the perpetrators, who was known to be a prominent warrior, was still at large. Tlacaelel's guilt was hotly debated. The nobility mostly defended Moctezuma's decision to imprison the general, while the knights and other full-time warriors quietly insisted on the man's innocence. There were very few who were undecided.

'You think he was in on this?'

'Tlacaelel has always had designs on the throne,' remarked Obsidian Snake. An overhanging roof provided a dry corridor along the side of a building. He ducked under the roof and led them past three mayeques who had taken shelter there, one sitting nonchalantly on an upturned basket and sucking on a green fruit.

'You think so?'

'It's not the first time the tlatoani has put his brother on trial.'

Axayacatl glanced at his cousin. 'Why would Tlacaelel wait until now to act?' he asked. 'He's not a young man anymore. If he wanted to rule, I would have expected him to make his move a long time ago.'

'He wouldn't have had many opportunities. The tlatoani is well protected and besides, he would have had to have made it look like an accident or at least ensure that he was in no way connected with the attack. The people would not have liked it.'

'Well, in that respect he has failed.'

'You're right. If the tlatoani's sons hadn't happened on the scene and recognised Tlacaelel's men, we might never have known of his involvement.'

'I heard it was two Jaguar Knights,' said Axayacatl, following his cousin up the courthouse steps.

'One of them was, yes. Heart of the Jaguar, no less than the commander!'

'Of course, cousin,' replied Axayacatl. 'He's the one everyone was talking about a few years back when he and some other Mexica were captured by the Chalca and won their freedom in a game of ullama. What about the other?'

'The commander of the Eagle Knights, Two Sign. This scheme was brewed high up in the establishment, my friend.' Obsidian Snake was shaking his head again. 'That's why the tlatoani suspects his brother. Even if Tlacaelel isn't the mastermind behind this, he has to bear some blame for knowing nothing about it when two of the attackers were his most trusted men.'

Axayacatl didn't hear the rest of what his cousin was saying. He'd stopped listening. He remembered the parchment he'd seen in Xiconoc's home, the one bearing the record of payments to a warrior he had mistakenly read as 'Looks Both Ways'. The illustration had shown a man's head in duplicate, looking to the left and to the right. Axayacatl had read this as 'the one who looks in two directions', but it worked equally as 'The Man with Two Faces' or, with the relevant calendar notations on either side, 'Two Signs', meaning someone born at midnight, the exact midpoint between two days of the horoscope. It wasn't a common name.

'I have to speak to Moctezuma,' he said urgently.

'I know,' replied Obsidian Snake looking puzzled. 'That's who we've come to see.'

'No. I mean I need to speak to him right now about the assassination attempt. I have some information he needs to know.'

Obsidian Snake spoke rapidly to the large warrior standing guard at the entrance to the main chamber of the courthouse, seemingly oblivious to the rain. They grasped each other's arms in what Axayacatl interpreted as the comradeship of brothers-in-arms. A few rapidly exchanged words and moments later, the big man let them pass into a cool, dry hall whose ceiling was held aloft by a row of eight grotesque sculptures twice the height of Axayacatl, four on either side. The walls around the edge were featureless aside from the long, vertical slit window openings that did little to deter the wind and rain. Puddles covered the flagged stone floor along one wall. The two men strode across the hall towards the far doorway that was guarded by a dozen more warriors bristling with every weapon imaginable. As they passed between the columns, Axayacatl tried to recognise the likenesses that were richly daubed in browns, muted yellow tones and russet. White eyes bulged accusingly across the space at their opposite number, as if they blamed each other for their incarceration in this bare and unexciting room.

'Not like any of the gods,' he remarked.

'Previous rulers of Ahuilizapan,' explained Obsidian Snake. 'They have incorporated deities though. See here? This is the staff of Black Tezcatlipoca. And here... the shield of Red Tezcatlipoca.'

'The style is nothing like our own.' Axayacatl spoke quietly to prevent his voice echoing and then wondered why he was bothering.

'No. It's... coarse,' said Obsidian Snake, copying Axayacatl's breathy voice.

They reached the far door where the guards were not content with the simple handshake that had seen them through the last one. They were Grey Privy Knights and they looked bored. One stepped forward to take control, presumably the leader.

'Hand me your blades and your tunics,' he said. 'Then take off your loincloths and let's see you shake them out.'

'What?' protested Axayacatl.' That's outrageous!'

'Orders.' The one in charge shrugged. 'No one gets close to the tlatoani without a thorough search.'

'Are we returned to the times of the Mad King? Is the tyrant Maxtla once again in charge?' Axayacatl stood with his fists clenched until Obsidian Snake shook his arm.

'Unusual times call for unusual measures. Come on. It will be quick.'

They submitted silently to the indignity of the strip search. Obsidian Snake didn't look concerned, even when the guards began to make fun of them. His time fighting with the Order of Manifest Light had given him a hard edge.

'No dangerous weapons there.' One burly warrior with massive forearms smirked.

'You're right. Those are a crime against manhood,' said another, trying to keep a straight face as his friends snickered. 'But we're not authorised to keep you out on that account.'

'Alright, that's enough,' said the first man to the others. Apparently he'd heard it all before. 'Sorry, my lords. They mean no disrespect. We've been here since first light and well... time passes very slowly.'

'That's alright,' said Obsidian Snake as he fastened his loincloth. He looked straight back at the leader. 'I understand. Your friends have big cocks because they're excited at seeing other men naked.'

The burly one stepped forward menacingly, but his commander got in the way.

'You can go in. Collect your weapons on the way out.'

Axayacatl passed through the doorway, herding his cousin before him. The confrontation was soon forgotten as he surveyed the main room in Ahuilizapan's courthouse. It was no more than twenty strides square. The walls were bare, whitewashed plaster. The only decorative item in the otherwise featureless room was a brooding tapestry that ran the length of the far wall. The black and gold thread was embroidered with a thousand seashells depicting an apocalyptic scene that Axayacatl guessed represented the end of the Fourth World.

The ruler of Ahuilizapan conducted his business from this room before the Mexica arrived. It was not extravagant and Axayacatl found himself wondering whether the conquest of Ahuilizapan had been worthwhile. He had imagined something more than this for a city that controlled the flow of trade from the coast. What was immediately more interesting to him was the fact that they had wandered in on Tlacaelel's trial. The general sat with his knees drawn up under his chin and his back to the bars of a cage that was only big enough to lie down in if he curled up to sleep. It was a dome made of stout vines on a flat base of logs that had been hauled into the centre of the room for the trial. Aside from the Grey Privy Knights who lined the room there were two dozen more warriors representing the Eagle and Jaguar Knights, dressed in their regalia, and perhaps fifty members of the Mexica nobility. Moctezuma's sons, Iquehuacatzin and Mahchimaleh, stood with their father below the gloomy tapestry.

Moctezuma was addressing the crowd, but his words were aimed at Tlacaelel. The regalia he usually wore in Tenochtitlan was pared back, replaced with simpler, cooler clothes for the stifling air of the jungle. A lightweight, charcoal cloak was draped loosely over his shoulders and reached down to his thigh. A high collar of midnight feathers rested on his shoulders with a flash of startling red in a band running around behind his neck. A broad loincloth of the same colour complemented the cloak but echoed the collar with a broad red stripe across it. The elegance of his clothes was complemented by one of his many wooden staffs that he had made into his badge of office.

'These two men were your closest advisors and yet you tell me that you knew nothing of their plans?'

Tlacaelel faced the questions calmly, but he looked old and tired. Axayacatl had not seen the general since he had set out for Totonaca with the army half a year ago. It did not seem so long ago, but the passage of a handful of moons compounded by imprisonment had not been kind to the man. He had been stripped of all but his loincloth and the man's skin seemed loose upon his frame.

'Jaguar had no part in the attack, so your supposed link to my involvement is only through one of the men, not two.'

'You dispute the account my sons have given?'

Tlacaelel turned his head, sloth-like towards Iquehuacatzin and fixed him with a spear-like gaze.

'I don't doubt the certainty with which they speak,' said the general. His head swivelled slowly back to look at Moctezuma.

The play with words was one that Axayacatl immediately understood. He could feel the hairs standing on the back of his neck and his arms as the implication sunk in. Tlacaelel believed the princes were somehow involved, but what did this mean for his own discovery? Two Sign was involved and he'd been taking money from Xiconoc, but he couldn't have been acting on orders from Moctezuma's sons as well.

'Why then is Jaguar in hiding?'

'Do we know that he's in hiding, My Lord? From the account given by Lord Iquehuacatzin it seems more likely that he is dead.'

'You forget that I know this warrior,' said Moctezuma. 'Heart of the Jaguar was held captive in Chalco and secured his own release by taking on their best ullama players and winning. He has shown himself to be most... resilient.'

'My Lord, if he is in hiding it's because he believes himself to be in danger,' said Tlacaelel from his cage.

'From who?' Moctezuma frowned. 'Two Sign and the rest of the traitors are dead. Or will you tell me that, like the jungle creature whose name he carries, this man is afraid of his own shadow?' That drew a few chuckles from around the room.

'I suggest we make a list of anyone who stood to gain from your death.'

'Like you, brother,' observed Moctezuma.

'It is a distressingly short list at the moment,' agreed the general. 'May we add a few more names to it?'

'That would suit you, wouldn't it?' Iquehuacatzin cut in. His voice took on a warning edge. 'Who do you propose should join you on this list?'

For the merest heartbeat, Axayacatl felt sure Tlacaelel was going to name Moctezuma's sons, but he did not. A long pause stretched out into an uncomfortable silence and then suddenly, Axayacatl found himself speaking out.

'Put my name on the list,' he called out across the hall.

Obsidian Snake grabbed Axayacatl's arm to restrain him but stepped away a heartbeat later when he realised it was too late. His cousin was already committed.

'Axayacatl!' exclaimed Moctezuma. 'When did you get here?'

'Just a few days ago, My Lord.'

'And what is this madness? Why have you spoken?'

'My Lord. Lord Tlacaelel means to make a list of those who profit by your death. I am your grandson and therefore I belong on that list.' Here was an opportunity to draw Iquehuacatzin out. The man was impossibly proud, but there was no guarantee he would react as Axayacatl hoped. It was a huge risk, maybe even madness, but it might just be worth it if the arrogant prince took the bait. What of Xiconoc though? Was he still at the centre of the plot? That would have to wait. Xiconoc was not here and Iquehuacatzin was; moreover, it did look as though he had something to hide. Very well, thought Axayacatl. For once, he felt strong. Iquehuacatzin already hated him so there was nothing to lose by tricking him into putting his own name forward. After that he could focus on Xiconoc and making the greedy merchant pay for the damage he had caused his family. Something Nezahualcoyotl had said came to mind, something about catching a snake by the head, not the tail. Xiconoc was a long way away. Here, Iquehuacatzin was the immediate problem and only time would tell which was the head and which was the tail.

Axayacatl waited, heart hammering in his chest, wondering if the prince would take the bait. Moctezuma was about to speak when Iquehuacatzin laughed derisively.

'You? What a peculiar upstart you are!' Iquehuacatzin's voice was puzzled condescension that played well to the room. There was a ripple of amusement.

Moctezuma waved for silence and bade Axayacatl approach him. Several courtiers stepped aside to allow him through, eyeing him with suspicion.

'You don't belong on this list,' stated Moctezuma.

Axayacatl suppressed his fear. 'So you say, My Lord, but look around you. Everyone is already wondering whether I am responsible. My name is on the list now, whether you like it or not—'

'Ridiculous!' interrupted Iquehuacatzin. 'A hundred Colhua relatives stand between you and the top of that list with me at the top.' His brother tapped him on the shoulder. 'My brother, Mahchimaleh, and me... at the top,' resumed Iquehuacatzin without a hint of an apology. 'The throne is our rightful heritage when our father passes away.'

Axayacatl caught sight of Tlacaelel at the back of the room, saw him smile and tip him the smallest nod. Moctezuma just watched.

'So my name is on the list,' raged Iquehuacatzin, 'but don't think you can point the finger of suspicion at me!'

Now it was time to pin both ends of the snake and see which was the head. This was Axayacatl's chance to take revenge on Xiconoc. The realisation he had had on the way to the courthouse was his weapon. There was a link between the merchant and the warrior Two Sign, he was sure of it. The only problem with linking Xiconoc with the plot was that it would let Moctezuma's sons off the hook. As much as he despised the two men, Axayacatl's resolve held firm. Freeing his family from the merchant's clutches was more important.

'Lord Iquehuacatzin, I had no intention of bringing you into this,' said Axayacatl, mustering as much innocence as he could. 'Lord Tlacaelel suggested a list of people who stood to gain from the tlatoani's death and it is you who volunteered your own name and placed it at the top of the list.' Axayacatl paused again, allowing the room to consider that fact. 'But I name another of the Colhua family as the traitor.'

The collective gasp was impressive and Axayacatl knew that he was committed beyond retrieval. His suspicion had to be correct or he would pay the price.

'My Lord, your brother was paying large sums of money to Two Sign,' said Axayacatl. 'I believe he had a hand in this.'

'Tlacaelel?' said Moctezuma, gazing towards the rear of the room where the general sat in his cage.

'No, My Lord. The name you must add to the list is that of your other brother, Xiconoc—'

'Run back to your mother's skirts, Axayacatl,' interrupted Iquehuacatzin. 'Leave the grown men to sort this out. We've heard enough of your foolish ideas.'

Moctezuma ignored his son and glared at Axayacatl. 'You speak rashly, young man, and I do not like the words that come from your mouth.'

'Send him away, Father. He's trying to sow discord in our family to further his own aims.'

'I will ask for your advice if I have need of it!' warned Moctezuma.

'My Lord,' called Tlacaelel. 'There may be something in what Axayacatl says. Two Sign was in trouble. He had run up some large debts. He had taken to gambling in a big way. I only learned of this recently and have not had time to confront him over it.'

'That may be so, but I will not have wild accusations bandied about, especially when it concerns members of my family.' He frowned at Axayacatl. 'Xiconoc paid Two Sign's debts? Are you sure?'

Axayacatl replied, emboldened by Tlacaelel's support. 'Yes, My Lord. It's well known that your brother keeps meticulous records. Search his house if you do not believe me. I have seen records that he made, evidence of payments to the Eagle Knight.'

'Listen to me, Axayacatl,' Moctezuma intoned gravely. 'Though you are my daughter's son, I will come down very hard on you if this claim proves false. Retract your words now and out of respect for your parents, I will forget this outburst ever happened. If you insist on sticking to this story, I shall have my brother's house searched. If nothing is found to support your claim, you will dance the steps of shame through the streets of Tenochtitlan and when the people have grown bored of pelting you with rotten fruit and beating you with sticks, I will have your tongue cut out to prevent you spreading any more malicious lies. Do you understand?'

'I understand,' he replied, fervently hoping the tlatoani's brother had not decided to clear out the evidence. 'Search Lord Xiconoc's place. You will find proof of what I said and more besides.'

'Bravely said!' Iquehuacatzin said in a mocking tone. He winked at his brother. 'Let's stock up on fruit, Mahchimaleh. That sounds like good sport.'

'Lord Moctezuma,' Tlacaelel called out from his cage. 'If Xiconoc arranged for this attempt on the tlatoani's life then perhaps your sons knew of it too.'

'What?!' exclaimed Iquehuacatzin.

Inside his cage, Tlacaelel gave a ghost of a smile. 'What is the purpose of your visit to Ahuilizapan? Why are you and your brother here?'

'I don't know what you mean. Lord Moctezuma, our father, invited us.'

'That's true,' rumbled Moctezuma, 'but only on the condition that you help setup trading links with the local rulers. You know how I despise the frivolity of your lifestyles, you especially, Iquehuacatzin. It was I who arranged for you to work for Xiconoc.'

Mahchimaleh frowned, his big eyebrows compressed in an ugly bar across his eyes.

Iquehuacatzin coloured. 'We did as you asked.'

'So you are helping to establish trade links with the merchants in the region.'

'Of course.'

'On behalf of Xiconoc,' Tlacaelel cut in, speaking from the back of the room.

Moctezuma finished up. 'You must have spent many days planning this trip with him.'

'Ah… yes,' replied Iquehuacatzin carefully, 'but we knew nothing of this treachery.'

Moctezuma nodded, looking pensive. 'I see. And while you've been here you've been busy helping his traders to make deals?'

'Yes… well, we haven't been here long.'

From the gloom, Tlacaelel laughed. 'You've been here thirty days or more! You arrived in time to see the bird-men fly.'

Moctezuma glared at Iquehuacatzin and Mahchimaleh. 'Hold your hands up in front of you.'

'Why?' Iquehuacatzin was sullen.

Moctezuma surged to his feet. '*Just do it!*' he roared.

Slowly, his sons raised their hands and held them out.

'I'm going to clap my hands,' said Moctezuma, 'and when I do, I want you both to speak a number. The number of meetings you have had with local chiefs, village elders or merchants to help further our trade links in the area. Keep your hands where I can see them so that you cannot signal to each other.'

Mahchimaleh glanced at his brother and licked his lips nervously, but Iquehuacatzin didn't see. He was staring back at his father with a look of pure loathing.

Moctezuma's hands came together. Clap.

'Two,' said Iquehuacatzin.

'Two,' echoed Mahchimaleh fractionally after.

'Splendid work. What were their names and where did they live?' Moctezuma rounded on his sons.

Iquehuacatzin's mouth worked as he tried to conjure some lies, but his father's patience had run out.

'Tell me something, *boys*. What did your uncle promise you if you helped to overthrow me, eh? Did he promise you a position on the Grand Council?'

Iquehuacatzin's look of contempt must have conveyed more than Axayacatl understood because the tlatoani threw back his head and roared with laughter.

'Ha! He promised you my throne! Yes? And you believed him?'

A malevolent glare was Iquehuacatzin's only response.

'Did he tell you all he wanted was lower taxes for his trading enterprise? Let me guess... he told you that Tenochtitlan should keep the spoils of war and give less to Texcoco. Do you think I haven't heard his crazy ideas?'

'Xiconoc is right.' Usually the quiet one, Mahchimaleh finally found his voice. 'The Triple Alliance is a disgrace and shames the people of Tenochtitlan. We carry the burden, while Texcoco and Tlacopan reap rewards they do not deserve. We do all the hard work. Look at what we've achieved here in Ahuilizapan while Nezahualcoyotl's forces take a handful of insignificant villages in the north. Why should we share our spoils with him?'

'Well, well, Mahchimaleh...' exclaimed Moctezuma. 'It sounds as though you've been doing some thinking, or at least listening to others. What did Xiconoc promise you? Or perhaps your big brother offered you one of the lesser cities of the lake.'

'You're holding us back, old man,' rejoined Iquehuacatzin angrily. 'These old compromises hark back to an earlier time when Tenochtitlan was weak. We don't need to keep Texcoco sweet anymore. We can take them and anyone else who stands in our way and rule the entire land properly.'

Moctezuma stepped forward and slapped Iquehuacatzin hard. 'And I thought you were the clever one.' He turned away from his son and stepped back onto the dais. 'Your mother will be very disappointed.'

Iquehuacatzin leaped for his father's exposed back, but Axayacatl was quicker. He had known that this moment would come and he sprang forward. He had no weapon to counter the outstretched dagger that suddenly appeared. Presumably the men guarding the room had been less inclined to strip-search the tlatoani's sons. Axayacatl barrelled into Iquehuacatzin whose entire focus was on his father. They crashed to the ground where Axayacatl had the sense to roll away, putting distance between himself and the blade.

'Seize them!' shouted Moctezuma.

The nearest guards reached out but were immediately dashed aside. Mahchimaleh's turn had come to take the lead. Silent

Mahchimaleh, who Axayacatl had always assumed was slow-witted, moved with lightning speed and animal ferocity. He caught the wrist of one guard who swung at him and spun him round, hurling him into another one of Moctezuma's men. Axayacatl tried to stand up and then felt the man's foot crash against his chest. He flew back, winded, and could only watch as the brothers dodged two more Grey Privy Knights and made for the doorway. There was a brief scuffle and before anyone else in the room could get close, the brothers had gone.

Chapter 35 – Tenochtitlan

The sheer number of dwellings that stretched as far as the eye could see, that was what struck Clawfoot when he returned to the valley. He hurried down the track towards the southern end of Lake Texcoco and the majestic sprawl of Tenochtitlan and its sister cities that wrapped around the far side of the lake, rooftops as numerous as the stars at night. The other contrast was the cool crisp air. No wonder that the armies of the Mexica Empire were sweeping the jungle people aside. It was impossible to imagine anyone but savages living in those hot and inhospitable conditions.

Jaguar's disappearance into the waters of the cave had been a sign. He had to be a demon or possessed by an evil spirit. Only a creature from the underworld would have chosen to make his escape through a flooded cave and somehow Clawfoot knew he hadn't perished. Tired, footsore and hungry after nearly five days on the road, the high priest's warning about what to expect if the mission failed rang in Clawfoot's ears. He urged himself to a limping run. It was bad enough that they had failed in the main objective, but if Jaguar had escaped and Feathered Darkness found out, Clawfoot knew his life would be forfeit. He knew that he would be better off taking his own life than to set foot inside the Serpent Wall without killing Jaguar. All now depended on the warrior's will to save his own family. Clawfoot had seen the look in the warrior's eyes when he'd threatened his family. It was just a matter of waiting there until he showed up.

Running was no longer possible. Every footstep was an effort of conscious willpower. Clawfoot's feet were a mass of oozing blisters, but the need to reach Jaguar's family kept him going. On the approach to Tenochtitlan along the southern causeway, his exhausted body forced him to a stumbling halt. He lurched off the road feeling dizzy and threw himself down on the bank to rest.

An elderly woman bent double under the weight of an enormous basket stopped to ask if he was well and offered him water. Irritated that she was making him look weak, Clawfoot drained the gourd, then waved the woman away. He breathed deeply trying to clear his head. People moved behind him on the road, going about their business and paying him no heed. In front of him stood a sea of silvery green reeds, rippling gently in the midday breeze. Little storms of flies swirled and eddied, then flared upwards before dropping back to repeat their endless dance. Down to his right where the reeds thinned out, a repair crew was shoring up a section of the causeway that had eroded. Slaves or mayeques, peasants dressed only in filthy loincloths, stood knee-deep at the water's edge, pulling up mud and roots to dress the crumbling bank. They called to each other as they worked, a constant stream of banter interspersed with good-natured laughter, the shimmering lake as their backdrop. Their easy camaraderie annoyed Clawfoot. No such friendships existed for him in the Order of Huitzilopochtli. The other priests kept their distance and when they didn't, it was because, like Angry Lizard, they had decided to act on some grudge, real or imagined. Clawfoot realised he was grinding his teeth. He forced himself to take another deep breath. None of it mattered. The priesthood was his life and it was his friend. He needed nothing else. He would finish this job and report back to Feathered Darkness. Clawfoot knew he was valuable to the high priest. There would be more work for him that could not be entrusted to the rank and file priests.

An iridescent green beetle crawled onto Clawfoot's leg. He brushed it off, then stood up. He patted his dusty robe down as best he could, aware that he must look like one of those disreputable soothsayers who plied their trade in the marketplace peddling dubious divinations and worthless charms. Feeling stronger for his rest, Clawfoot rejoined the foot traffic heading in to Tenochtitlan, buoyed up with the knowledge that Harbour Street wasn't far away. The thought of Jaguar walking into his own home to find him waiting there filled Clawfoot with a savage joy.

At the broad shoulder of barren ground where the causeway joined onto the island of Tenochtitlan, Clawfoot paused to scan the entrance to the city. It occurred to him that Feathered Darkness may have posted men of the Silent Watch here to wait for his return. It was unlikely; after all, one entire cycle of the moon had passed while he'd been away. Still, the prospect of being intercepted and hauled in front of the high priest now was too horrible to contemplate. Two men with spears were standing guard at the archway into the city, but they were regular city guardsmen posted by the clans, not the high priest's men. Clawfoot felt the hairs on the back of his neck rise even though there didn't appear to be anyone else spying on the road. *Best to be safe*, he thought.

An old man approached from the south carrying an enormous bundle of firewood tied with a stout hemp rope and slung over his back. His face was burdened by a mountain range of frown lines and partially covered by sweat-stuck fine, grey hair. Clawfoot fell in with him and engaged in eager conversation. He would look less conspicuous if he was travelling with someone. At first, the man was suspicious.

'I'm in training,' explained Clawfoot, trying to gain the other's confidence. 'My master has instructed me to go out and spend all day providing the good people of Tenochtitlan with horoscopes.' They were only a few paces from the archway into the city now. The guards weren't even remotely interested, but it wasn't them that worried Clawfoot.

'For free?'

'Yes, indeed. My master is very harsh,' said Clawfoot, looking downtrodden. 'Of the five hundred or so predictions I have provided in the last year, only five later proved to be incorrect. Three of them because the supplicant misremembered their own birth day. Even that is not good enough for my teacher, the wise and forever angry Eternal Flame.'

'That does seem tough, Venerable Father,' said the porter, raising his eyebrows and deepening his frown briefly. 'I humbly accept.'

They were passing between the guards now.

'What is your birth sign? You remember it well, I trust.'

'Of course. Water, third day in the House of the Rabbit.'

'Hmm, and today is...' Clawfoot paused, mentally checking the number of days since he had left Ahuilizapan. 'Cuauhtli, the Eagle, and the ninth day in the House of Grass. So we have the Eagle, who protects fighting men, represents action and freedom and whose guardian is Xipe Totec, our Lord the Bringer, He of the Flayed Flesh.'

The porter grimaced, accentuating the furrows on his brow again.' What does that mean, Venerable Father?' He shifted the load on his back so he could better observe Clawfoot.

The guards were behind them and a plaza opened up with a main street running to the north and side streets in just about every other direction. This was Teopan and Harbour Street wasn't far away.

'It means that you must be careful who you do business with today. Fight for a better deal for your wares but avoid getting into trouble with people in authority such as clan elders or the city watch.' Clawfoot smiled beatifically, ignoring the fact that priests also counted in that group. 'Do you have a buyer for this wood?'

'Yes, I always deal with Huezacatca in the Street of Shadows, in Moyotlan.'

'Maybe the telling relates to him,' ventured Clawfoot.

The porter set down his load on the kerbstone of a planter, one of four that bordered the edges of the plaza. He scratched his head. 'Well, that would be worrying. He's never given me any trouble before. Always pays a fair price for a load.'

'Well, be on the lookout,' insisted Clawfoot. 'Perhaps there is someone else out there who will give you a better price. I must leave now. May the gods protect you!'

Clawfoot took his leave, hopeful that the lengthy conversation would have appeared dull and uninteresting to anyone watching. At the edge of the plaza, he found a stall selling tamales stuffed with mushrooms and charred peppers and invoked his right as a priest to a free meal. The sweet flavour of the peppers mingled with savoury mushrooms was like an elixir to Clawfoot's undernourished body. The prospect of taking Jaguar on was suddenly less daunting. When he had finished eating, he negotiated the narrow lanes among whitewashed houses until he found Harbour Street. The commercial district annoyed Clawfoot. It was a haven for artisans selling worthless brooches, bracelets, ear and lip plugs and other such worldly trivia. He soon located the workshop, which occupied a place on the main thoroughfare. He crossed the street, gently pulled aside the cloth door hanging and stepped inside. A short woman in a green dress was singing to herself quietly as she sluiced water over some bowls. She looked up from her cleaning.

'Are you lost?'

Clawfoot didn't reply immediately, instead choosing to inspect the room for signs that Heart of the Jaguar might have already returned. He could sense the woman's discomfort rising, so he waited longer, enjoying the level of authority granted to him by his priestly attire, tatty though it was. At last he turned his gaze back to the occupant.

'You are not Heart of the Jaguar's woman.'

She shook her head. 'I'm his sister.'

Irritation flared as Clawfoot realised she was not going to use the honorific title. Now he understood why his teachers disliked him. 'What's your name?'

'Little Beetle.'

His questions were unsettling her, so he decided to ask more. 'Is he here?'

'Who? Jaguar?'

'Yes. Has he returned from the war?'

'No. Not yet.'

The woman wasn't volunteering any more information than was absolutely necessary and that needled Clawfoot who expected total cooperation. He nodded, affecting indifference.

'Where is his wife?'

'Not here. Look, who are you? Why do you want to know where she is?'

'I have a message,' replied Clawfoot.

'You are a priest, are you not?'

'I am. Are you going to call me Venerable Father?'

Little Beetle gave him an odd look. 'You've travelled a long way, haven't you, Venerable Father?'

There was something disrespectful in her tone that made Clawfoot wonder if he'd broken some unwritten code by entering the house uninvited. He had never had any personal space, either living rough or in the priesthood.

'Totonaca,' replied Clawfoot, brushing absent-mindedly at the layers of dust that clung to him.

'Oh dear! I hope it's not bad news,' said Little Beetle, suddenly concerned.' Were you with the army, Venerable Father?'

'The message isn't for you,' said Clawfoot brusquely.' It's for Jaguar's woman. Where is she?'

'Gone to the family's smallholding.'

'Gifted to him for his successes in battle, no doubt. And where, exactly, is this smallholding?' It felt good to be away from the chaos of the jungle. He understood the city and its people, the way they lived in constant fear. Huitzilopochtli's reign over all creation was much firmer here in Tenochtitlan than it had been out in the wilds of Totonaca.

Clawfoot drew himself up, discovering that he towered over her and then realised he had made a mistake. Initially wary, Jaguar's sister had warmed to the idea of a messenger, but his sudden and ill-fitting arrogance had filled her with mistrust again.

'To the west,' Beetle said, clearly stalling.

Clawfoot crossed the space in a heartbeat and pushed her up against the wall. 'Tell me where she is or I will crush you, LittleBeetle. Do you understand?'

'What are you doing to my wife?' said a deep voice.

Clawfoot pinned Little Beetle's throat to the wall with one hand and whipped out his thin blade with his other hand while he turned to assess the threat. The newcomer was a tall man dressed in a soot-blackened leather tunic with an unusually long front that must have been made to protect his thighs and knees. It looked as though he was constructed of grime. *Strong but not used to fighting*, decided Clawfoot, observing the man's stance, *and he's tired too*.

'Nothing, as long as she tells me what I need to know.' Clawfoot hardened his gaze.

Beetle whimpered and her husband took a half-hearted step forwards.

'That's right. Come on over here where I can keep an eye on you,' said Clawfoot, gesturing at the wall. 'What's your name, big man?'

'Arrow One. Please... don't hurt her.'

The man was broken, as easily as that. Clawfoot made a soothing noise or at least that's what he aimed for. As soon as he had both of them in his field of vision, he slid his blade up to the corner of Little Beetle's eye.

'Please,' she whispered. 'I told you everything I know.'

Disrespect, that's what it was. These people didn't understand their place. Clawfoot's ire overwhelmed him. It was a small movement – a slip of the hand really – but it was enough to puncture the woman's eyeball. She shrieked and tried to put her hands up to her eyes, but Clawfoot prevented her with the point of his dagger, jabbing until her hands were dripping blood. Her body sagged as she dissolved into hysterics, sobbing. Her right cheek was a mess of tears and a gelatinous fluid shot through with streaks of red. She would have slumped to the floor if it hadn't been for Clawfoot's grip. He moved the point of his blade beneath her other eye and hissed at her to be quiet.

Arrow One had turned white. 'Please!' he begged, sagging to his knees. 'What do you want of us? We have done nothing wrong.'

Clawfoot ignored the husband. He wouldn't intervene if he hadn't acted by now.

'That was for lying to me.' He used his most menacing voice. 'Your brother owns land bequeathed to him by the tlatoani and you claim you don't know where it is? You lost one eye to stupidity, but I think you're clever enough to keep the other one.'

'I'll tell you,' said the tall man. He had tears in his own eyes and was wringing his hands. 'Please let go of her and I'll tell you what you want to know.'

'Don't do it,' whispered Little Beetle. 'I don't know what he wants with Precious Flower, but it isn't good,' she added, before Clawfoot could stop her.

Clawfoot was pleasantly surprised at the woman's fighting spirit. She and Jaguar had come from the same family, that much was certain. His anger subsided, sated by the intoxicating power of violence. He flipped the knife over in the blink of an eye, slid the blade into Beetle's mouth and pulled it out sideways, slicing her cheek all the way to her back teeth.

This time it was Arrow One who shouted. He had fallen face-first on the floor in terror. 'Xalatlaco! Merciful Creator Pair and in the name of Quetzalcoatl, please stop! Precious Flower has gone to Xalatlaco! Please, I beg you to stop.'

'Directions,' hissed Clawfoot. 'I don't know this place.'

'There's a small village in the foothills southwest of Coyoacan.' Beetle's husband rattled off the response, breathless in his eagerness to comply. 'Take the road to Toluca but south where it meets a small river. Please... please leave my woman alone now.'

Clawfoot let go of Little Beetle who was shuddering and weeping uncontrollably, tears spilling onto her ruined mouth. He stepped back smartly and watched as Arrow One moved to comfort her.

'When you see Jaguar, tell him I'll be waiting for him at Xalatlaco.' He curled his lip disdainfully and swept from the depressing little home, cleaning the blade on the black cloth of his robe and sliding it into its wooden sheath. There could be no doubt that Arrow One had been telling the truth. Priests deserved respect, but it was earned on the edge of a blade.

Chapter 36
The Western Mountains

Precious Flower dropped the adze and looked at her hands. They were rough and the fingernails were torn and broken. Farming life was even less kind to them than toil in the workshop. Still, the countless rows of maize seedlings filled her with pride. If only Jaguar were here to see the work that she had done. Of course, she would never be as good at farming as she was at carving jade, but she might grow to love it almost as much.

This field was planted. Everyone else had moved on to another area except for Precious Flower who was determined to clear out the irrigation ditch. This land was prone to flash flooding, which was no use to the crops. In the spring deluge, the irrigation channels trapped the water, allowing it to soak into the ground. In the summer, a stream was diverted twice a day to moisten the parched earth. This ditch was a tangle of dry twigs and vicious thorns that would clog it if left uncleared. She eyed the brush suspiciously. It was exactly the kind of place where snakes made their homes. What she needed was an expert snake catcher.

'Blade? Where are you?' she cried.

'Here, Mama!' called a tousled head from nearby. Blade had discovered an ants' nest further along the ditch and was busy excavating. He stood up so that Precious Flower could see where he was.

'Have you got your snake-catching stick with you?' she asked.

'Yes, Mama.'

'Well, get over here then! Poke around in that brush and see if anything comes out.'

'Have you seen a snake?' asked Blade, eyes wide with excitement. Since his lucky triumph on the road to Xalatlaco when he had caught a rattlesnake, Blade had appointed himself as chief of vermin control.

'No, and I don't want to either. I don't want a repeat of what happened on the way here. You scared me half to death!'

'I was scared too, at first, but I caught it didn't I?'

'Yes, my brave little warrior; you did, and I'm very proud of you. Even Fast Rabbit was impressed.'

Blade looked very pleased with himself as he went to retrieve his catching pole. It was a head taller than he was and had a forked end.

'Be careful,' said Precious Flower.

'I will.'

Blade wielded the catching pole confidently but without producing any quarry.

'Is it safe?'

'I think so, Mama, but be careful,' said Blade solicitously. 'It's in shadow down there, so they might be sleepy.'

Precious Flower smiled. She was delighted that Blade was taking his job so seriously. Fast Rabbit had been full of praise for the boy's capacity for learning and the responsibility clearly made the boy feel important and grown-up. She passed him a gourd.

'Have a drink. It's getting hot.'

'Mama, can a farmer be a warrior too?' Blade asked after he had drunk his fill.

'Yes, my pouncing jaguar, but only in times of crisis.'

'Why?'

'Because the business of growing food is so important. Without food our armies will starve.'

Blade gave this some thought. 'But if the farmers are killed there will be no one to grow food for the armies.'

'That's true. It's a complicated business, isn't it?'

'Yes, Mama.'

'That's why Tlacaelel and the other wise men on the council are in charge,' said Precious Flower. She picked up her adze and climbed down into the ditch where she started hacking the tangle into smaller pieces.

Blade said something, so she had to stop. 'Please would you repeat that? I didn't hear because of all the noise I was making.'

'Oh, yes.' Blade sat down and dangled his legs over the edge of the ditch. 'Have we always had this land, Mama?'

'No, Blade. Twice a year the tlatoani gives out land to brave warriors who have done great deeds. Your father received this plot five years ago, not long before you were born.'

'So the tlatoani owned it before that.'

'Yes, well, no. This land was taken from our enemies as a punishment for opposing us.'

'Where are they now? The people who owned it.'

'I don't know, Blade. Sometimes, our enemies become our friends and if that happens and they help us fight our enemies then they can earn new land back.' Precious Flower stooped and pulled out twigs and weeds, throwing them onto the bank.

'And if they don't become our friends?'

'Well, then you know what happens to them, dearest, don't you?'

'They go to feed the gods.'

'That's right, my little warrior. Now, let me clear this awhile and...'

There was movement on the horizon. Out of the shimmering heat haze, a lone figure approached along the dusty road from Tenochtitlan. Precious Flower's heart skipped a beat. Perhaps it was Jaguar, finally returned from the campaigns in the east. She watched as a faint breeze plucked at the distant figure's cloak. It was a man but too slender to be Jaguar and his gait was all wrong. Precious Flower chided herself for being so silly. There was no reason to think that any of the warriors would be back for many moons to come.

A bead of sweat trickled down Precious Flower's forehead and a fly buzzed, trying to land again. She ignored both and closed her eyes. She formed a picture in her head of Jaguar as she had last seen him outside the workshop. They had embraced, awkwardly because of the sword and bag of provisions slung over Jaguar's shoulder. He had smiled that foolish, boyish smile of his and kissed her lovingly. Precious Flower remembered the gentle strength of that hug and the promise it offered of good times to come.

When she opened her eyes, the traveller was closer and Precious Flower could just make out his face. Her heart lurched as she recognised the young priest visited her in her in Tenochtitlan. He was still some distance away. Perhaps he hadn't seen them.

'Blade! Come with me now!'

'Why, Mama? What's the matter? Did you find a snake after all?'

'No, Blade, but we must run back to our house.' She caught hold of Blade's hand in one of hers and lifted the hem of her skirt with the other. 'Quickly now.' Together they flew over the ruts and rough lumps of dried earth.

'Mama! I dropped the stick,' wailed Blade and twisted, trying to look back over his shoulder.

'We'll come back for it later,' cried Precious Flower. She tried to keep Blade upright, pulling his arm high to help his short legs clear the uneven terrain.

'Why are we running? Why can't we go back for it now?'

Precious Flower tried to keep the terror from her voice. 'There's a bad man coming. We have to hide from him.' What was the priest doing here? Had he tracked her all this way and if so, why had it taken so long? They were nearing their little mud-walled home now. How she wished it was near to the village instead of being stuck out on its own. Would it be possible to change course and head towards the others instead? Precious Flower didn't think so. They would have to cut across the priest's path and he'd meet them long before they reached the safety of the village. No. They would have to get to their little hut and hunker down inside...hope he went to the village first to ask for directions. Fast Rabbit and some of the others would be there. They would turn him away or come with him to find her, at least that way she and Blade would be safe. They leapt the ditch that marked the edge of the field and got to the lowly building. Blade was just about to go inside when Precious Flower had an idea.

'No. If he's coming for us, he may think to look in here. Let's hide in bushes behind the well.'

Precious Flower and Blade skirted round the hut and made for the well, which lay at the centre of a shallow depression in the earth. The well! It was at least the height of a man down to the water and Fast Rabbit had said that once at the bottom was only waist deep and they could climb back out using the footholds in the stone wall that reinforced its sides. She was about to veer off towards it when it occurred to her that anyone who had travelled from Tenochtitlan would be thirsty and the first place they would go would be the well. Precious Flower looked back and saw no sign of the priest. Good, she'd put their home between them. They were hidden as they dashed across the final twenty paces past the well and into the stand of straggly bushes.

'In here, Mama?'

'Yes, Blade. Push as far as you can inside and sit down.'

'Alright, Mama, hold my hand. Don't be afraid now. He won't find us here. I'm very good at hiding. When I play back home with—'

'Hush now, dearest. I know…you win almost all the time, but now we have to be quiet. Can you do that for me?'

Precious Flower sat down, snapping some dry branches as she did. She tried to slow her breathing down. Even her heartbeat sounded thunderous in her ears.

'I hope there are no snakes in here, Mama,' whispered Blade. 'I haven't got my stick with me.'

Chapter 37
The Jungles of Totonaca

The thrill of a burning had drawn a large crowd, but the atmosphere was tense. The ordinary citizens of Ahuilizapan weren't exactly devoted to their tlatoani, but neither were they content to have his replacement foisted on them by their new Mexica overlords. The two orders of knights were out in full strength to keep the peace.

Shield of Gold knew that such rituals took place in Tenochtitlan from time to time, but he had never seen one. As Tlacaelel's messenger he would have a grandstand view of the spectacle. The general and Moctezuma, so recently reconciled, stood a few paces away, watching the proceedings from under an awning. Shield of Gold saw Tlacaelel looking at him. A wisp of his usually immaculate queue had slipped from its tie and a clutch of grey hairs curled over his ear. The general smiled, but the strain that he had been under was evident from the lines in his face and the deep shadows beneath his eyes. Axayacatl was also with them. His recent contribution to exposing the wayward princes had catapulted him into the tlatoani's inner circle.

Last Medicine was next to Shield of Gold. He was watching as Ahuilizapan's head man was corralled inside a ring of burning wood, but his rheumy eyes didn't look entirely focused.

'Why is Imixquitl being sacrificed?' Shield of Gold asked the veteran.

'Eh?' Last Medicine came to and looked at Shield of Gold with a thoughtful expression. 'Oh...well, we can't have the people of Ahuilizapan thinking that our own people carried out this attack on our ruler,' he explained. 'So we blame theirs. We've carried out a thorough search and turned up a local man who was involved in the attempt on Moctezuma's life and can implicate him.'

'But none of the attackers survived,' Shield of Gold pointed out.

Last Medicine shrugged. 'Then this one supplied some weapons. It doesn't matter. What's important is that he has sworn it was all arranged by their own ruler.'

'Why did he say that?'

Last Medicine gave a sad smile. 'Because we have his family imprisoned and he wants us to set them free.'

'So Tlacaelel sets an example of Imixquitl and shows our new conquered territories how we deal with dissent,' concluded Shield of Gold.

It was a ruthless side to the general that Shield of Gold hadn't seen before. He watched the six Mexica warriors who had won the right to put the ruler of Ahuilizapan to death use long water-soaked poles to nudge the blazing pyre closer to the centre of the arena. Shield of Gold was filled with horror and admiration in equal measure as the noble lord stood still, arms folded, even as his hair began to curl under the onslaught of the heat. It couldn't last, of course. Another shove sent embers spilling over his feet causing him to dance and jerk uncontrollably, while the flesh on his limbs began to scorch and the edges of his loincloth singed. Then, suddenly he leapt, as though trying to escape from the encroaching circle of flames. He didn't make it. He fell and a string of terrible shrieks raked the watching crowd.

It was too much for Shield of Gold. Last Medicine noticed him turn away.

'It is often necessary to remove the previous ruler and many of his people. They rarely bend to our will. Their allegiances are always somewhere else, but if we choose a new ruler...he will be wholly our man.'

'For how long?' asked Shield of Gold.

Last Medicine threw back his head, eyes squeezed shut beneath his hoary eyebrows, and laughed. The puckered scars on the old man's neck bobbed grotesquely. Shield of Gold swallowed uneasily. The veteran put a hand on his shoulder.

'You're too clever to be a messenger. Lord Tlacaelel will have to find something for you to do that's more worthy of your abilities.'

Shield of Gold tried to think of a reply, but he was spared when Tlacaelel and Axayacatl broke away from the tlatoani and approached. Moctezuma, still closely protected by a cadre of Grey Privy Knights, was gesturing across the black smoke that was curling up from the arena. It was impossible to hear what he was saying, but his manner suggested he was not pleased. Lying prostrate at his feet were three members of Imixquitl's family, doubtless terrified that they would be next to dance among the flames. Musicians were processing around the edges of the arena playing flutes and drums.

'Here's the young man who set me free,' exclaimed Tlacaelel. 'I owe you my thanks, Shield of Gold.'

Shield of Gold inspected his feet, embarrassed. 'My Lord, it's mostly down to Lord Axayacatl and Jaguar.'

'Not true,' chided Axayacatl, tilting his face on one side. 'I had some information on Lord Xiconoc's involvement with the Eagle Knight, but it was you who brought the news from Jaguar that Two Sign was deep in debt. That helped to convince the tlatoani that none of this was Tlacaelel's doing.'

Tlacaelel spoke to Last Medicine. 'Did you know Two Sign was in so much trouble?'

'No, Lord Tlacaelel, I did not. He was never a man of many words, but after his son was taken from him he withdrew even further.'

'He should have said something. I could have helped. He's not the first person ever to be caught out by a love of gambling.'

'He was a proud man, Lord Tlacaelel,' offered Last Medicine. 'I'm sure he thought that he could handle it, right up until he realised that the debt was too large for him to deal with on his own. Then it would have been too shameful to admit to anyone, especially to you.'

Tlacaelel nodded thoughtfully and then turned to Shield of Gold. 'What of Jaguar? Where is he?'

'He's gone, Lord Tlacaelel.'

'Gone?'

'Yes, returned to Tenochtitlan.'

'I thought you said he was badly wounded.'

'Yes, My Lord, but he was worried for his family. He said they are in danger.'

'From the princes?'

Shield of Gold hesitated, wondering how much of this Jaguar would have wanted him to reveal. Inside the arena, dancers had filed in behind the musicians. They were standing in a circle facing outwards, swaying and windmilling their hands, displaying the red feather bracelets and gold braids that circled their wrists, necks and waists. In the centre of it all, sweating slaves used poles to push the hot ash to one side while two priests used another pole to hook out the twisted and blackened remains of Imixquitl. 'No, My Lord. Jaguar believed that Clawfoot was going after them.'

'Have you told the tlatoani about the young priest?' Last Medicine asked the general.

'Not yet. I need to be sure about this. The tlatoani is not in a forgiving mood right now. He will want to see a lot of blood spilled over this and if I falsely accuse the priests, all of that blood will be mine.' Tlacaelel looked at Shield of Gold. 'Is it true that you've known this young man Clawfoot for many years?'

'Until he showed up in Ahuilizapan, Lord Tlacaelel, I had not seen him for five years. We were part of a gang, orphans mostly.'

'And Clawfoot was one of the gang.'

'Yes, My Lord. Clawfoot was the leader.'

'What was he like?'

'He was a good leader. A little bit distant, but he always worked hard to keep us together. He was fearless. I never saw him scared of anything until that night the priests took Indigo.'

Axayacatl, who had been watching intently, cut in. 'The priests took one of the gang?'

'They ran an operation to clean up the streets,' explained Tlacaelel. 'You have to remember that it was a very hard time. A lot of people died in the famine and many of the children who lost their parents took to the streets. Please continue, young Shield of Gold.'

'Well, I remember how scared and angry Clawfoot had been that night, which is why I was so surprised to see that he'd joined the priesthood himself, the Order of Huitzilopochtli, I believe. When I asked him why he had become a priest, he said that they had taken him too.'

'Hmm, I see. Did you ask him why he was in Ahuilizapan?'

'Yes, Lord Tlacaelel. He said that he was part of the mission to enlighten the local people about Huitzilopochtli and other deities.'

'The Ray of Truth,' concluded Tlacaelel.

'Yes, that's it.' Shield of Gold nodded. He felt more self-assured now that his voice had settled into a permanent deep timbre. 'Except, I did not believe him entirely. It felt as though he was trying to hide something, so later, I went to find Gathers the Dawn, the priest responsible for the Ray of Truth, and I spoke with him. He told me that Clawfoot showed up long after they'd all arrived, carrying special orders from the high priest, but that he never took part in the efforts to convert the local people.'

'If what you say is true, then Feathered Darkness may be at the heart of it all. I will need to go and speak to Gathers the Dawn—'

'Er...excuse me,' interrupted Axayacatl. 'Who is Gathers the Dawn?'

'The Lord-High Spiritual Assessor, the priest in charge of converting the locals,' explained Last Medicine.

'Wait, wait, wait,' said Axayacatl. 'Iquehuacatzin and his brother were working for Lord Xiconoc with help from a priest—'

'Or perhaps several priests,' Last Medicine cut in.

'And those priests were sent here by Feathered Darkness, the High Priest of Huitzilopochtli! Can that be right?'

No one spoke for a while. Last Medicine rubbed his neck, fingers gingerly massaging the gouged and puckered scar tissue beneath his ear and then he spoke, his voice a deep rumble. 'That would mean Lord Xiconoc and the high priest planned this together.'

Axayacatl frowned. 'Is that possible?'

'Oh, it's possible,' replied Tlacaelel. 'Feathered Darkness' predecessor tried something similar. The priests can't help but meddle in the affairs of state.'

'What now?' asked Last Medicine.

'Clawfoot must be caught and questioned.'

Last Medicine sucked air through his teeth. 'I'm not certain that even you have that authority, Tlacaelel. Even if you do, there's no guarantee he'll talk.'

'No, perhaps not,' replied the general, 'but I can put him in front of the tlatoani and *he* can ask the questions.'

'It may not be necessary to question him,' said Shield of Gold. 'If he was one of the assassins, the tlatoani may recognise him.'

Tlacaelel beamed. 'Good thinking, young man! Now…I must go and send out some men to round up this rogue priest. You say he's headed for Tenochtitlan?'

'Yes, My Lord. He's looking for Jaguar, so find him and Clawfoot may come to you.'

'Right. Thank you for your help, Shield of Gold. Your honesty and spirit will serve you well.'

The general asked Last Medicine to explain his absence to Moctezuma and left. Drums took up a stately rhythm and the dancers slid sideways in stealthy steps. Axayacatl, Last Medicine and Shield of Gold watched the proceedings for a few moments before Last Medicine looked at Shield of Gold thoughtfully and spoke again.

'You're going to have to be careful,' he said, lowering his voice. The people around them were wrapped up in the preparations for the next spectacle in the arena. 'Don't tell anyone else what you know of this. Also, stay away from Jaguar until things calm down. While Moctezuma's sons are at large, they are a danger. If they find out that they can get to Jaguar through you…' He didn't finish the sentence.

'What use is silencing Jaguar now that the truth is out?'

'Revenge is motive enough for those two, Shield of Gold,' said Axayacatl. 'Last Medicine is right. There's no telling what they will do next. I never liked them before, but now I know why.

351

When we were young I used to blame it on their mother, putting ideas into their heads.'

'And now?' asked Shield of Gold after a long pause.

Axayacatl smiled. 'You had a difficult upbringing, did you not?'

'I had no upbringing at all, Lord Axayacatl. I never knew my mother...' Shield of Gold shrugged. 'My father and I had nothing. My father went lame. We only ate when I could find scraps thrown out for the dogs or beg some stale tamales from the stallholders in the market.'

'I have never had anything but the greatest respect for the macehualtin.' Axayacatl looked at Last Medicine who nodded in agreement. 'You live from day to day, unsure that you will eat but for the labour of your hands. We nobles know nothing of hardship and it makes us arrogant. Moctezuma's sons were born and bred to rule, part of a special family. Can you imagine what that's like?'

Shield of Gold shook his head.

'It wasn't their mother who made them what they are. It was all of us: their father, their uncle, all of the nobility. They were taught to expect great things. Should we be surprised that they see their father and their uncle as obstacles?'

'What about you, Lord Axayacatl? Weren't you raised to rule?' For a moment, Shield of Gold thought he'd gone too far, then Axayacatl's frown softened. Tlacaelel closed his eyes and squeezed the bridge of his nose, as if he had a headache. Or perhaps, thought Shield of Gold, it was the shrill note from the reed pipes that pained the man.

'Yes, of course,' said Axayacatl after a pause,' but my situation is different. My descent is too far from the royal lineage in spite of what I said to provoke Iquehuacatzin into declaring his desire to inherit the throne. Even Lord Tlacaelel has prior claim to the throne before me.'

'Lord Axayacatl, if the tlatoani's sons crave power then surely their uncle stands in their way?'

'Of course. That's why they were so keen to point out that Two Sign and Jaguar were Tlacaelel's men. They had to undermine him.'

'What will they do now?'

'I expect they will seek sanctuary with our enemies, perhaps in Tlaxcala where they will claim to offer an advantage that can be used against us.'

'And then what will happen to them?'

Last Medicine beat Axayacatl to an answer. 'If the Tlaxcala believe they can be used against us, they will be feted as princes in exile, but it's just as likely that they'll be put to death.'

Shield of Gold frowned. 'And Xiconoc?'

'What do you mean?' asked Axayacatl.

'Do you really think he is involved?'

'Yes. I saw the evidence in his home. Moctezuma's sons are headstrong and ambitious. They could simply have waited for their father to pass away, but Xiconoc's time is running out. He's younger than the tlatoani, but not by much.'

Last Medicine rejoined the conversation. He'd been watching Moctezuma dismiss the late Imixquitl's inner circle. 'You'd better hope there's still something there for the tlatoani's men to find.'

'I know,' replied Axayacatl with a worried look. 'It will not go well for me if they don't find anything.'

Shield of Gold didn't know what to say and Last Medicine wasn't known for his cheerful rejoinders, so the three of them turned their attention to the entertainment that was reaching some kind of climax.

The dancers whirled, weaving past each other in a show of flailing beads and finery, while four men with conch shells raised their heads in unison, sending a sonorous blast across the crowds. Shield of Gold held his breath, trying to outlast the mournful note. He did not succeed. Drummers swelled the clangour with a furious assault that reached a crescendo just as the conch blowers' breath ran out and as one, the dancers gave a cry and cast themselves face down upon the floor. The audience sat in stunned silence.

The echo of that last shout was still reverberating in everyone's ears when Moctezuma stood to make a closing speech. He talked for a while about a new and prosperous relationship between the people of Ahuilizapan and the Mexica. He urged the local people to support their new ruler and support him in the payment of tribute. As long as commerce continued and the flow of precious goods back to Tenochtitlan was plentiful, there would be no problems. In return, the Mexica Empire would offer its protection to the people of Ahuilizapan and its own vassal states, but, Moctezuma warned in a voice laden with portent, if the people of Ahuilizapan should fail in their responsibilities and renege on the new treaty, they could expect swift retribution.

At that exact moment, a group of Mexica warriors, Jaguar Knights dressed in their finest spotted skins, hoisted a long and slender post aloft using four ropes tied to a spot halfway up it. Impaled on the top of the pole was a charred lump that might have been Imixquitl's head. Moctezuma gave a signal to someone on the far side of the arena and then sat down. The three noblemen who had so recently been spoken to by Moctezuma stepped forth and crossed to below Moctezuma's seat. As one, they kneeled and then lay face down upon the floor where they kissed the dusty ground. When they were commanded to rise, they explained that by the gracious decree of Ilhuicamina Moctezuma, tlatoani of all Mexica and the lands of the Fifth World, had appointed them to rule Ahuilizapan on his behalf. They begged their people to see sense, exhorting them to celebrate the rise of the new order and when their speeches were done, the conch shells blew again to signal that the day's events were over.

Shield of Gold was about to follow the crowd out when Last Medicine stopped him.

'If you do manage to get a message to Jaguar, tell him to get his family out of Tenochtitlan...take them somewhere safe. He will be safe while he's with his men, but we cannot protect his family night and day. They may be in danger, not just from the priests, but also from Iquehuacatzin and Mahchimaleh as long as they are alive. Those two will still have many friends in the city.'

'They will remember Jaguar's part in this?'

Last Medicine shrugged. 'Iquehuacatzin is used to getting his way. Do not underestimate his ability to hold a grudge.'

Chapter 38
Tenochtitlan and the Western Mountains

Jaguar could derive no pleasure from his return to the shores of Lake Texcoco. The familiar smells and bustle of Teopan went unnoticed. He was weak and feverish. He couldn't move his left arm properly. The wound inflicted by Two Sign had been exacerbated by the long climb out of the flooded cave and even though he had bandaged it carefully he just knew it wasn't healing properly. Somewhere along the way, he had lost his shoes, maybe all the way back in the cave. His mind wasn't working properly. A single purpose had driven him to this point. He had to get back before Clawfoot did... had to protect his family.

When Jaguar finally staggered across the threshold into his own home, the scene that greeted him defied comprehension. He blinked. The main room was filled with people, women mostly. A hush fell over the room as soon as they noticed him. It was a strange kind of silence, one that Jaguar could only partially attribute to his wild and unkempt appearance. Something terrible had taken place here and knowing it filled Jaguar with fear.

'Where is she?' he yelled.

The eyes all looked to the doorway into the next room. Ignoring the protests – no one seemed to recognise him – Jaguar thrust the flimsy fabric aside and went through. The meagre light that came in from the tiny window revealed the broken-looking figure of Arrow One crouched over someone in the low cot. He looked like an old man, staring up at Jaguar from sunken, red-rimmed eyes, but he gave no sign of recognition. Jaguar only realised that the person lying in the bed was his sister when he knelt down to take a closer look. A bandage covered most of Little Beetle's face. She was hot and her clothes were wet to touch.

'She has a fever, brother. What happened to her?'

'I'm sorry, Jaguar.' Arrow One finally found his voice. 'I'm so sorry!'

'By the blessed powers of Quetzalcoatl! What happened?'

'A man...' Arrow One's voice faltered. 'A young man came in here looking for you, looking for Precious Flower. He wanted to know where you were.'

'A priest?'

'I don't know who he was, Jaguar, perhaps a priest, yes. He was very angry. I...' Arrow One stopped. He looked at Jaguar with anguish creasing his features. 'I had to tell him. I'm so sorry.'

Jaguar wasn't sure what his brother-in-law was saying. It didn't make much sense. 'Where's Precious Flower?'

'At the farm, but—'

'Good,' said Jaguar interrupting. 'How is my sister? Will she live?'

Arrow One's voice shook. 'Yes, the healer says with luck, her cheek will heal closed, but her eye is lost, but wait...'

Hot rage took hold of Jaguar. This was the work of Clawfoot. His mind whirled, wondering how he would get at the priest if he had retreated behind the Serpent Wall. He would have to watch and wait for the demon to come out. Then Jaguar caught what Arrow One was saying.

'...gone after Precious Flower. Oh Mictlan spare me! It was my fault. I had to tell him or he would have killed your sister.'

Jaguar stared sightlessly at Beetle's husband. He might have said something; he wasn't sure, but then he turned and shoved through the press of strangers in his house. He paused outside for a moment, trying to work out the best course of action. *There really is only one course of action*, he thought...the one he had set out to do when he left the jungle. He had to get to Precious Flower before Clawfoot did. He began to trot uncertainly towards the southern causeway, wincing at the discomfort in his side. He managed to suppress the pain after he'd settled into some semblance of an even gait.

It was early evening when Jaguar reached the far side of Coyoacan. He'd stopped off briefly for some food and water, but there was no time to rest. He pushed himself to jog again. By forcing himself into a good rhythm, the aches and pains could be banished for a while as the dust and stones glided by beneath his feet. Eventually the light disappeared completely and Jaguar had to walk again or risk twisting his ankle.

The stars grew bright and the thin arc of Coatlicue rose and shone her baleful light across the rocky landscape. Jaguar kept walking. The cool night air was like a draught from a clear mountain stream. For a while it sustained Jaguar, but as the heavens marched across the sky, his head grew fuzzy again. He nearly fell over several times. Once, he stubbed his toe and woke up to find he'd staggered off the track.

There was a point during the night when Jaguar believed he had been walking for all eternity. He could vaguely recall setting out from a storehouse in Ahuilizapan eons ago when Tezcatlipoca and Quetzalcoatl had fought over the creation of the world. Jaguar had traversed mountain ranges as they had risen and glanced behind him on his journey to see the same peaks eroding away into the hungry rivers. Kingdoms had risen and fallen into ruin, a succession of rulers cresting like a wave upon their own success and then crumbling into inadequacy as their neighbour states tore them apart as they still writhed. Forests marched upon the barren plains in times of rain, then shrank away leaving desiccated stumps when the years of drought returned. Jaguar watched it all and still kept walking. Finally a pink dawn raged behind him, echoed in the incandescent strips of cloud ahead. Cold night air was gradually banished by the rising sun, so by the time Jaguar caught sight of the tiny settlement of Xalatlaco, his back was burning hot.

He had only visited the village twice since the tlatoani had gifted it to him, but that was enough. Its tranquil paths and modest houses were stamped into his memory. A place of peace the like of which the capital would never match. He approached along the main road and soon found the turning that led to his land and the modest hut he shared with Precious Flower when they were here. All looked silent. Jaguar's heart began to lift. Just then, a figure stepped from the door of the house, thin and purposeful, swathed in a priest's travelling cloak whose corners flicked and twitched in the gathering breeze.

'You!' cried Jaguar, unable to run the last few paces. 'Stop!'

It was only as he drew up in front of Clawfoot that Jaguar realised he had no weapon. He'd lost his sword in the cavern the last time they had fought. He didn't even have a knife with him. *The journey home must have taken more out of me than I realised*, he thought.

'You made it back then, old man,' said Clawfoot with a mocking smile.

'My family?'

'They tried to hide, but I found them and persuaded them back in here.' Clawfoot jerked his thumb over his shoulder.

'If you've touched them... Precious Flower!' Jaguar called out, but there was no response. 'Blade?'

Clawfoot's smirk drove all thoughts from Jaguar's head. He rushed Clawfoot and they both crashed against the wall of the house. He felt something punch into his back and realised he'd been stabbed before the pain hit. His back went into spasm and the next breath felt wrong, half-formed somehow. He'd seen enough fights to understand his lung was punctured and knew that he would lose very soon due to a lack of air. If he could not get the better of Clawfoot in the next move or two, he would weaken and collapse. Just as importantly, he had to prevent Clawfoot from stabbing him again.

Jaguar knew that in his weakened state, with no weapon, his weight was the only advantage he had over the slender priest. With his arms still locked around Clawfoot, he spun to unbalance himself and try to land on top of Clawfoot. The ploy was only partially successful. Clawfoot hit the ground first and although Jaguar landed half on top of him, his damaged shoulder struck the ground at the same time. A roaring sound filled his head and his vision reddened at the edges, threatening to draw him down to darkness. When it cleared, he realised that Clawfoot had drawn back his arm to strike again. He had no means to protect himself. One hand was trapped under Clawfoot and the other hand hung useless.

Jaguar saw Clawfoot gaze at his knife with a puzzled expression. With an effort, Jaguar focused on the weapon and realised that the blade was missing, snapped off cleanly at the hilt. Before he could react, Clawfoot hit him in the face with the blunt handle and struck him again and again. Another blow crushed Jaguar's nose and then an eruption of crimson spray splashed Clawfoot's face. The attacker was more surprised than the victim, which was enough to give Jaguar an opening. He twisted, brought his knee up to Clawfoot's stomach and ground it down as hard as he could. Now it was the young priest's turn to scream and writhe in pain, freeing Jaguar's right hand at last. He clamped it round the youth's exposed throat and moved to pin him securely to the ground.

'Why?' wheezed Jaguar. His breathing was quick and shallow and he could taste the blood in his mouth. 'Why did you do it?'

Clawfoot beat feebly at Jaguar's arm and then bucked, trying to throw him off. For such a skinny person, he put up a good struggle, but after what seemed like an eternity to Jaguar, the young priest tired.

'Why?' asked Jaguar again, wincing at the pain in his back. He realised where the priest's blade was. It had snapped off inside him.

'Why did I kill your family?' Clawfoot's voice strained through his tortured throat.

'Arghh!' roared Jaguar, trying to block out the words he didn't want to hear. 'Why did you try to kill the tlatoani?'

They weren't alone anymore. A small crowd was gathering, drawn by the noise. Jaguar only noticed legs standing well back. He guessed they weren't willing to intervene when neither of the brawlers looked familiar.

'I didn't, old man,' hissed the priest, now purple-faced.

'You did. I was there, remember?'

'I can't breathe.'

Jaguar loosened his grip a fraction.

'It's the priests again, isn't it? What does Feathered Darkness want? His master died for a lesser offence. Is he so keen to follow the same fate?'

Clawfoot's voice was hoarse. 'No, the high priest wanted nothing to do with it, but he had no choice.'

'What do you mean?'

'Moctezuma is getting old. He won't be around forever. New powers are rising, hungry for his place, and Feathered Darkness did not want to anger them lest they held it against him later on… held it against the priests later on.'

'Who do you mean? What powers?' snarled Jaguar.

Clawfoot shook his head. Jaguar began to squeeze again until the young priest's eyes began to protrude. Still he would not talk.

'Alright then, why come after me?'

'You saw me there,' choked the youth. Jaguar eased off again so he could finish. 'No one can know that the priests are involved.'

'So you had to get rid of me. You had to shut me up.' Jaguar tried to shout out loud again to hurl his anguish at the gods, but all that came out was a wheezing rattle. He couldn't get any air. One side of his chest wasn't working. Blood dripped from his shattered nose and every time he breathed, a few more droplets beaded Clawfoot's face. 'What have you done to my family?'

A careworn man limped forward. 'Jaguar? Is that you?'

Jaguar recognised Fast Rabbit but found no words to use.

'By the Flesh of Xipe Totec, you're in a bad way! What are you doing here and who is this boy?'

Then Jaguar remembered what he needed to do. 'Hold him for me, Fast Rabbit. He's a priest… a bad one. He tried to kill the tlatoani. He must not escape. I have to see if…' But he didn't have enough breath left to finish the sentence.

Fast Rabbit summoned two burly mayeques who took a firm grip of Clawfoot.

Jaguar struggled to his feet and promptly fell over.

'Let me help you.' It was Fast Rabbit, levering him to his feet. 'You have a chest injury of some sort, it looks like you're missing a finger, you've got a puncture wound in your back and your face…well, I've seen prettier turkeys.'

'We need to get… help me check my…' Jaguar gave up and pointed at the hut.

'Come on. Lean on me. Put two damaged men together and you have a whole good one, eh?'

Jaguar didn't understand what the man was saying. His world had shrunk to the doorway and what lay inside. Maybe they weren't here. Maybe Precious Flower and Blade had been out in the fields or had fled when they saw the strange priest approaching. That would explain why they had not come out to see what all the noise was. They simply weren't there.

But they were. Precious Flower lay just inside, cradling Blade's head in her lap. Jaguar thought they might be asleep, but the vast pool of blood that covered the floor said otherwise. Clawfoot had opened the boy's throat and had then turned on the mother. Her last dying act had been to hold her son close and comfort him. Jaguar fell to his knees and rested his own head on Precious Flower's lap, next to his son, too weak to cry out. He convulsed a couple of times, the pain in his damaged chest so violent it even denied him sorrow.

'I was too late,' whispered Jaguar. 'It's my fault. I should have run faster.'

'Come.' A hand rested on Jaguar's shoulder.

'No. They're all dead! Don't you understand? I have nowhere to go. I belong here with them.'

'No, listen to me.' It was Fast Rabbit, insistent. 'They aren't all dead. Come with me.'

Jaguar felt himself manhandled from the house. He couldn't see anything, but he didn't care anymore.

'Look! Look there.'

Jaguar tried to follow where Fast Rabbit was pointing. He tried to clear his eyes with the back of his hand. A woman he did not recognise stood at the edge of the crowd with an infant cradled in her arms. He looked to Fast Rabbit for help.

'Your daughter is safe,' said the veteran. 'My wife was looking after her while the others worked the fields.'

Jaguar remembered. Precious Flower had been expecting. They'd had another child.

'Graceful Bird?'

'That is her name,' said the woman who was holding her.

Jaguar peered at the squashed features of his daughter and saw Precious Flower staring out. She was so beautiful, so perfect it didn't seem possible.

'What shall we do with this one?' interrupted Fast Rabbit. He spat at Clawfoot.

Jaguar wasn't paying attention. All he could see was the baby, his child. A child with no mother. His eyes stung. Each breath made a spear of flame in his back and there was a dull ache in his chest. He had to stay alive.

'Peg him out for the vultures,' one of the local men was saying.

'No. Kill him now.' That was Fast Rabbit's wife, leaning forwards and speaking quietly so only Jaguar could hear her. 'Justice for what he's done to Precious Flower and Blade.'

Jaguar looked at her, not quite focusing. Something she had said made sense. Justice. That was it, except that it was the courts that dispensed justice under the guidance of the tlatoani. *I feel so weak,* he thought. *Have to rest... have to ask someone to pull the blade from my back.* When his voice came, it was the merest whisper.

'No.' Jaguar felt like he was drowning. 'Tie him up. I'll take him... back to the city... when I...when I've had a couple of days' rest. The High Council will want to speak to him. The tlatoani will decide what to do with him.'

There were cries of protest and then in the next instant, Clawfoot had twisted free from the grip of one of the men holding him and punched the other in the throat. Suddenly, he was free and slipping out of reach. Fast Rabbit stepped in front of Jaguar defensively, a hatchet materialising in his hands.

Clawfoot stopped, his eyes darting about, watching as a dozen people took a step towards him with murderous intent.

'You're dead anyway,' snarled Clawfoot, 'but I'll be back this way to make sure.' Then he was gone, sprinting away before anyone could react. The two mayeques who had been charged with holding him gave chase, but they were stocky men, not built for speed, and it wasn't long before they realised it was futile.

Jaguar took a step towards Fast Rabbit's wife. He wanted to hold Graceful Bird in his arms. He reached out to take hold of his daughter's hand, but the dust rushed up to greet him.

Chapter 39 – Tenochtitlan

Clawfoot stared down at the table again, unable to keep himself from the horror.

'You see,' said Feathered Darkness.' I really meant it when I said that I would give you up to the Master Curator if you failed.'

Clawfoot heard the words but understood nothing. The oppressive room deep below the temple crowded his senses and the ropes that bound him to a stout wooden post had been pulled tight, making it hard to breathe. Torches burned in sconces on the wall of the room, shedding their fitful light on the proceedings. Every fibre of Clawfoot's being was focused on the skeleton hand strapped down against the heavy wood and the tourniquet that marked the point where his flesh and his arm began.

'I never wanted it to end this way,' continued the high priest.

He stooped a little under the low ceiling, which, with his pitch-black robes, gave him the air of a lean crow surveying freshly discovered carrion. He looked across at the only other man in the catacomb. The Master Curator was a stolid man with a pockmarked face, a paunch and the air of someone who valued new experiences above human qualities. The man nodded and moved around to Clawfoot's side where he began loosening the straps that had kept his arm tight against a makeshift trestle.

'Then again, I never really thought you would succeed.' Feathered Darkness ran a hand through his luxuriant black hair before continuing. 'Which gave me something of a problem. I don't want to lose you, but...'

Clawfoot looked up at the high priest, uncomprehending.

'Lord Ilhuicamina Moctezuma and his scaly half-brother are sure to stop by and ask me why one or more of my priests were involved in an attempt on the tlatoani's life and when he does, I need to be able to make it clear that I knew nothing of the heinous crime until after it had occurred. Then, when they ask me to give up the traitors to face justice, I can parade you in front of them.' Feathered Darkness pointed at the remains of Clawfoot's hand.

Clawfoot's arm was free. He lifted it, then lowered it, unable to bring the abomination any closer.

'You have to admit that it's neat.'

The sentence hung between them for a while. The high priest knew what they were all thinking. Even the Master Curator could not tear his eyes away from his own handiwork.

'No, not that,' scoffed Feathered Darkness, looking down. 'Well, it is very tidy really. I'd never have believed it could be done with so little blood.' He gave an appreciative nod to the Master Curator. 'No, I meant my solution is neat. After all, who would believe, looking at you now that you haven't been punished? Graven Sky says he hasn't found a way to keep his subjects alive for more than a few days after he skins their heads. Even if the worst of the bleeding can be staunched, they always develop some terrible infection. This way, after I have paraded you before the tlatoani, rattling your finger bones in shame, we can get you back here and finish the job neatly, take off the bony bits and make a neat stump at your wrist. With luck it will heal over and I'll get my brightest pupil back.' The high priest beamed.

It was impossible to say where the real world ended and where the nightmare began. Clawfoot had returned to Tenochtitlan expecting retribution of some kind for his failure. He had nowhere else to go. The decision to live his life as a priest had been cemented when he had said goodbye to Little Maize for the last time. He had expected Feathered Darkness to offer him up to the gods. To have seen his own heart held aloft as Huitzilopochtli claimed him would have been terrifying but short-lived and honourable. That anyone could have dreamed up this hell was inconceivable. The tourniquet had hurt at first; cut deep and made his hand turn the colour of an autumn storm. When Clawfoot had understood what the two men had planned for him, he had wanted to beg for mercy. He could have blamed his failure on the idiots who'd been assigned to him or on the Eagle Knight, but instead he said nothing. This was just another test, whether of earthly or heavenly design didn't matter. Once all feeling had left his hand, the Master Curator had begun his work, cutting and paring back the flesh, sparing only the tendons and ligaments that held his digits together. The tourniquet had done its work. Clawfoot felt nothing except the cold sweat upon his brow and the bile creeping up his gorge.

'I am surprised that you said nothing,' continued Feathered Darkness. 'You have shown great strength of character beyond what even I thought you were capable of.'

At the other end of the room, the Master Curator stoked a stone brazier until the flames began to crackle and sparks brushed the soot-blackened ceiling. A copper knife was poised at its edge, blade glowing in the conflagration. Feathered Darkness came over and lifted Clawfoot's ruined hand up, seeming pleased with the effect.

'Move your hand,' he commanded.

The high priest could not be denied. The flensing job was partial, in order to leave the tendons in working order. In places the knuckle bones were pristine white, scraped clean, but in other places, strips of pink flesh clung to tough fibres, already yellowing as they began to dry. The skeleton hand looked unnaturally long. Clawfoot clenched the muscles in his arm. Sinews tightened, pulling through the flesh, despite the constricting band of leather, and the bony segments of his fingers made a claw. He felt his stomach lurch and had to turn away.

'Graven Sky will seal the cut flesh now so he can remove the tourniquet.'

The Master Curator waddled over holding the copper knife wrapped in a cloth.

'I'm warning you now,' he said. 'When I take that band off, that's when the pain will start.'

There was nothing to say to that.

'After a few days, we'll have to take the whole thing off and seal the wound over properly or you will die.'

'How many times have you done this, Graven Sky?' Feathered Darkness asked.

'What, hands?'

Feathered Darkness nodded.

'Five times...on humans. I tried on monkeys first.'

'And how many have survived?'

'Er, none. One went mad while I was cutting and bashed his head against the post there until he stove his own head in. That's why I had to fit that,' said the Master Curator, pointing a fleshy finger at the padded cloth wrapped around the post behind Clawfoot's head. 'One died from the pain when I took the tourniquet off...screamed and screamed then suddenly fell down dead. One wouldn't eat or drink and died after three days and the other two got infections. Green roots of sickness spread up their arms, smelled terrible. The strongest one lasted eight days.'

'It's not been very successful, has it?' observed the high priest and without waiting for an answer, he turned to Clawfoot. 'So I depend on you to get through this, be the first one to make it. I'd hate for all of Graven Sky's work to be for nothing. Besides, I need you at my side. The senior clerics are all but useless to me except for the simplest of tasks. They're quite incapable of doing anything unusual. Most come from very traditional families and none of them have your enthusiasm for difficult jobs.'

Clawfoot swallowed drily. He tried to say something. His mouth worked, but no sound emerged.

'What's that?'

Clawfoot tried again. 'I did what you asked,' he rasped. 'Xiconoc will know that we tried to help him.'

Feathered Darkness laughed harshly, a crow-like cackle. 'That's the funny thing,' he said. 'It turns out he's gone and died. His new wife stove his head in with a rock and then drowned him. It's the scandal that's been the talk of the city for days.'

'Little Maize?' croaked Clawfoot.

'Indeed, your old friend. She killed her husband and then disappeared without a trace. Thanks to her, all our efforts have been wasted. We could have avoided all this pretence of being on his side.' The high priest gave a short bark. 'Such is the fickle nature of our Lord Huitzilopochtli.'

Clawfoot groaned.

'Don't trouble yourself, brother. Save your strength. You'll need it.'

With that, Feathered Darkness grasped Clawfoot's hand in both of his and held it tightly. The Master Curator waddled over holding the copper knife wrapped in a cloth and pressed the smoking blade against the ragged flesh at Clawfoot's wrist. The glowing blade hissed and spat, dark fibrous smears blackening its orange surface, while the stench of cooking flesh coiled around the room. There was only a dull ache at the end of Clawfoot's arm, but that, combined with the smell, was suddenly too much for him and he passed out.

It could only have been moments later when he awoke. The high priest and his torturer hadn't left their places.

'He's back,' said Feathered Darkness. 'Excellent! Now take off the tourniquet.'

The Master Curator loosened the first band that held a stick in place and then unwound it until the second band, the tight one, was entirely loose. He slid one over the bones of Clawfoot's hand and undid the knot on the other. Feathered Darkness peered at the result.

'No blood,' he remarked, almost sounding disappointed.

'No. It's a good one,' said the Master Curator, beaming with pride. 'You must show him off to the tlatoani while he's like this.'

'Of course. He's due back in the city in a couple of days.' Feathered Darkness gave a mock bow. 'One miscreant, justly punished, My Lord,' he said, effecting a subservient voice.

Clawfoot felt a tingling sensation in his hand, the skeleton one. In a few heartbeats, the tingling became an itch and moments later it grew to be a mauling, incandescent flame of pain that scorched at the end of his arm. Clawfoot heard the keening sound escape his throat and listened as it rose in pitch until it became a throat-rending, rib-rattling shriek that nearly tore him down the middle. Still the agony spiralled up into the vault of his soul, shredding as it went.

Feathered Darkness approached and embraced Clawfoot tenderly with one hand holding his head against his chest.

Tied to the post and held firmly by his mentor, there was little Clawfoot could do but draw another breath and scream again. He felt the top of his head might crack with the force of it and this time there was no let up. He screamed and screamed, flailing his damaged hand about as if it was on fire and all the time, Feathered Darkness held him like a parent might hold a child who was shaking with a fever. Clawfoot shrieked and screamed until black blots began to cloud his vision and made a dark tunnel that finally closed and shut his window on the world.

Epilogue
The Western Mountains

Little Maize shivered. *It must have something to do with the elevation of Chatacatl,* she thought. The air was a lot clearer here in the mountains than in the valley and it was so cold this morning that it actually hurt to draw breath. She didn't mind. She was alive and free for the first time in nearly six years. She rolled her shoulders against the weight of the yoke and its water buckets. Stones on the narrow trail crunched beneath her feet. The trick was to savour the feeling as long as possible. There was no way of knowing how long it would last. Outsiders had passed through the village only yesterday, bringing renewed terror to Little Maize. She hadn't left her house all day. There was no way of knowing whether there had been an extensive search for her and if there had, whether it was still ongoing, but that was no reason to be complacent. Death of a member of the royal family would surely have made shockwaves all around Lake Texcoco and her disappearance had made her the obvious suspect.

The village chief was walking down the path towards Little Maize. She nodded and made way so the old man could get by, grateful for a chance to recover her breath after the climb up from the stream.

'Good to see you, Dancing Star,' said the elder, using her assumed name.

Little Maize was grateful for the kind words. The small community had quietly accepted her even though she was an extra mouth to feed. They must have seen something in her, some resourceful streak, and judged that she would eventually earn her keep.

'How is the sleeper?' asked the old man.

'Still not woken, My Lord, but his skin has lost its deathly pallor.'

'Is he still having nightmares?' he added.

'Yes, My Lord.'

'Please,' insisted the old man. 'Do not call me that. You are not in the city now. My name is Thoughtful River.'

Little Maize averted her eyes shyly. It was hard to break with the years of training.

Thoughtful River gave a kindly smile full of honest brown teeth. 'The village is very grateful to you for agreeing to look after him. I am sure you have saved his life.'

'I don't want to be a burden,' Little Maize replied.

'You are not, my child. When he is well he can look after himself and we can find more interesting work for you...that is, if you wish to stay.'

Little Maize nodded. 'Yes, yes, I do. Your village is beautiful and I have no other place to call my home.'

'Good,' said the old man. He looked around and breathed out a plume of frigid air from his nostrils. 'It's getting cold. I'll send my sons over with some more wood before it gets dark.'

'You've been very kind. I will repay your hospitality.'

The chief waved one hand lazily at Little Maize. His craggy features twitched into another half-smile. He sucked on his teeth, nodded a farewell and then set off down the path. Little Maize hoisted the yoke onto her shoulders and threaded her way across the stony ground to the ramshackle house she'd been allotted, little more than a crumbling shack on the edge of the village. The stone walls were blotchy with sulphur-coloured lichen and in serious need of repair. A thatch of vigorous weeds infested the turfed roof and hung untidily over the sides giving the building a forlorn appearance.

Little Maize pushed the heavy drapes aside and went in. She put the bucket down next to the hearth. The fire she had rekindled from last night's embers was flickering fitfully, so she added a handful more twigs.

'Hello?' came a weak voice from the far wall.

Little Maize nearly jumped out of her skin. She just couldn't shake the constant nagging fear that Tenochtitlan's judiciary would track her down. Her heart steadied when she realised that the invalid had finally woken. She crossed to the corner of the room. Light from the two tiny windows barely penetrated this far back, but she could see that his eyes were open.

'You're awake at last,' said Little Maize, her voice matter-of-fact, even though she had been convinced he wouldn't make it. The moon had waxed and waned nearly twice while the man had lain in this corner, barely alive. He had staggered into the village, badly wounded and an infection raging in his blood. His appearance in the remote mountain village caused a commotion and soon, a small crowd had gathered. Though the man was wearing nothing more than a loincloth and a blood-soaked tunic, it was plain to everyone from the man's muscular body and scars that he was a warrior or perhaps had been. The climb from the valley floor had sapped the last of his reserves and as he fell to his knees, he had held out the bundle he was cradling in his arms. It was an infant, a baby girl, weak with dehydration.

'Water...please?'

Little Maize fetched a pitcher and filled the cup that lay beside him. He drank weakly until the cup was empty and held it out for a refill. Little Maize obliged him, then turned to add some more wood to the fire.

'Where am I?'

'Chatacatl,' replied Little Maize, focused on her task. This wasn't what she had wanted to do. She would willingly have undertaken any job the villagers had given to her, no matter how hard, as long as it didn't involve sharing her home with a stranger, but what choice did she have? Her escape from Tenochtitlan had been arduous and terrifying, fearing arrest at every step. She had never been outside the city before, but it was clear that she needed to put a lot of distance between her and her crime. At last, exhausted by the long trek into the mountains, she had stumbled into this village. She had begged the elders to take her in, promising to pull her weight. The women of the village had wrapped their arms around her and told her not to worry; she would be made to feel useful. No one had asked her any questions about where she had come from; they had all sensed her pain and decided to wait until she was ready to talk. Instead they had taken her in and allotted an empty, dilapidated house to her. They had told her she could take her time repairing the worst of the damage and making it habitable and in the meantime, they would think of a way for her to contribute to the community. She had only managed to repair the worst of the holes in the roof when the wounded warrior had arrived in town and Little Maize had been charged with taking care of him.

'He will surely die,' said the villagers shaking their heads sadly. Little Maize had fervently hoped that he would, but it had never occurred to her to speed him on his way. Two matronly women visited Little Maize's shack every day bearing herbs and poultices. They attended to his wounds, while Little Maize pulped squashes and corn gruel to coax down his throat. Many days passed with the only sign that the man was not dead was his shallow breathing and weak cries in the dead of night. All this time, Little Maize had been looking forward to proving everyone wrong. She would show them how useful she was. She dribbled water into his slack mouth, she wiped the thin yellow faeces from the man's increasingly emaciated buttocks. She changed the dressing that wrapped his chest, holding his torn flesh against his ribs and soaking up the thin drizzle of discoloured ooze from the hole in his back. She changed the hay in his bed and washed the blankets to rid the house of the stink of putrid flesh and looked forward to the day the man would wake and the villagers would marvel at what she had done.

Now the warrior was awake and all Little Maize could feel was irritation. She sensed him stirring and looked over. He was searching around, growing panic in his eyes.

'Where is she?' he said, his voice stretched with despair.

'The little girl is safe. Is she yours?'

The man nodded. 'I want to see her.'

Little Maize came over to him and eased him back onto the bed. 'You need to rest. I'll make sure she's brought to you later today.' She tried to hide her anger, knowing it was irrational. 'What's her name?'

'Graceful Bird.'

'That's a lovely name. Graceful Bird is well. One of the women of the village is looking after her. She had her fifth child two moons ago, so she is with milk. Your little girl has grown chubby since you arrived here.'

'How long have I been lying here?' breathed the man.

'Since Tecpatl, seventh day in Malinalli.'

'And what day is it now?'

'Cuāuhtli, eleventh in Cōātl.'

'By the bones! Nearly twenty days! Have you been taking care of me all this time?'

'Yes.'

The man was pitifully grateful.

'Don't thank me. It wasn't my decision,' said Little Maize and then cursed herself. She had no wish to reveal anything of her own circumstances. 'My name is Dancing Star,' she added, hoping to change the subject. 'What is yours?'

'Heart of the Jaguar,' said the man. 'Everyone just calls me Jaguar.'

He closed his eyes, exhausted with the effort of speaking. It looked as though he had fallen asleep. Little Maize took hold of her emotions. She had known this day would come.

'We didn't think you were going to make it,' she said, as much to herself as to her patient. In truth, he had either been going to die or get better. Either way she had been looking forward to getting rid of him...getting her little shack back to herself.

The man opened his eyes. 'I'm not surprised.' He was staring at the ceiling. 'I dreamed of a paved road lined with flowers and the people of Teopan cheering me on. All my neighbours and my relatives were there.' He turned his head and looked at her. 'The path descended underground and became dark. I realised I had left all the people behind me.'

Little Maize hadn't expected to feel anything but the satisfaction of being rid of her burden, instead of which she was fighting disappointment. Now that the man was talking, he seemed quite ordinary, a little like Clawfoot had been before the priests had got a hold on him, only older. She was being silly, she knew. She decided to make him something to eat. There was half a squash and two peppers in the alcove in the stone wall that acted as a larder. It would have to be soup again. Later, she would go and speak to River, tell him the news and ask for some more provisions. Now that the man was awake, she expected he would need a great deal more food.

'I'm very grateful to you, Dancing Star,' breathed the man. He was looking at her again. 'I owe you my life. I don't wish to trouble you. I will leave in a few days...when I am stronger. How can I repay you?'

Little Maize smiled then, a warm and easy smile. She couldn't remember the last time she had felt such genuine warmth for another person. 'You were badly wounded, Heart of the Jaguar. It will be many days before you are strong enough. There will be time to speak of such things.'

'I'm sorry. It must be terribly inconvenient for you, with me taking up so much space in your home.'

'It's not really my home,' admitted Little Maize. 'I'm an outsider like you. I only arrived a few days before you did.'

'From the city?'

'Yes.' Little Maize didn't want to say anymore. She turned away from him and filled an earthenware pot with water, placing it on the fire to heat. The man sensed her unease.

'I'm sorry,' he said. 'I didn't mean to pry.' A little later he added, 'It sounds like we're both on the run.'

'What happened to you?' asked Little Maize. 'You looked as though you'd been in a battle. None of us could understand how you came to be carrying a baby when you'd just come from a war.'

The warrior sighed. A sound that welled up from deep inside him, somewhere that had been torn apart.

'I was with the army in Totonaca until recently. Some people tried to kill the tlatoani.'

Little Maize held her breath, thinking of Xiconoc's body floating in the reeds. 'Is he...?'

'He's fine,' replied Jaguar, tiredly. 'They were defeated, but one of them threatened to take his revenge out on my family. I had to return to Tenochtitlan, but...'

Little Maize could see the warrior was struggling. He should be left in peace, but she had been caring for him and carrying out intimate cleaning for many, many days and she needed to know. She cut up the vegetables and placed them in the pot, then poked two more logs onto the fire, knowing that the tale would continue. Now that he had started, Jaguar looked as though he needed to see it through.

'I didn't get back in time. The madman cut open my sister's face and then he murdered my wife... my son as well,' continued Jaguar. His voice was small and tight. 'I wasn't there for them. I wasn't able to protect any of them.'

Little Maize heard the pain and the self-reproach. She stirred the pot, trying to imagine what it was like when someone you loved was killed. She sighed.

'I suppose that's worse than never having had a family.' She thought of Clawfoot and the gang. It had all been such a long time ago. Whatever meaning it had once held for her had gone. 'I never knew my parents. My first memory is of searching through a rubbish pile for something to eat. I must have been four years old. There was an unripe maize cob with a crushed end. It was the most wonderful thing I'd ever set eyes on.'

There was a long silence. The pot was steaming gently, sending tendrils of steam into the rafters of the hut, mixing with a thick plume of blue smoke from the fire. She wiped her hands on the edge of her cloak and looked over at Heart of the Jaguar. He was fast asleep again, his mouth slightly ajar. She wondered if he'd heard what she'd said. She bent down and pulled the blanket back over his chest.

'We've both had hard times,' she said. 'Perhaps the gods will look more kindly on us now.'

THE END

Author's Notes

As with *Codex One: New Fire*, I'm keen to point out that this novel is not intended to be a weighty, scholarly work. The historical context is there to create a sturdy, believable warp through which the fabric of the tale is woven. The word 'Aztec' is not used anywhere in this novel because this term was only coined after the Spanish conquest.

One of the consistent observations made by readers of *New Fire* was the difficulty of reading Nahuatl names. It didn't help that they were sometimes used interchangeably with their English translations for a handful of the characters and the only translation was in the back of the book. I have tried to suppress this latter behaviour in *Dark Water*, but there is little I can do to address the first problem of our lack of familiarity with Nahuatl. Calling Mexica warriors 'Jim', 'Bob' and 'Mike', although a humorous idea, would undermine any attempt to give an authentic feel to the story.

Ahuilizapan is the modern day city of Orizaba. I have not been able to establish what Zongolica was called – if it even existed – before the Spanish conquest of Mexico, so I have kept its modern name.

The word 'trecena' is spanish work for the thirteen day period that was as close to the concept of a week that we have in modern times.

Moctezuma did have sons called Iquehuacatzin and Mahchimaleh, but I have found few references to them in historical sources. One source, *Factional Competition and Political Development* by Rudolf von Zantwijk, claims that they embezzled state funds and ran away when their theft was discovered. I decided to rewrite that version of events to give me the foundation for the assassination plot.

There is no record that I can find of Xiconoc's treachery, but what great empires are without a deadly internecine feud?

376

Lightning Source UK Ltd.
Milton Keynes UK
UKOW02f1249260415

250347UK00002B/31/P